The Rancher's Daughter

Holly Copella

ISBN:
ISBN-13: 978-1-947694-34-7

To Emma Hughes

&

Mr. B.

ACKNOWLEDGMENTS

Copella Books: First Paperback Edition 2025
Cover Artist: Daniela Owergoor
Dani-owergoor.deviantart.com
Horse Photographer: Tommy Dunleavy
Printed by KDP, an Amazon.com Company

PUBLISHER'S NOTE

Chapter 1

New Year's Day. It was three o'clock in the morning, and an hour after the casino had officially closed. With the evening's celebration ending only an hour earlier, the place was left in disarray. Confetti and the remnants of party poppers were scattered along the floor, left for the morning clean-up crew to deal with. It was a long night, and everyone just wanted to get home. The small casino's gaming floor was approximately five thousand square feet with a wide selection of slot machines along the far wall. The rest of the space remained open and filled with professional-grade table games. Enormous stained glass windows, being the only windows, were located along the two side walls and were impossible to see through. A large, elaborate bar occupied the entire front wall near the main entrance, while the enclosed casino cage was situated against the far wall. The carpeting wasn't nearly as gaudy as that in a traditional casino, and the lights were only a series of ceiling fans rather than crystal chandeliers. Clearly, this wasn't a proper or even a legitimate casino.

The lone worker, Sebastian, was in his mid-to-late twenties, standing a little under six foot tall with a solid build. Looking somewhat like an Italian mobster, the moderately handsome man wore an expensive suit, his dark hair slicked back and his face clean-shaven. Sebastian stood behind the counter of the casino cage, counting money, the last of the cash from the profitable day's take. As he bundled the bills by the thousands, he looked at his watch several times. Perhaps it was the late hour or being alone with all the cash that seemed to have him on edge. Sebastian's cell phone vibrated on the counter near him, prompting him to pause and view the new, incoming call. He smiled and immediately answered it.

"Hey," he announced with a certain warmth, indicating the caller was someone with whom he possibly had an intimate relationship. "I'm almost finished here." There was a brief pause as he listened to the caller. "No, I'll come and get you. Just be ready, okay? I want to leave as soon as possible." His smile increased, resembling a schoolboy grin at the response from the person on the other end. "I love you too. See you soon."

Sebastian disconnected the call and set his cell phone on the counter while he finished stuffing the wads of wrapped cash into the second locked bag. The fullness of the bags indicated they'd had a very profitable night. Over a quarter of a million dollars in revenue. All tax-free. What the government didn't know about, they wouldn't miss. Sebastian zipped the bag shut and pressed the lock down, securing it. As the lights flickered, he looked up, seeming slightly skittish while alone in the building so late at night. When the house lights remained on, and he didn't see anyone within the casino, he relaxed and carried the locked money bags to the safe, only a few feet behind him. As he neared the safe, he glanced up and noticed that the red light on the security camera was off. It was never off, recording twenty-four-seven.

"What the hell--?"

It took him only a split second to realize the implications of no camera light. It meant someone physically turned off the camera! Sebastian threw the bags to the floor and immediately reached for a hidden gun inside his shoulder holster while turning toward the cage door. Two nearly silent shots were fired, both striking him in the chest. As he collapsed, dropping his weapon, he caught a glimpse of a woman at the far end of the casino darting from the room. With his last breath, he looked up as his shooter stood over him, then watched as the gun was aimed at his face. Another nearly silent shot was fired, ending Sebastian's life. His assailant snatched the locked bags and took off across the room.

Within the silent, empty casino, Sebastian's cell phone vibrated with a new incoming call. The name on the caller ID read "Asshole," lighting up the screen as well as the entire area around the counter. The phone was quickly and quietly lifted from the counter, and with the press of a button, the call was immediately silenced.

Chapter 2

Fourth of July. Morning. The Winchester cattle ranch spanned over one thousand secluded acres, featuring a long driveway that led back to the old homestead, a massive twenty-stall barn, an equipment building, a hay barn with ten stalls, and a twenty-bed bunkhouse. The two-story, eight-bedroom plantation home had a large wraparound porch and tall windows on both floors. There were several rocking chairs and double rocker benches along the front porch, while many large, colorful hanging plants hung from the openings. Within the house, the old, refurbished country kitchen had refinished hardwood floors, many cupboards, granite countertops, and an island counter. In addition to the large, thick table with seating for ten, there was a spacious pantry, a back kitchen door leading to a mudroom, and a smaller back staircase.

A young, attractive woman in her early twenties hurried down the back stairs and entered the kitchen. Skyler Winchester wore her long dark hair pulled back into a messy ponytail, dressed for a day on the farm. Sky's uncle was already up and preparing scrambled eggs and bacon for breakfast. Her Uncle Nash was a shorter man, standing about five foot seven, with slightly thinning dark hair and a full beard. Although he was only in his late forties, he had a considerable amount of gray in his beard, which may have made him appear older. Uncle Nash was a bit like a little dog. The smaller the dog, the bigger the bark, and, when provoked, her uncle liked to bark. Nash smiled when he saw her.

"Good morning, sunshine," he announced cheerfully. "You got in late last night."

Sky laughed and poured two mugs of tea. "Keeping tabs on me?" she teased while taking the mugs to the table.

"No," Nash replied while grinning. "Just enough to worry."

Nash placed scrambled eggs and bacon on three plates, but only brought two of them to the table. He set one plate in front of her and joined her at the table. Sky eyed the third plate still on the counter, then looked at her uncle.

"Aunt Selma sleeping in this morning?" she lightly teased.

Nash snorted a laugh. "Why should this morning be any different?"

"I envy her," Sky reported while digging into her breakfast. "I'd love to sleep late. Unfortunately, it's physically impossible. Once the sun comes up, so am I."

"You get that from your father," Nash informed her. "He came from a long line of cattle ranchers. It's in your blood."

"Not my mother, though, huh?" she asked with a sly grin.

Nash laughed and shook his head. "No, our side of the family is used to being pampered," he remarked. "Sleeping late. Hustle and bustle of the city. Nice clothing."

"You aren't really describing my mother," Sky remarked.

"Well, she shared your father's dream," Nash replied while remaining cheerful. "She was an honest-to-goodness city girl until she met your father after he got out of the service. She'd given up her Park Avenue ways long before you were born." He then sank into thought. "But your Aunt Selma--?" Nash made a face. "She misses the city life. Mostly the shopping, I presume."

"You should spend a few days in the city," Sky reported. "She'll enjoy it, I'm sure."

"I suppose I can afford it." Nash laughed while eating a strip of bacon. "All of my stocks have been performing well," he informed her. "Financially, moving out here was the best decision I'd ever made." He leaned across the table closer to Sky. "Your aunt doesn't max out the credit cards like she used to." He then winked and leaned back with a chuckle.

"Well, I really appreciate everything you and Aunt Selma did for me after my parents died," she replied. "I know it wasn't easy for Aunt Selma to give up city life, but I'm glad I didn't have to leave."

"You were fifteen," Nash remarked, matter-of-factly. "No man in his right mind would pull a teenage girl away from her horses." He shrugged without care. "Besides, for my job, I only need a laptop and the internet."

"I know," Sky remarked. "But it was still a sacrifice, leaving your home in the city like that."

"The city isn't going anywhere," Nash reminded her. "We'll be moving back in two years." He groaned softly. "And then my credit card will be back to being maxed out."

"You could move back sooner, if you really wanted to," Sky informed him. "I know I don't take full possession of the ranch until I'm twenty-five, but

Ryder could go back to handling the estate finances until then."

"Ryder," Nash scoffed with detest. "I don't like that guy, and I certainly don't trust him. I can't, for the life of me, figure out why your father even considered putting him in charge of the estate."

"I'm guessing because Ryder is the only estate lawyer in these parts," Sky replied, then shrugged. "And, in my father's defense, he wasn't exactly anticipating dying at his age."

"Well," Nash announced as he finished his breakfast. "I'm not letting that shyster get his hands on your finances. I'm perfectly happy remaining your property manager until the ranch is turned over to you. Aunt Selma and I will survive another two years here in the country." He then reconsidered the comment. "Well, I'll survive. Your Aunt Selma could be touch and go."

An attractive woman in her early forties glided across the kitchen wearing a white silk nightgown with a matching robe. Selma was a short, petite woman in her mid-forties with wavy, deep auburn hair that hung down several inches past her shoulders. Her fiery hair stood out against her ivory alabaster skin and blue eyes. Judging by her appearance, Aunt Selma clearly enjoyed expensive makeup, eyelash extensions, and a wealth of jewelry. Even first thing in the morning, she looked like a goddess from some fashion magazine.

"If you're so worried about me, we could always rent a place in the city," Selma announced while placing her breakfast plate in the microwave. "Split our time between here and the city."

Nash groaned and sipped his tea. "Renting an apartment in the city isn't cost-efficient," he reminded her. "Buying a place makes more sense."

Selma poured a cup of coffee for herself, then eyed Nash while grinning. "Buy or rent; it makes little difference to me," she informed him, turning enthusiastic. "I'll start checking real estate listings this afternoon."

"Not what I meant, *Petunia*," Nash remarked, clearly mocking his wife. "We'll buy a nice place in the city--in two years. Houses are at an all-time high right now. If you want a nice home, it makes more sense to wait."

"You're killing me, Nash," she pouted as she removed her plate from the microwave and then joined them at the table.

"Between our monthly trips and your visits with your brother and his wife, you spend half your time in the city already," Nash remarked. "I hardly think you're suffering."

Selma glanced at Sky and raised an arrogant brow. "Tell him, Sky," she remarked while indicating Nash. "Tell your uncle a woman needs to be pampered and spoiled."

Sky hid her smile and laughed. "You may want to keep me out of this," she replied. "My idea of pampering is giving my horse a bath."

"Tell me you didn't enjoy those bath bombs I brought for you the last time I went to the city," Selma remarked.

Sky squirmed in her chair and then grinned. "Okay, they were kind of nice."

"Kind of?" Selma announced. "Who spent an hour in my garden tub?"

"Fine," Sky blurted out while hiding her smile, then groaned. "My skin felt like a baby's bottom. It was pretty awesome."

Selma indicated Sky while grinning at Nash. "There you have it," she announced. "The conversion has begun."

Sky then looked at her watch and groaned. "I'm going to be late."

"Late for what?" Selma asked with surprise.

"To harass the ranch hands and take tons of photos," Sky replied cheerfully while springing up from her chair. "I love getting out with the guys first thing in the morning while they're wide awake and fully caffeinated." She then shrugged. "And still somewhat shower fresh."

"Those poor men," Selma muttered and shook her head.

"Believe me," Sky remarked with a low chuckle while taking her dirty dishes to the sink. "They don't mind."

"Don't forget Marcus's Fourth of July party tonight," Selma reminded her. "I hear he went all out this year and is even having a professional fireworks display."

"That should scare all his million-dollar racehorses rather nicely," Sky muttered, then groaned and eyed her aunt. "Do I really have to go?"

"Yes," Selma insisted. "Marcus adores you. He'll be absolutely heartbroken if you don't come."

"Adores?" Nash muttered under his breath. "Is that what they're calling creepy old guys who stalk young girls these days?"

Selma either didn't hear her husband or chose to ignore him.

"Do I have to wear a dress?" Sky almost pouted, knowing the answer before she asked.

Selma glared at Sky and raised her brow, indicating her answer. Sky groaned and listlessly headed for the kitchen door. She then hesitated and looked back at her aunt, now interested.

"Is it true Marcus hired a new guy?" Sky asked.

Selma was slightly surprised by the question and appeared almost pleased that her niece was inquiring about a man.

"Several of them, as a matter of fact," Selma replied cheerfully, her enthusiasm evident as she appeared ready to leap from her seat at the prospect of Sky's curiosity. "Are you interested in meeting them? I heard a couple of them are rather nice looking."

Sky stared back at her aunt as if she were speaking a foreign language. "Well, yeah, but I'm not sure what being good-looking has to do with it," she remarked.

It was Selma's turn to appear puzzled. "It doesn't?" she asked.

"He hired a new horse trainer," Sky reminded her aunt, and just about bubbled over. "Now, that's someone I'd enjoy talking with."

"Oh," Selma muttered, now disappointed, and then waved her off. "Yes, I'm sure you'd have horse-related things to discuss with some new trainer."

As Sky turned toward the back door, she hid her smile. She wasn't sure why she secretly took pleasure in disappointing her aunt when it came to her lack of a love life. Perhaps it had to do with Selma pushing for her to acquire one. Sky's love life was currently zero-one, and she wasn't ready to put her heart out there again just yet. Selma would have to be disappointed a while longer.

Chapter 3

Sky rode her horse, Admiral, along her usual morning route. She was quite possibly the worst creature of habit, enjoying the familiar and even the mundane. As long as she had time to ride, enjoy her horse, and take scenic pictures, she was perfectly happy with her life. Admiral was a tall, broad-chested, blue roan gelding with a black face, four black legs, and black mane and tail. He was a handsome boy, and with the way he arched his head while jigging rather than walking, suggested he knew it too. Despite Sky's love for photography and the thousands of pictures she'd taken over the years, she only shared them with her Uncle Nash and a few others. Her Aunt Selma, the ultimate city girl, thought all her photos looked the same. Fields, woods, streams, cattle, and cowboys. Maybe they all looked the same to Aunt Selma, but each one was different.

With her heart in the right place, Aunt Selma tried to steer her toward taking photos of women in fancy dresses, weddings, and screaming babies. Those things didn't interest Sky. Rather than continually telling her aunt she didn't care for those things, she simply stopped sharing her photos altogether. It made life easier for everyone concerned. Sky rode into one of the larger pastures where several ranch hands were tending to the big herd of cattle. The large open field was lush with thick grass and surrounded on three sides by woods. More than four hundred head of steer were grazing under the watchful eyes of five ranch hands working that morning. Five additional ranch hands worked on a rotating basis, maintaining minimal coverage overnight. Sky took several pictures of the men tending to their duties and even got a few action shots.

Once the men noticed her, as usual, they put on a show for the camera. She actually enjoyed those moments. They made for great photos and fun stories. Once she stowed her camera in her saddlebag, two ranch hands rode across the pasture to greet her. The first man, Jerry, stood about six foot tall with a moderately athletic build, as with most rugged ranch hands. Hard work kept the men in shape almost as much as it beat them up. He was in his late twenties, with short, dark hair, short sideburns, and a few days' worth of stubble that he often referred to as a beard. His rugged good looks and lack of refinement only added to his boyish charm.

The second ranch hand, Tom, was slightly shorter than average, standing at five foot nine, with the same athletic build. The cowboy, in his late thirties, seemed more like a cartoon character than a person, with a larger-than-life personality to match. His language was the only thing more colorful than his personality. His sandy brown hair was buzzed close to his head, matching his facial stubble. Although not as imposing or as handsome as Jerry, he was actually more popular. Yes, they were Tom and Jerry. Although nothing like the old cat and mouse cartoon characters, it was still fun tormenting them about it.

Tom was grinning a bit like a schoolboy while sizing her up. He obviously had something he wanted to say, and it was usually something slightly crude or meant to embarrass her.

"I hear Cinderella is attending the ball at Prince Charming's castle tonight," Tom announced a little too cheerfully.

Sky groaned and rolled her eyes. "You guys hear and spread more gossip than all the old women in town combined," she remarked.

"Can't help it," Tom replied while grinning deviously. "The boys and I are just trying to envision you in a fancy dress."

Although Jerry wanted to join in on her torment, he attempted to hide his smile and play nice. "Behave, Tom," he insisted. "That's your future boss you're teasing."

"No, thank you," Sky huffed, then looked around. "I don't want any part of 'management'. I like things exactly as they are. With Abbott and Costello running the show."

Tom and Jerry each snorted a laugh at the comment. They actually liked running the show as well. Why fix what isn't broken?

"You don't think you'll take over when your Uncle Nash hangs up his calculator and ledger?" Jerry asked.

"God, no," she gasped. "I'll worry about that when I have to and not a second before."

"Nash isn't going anywhere," Tom remarked with a chuckle. "He enjoys it too much."

"He enjoys Aunt Selma, too," Sky reminded him. "If he wants to keep her happy, he's eventually moving back to the city."

Both men groaned.

"Who'd want to live in some stuffy, crowded, noisy city?" Tom scoffed.

"I couldn't say," Sky replied. "Far too peopley for me."

Both men laughed.

"Catch you guys later," she announced, then sent her horse into a canter toward the woods and her favorite trails.

§

It was almost noon by the time Sky returned from her extended horseback ride. As she rode her horse toward the barn, she saw a familiar, black mid-sized sedan parked in front of the house. Sky smiled, knowing it was her Uncle Cyrus stopping by for a visit. Most times, he'd stop by on his lunch break from work, but since it was a holiday, the bank was closed, making his visit completely unexpected. Cyrus was her Aunt Selma's oldest brother, so technically, he was not a blood relative, but she was always close to him and Selma's younger brother, Carlton. Cyrus worked and lived in town while Carlton lived in the city for the last decade or more. Although she loved them equally, she did see more of Uncle Cyrus. Sky unsaddled her horse, gave him a quick brushing, and then put him in the pasture for some well-deserved playtime. Once her horse was enjoying some pasture grass, Sky headed to the house.

After depositing her riding boots in the mud room just off the kitchen, Sky entered in time to catch her aunt and her Uncle Cyrus finishing up their lunch. Uncle Nash was probably already back in the home office working on bills and other house management affairs. Her Uncle Nash was good at ducking out when Selma's brothers came to visit, since the gossip was usually too much for him. Uncle Cyrus immediately grinned when his niece entered the kitchen. Cyrus was a handsome man in his mid-forties, with dark hair peppered with gray, particularly in his sideburns, which gave him a certain sophistication and charisma. He barely stood five foot ten with a lean physique and broad shoulders. Looking much like an olden day movie star, there was no denying Cyrus was charming and quite the ladies' man, which might explain why he was currently on wife number two.

"Hey, kitten," Cyrus announced cheerfully and stood in time to greet her.

Uncle Cyrus had been calling Sky 'kitten' since she was a little girl. She would often play with the cats on the farm for hours, earning her the nickname "kitten." They exchanged a quick hug, which they usually did whenever they visited or ran into each other, even in town. Although, despite her frequent visits to town, she didn't often find herself at the bank. Likewise, Uncle Cyrus didn't often find himself at the feed store either.

"Hey, Uncle Cyrus," Sky replied, then headed to the counter and poured a glass of iced tea for herself before joining them at the table. "Aunt Selma didn't mention you were coming by for lunch today. If I had known you'd be here, I would have gotten home sooner."

"It was a last-minute thing," Cyrus informed her while managing a tiny smile. "Your Aunt Fran wanted to borrow Selma's fancy red handbag for Marcus's big Fourth of July shindig tonight."

Sky perked up and looked around. "Is Aunt Fran here?"

"No, she sent me here to fetch it for her," Cyrus replied. "She had to work the morning shift at the hospital, but you'll see her tonight at the party." His grin cheapened. "Selma tells me you're actually going along tonight."

Sky groaned and rolled her eyes just thinking about it. "Being bullied into it, I assure you," she informed him, and immediately received a 'tsk' from her aunt.

"It's the Fourth of July," Selma insisted. "You certainly don't want to sit here all alone on the holiday."

"Besides," Cyrus added. "You might get some good pictures of Marcus's fireworks display from the ballroom patio."

"I'm forbidden from taking my camera," Sky muttered before casting a quick, sideways glance at her aunt.

"Don't get her started," Selma lectured her brother. "That camera is big and distracting. It certainly won't fit in any purse."

"I don't carry a purse," Sky reminded her.

"Exactly why you're not dragging that monstrosity along," Selma replied.

Uncle Cyrus glanced at Sky and offered a sympathetic look. He knew what Selma was like. They grew up together.

"Before the two of you start ganging up on me," Selma announced and stood, "I'd better go get that purse."

As Selma headed up the back stairs, Cyrus smiled at Sky and leaned across the table closer to her.

"Any new and exciting photos to share?" Cyrus asked.

Sky grinned, picked up her camera, and sorted through her more recent digital photos. "I got some really cool roping shots with the guys," she informed him. "And you wouldn't believe all the wildlife I saw in the woods on my ride."

Cyrus checked out the digital photos from her morning ride. "You almost make a cowboy's job look glamorous," he teased.

Sky laughed and showed him more photos. "These are my favorites."

"I assume Tom didn't appreciate this particular picture," Cyrus teased while indicating a photo of Tom taking a tumble off his horse.

"It happens to the best of us," she insisted while maintaining her smile. "Any reason for the guys to pick on each other, I assure you."

Chapter 4

Marcus's three-story, multi-million dollar mansion was nestled on a large clearing that was both secluded and set back from the road. Although he owned several hundred acres, the two acres of land surrounding the mansion were professionally landscaped, which included a two-level patio and a pool designed to resemble a large coy pond, complete with a waterfall. In addition to the pool and terrace, there was a two-thousand-square-foot pool house and a private tennis court. A broad, lit path extended more than two hundred yards to the indoor riding ring attached to massive, two-story horse barns on either side, which housed forty horses. There were several groomed pastures enclosed with black, four-rail fencing, and a smaller-scale thoroughbred race track located further from the barn, used for practice runs and training.

Within the mansion, the ballroom was something out of a fairytale with a tall ceiling, massive windows lining the entire wall along the patio, half a dozen crystal chandeliers, and paintings on the interior walls. The dark wooden parquet floor was highly glossed and stunning. The ballroom was filled with more than two hundred well-dressed men and women drinking and socializing. All the prominent people in town, as well as many from the city, were in attendance. Servers carried trays of appetizers and champagne around the room to the wealthy guests. There was also a massive buffet table and a large bar, staffed by two bartenders. Not surprisingly, both bartenders were young, attractive women, dressed in somewhat revealing outfits, which was possibly why the bar was crowded with male patrons.

Marcus liked to act the part of a sophisticated businessman, but the truth was less flattering. It was common knowledge he was a notorious womanizer, which wasn't even his worst trait. His womanizing ways undoubtedly revealed why his parties had an unusually high number of beautiful, sexy women, all surprisingly without dates. There had been plenty of speculation about who or *what* the glamorous, single women attending his parties actually were. Alongside her aunt and uncle, Sky entered the ballroom wearing a simple, black, thin-strapped dress that revealed just enough cleavage to garner attention without being too revealing. The knee-length dress had a long slit halfway up her right thigh. She finished off the look with plain black, one-inch heels, her grandmother's pearls, and her hair hanging down beyond her shoulders.

Selma wore an emerald green, strapless, form-fitting dress that had a plunging neckline and a high slit up the side. She completed her ensemble with her red hair in a French twist, two-inch green heels, and a matching set of emerald jewelry. Aunt Selma was immediately swarmed by several prominent figures from their small town, as well as affluent men and women from the city. She was well-known and well-liked at Marcus's parties. Her knowledge of the finer things, like art, jewelry, and clothing, attracted *her* kind of people, who were also Marcus's kind of people.

Uncle Nash patted Sky's hand, which was linked onto his arm. "I'm going to get us some drinks," he announced. "Look after your aunt."

Before Sky could protest or beg to go with him, Nash swiftly crossed the room. While Selma played socialite, Nash purposely got lost in the sea of men at the bar. Now, Sky was left floundering alongside her aunt, immediately bored. It was bad enough she had to attend the party *and* wear a dress, but the boring guests were the worst. Salvation appeared when Sky saw her Uncle Cyrus and Aunt Fran waving from across the room. They immediately made their way through the crowd and joined Sky. Selma gave a polite, acknowledging nod but continued her in-depth conversation with the elites. Sky's Aunt Fran could only be described as a 'glamorous' beauty. She was over five foot seven with a slender build and ample cleavage. Add in her two-inch heels, and she was over five foot nine. Her raven hair was long and wavy, falling past her shoulders. In her low-cut, thin-strapped, red sequin dress, matching high heels, and borrowed purse, she was possibly the showstopper of the gala.

"You look lovely tonight, Sky," Fran gushed, rarely seeing Sky in a dress. "Is that a new dress?"

"Yes, straight from Aunt Selma's closet, which is why it's so short," Sky replied while grinning. "Is that the dress you bought when you visited Uncle Carlton and Aunt Beth?"

"Yes," Fran squawked proudly. "If your Uncle Cyrus asks, I'd gotten it on sale."

Cyrus groaned and rolled his eyes at the comment he was obviously meant to hear.

"Well, I'm sure he'd agree that you're worth it," Sky remarked.

Despite the sideways glance she'd received from Cyrus, he hid his tiny, humored smile. Fran giggled at the comment, then eased her way into Selma's conversation with a wealthy-looking couple. Cyrus released a low sigh, frowned, and looked around.

"Once again," Cyrus remarked. "Marcus outdid himself. All the right people, enough food to feed a small village for a month, and the world's slowest bartenders." He shook his head. "Thank God I had a double before we left home. I can't do these things sober."

Sky eyed her uncle, then laughed. "Uncle Nash went for drinks," she informed him. "I doubt I'll see him the rest of the night."

He chuckled while looking around. "Seriously--?" Cyrus demanded just loud enough for her to hear. "Who are all these people? I think I recognize six people. And that's including you, Nash, Selma, and Fran."

"Have you ever heard of crisis actors?" Sky asked Cyrus.

Cyrus finally looked at her, slightly puzzled. "Of course."

"Well, these are party actors," she insisted.

He snorted a laugh. "You just made that up."

"Yeah, I kind of did," Sky replied and again looked around. "But I'm almost positive Marcus doesn't personally know those dozen attractive, stacked women floating around the room and flirting with all the guys."

Cyrus nearly gave himself whiplash scanning the room. His expression suddenly dropped. "I thought something seemed *off*," he remarked.

"What did you expect from the guy who owns half the town?" she remarked.

Although theirs was a small town, it came with big city problems. The town was run by the corrupt mayor, whose strings were being pulled by Marcus, the wealthiest man in town. Enforcing Marcus's law of the land was the sheriff and his deputies. By the time their host, Marcus, finally greeted Selma and Sky, Cyrus and Fran had already made their way to the buffet table. Marcus was a tick under six foot tall with a lean, athletic build. He was in his mid-to-late thirties, with medium-brown, neatly trimmed hair, a clean-shaven face, and wore expensive clothes. Despite being handsome and charming, his grip on the town made him unappealing. Upon his arrival, he was shadowed by his second in command, Tony.

Tony was over six foot tall and moderately muscular, which was a long way from his slender build during his high school days. Despite only being in his early twenties, he looked much older and a little rough. He wore his dark hair in a buzz cut and kept a light coating of facial stubble for that intimidating look. Although there was a handsome man underneath his rugged exterior, his hardened shell made it hard to see. Sky internally groaned at the mere sight of Tony. As with most of Marcus's 'yes' men, Tony was a relatively decent-looking man with a deplorable personality. Actually, he lacked personality. He was more like a guard dog than a man. If he actually smiled, his face would probably crack. Marcus extended both hands to Selma, which she eagerly accepted.

"Selma, my dear," Marcus announced while grasping her hands, then dramatically kissed both her cheeks. It was a high society *thing*. "You look absolutely stunning."

"Marcus, charming as ever," Selma replied cheerfully.

Marcus then looked at Sky and extended his hands to her as well. "And, Skyler. I'm so happy you joined us."

Sky forced a smile and reluctantly placed her hands in his. As he leaned in and kissed both her cheeks, she internally cringed. She couldn't, for the life of her, figure out why her aunt liked Marcus. He was as fake as they came. Everyone knew he ruled their little town and owned the police. Although his racehorse farm was legitimate, he had many side gigs that weren't.

"Aunt Selma made me come," she casually replied with a smile. "And I prefer Sky."

Marcus laughed at her witty remark as if it had been in jest. Pity he didn't know she was being serious.

"Yes, of course, Sky," Marcus replied. "Forgive me." He immediately roused his best smile while taking in another sweeping eyeful of her. "You look beautiful in that dress."

With Marcus's compliment, she could almost feel Tony's eyes ravishing her, as if he was suddenly made aware of the dress she was wearing.

"Thank you," Sky replied, attempting to be polite. She internally fidgeted, looked around, and then met Marcus's gaze, almost catching him checking out her cleavage. "I heard we'd be meeting your new hires tonight."

"Yes, of course," Marcus announced cheerfully. "I hired three new men in charge of estate security. They came highly recommended."

Sky had to wonder who recommended them. The Italian or Russian mob?

"Unfortunately, Vaughn couldn't join us," Marcus announced.

Tony sneered at the mere mention of the new man, which Sky found a bit interesting. If Tony didn't like him, that either meant he was a good guy or far worse than anyone could imagine.

"The other two are around somewhere," Marcus explained.

"Did the police ever find that employee of yours who robbed the Lake House Bar on New Year's Eve?" Selma asked.

Sky internally chuckled at the police comment as if the police would have found him first. Anyone stealing from Marcus would be hunted down, driven out to the desert, and buried with a nice new Colombian necktie.

"No, I'm afraid not," Marcus replied with a somewhat dreary sigh, although he really didn't seem too broken up.

There was little doubt that his comment was code for 'captured, slain, and buried'.

"You know how it goes," Marcus continued.

Sky was sure the answer was 'six feet under'. Marcus eagerly looked around the room, possibly wanting to end the conversation, and motioned for two serious-looking men to join them. Sky wasn't too surprised to see his new hires looked like every other man on Marcus's payroll. Just two more 'enforcer' types. Who did Marcus think he was fooling? He no longer bothered to hide it. Aunt Selma eyed both men, struggling to hide her surprise. Her aunt was obviously thinking the same thing regarding the two new men.

"This is Ox and Moose," Marcus announced somewhat proudly.

Selma and Sky were taken aback by their names. Certainly good pet names for his new attack dogs. Moose was a tall and moderately muscular man in his mid-thirties with a definite 'wise guy' look about him. His dark, slicked-back hair and clean-shaven face somehow made him appear even more intimidating. His quiet demeanor and rugged good looks added to the overall menacing package. Ox was aptly named. He was a brute of a man in his early-to-mid thirties, standing well over six foot four and with enough muscle mass to make him as intimidating as his name suggested. He had short dark hair with some gray in his medium-length sideburns. He was as serious as he was imposing and definitely not someone Sky would want to cross. Although both men appeared polite enough, they didn't seem interested in being there any more than Sky was. And intelligent conversation certainly wasn't one of their job qualifications.

"Actually," Sky announced while eyeing Marcus. "I was hoping to meet your new horse trainer. Maybe he could show me some of the horses."

Tony snorted a laugh, finding humor in the comment. Sky cast a sideways look at him and sneered, instantly silencing him. He knew better than to ruffle her feathers in front of Marcus.

"Yes, well, he said he'd try to make it to the party," Marcus informed her. "Unfortunately, he's been quite busy since I hired him. But I'd be more than happy to show you the horses after the party."

"I don't think I'm going to be staying that late," Sky replied rather bluntly. "Would you mind if I took the self-guided tour?"

Sky didn't have to look; she could almost hear her Aunt Selma rolling her eyes.

"I could show Sky the barn and horses," Tony offered, almost too eagerly.

Sky internally cringed at the mere suggestion and met Tony's gaze. He locked eyes with her for possibly the first time since their arrival, and she immediately saw something foul behind his eyes, maybe even a hint of a smirk.

Marcus tensed slightly at the suggestion but maintained his smile. "That's quite all right, Tony," he announced. "You have guests to attend to. Sky knows her way around horses."

Chapter 5

Sky enjoyed the lengthy evening stroll out to the barn on the well-lit, stone-lined path. She hated attempting to walk the path in high heels, but she was happy to escape the party. If she tried, she could milk the self-guided tour for at least an hour. As she neared the barn, a man hurried past her, barely noticing her as he almost knocked her down. She watched the slightly shorter, well-dressed man hurry back to the house and the ongoing party. Perhaps he had a disagreement with one of the thoroughbred mares. She was about to enter the barn when a second, much larger, casually dressed man in a black cowboy hat appeared and nearly collided with her. Thankfully, he only winged her. He had to be Marcus's new trainer. The man who almost knocked her off her feet was in his late twenties to early thirties, stood well over six foot with a solid, athletic build, and had amazingly broad shoulders.

As with most cowboy types, he was very masculine and manly, emitting enough testosterone that even Sky took notice. His short, dark hair was mostly hidden beneath his black cowboy hat, which only added to his magnetic appeal. His sparse yet well-maintained beard was showing a few strands of gray, which actually made him more appealing. Sky couldn't deny it had been a while since she took notice of the way a man filled out his jeans. Despite being a sucker for a cowboy, this man had something more than that. His outward physical appearance aside, he looked to be in a foul mood.

"The barn is off-limits to guests," he informed her somewhat curtly.

"Marcus said it was okay," she informed the man, then smiled. "You must be the new trainer Marcus was bragging about. I've been looking forward to meeting you."

He stared at her a moment, then offered a polite smile. "You have?" he asked and seemed humored by the comment. "Well, if it's okay with Marcus, I guess it's okay with me. I'll show you around."

Sky smiled and followed the man into the massive barn. She'd been inside Marcus's barn a year or two ago, but she didn't remember it being so big. The barn interior was nothing short of awe-inspiring. The natural knotty pine wood panels were stained and highly glossed, giving them a look that almost resembled a fine home. There were ten lavish, oversized horse stalls on each side of the stamped, concrete aisle, as well as two grooming stalls, two wash stalls, and two tack rooms. The attached indoor riding ring was approximately thirty thousand square feet, with a dirt walkway surrounding the entire arena. The tall, vaulted ceiling featured clear panels, allowing for plenty of natural light, as well as numerous ceiling lights for nighttime work. The windows on the attached second floor of the barn undoubtedly were part of a spectator lounge or possibly living quarters. On the far side of the large indoor arena was the other twenty stalls with the same grooming stalls, wash bays, and tack rooms as the front portion.

A lone horse was standing in the riding ring wearing a western saddle, which seemed odd for a racing barn, but Marcus did keep saddle horses to help with leading and exercise. The gelding was a tall, black beast that was quite possibly a Friesian. It had a long, flowing mane on its thick, arched neck, and an equally impressive tail. The feathering on its fetlocks almost confirmed the horse's breed. Sky approached the ring and eyed the horse.

"Who's this handsome fella?" she asked.

"This is Diablo," he replied proudly. "I've been training him for a few weeks now, but he's a bit of a handful."

"What's he doing wrong?" Sky asked while marveling at the horse.

"He thinks he's one of the racehorses, but he's clearly a war horse," he replied. "I can get him to walk and trot, but when I ask him to lope, he wants to charge into battle. A real ball buster, if you get my meaning."

Sky cast a quick look at the man, almost humored, because she did know what he meant. "Sounds like he needs to have the piss run out of him," she announced.

He snorted a laugh at her crude suggestion. "You don't think I've tried?" he remarked. "Honestly, he's more of a stubborn prick than I am."

Sky had a good chuckle at the comment. "Horses learn faster than men."

He raised a brow and cocked his head, along with a sly sort of smile. "Is that so?"

Sky cast another look at the handsome man and noted the way he smiled. She couldn't deny he had a nice smile.

"Sometimes, men just like to butt heads," she informed him. "And the horse picks up on that. If he's an alpha male, he might be challenging your leadership."

"I can see that," he replied. "He does remind me a little of me."

"Mind if I give it a try?"

The man stared at her a moment, then eyed the dress, somewhat humored. "I think you're a little overdressed," he announced, then indicated her shoes. "Although I'd gladly pay money to see you ride in high heels."

Sky smiled as she slipped off her shoes, then handed them to him as she entered the riding ring in her bare feet. He eyed her shoes in his hand, then hurried after her.

"You're going to get me into a lot of trouble if you fall off," he insisted and studied her in the dress. "And that dress really isn't made for riding."

"Interesting," she remarked. "Because I'm not really made for dresses."

"I respectfully disagree."

Sky looked back at him and the sly grin on his face. She hid her embarrassed smile, somehow enjoying the small compliment, then turned toward the horse and lovingly ran her hand over its thick neck beneath the long mane.

"That's a good boy," she announced softly to the horse.

The horse checked her out and appeared almost as interested in her as his human counterpart had been. Sky hiked her form-fitting dress up as high as it would go without revealing her panties.

"Well, if that doesn't get his attention, nothing will," the man remarked.

Sky looked back at him and smirked. "No peeking," she scolded.

"Too late," he replied, unable to hide his grin.

Sky grabbed onto the saddle horn and mounted the tall horse without using the stirrups.

"Okay, I'm impressed," he announced.

She didn't bother using the stirrups since they were too long for her anyway. "I've been riding since I could walk," she informed him as she gathered the reins, then turned the horse and trotted around the ring.

The man held onto her shoes and watched her trot the entire length of the massive riding ring. She then sent the horse into a lope. True to form, the horse attempted to deer hop and bolt. She collected the horse and slowed him. The horse responded and maintained the lope.

"Okay, that's not right," he announced. "He's just trying to make me look bad."

"Like most men," she informed him. "He wants to please the ladies."

"He's a gelding," the man reported with an added chuckle. "Trying to get him laid would be like adding insult to injury."

"Well, there's part of your problem," she remarked while loping the horse around the large ring. "There's more to pleasing a woman than just sex."

"See," he announced, folding his arms across his chest. "I hear you talking, but you're just not making any sense. In all fairness, though, I didn't hear much of what you said after you pulled up your dress and flashed me."

She stopped the horse near him and shook her head. "You're not like any horse trainer I've ever met," she remarked, then swung off the horse's back in a flying dismount.

Before she reached the ground, she felt his hands on her hips, guiding her safely to her feet. She jumped with surprise and spun around, facing him. He didn't give up an inch of space while staring into her eyes and grinned as he helped guide her dress back into place.

"That's because I'm not a horse trainer," he told her, his hands settling on her hips. "I'm Marcus's new head of security."

She stared at him as his hands firmly held her hips with maximum contact, and his eyes never left hers.

"You're Vaughn," she scoffed with some surprise and a little irritation before turning stern while removing his hands from her hips.

"And by what I just saw," Vaughn announced. "You must be Skyler Winchester or, more famously, the rancher's daughter."

She easily slipped out from between him and the horse, since the horse was more willing to move away from her.

"How did you know that?"

Once she was a few steps away from him, she turned only to find him directly behind her, once again crowding her.

"Tony described every inch of you in vivid detail," he replied while maintaining his grin. "And he wasn't wrong."

"Careful, Vaughn," she announced without backing down. "You can be castrated too."

His smile didn't falter. "Oh, I doubt you'd want to do that," Vaughn insisted. "It'd be a lot more fun for you if you left me intact, I promise."

Sky locked eyes with him, then affectionately placed her hand on his chest while moving in closer. Vaughn maintained his grin as he lowered his mouth to hers. Without flinching, Sky effortlessly rammed her knee into his groin. Vaughn let out a loud groan and clutched himself. To her surprise, he didn't go all the way down. That was a bit concerning, but she didn't let it ruffle her.

"I guess when Tony told you *all about me*, he left out a few details about the sort of relationship he and I have," she remarked. "Since I don't know whether

Tony did it to piss me off or put you in the crosshairs, I'll cut you a break and not tell Marcus about this, but don't let it happen again."

Sky turned, snatched her discarded shoes from the ground, and walked out of the riding ring. Although she seemed confident, her heart was racing. Since she hadn't disabled him, she was a little concerned about his recovery time, and she didn't need him turning angry and chasing her down. Thankfully, he didn't follow her.

Chapter 6

Sky paused on the path from the barn near the house and took a moment to slip back into her high heels before rejoining the party. She saw some of the guests already spilling out onto the patio, awaiting the upcoming fireworks display. Sky was about to continue to the patio when she heard raised voices behind the pool house. She hesitated and suddenly felt compelled to eavesdrop. Sky took a couple of steps off the path and peered behind the pool house. The pissed off man she had nearly collided with on her way to the barn was very heatedly talking with Marcus's two other goons, Roscoe and Foster. Sky knew Tony's sidekicks had to be somewhere around the mansion. Roscoe was a tall and beefy guy in his late twenties, but also a bit of a pretty boy for a goon. His medium brown hair was kept short yet slicked back, and he was meticulously clean-shaven. Not surprisingly, his good looks and toned body came with a large ego, but he came up short when it came to intellect.

Foster wasn't nearly as tall nor as beefy as his counterpart and far from handsome. The man, in his late thirties, had dark hair that was slightly longer, with unkempt waves, and excessively bushy eyebrows. His ego wasn't nearly as big as Roscoe's, and he was possibly twice as dumb. Fortunately, Foster wasn't hired for his intelligence, but rather for his ability to intimidate people. Now that she had a better look at him, the man she had literally run into outside the barn was well-dressed, in his mid-to-late thirties. He was somewhat shorter in stature with neatly trimmed dark hair and a clean-shaven face. Built athletically slender and a bit mousy, Sky was left wondering if this was Marcus's new horse trainer, although seeming more like a taller jockey.

"He's completely disrespectful," the mousy man lashed out to Marcus's much larger goons. "I can't work under these sorts of conditions!"

"You need to calm down before approaching Marcus," Roscoe informed him. "Marcus doesn't tolerate hot tempers and certainly not at his parties or around his guests."

"Good way to get yourself fired," Foster muttered, already seeming bored with the entire conversation.

"I could get fired?" the mousy man exploded. "I'm not the one with the deplorable attitude!"

"Well, that's debatable," Foster scoffed under his breath, further firing up the mousy man.

Roscoe attempted to calm the man before Foster could say anything more to fire him up. "Wait until tomorrow morning, after Marcus has had his coffee, and have a calm discussion with him about the situation."

"There's no way in hell I'm getting fired," the mousy man cried out. "Marcus needed my help and is paying me a hefty sum for my services. I'm very good at my job, and I'm not about to take any crap from some arrogant asshole. If my terms are unacceptable, he can find someone else!"

Foster rolled his eyes and seemed to be waiting for the perfect time to bolt or punch the guy, while Roscoe remained diplomatic.

"I doubt he'd want to do that," Roscoe insisted. "But if you lead with that, Marcus won't appreciate your hostility." He drew a deep breath and cut the man off before he could fire back with another angry rant. "Just pull yourself together, have a couple of drinks, and wait until morning to talk to Marcus. You'll thank me for it."

The mousy man fought his urge to explode, considered the advice, and finally nodded. "Okay," he replied. "I'll take your advice. It is a party, after all. It can wait until morning."

Roscoe patted the man on the shoulder and nodded him back to the party. Before they could make their move, Sky hurried back to the path and bolted for the patio. She tackled the steps a bit faster than she would have preferred in high heels, but managed it without falling on the stone. Sky composed herself as she walked past dozens of people on the patio and headed into the ballroom through the first set of open glass doors. With over one hundred guests still milling about the ballroom, Sky had a difficult time locating her aunt and uncle through the sea of black tuxedos and satin evening gowns. Checking the bar for Uncle Nash was the safest bet, but there were dozens of men still surrounding it, and her uncle wasn't exactly tall enough to stand out.

As she made her way across the ballroom, she spotted Marcus. Before she could change direction and keep from being noticed, he'd already spotted her and was approaching. It would be rude to make her escape after she had already made eye contact. She put on her best false smile and accepted her fate.

"How was your tour of the barn?" Marcus asked as he paused before her.

Despite her taking a step back, putting a little distance between them, Marcus immediately closed the gap.

"You have an amazing set-up," Sky informed him. "Beautiful training facility. I even got to meet one of your trainee horses, Diablo."

Marcus stared at her a moment as if she'd spoken a four-letter word. A strange smile crossed his face, a poor attempt to conceal his odd look.

"Diablo, huh?" Marcus remarked before gently scratching his brow. "Can I assume you met Vaughn as well?"

It was her turn to look puzzled. "Yes, I did," she replied. "How did you know?"

"Diablo is Vaughn's hard-luck case," Marcus informed her while hiding his slightly humored look. "He got the horse for next to nothing. Probably because it almost killed its last owner. I guess he sees that beast as a challenge. My new trainer thinks we'll eventually find Vaughn broken or dead at the hooves of that horse."

Sky stared at Marcus for a moment, slightly baffled by the comment. At least in the arena, the horse didn't seem that bad. Of course, a horse is only as good as the person riding it, and Vaughn, being the rider, was possibly the problem, even though she didn't have a chance to see him ride.

"Clash of the egos," Sky remarked. "I've seen it too often with horses and stubborn men."

"Stubborn is being polite," Marcus replied, then snorted a tiny, humored laugh. "Did Vaughn behave himself?"

Marcus's simple question felt like a trap and required a moment of thought. Was he asking because Vaughn was a known pervert? Or did Marcus fear she found Vaughn attractive? It sort of felt like a trick question. Sky preferred giving new guys a chance for redemption, so she wasn't ready to 'out' Vaughn's behavior just yet.

"He's a little intense," Sky casually replied, then shrugged. "But so are all the guys at the ranch. I know how to handle 'intense'."

Marcus chuckled, appearing pleased. "Yes, you do have a reputation," he remarked. "Maybe I should have warned Vaughn about you and not the other way around."

"Maybe someone already had," Sky insisted, but didn't elaborate on her thoughts.

There was an awkward silence, almost as if Marcus had read her thoughts. Although he managed a smile, she could see some bitterness behind his eyes.

"Tony knows better," Marcus insisted in a tone that chilled her. "And if Vaughn ever gives you any trouble, you let me know, and I'll handle it."

"I appreciate that," Sky replied and even managed a smile, all while wondering if 'handle it' was code for a long drive through the desert. "But I think Vaughn and I have a pretty good understanding. I'll leave him alone, and he'll leave me alone."

"I'm glad to hear," Marcus replied and seemed to relax.

Why did Sky get the feeling she just saved Vaughn's life by not telling Marcus what happened in the barn? She suddenly remembered why she didn't like being left alone with Marcus. It always ended with her feeling as if she were having a conversation with "The Godfather". The same mousy man she'd heard heatedly talking with Roscoe and Foster approached Marcus. He had a half-empty glass of scotch in his hand and appeared more relaxed than he had only a few moments ago. Marcus saw him and seemed to be pleased.

"Here he is," Marcus announced while indicating the mousy man. "Sky, I'm pleased to introduce my new horse trainer, Elias Hammond." He then indicated Sky. "Hammond, this is Skyler Winchester."

Hammond smiled politely and shook her hand. "Miss Winchester," he announced. "It's a pleasure to meet you finally. I've heard so much about you."

It was apparent he didn't remember nearly plowing her down on the path outside the barn less than an hour ago.

"Marcus tells me you're an equine enthusiast," Hammond remarked.

"Among other things," Sky replied.

Marcus was always careful to exclude her ties to the cattle ranch in every conversation he had around her, although she was never sure why. Long before her parents died and the ranch went into a trust for her, she was fondly referred to as 'the rancher's daughter'. Perhaps she should have been offended by the complete lack of association with her family's ranch by others. Still, she preferred her Uncle Nash taking on all the day-to-day ranching responsibilities anyway. He managed it well, and she never had to worry about anyone calling her 'boss'.

"Yes, she's an excellent amateur photographer," Marcus interjected, then looked back at Sky. "Perhaps you'd like to come out to the farm and take some photos of Hammond training and working the racehorses."

"I think that'd be a lot of fun," Hammond announced.

Sky smiled and nodded, although not actually agreeing to it. It did sound like a fun assignment, except Marcus would probably follow her around most of the time. But at least it wasn't another offer to take pictures of someone's screaming child throwing a tantrum.

"I might take you up on that," Sky replied while making a mental note that neither Marcus nor Tony hung around the entire time, hovering over her shoulder.

Marcus then noticed a larger crowd of people heading out of all three sets of glass doors to the patio. He looked back at Sky and grinned.

"The fireworks will be starting soon," Marcus announced. "Did you want a drink before heading outside?"

"No, I'm good, thank you," she insisted, then cast a quick look around the rapidly emptying ballroom. "I should catch up with my aunt and uncle before they think I ran out on them."

"Your aunt is already outside," Marcus informed her, then extended his elbow to her. "Shall we join her?"

That was the last thing she wanted, and she wasn't going to encourage Marcus's romantic delusion of them standing outside under the stars with fireworks going off in the distance. Sky glanced toward the bar and responded, despite not seeing her uncle.

"I think I see my uncle now," she informed him. "We'll join you outside."

Marcus offered a disappointed but acknowledging nod, motioned Hammond toward the doors, and then headed for the patio. Once Marcus passed through the doorway, she scanned the nearly empty room but still didn't see her uncle. Perhaps he was already outside, and she'd missed him. She turned toward the patio doors and nearly collided with Tony. Despite internally jumping, she remained composed in front of the intimidating man. Considering she hadn't seen him a minute ago, he clearly put himself in her path to force a conversation.

"Looking for someone?" Tony asked while smirking in a way that sent shivers down her spine.

She wanted to respond with, 'not you', but that would be pushing the envelope. She needed to play nice.

"My uncle," she replied.

"Want help finding--?"

"I'm good, thanks," Sky informed him, then took a step around him.

Tony took a step backward and again put himself in her path. "You don't have to be rude, Sky," he reminded her.

"Rude is the only language you understand," she reminded him, then straightened proudly. "Now, will you move out of my way?"

"When you disrespect me, Marcus automatically thinks I did something to upset you," Tony remarked. "It destabilizes my reputation with him every time we're in the same room together."

Sky stared at him a moment before cocking her head. "Well, I don't respect you," she informed him. "I have no reason to respect you." She then folded her arms across her chest and raised her brows. "And if you don't want me to be rude, go back to ignoring me. It's a win-win for both of us."

Tony refused to back down or move out of her way, turning it into a game of 'who blinks first'. Sky refused to give in to Marcus's hired goon, but it was going to get awkward fast. Nash mysteriously appeared alongside Sky and eyed the tense exchange.

"Is there a problem?" Nash asked in an oddly threatening tone.

Nash wasn't a big man, but he didn't let his short stature stop him from standing up for his niece. He wouldn't last long in a fight with Tony, but he'd still stand up all the same. It also didn't hurt that his name still carried some weight around town.

"No," Sky announced with little emotion, but didn't take her eyes off Tony. "Tony was just looking for Marcus." She raised her brows commandingly. "He's outside on the patio."

Tony stared at her a moment longer, then finally turned and headed for the first set of patio doors to join the others. Nash, Sky, and one or two other people were soon the only ones remaining within the ballroom. Nash partially turned to face his niece, giving her a slightly skeptical look.

"Do I want to know?" Uncle Nash asked.

"Tony has a fragile little ego," she replied, then released the tense breath she'd been holding. "He always thinks I'm telling Marcus bad things about him."

"Correct me if I'm wrong," Nash remarked. "But doesn't Marcus already know all the bad things about Tony? The *bad things* are part of his job, as a matter of fact."

"You know what I mean," she reminded him, but managed a tiny laugh.

Nash frowned and shook his head. "I can't believe you actually dated that bastard," he muttered.

"In my defense," Sky announced. "We were in high school at the time, he was only eighteen, and he wasn't nearly as bad back then."

"Maybe not as bad, but he was still a bastard," Nash reminded her. "I never liked the guy."

"I'd rather forget about that part of my life," Sky insisted. "I don't know why he does such a great job of ignoring me sometimes and then, other times, he's in my face."

"I know you don't want to hear it," Nash informed her, "but when you dress up, a lot of men take notice. Just because the two of you aren't dating anymore, that doesn't mean he's not jealous when other men check you out."

"You're right," she replied, sighing. "I don't want to hear that. If that were true, I fear what would happen if another man actually took a genuine interest."

"Given Tony's deplorable disposition since he started working for Marcus," Nash announced. "It's a scary thought."

The ballroom lights suddenly dimmed, indicating the fireworks were about to start.

"A worry for another day," Nash announced, then grinned and extended his arm to her. "Join me on the patio?"

Sky smiled, linked onto his arm, and walked onto the patio with her uncle as the first fireworks screeched into the sky.

Chapter 7

Bear Creek. Monday was Sky's usual day to stop in town, pick up some household supplies at the general store, and have lunch with her friends. The wranglers regularly picked up the necessary ranch supplies at the feed and tack store, so they did the heavy lifting. Quite literally. There were several businesses along the main drag, including the courthouse, sheriff's station, local bank, and a pharmacy. On one of the secondary roads was the general store, feed mill, and diner. As Sky drove her gray, two-door Jeep 4x4 into town, she saw Jerry and Tom at Gus's Feed and Tack Store, loading grain and salt blocks onto the ranch pickup truck. She tooted her horn and waved to them. Most of the ranch hands were like brothers to her since some had been around when she was just a little, pain-in-the-ass kid. As a matter of fact, all but two of the new guys worked for her father before his death.

Even though the ranch would officially be hers in two years, she never really felt as if she were their boss. Her uncle gave Jerry, the foreman, minimal instructions and let him run the ranch as he saw fit. Nash mostly took care of the books, although he had been including her in the finances for the last two years. She could probably do his job, but it didn't really interest her. Sky wished her uncle could continue running the ranch forever, but she couldn't ask him to stay on. Aunt Selma really wanted to get back to the city, and it would be unfair to the woman who'd given up the last eight years of her city life to live on a ranch in the middle of nowhere. Sky pulled up to Bear Creek Mercantile, the old-fashioned general store, which was just next door to the feed store. She groaned when she saw one of Marcus's pickup trucks parked out front. She tried to plan her visits when his men weren't in town. It made for a less stressful environment. Unfortunately, it didn't always work that way.

Everyone in town walked on eggshells around Marcus's enforcers. *Enforcers.* If she were ever heard uttering those words aloud in front of Marcus's men, they'd turn ugly, but everyone knew what they were. Now, there were three more of them to spread the joy. Sky couldn't just sit in her Jeep and wait for them to leave, so she sucked it up and got out. As she entered the general store, she could hear Marcus's men loudly carrying on just one aisle over. It was almost certain they'd chased all the nice people from the store that morning with their foul mouths, leaving Ron, the store's proprietor, to deal with them. The store interior was just as old-fashioned as the outside suggested. The old hardwood floors were in desperate need of varnish and wax, and creaked with just about every step. There was always the distinct sound of thumping cowboy boots up and down every aisle. Sky actually liked the sound.

The store carried a wide range of items, including junk food, cold drinks, deli meats, local produce, canned goods, and toiletry products. Ron stood behind the counter with an all-too-familiar scowl on his face. He looked that way whenever Marcus's men sauntered into his store. Ron resembled an old farmer in his worn baseball cap, flannel shirt over a faded t-shirt, and grass-stained blue jeans. He was in his early to mid-fifties, with short brown and gray hair and a matching trimmed beard. Although a little frumpy, he was still physically fit and possibly more of a powerhouse than most men half his age. Sky was certain he could handle his own in a fair fight. Ron smiled at Sky as she entered, although his smile was weak and uncomfortable.

"Morning, Sky," Ron announced, then grimaced while giving a slight nod to the nearby aisle. "Maybe you'd rather come back in half an hour."

Sky offered a sympathetic smile. "Not my first rodeo," she informed him, then headed for the health care aisle.

She just needed a few items for herself and her aunt. Sky picked up a bottle of shampoo and conditioner and then found some bath salts. They weren't nearly as exotic as the ones her aunt would buy in the city, but they didn't cost nearly as much either. Sky heard angry, raised voices from two men in the next aisle. Most of the time, Marcus's men were just loud and rude. There weren't many men left in town who'd dare argue with them, that was certain. It was really none of Sky's business, and she wasn't about to get involved either. She was saving her 'get out of trouble free' card when it was her own ranch hands at risk. It hadn't happened yet, but she was sure they'd step into that particular trap eventually, especially at the bar.

As she emerged from her aisle while heading for the register, she still heard the arguing male voices in the next aisle, possibly heading in the same direction. Sky paused at the end of the aisle and decided it was best to wait out the storm. Tony and Vaughn no sooner appeared from the first aisle when Tony spun in anger and poked Vaughn in the chest with his thick finger.

"Stay the fuck out of my business, Vaughn," Tony snarled in anger without taking his squinting, hateful eyes off Marcus's new man. "Or I'll knock those pretty teeth down your throat."

Although Vaughn and Tony were the same imposing height, Tony had a little more muscle mass behind him. Vaughn was no slouch, built a bit like a brick shithouse, but Tony was definitely the stronger man.

"Put your hands on me again, and we'll find out," Vaughn snapped with all the arrogance expected from one of Marcus's enforcers.

It was like watching two dogs with ruffled scruffs staring each other down. Sky didn't give Vaughn very good odds against Tony, but she had to admit, he mastered the art of intimidation. The way he looked at Tony even made Sky shudder a little. Poor Ron remained behind the desk, watching the situation unfold, fearing the desecration of his store if the two men clashed.

"Watch yourself, Vaughn," Tony snarled, then turned and headed for the check-out counter with his box of condoms and an energy drink.

Rather than go in front of the counter to pay for his items, Tony headed behind the counter, grabbed two packs of cigarettes, and walked out of the store. Marcus's men were notorious for taking things without paying for them, and there was no questioning them either. Marcus owned the town, and his goons ran it. Vaughn approached the counter with a scowl on his face and placed a bottle of aspirin on top. Ron eyed him, somewhat surprised, then cautiously scanned the item.

"That'll be six-fifty," Ron announced.

Vaughn removed his wallet and placed some cash on the counter. "Start a tab for each of the guys," Vaughn informed him. "Send the bill to Marcus at the end of each month." He snatched his change. "No more free rides for the boys."

Ron stared with surprise, then nodded and watched Vaughn grab his bottle of aspirin and leave. Once he was gone, Ron cast a look at Sky, who was equally baffled.

"Well--" Sky huffed with surprise. "I don't know what that was all about." She approached the counter and set her purchase down for Ron to ring it up. "But it has to be too good to be true."

"Maybe Marcus is cleaning house," Ron reported in a serious tone.

Sky and Ron exchanged looks, then immediately erupted into laughter.

"If that's the case, it's only a matter of time before that new guy has an accident," Ron coldheartedly informed her. "Pity, too. He seems nicer than the rest of them."

"I wouldn't be too quick to sing Vaughn's praises," Sky remarked, then sneered, recalling her encounter with him. "He's just an upgraded version of Tony. Doesn't really mean he's much better."

"You want this on your tab?" Ron asked.

Sky nodded.

"I guess that's where you and I differ," Ron reported. "Too many locals are fed up with Marcus's dealings. He owns half the town. Rent is getting too high. Add in the additional cost of his hired goons' 'five finger discounts', and it's getting to the point where most would rather just cut their losses and move." He shook his head. "Thought about it myself. Marcus wants the whole town? He can have it. Let him run all the businesses at a loss and see how he likes ruling a ghost town."

"I hope it doesn't come to that," Sky replied while frowning. "I'd hate to see you go."

"I'll hold out a little while longer," he informed her. "Gus at the feed store and Jasmine at the diner pretty much feel the same. Marcus has been trying to get them to sell their businesses, at a loss, then rent the space like I do." He shook his head. "Biggest mistake I ever made. Didn't stop them from harassing me anyway."

"I'm sorry, Ron," Sky announced with genuine sympathy. "I wish there were something we could do to stop the bleeding, but we're all pretty much screwed around here."

"If I were young like you, I know I'd leave the first chance I got," Ron remarked.

"Yeah, but I'm bull-headed like my father," she reminded him.

"Well, just watch yourself, Sky," Ron announced and shook his head. "You're not as untouchable as you may think. You don't want to mess with these guys. Eventually, Marcus will lose interest in you, especially once you find yourself a boyfriend. I don't want to see you harassed by those half-wits, and it's only a matter of time before Marcus goes after the big land owners."

"Winchester Ranch currently employs ten ranch hands," Sky remarked, then smirked. "Got room in the bunkhouse for twenty men. There are a thousand acres, forty rifles, and two backhoes. You do the math."

Ron snorted a humored laugh and shook his head. "You sound just like your father," he remarked. "Except he may have followed through with that sort of threat."

"Desperate times, Ron," she announced with a sly smile.

§

Sky finished up at the general store about an hour before she was supposed to meet her friends for lunch at the diner, so she decided to kill some time by checking on her ranch hands at the feed store. Even though Jerry and Tom were loaded up and ready to go when she arrived, they were enjoying a cup of coffee and a little conversation with the feed store owner. Gus was an older man in his late fifties with surprisingly dark hair and almost no gray. He was short and lean, being a laborer all his life, but dressed neatly in a collared, button-down shirt and took care of himself. Despite being an old farmer, Gus was a slightly meek and non-confrontational sort of guy. As Sky approached, Gus nudged Jerry while indicating the young woman.

"Look alive, here comes your boss," Gus teased, receiving laughs from both men.

"Not me," Sky announced boldly, then hoisted herself upon the open tailgate of the ranch truck. "Did I interrupt anything good?"

"Gus has a girl," Tom informed her while suggestively raising his brows.

"Locked in his basement?" Sky asked, then eyed Gus. "I already heard about that one."

"I don't *have* a girl," Gus retorted, despite his inability to look at Sky and the tiny grin he was attempting to hide.

"Don't be so modest, Gus," Jerry announced cheerfully. "From what you told us about her, she's crazy for you."

"Now, I have to hear about this one," Sky remarked and made herself comfortable while keeping her eyes trained on the slightly embarrassed, lovesick feed store owner.

"Not much to tell, *yet*," Gus informed her, then shrugged while attempting to hide his smile. "We went out twice so far and had a really good time. We're going out again this Friday."

"To the city," Tom added.

"For dinner and a show," Jerry revealed.

Sky cocked her head and grinned at Gus. "Oh, that sounds pretty serious to me," she announced, joining in.

"Third date," Tom informed her while suggestively raising his brows.

Sky eyed Tom, slightly puzzled.

"Stop," Gus groaned. "You're embarrassing me and your boss."

"Not their boss," Sky quipped to Gus without taking her eyes off Tom. "What's the significance of the third date?"

All three men suddenly seemed uncomfortable with her question. When she stared at the three men, it became clear she wouldn't let up until someone answered her.

"It's kind of a standing joke," Jerry explained, then gently cleared his throat. "Third date. You know. Sex."

There was an awkward silence as Sky processed what Jerry was attempting to say without actually saying it.

"Uh, I don't think so," Sky informed him.

"As if you'd know," Tom announced. "You barely go on first dates, let alone second ones."

"Tom--" Jerry scolded under his breath.

Tom eyed his friend and immediately cocked his head to one side. "You think she doesn't know that she doesn't date much?" he demanded.

"He's right," Sky reminded Jerry before looking back at Tom. "But, if I did, I don't think I'd be putting out on the third date."

"That's why it's a standing joke," Gus attempted to cover and even managed a tiny smile. "It's just stupid guy talk."

"I guess I'm not 'guy' enough," she replied, then jumped off the tailgate. "Enjoy your date." Sky then grinned. "I hope you get lucky."

As Sky returned to her Jeep, Gus chuckled at Jerry and Tom's embarrassment.

Chapter 8

Jasmine's Diner was a historical, single-story train station that was restored and repurposed into the town diner many decades ago. The exterior walls were made of old barn wood, painted red, and the building still had the original, covered wooden platform out front. There were two newer benches on the platform, along with the original train clock. The former teller windows were now double-pane glass with thick frames painted hunter green, and it was rumored that the old train tracks remained buried beneath the stone parking lot. As Sky pulled up to the diner, there were only a few cars in the small parking lot, indicating that the restaurant wasn't very busy despite the early lunch hour. She saw her friend's car parked out front and headed inside. Just past the cash register, located on the dessert case, was the large counter with plenty of seating opposite the half wall to the kitchen. The front windowed wall featured only booth seating, while the rest of the area had tables and chairs.

Once she entered the diner, Sky heard Marcus's men in the back, which may have contributed to the lack of customers at a normally busier time. Sky cast a glance at the six familiar men in the back, but easily brushed them from her mind. She saw her friends, Dixie and Marlon, at the opposite end of the diner and joined them at their back booth. Dixie was barely five foot two and usually wore two-inch boots to increase her height. Although she was the same age as Sky, she looked much younger, sometimes passing for a high school student. Being a short, petite, blue-eyed girl with straight blonde hair that just about touched her shoulders, Dixie attracted plenty of attention. That Dixie never actually went out with any of Sky's ranch hands always baffled her. Sky didn't pretend to understand, but she also didn't meddle in other people's love lives, hoping they would return the favor with her.

Dixie's brother, Marlon, was a tall, classically handsome man in his mid-twenties with broad shoulders and an athletic build. Unlike his sister, he had short dark hair and a close-trimmed beard. Despite his good looks and business-savvy wardrobe, he was pretty down-to-earth with less of an ego than one would think. Although the town's single female population should have swarmed him, his timid nature made him somehow less appealing to the younger women. Shamefully, many of the single women in town were attracted to Marcus's hyper-aggressive men. Perhaps they were afflicted with the 'bad boy' syndrome that was going around. Sky's friends seemed less than enthusiastic about eating at the diner that was currently *under siege* by Marcus's 'bad boys'.

"Maybe we should go someplace else for lunch," Marlon muttered while casting looks at the table at the far end of the diner.

"Stop looking that way," Dixie scolded her brother. "They're liable to think you're looking for trouble and pick a fight."

"Don't worry about them," Sky announced sternly to her friends. "They won't bother us. For some unknown reason, Marcus likes me."

"You're part of the 'in' crowd," Dixie reminded her. "That gives you a free pass."

"Yeah, right," Marlon muttered with a soft snort. "Marcus wants to get in her pants. That's why she gets a free pass."

"I wish you'd stop saying that," Sky remarked, rolling her eyes. "He's got to be at least forty. Makes me nauseous just thinking about it."

"You do know that most of his girlfriends are your age," Marlon reminded her.

"Makes me wonder why he seems interested in me," Sky insisted, slightly dumbfounded. "He has an entire stable of beautiful women waiting on his beck and call. Why would he want someone like me? I'm certainly not show pony material."

"How do I put this politely?" Marlon asked and sank into thought.

"They're high-priced call girls," Dixie informed her, not skirting around the issue as her brother had.

"I would have phrased it more politely," Marlon muttered.

"You're from one of the respected families in town," Dixie reminded her. "And your rumored virgin status excites him."

"Okay, that's just plain gross," Sky muttered while making a face.

"You need a boyfriend," Marlon informed her. "Whether or not you're actually sleeping with said boyfriend is irrelevant. Eventually, it'll be assumed you're not one of the few remaining virgin sacrifices, and he'll lose interest."

"Great," Dixie announced somewhat cheerfully while eyeing her brother. "I nominate you to be her pretend boyfriend."

"Not me," Marlon gasped. "It'd be a toss-up over who'd kill me first. Marcus or Tony."

"They don't own me," Sky scoffed while shifting uncomfortably in her seat. "Besides, I'm not interested in any of the guys around here." Sky hesitated and felt compelled to backpedal on the comment. "No offense, Marlon."

"None taken," he replied without missing a beat. "I'm actually rather grateful."

Dixie frowned and swatted Marlon on the shoulder closest to her. He yelped with discomfort and rubbed where she'd hit him.

"I mean, I love the guys on the ranch, but they aren't really my type," she explained, then frowned at the thought. "I'm not even sure I have a type." Sky waved them off. "Something to worry about another time."

The waitress, Jasmine, approached with three iced teas while seeming a little frazzled. Jasmine was a slightly shorter, attractive woman in her mid-thirties with dark shoulder-length hair and big brown eyes. She was as spicy as she was curvy and could hold her own in any conversation, never fearing to speak her mind.

"Are you sure you guys want to be here?" she asked while nodding toward the back. "Environment is a little hostile right now."

"What's going on?" Sky asked while eyeing the diner owner. "They're usually loud and obnoxious. Kind of quiet over there."

"Yeah, quiet, like the eye of a hurricane," Jasmine informed them. "There's some unpleasantness among those six. Death glares and harsh whispers. Real 'calm before the storm' shit going down."

"I'm guessing Tony and Marcus's new crew aren't playing well together," Sky informed her. "I caught a pre-show at the general store. Seems like they're re-establishing the pecking order."

"Well, it's not looking good," Jasmine informed them. "Get ready to take cover if they go at it."

"There's always in-house fighting among Marcus's men," Marlon remarked. "Too many toxic personalities clashing."

"I've seen them like that," Jasmine reported and shook her head. "This feels *different*."

After Jasmine left the table to place their order, Dixie leaned across the table closer to Sky to speak privately, even though there was no one around.

"Did you meet Marcus's new guys at the party on Saturday?" Dixie asked. "What's their deal?"

"No deal, really," Sky informed her friend and shrugged. "Ox and Moose appear to be housebroken, and Vaughn is a narcissistic pig suffering from delusions of grandeur."

"Oh, so the type I usually attract?" Dixie remarked with a tiny, humored smile.

"Except this guy makes bad guys look decent," Sky informed her.

"I already told you, he's my type," Dixie announced and snorted a laugh. "No need to sell it."

"He's working for Marcus," Marlon muttered. "Obviously, not a choir boy."

"Pity," Dixie remarked. "I caught a glimpse of that Vaughn guy when we came in. He's kind of sexy."

"Well, don't let Vaughn's dashing good looks fool you," Sky remarked while staring at her iced tea as she stirred it with her straw. "He's not Marcus's average attack dog. He probably collects heads in jars."

When Sky looked up, Dixie and Marlon were staring just behind her with slightly horrified expressions. Sky looked to her left and saw Vaughn standing only a foot from their table with a chilling smile on his face.

"Skyler Winchester," Vaughn announced somewhat cheerfully but with a sinister tone. "I was hoping to run into you again. You left in such a hurry on the Fourth of July, we didn't get a chance to finish our conversation."

Sky tensed but returned the smile, deciding she was all-in. "Vaughn," she announced in the same sarcastic tone he used. "What a pleasant surprise. We were just talking about you."

"Yes, so I heard," Vaughn announced somewhat deviously. "Good looking, above average, and something about 'head' that I probably shouldn't repeat."

"I'd ask you to join us, but I'm sure Tony has other plans for you," Sky announced somewhat cheerfully. "I'll be sure to send flowers to the hospital *or the cemetery*. Whichever."

"I wouldn't bother," Vaughn replied while grinning. "Tony doesn't really care for flowers." Without warning, he slipped into the booth alongside her, easily sliding her down the seat when his hip collided with hers. "Thanks for the offer, but I can only stay for a minute or two."

Sky felt a slight cold chill down her spine at his closeness and his words. She reluctantly moved further down the seat so her leg wasn't touching his. Vaughn immediately slid down the seat, pressing against her leg again while smiling at her friends.

"You must be Marlon and Dixie, Skyler's friends," Vaughn announced, matter-of-factly.

Marlon and Dixie seemed taken aback, possibly wondering how he knew who they were.

"The rest of the guys at Marcus's ranch filled me in on all the good town gossip," Vaughn cheerfully reported, then cast a glance at Sky, who was trapped on the booth seat alongside him. "I hear you go horseback riding a lot in the morning near the back edge of Marcus's property. We can go riding together. I'd love to finish our conversation from Saturday night." He then slapped his hand on her thigh and gave it a firm squeeze while grinning. "I'll clear my entire morning schedule. It's a date." He looked at Marlon and Dixie. "It was really nice meeting Skyler's friends, but I have to be going." He then slid out of the booth and smiled at Sky. "And I'll see you tomorrow morning." Vaughn then winked and walked away.

"Was he actually being friendly?" Dixie asked while cringing.

"No," Sky muttered. "That was a polite threat."

"Why would you think he was threatening you?" Marlon asked.

"Because I kneed him in the groin Saturday night," Sky replied.

Marlon groaned and sank into his seat while rubbing his eyes. "Why, Sky?" he asked, then peered at her. "Why do you always poke the bear?"

"I didn't poke the bear," she snapped back in anger. "He had his hands all over me. I needed to establish boundaries, and these guys don't take 'go to hell' for an answer."

"Maybe you'd better ride a different trail for a few weeks," Dixie suggested.

"I'm not going to let him intimidate me," Sky informed them. "I'll take a shotgun with me. If he crosses onto my land, I'll shoot him."

"You don't think that will escalate things?" Marlon demanded.

"Not really," Sky replied almost casually. "Not if he's dead."

Jasmine delivered their food once Marcus's men left the diner, seeming relieved that they were gone. "Everything okay here?" she asked with some concern at Vaughn's visit.

"Nothing I couldn't handle," Sky reported.

"Just digging her grave a little deeper," Dixie informed her.

Jasmine looked out the window and groaned. "At least they waited until they got outside," she muttered. "Saves me the cleanup."

Alerted by the comment, Sky, Dixie, and Marlon looked out the window. Vaughn and Tony were now shouting at each other. Each was backed by his men standing behind him. Tony's men looked angry while Vaughn's men stood by with stone-cold expressions on their stern faces. Tony suddenly took a step toward Vaughn while swinging his paw sized fist. Vaughn ducked the swing, then popped back up, punching Tony in the face with his left fist and then once with his right for good measure. Tony stumbled back a step, appearing enraged. His men jumped in front of him and held him back while he screamed profanities at Vaughn. Vaughn stood his ground and stared at him, lacking any emotion. Apparently, he made his point.

"Okay," Marlon remarked and minded his food. "That was kind of scary."

"I thought for sure Vaughn would be kissing the pavement," Sky muttered.

"I guess he's even tougher than he looks," Dixie announced.

That little display in the parking lot was enough to give Sky a moment's pause. She now knew she couldn't underestimate the man. If she thought Tony was dangerous, she had to assume Vaughn was worse. If she didn't want to be intimidated by the man, she was going to need one hell of a backup plan for her morning ride tomorrow.

Chapter 9

The following morning, Sky rode her usual pattern and routine. She wasn't going to give the schoolyard bully the satisfaction of scaring her. That wasn't to say she didn't have a backup plan as well as a shotgun. She did, however, leave her camera at home that morning so it wouldn't get accidentally broken. After she checked in with the guys watching the herd, she continued onward with the rest of her ride. She eventually rode across the field that was adjacent to Marcus's land and immediately noticed the horse and rider just beyond the woods. The rider was too far away to know if it was Vaughn wearing the black cowboy hat, but she easily recognized his horse, Diablo. The horse, much like her own, was unmistakable. Sky stopped her horse and stared at the distant horse and rider.

There was a strange moment where they just stared at each other across the distance. It felt like a pivotal moment for them, setting the tone for any future interactions. Sky knew that she couldn't back down, or he'd own her. Her cell phone rang in her pocket, almost startling her. Sky hesitated, then removed her phone and looked at the caller ID. It said 'unknown', but she could see Vaughn with his hand to his ear. She accepted the call and placed the phone to her ear.

"Yeah?" she gruffly responded.

"Do you actually have a shotgun strapped to your saddle?" Vaughn asked over the phone, sounding somewhat humored.

Sky removed the Browning twelve-gauge pump-action shotgun from the saddle holster and rested the stock on her thigh.

"Kind of looks like one," she replied. "Would you like to see it up close and personal?"

"Depends," Vaughn replied over the phone. "Are you inviting me over for a play date or threatening bodily harm?"

"I'm going to go with 'threatening bodily harm'," she replied.

"Aren't you paranoid?" Vaughn remarked with a low chucklc that sent shivers down her spine.

"I don't like being stalked," she informed him through the phone while staring at him across the large field. "And I don't tolerate trespassers."

Vaughn chuckled over the phone, sounding amused. "I thought we arranged a riding date," he remarked. "How is that stalking?"

"You inviting yourself is not 'arranging' a riding date," she replied.

"Technically, you never said no," Vaughn reminded her.

She could almost hear his cheap grin through the phone. "I doubt you'd accept that answer," she replied. "Are we through here?"

"I suppose so."

Sky disconnected the call, then snapped a picture of Vaughn on his horse before replacing her cell phone, but kept the shotgun resting on her thigh. She didn't attempt to leave as she stared across the field. Sky couldn't deny, at least to herself, that the distant image of him on his warrior horse was almost picturesque. Vaughn tipped his hat, then turned his horse and trotted back into the woods for a trail that would lead him back to Marcus's estate. The moment he disappeared, four ranch hands galloped over the horizon behind her and stopped their horses alongside her.

"Everything okay?" Jerry asked while staring at the woods on Marcus's land.

Sky smiled and nodded. "Yeah, everything is fine," she replied. "Thanks for having my back."

"Always," Jerry replied, returning the smile.

"Was that your new friend?" Tom asked while nodding toward the distant woods.

"Trust me," Sky muttered. "There's nothing friendly about that one."

Chapter 10

One week later. The Lake House Bar was aptly named, as it was a house overlooking a lake. The former large, three-story home had been converted into the locals' bar twenty years ago. Although it still looked like an old farmhouse, there were large neon beer signs in the windows. It featured a small, covered porch in the front, along with ample dirt and stone parking. To the right of the building was a long hitching post made from an old telephone pole that extended the entire side of the structure. The area between the hitching post and the woods was mostly dirt and grass with a well-worn path created by many patrons riding in on horseback. Sky's large, blue roan horse was visibly seen tied to the hitching post alongside several others.

The interior of the country-themed bar was designed to resemble an old Western saloon, featuring wooden floors, barnwood walls, and exposed ceiling beams. A large bar occupied most of the right side, while a small dance floor was located closer to the left side, near the hallway to the bathrooms. An old jukebox played a mix of older and current country hits while the crowd, comprising both younger and older men and women, socialized and line-danced on the wooden dance floor. Toward the back of the bar were several unmarked doors, possibly leading to the kitchen and the upper two floors. Not far from the unmarked doors were two pool tables and a table near the back, where a group of six men played poker. The local bar was the happening hot spot every weekend, and most weekdays too. It was a small town with little for folks to do to blow off steam after work, with most of the town's population involved in some form of ranch or farm work. Many of them were single men in their twenties and thirties.

Sky hung out with Dixie and Marlon at a table near the back, not far from the area containing the busy pool tables. Sky didn't usually drink when they went out, but tonight she was drinking whiskey, straight up. She needed to dull her thoughts, even if just for a few hours. All three occasionally cast their eyes upon the unsanctioned poker game, played out in the open. Dixie shook her head while frowning in displeasure.

"I can't believe they get away with playing poker out in the open like that," Dixie remarked. "There are half a dozen signs around the place saying 'no gambling'."

"It's not as if the sheriff intends to bust up the game any time soon," Sky informed Dixie, then gave a slight nod to the large table in the back. "Considering he's the player with the most chips."

Still in uniform but wearing a black jacket to mostly cover it, was their local lawman with his large stack of poker chips and a 'my shit don't stink' grin on his face. Sheriff Burke was over six foot tall, rugged, and somewhat imposing. Although he was only in his early thirties, he appeared to be a rough customer, with dark, unkempt hair and an unshaven face. He often looked as if he'd been drinking and was not really someone you wanted to approach.

"If it keeps the peace, let them play," Marlon muttered, then casually looked around the crowded bar. "For a Saturday night, it's oddly mellow for a change."

It was true. Everyone seemed relaxed and for a very good reason. None of Marcus's men were present to ruin everyone else's good time. It didn't happen very often, but it was a rare treat when they didn't show up.

"I heard some whispers around town that Marcus's new head of security and Tony still aren't playing well together," Dixie informed her brother.

"If we're lucky, they killed each other," Marlon remarked.

"Or Marcus put them in a timeout," Sky muttered.

"Not having either of the toxic men around certainly is refreshing," Marlon replied.

"I, personally, haven't seen either since last weekend," Sky remarked, then held up her drink. "And I can't say I mind."

Dixie giggled and clinked her glass to Sky's before both drank. Although Dixie was enjoying Sky drinking heavily alongside her, Marlon eyed his friend somewhat suspiciously.

"You're drinking quite a bit tonight," Marlon remarked. "Is everything okay?"

Sky managed a smile and casually shrugged. "Without Marcus's intolerable men hanging around and a bunch of my guys at the bar, I feel comfortable having a few."

Sky didn't have to worry about driving since she rode her horse to the lake bar, as she did most times they went out, and her ranch was actually only a short ride from the bar. Marlon didn't seem convinced by her response, but let it go. Sky had slipped into a darker world tonight, but didn't feel like sharing her depression with her friends, especially when they were having a good time. When Sky's ranch hands approached the table to entice them to line dance, Dixie was thrilled. Although Marlon reluctantly joined them on the crowded floor, the guys couldn't convince Sky to go with them. She wasn't really into line dancing, and especially not tonight. Honestly, she just wanted to get a massive buzz on. Sky watched her friends and her ranch hands enjoying themselves while she continued to drink.

It was eight years ago tonight that Sky's parents were killed in a car crash just a few miles from town. There was no one to blame. It was late, dark, and a heavy thunderstorm had rolled in while they were on a winding, wooded back road. Indicated by a shattered headlight containing tuffs of animal hair, they'd swerved to miss a deer. Her mother died instantly, while her father died on the scene after the paramedics arrived. Sky's sorrow was interrupted by the young waitress, Ruby, who had paused at her table. Ruby offered a sympathetic smile and placed a double whiskey on the table before her, despite not having requested it and having yet to finish the one in her hand.

Ruby was a beautiful young woman with a slightly athletic build, which she showcased by wearing low-cut tank tops, increasing her chances for excellent tips. Her brown hair was slightly wavy and fell just below her shoulders. She wore just enough makeup to gain the attention of heavily drinking cowboys and their generous tips. Sky drained the rest of her drink and placed the empty glass on Ruby's tray.

"Thanks," Sky replied just barely loud enough for the young woman to hear.

"That one's on me," Ruby informed her, then turned oddly sympathetic while forcing a tiny smile. "I miss them too."

Sky nodded but didn't respond. As Ruby left her table, Sky was left with mixed emotions. Ruby had been Sky's best friend growing up, long before Dixie and Marlon moved to town. She knew Sky's parents her entire life and was the first one at her door the morning after Sky's parents were killed. The two of them cried together for hours. Unfortunately, their friendship came to an ugly and abrupt end just after graduation when Sky found out Ruby had slept with her boyfriend. Sky and Tony dated their entire senior year in high school and were considered the perfect couple. Everyone assumed they'd even get married, including Sky and Tony. Then, Marcus happened. He built his mansion and racehorse stable. Suddenly, half the men in town were lining up outside his door to fill positions. Tony was first in line, which is when he started his transformation from a nice guy to Marcus's goon. The change was rapid.

Within a couple of weeks, Tony became hungry for money and power. Along with that hunger came an invigorated sex drive. Sky wanted to wait until she was married, which Tony always seemed to be okay with until he suddenly hooked up with Ruby. Sky's relationship with her boyfriend and best friend ended in an instant. Possibly the most ironic part was that Ruby and Tony never got together after Sky dumped them both. Maybe, if the two had been in love, Sky would have understood better what happened. Did Tony or Ruby think it was worth it? Apparently, Sky didn't mean much to either of them. It took a year or two before Sky could even look at Ruby, let alone talk to her. Now, they were *acquaintances*. Nothing more. With all the bad memories flooding her mind, Sky wasn't sure she could drink enough to forget everything, yet she somehow finished the last drink and ended up with another.

The mood within the barroom suddenly shifted, and that could mean only one thing. Sky followed the commotion and saw Vaughn, Ox, and Moose standing at the bar. Vaughn was clearly drunk, and his men were attempting to get him to leave with them. It was strange because they weren't in the barroom all evening, so where they had come from was anyone's guess. There had always been speculation that Marcus ran illegal gambling and possibly prostitution somewhere within town, but none of the locals seemed to know anything about it. At least, if they did, they weren't admitting it. It then dawned on Sky. Was it possible that Vaughn and his men emerged from a secret room inside the bar that she was unaware of? There were several locked doors marked 'private' within the bar. Any one of them could lead to the basement, which could be where this so-called gambling parlor was located.

Being mostly drunk didn't calm her curiosity any. Honestly, she was on her way to feeling no pain, which made her immune to anything that might not be in her best interest. Sky took her drink and moved closer to the bar. She heaved herself onto one of the stools for a front row seat. Although she had seen Vaughn angry before, she'd never seen him drunk. It was interesting to watch. For the first time, he didn't appear to be in control of his emotions. What he was mad about was anyone's guess. That's when she saw Tony and his two men, seemingly appearing from thin air as well. There had to be a secret entrance in that area! If she hadn't been drunk already, maybe she would have seen someone emerge from one of the 'private' doors. Tony suddenly lunged for Vaughn.

That's all it took. The two men violently punched each other, easily dispersing the crowd that had been standing around them. Both men flew across a nearby table, sending bottles and glasses flying and shattering against the floor. Nearby men and women sprang to their feet and attempted to flee the war zone. Both men fell from the table and onto the floor with a crash in a flurry of flying fists. Considering Tony was sober, he didn't seem to be dominating the fight against the drunken man as much as one would have thought. Men were shouting and cheering them on, although it was unclear if any of the locals cared who won. They just wanted to see the two men beat the piss out of each other for their own amusement. The two thugs were soon back on their feet. Vaughn punched Tony with a left, then a right, and knocked him backward against the bar, nearly hitting Sky on her barstool. She was suddenly regretting getting so close.

Vaughn could have easily finished off Tony, but he chose to take a step back and compose himself. Tony's men quickly stepped in and encouraged Tony to return to parts unknown with them. All three vanished without a trace, and Sky still couldn't figure out which door they went through. Once they were gone, Ox and Moose checked on their boss. He held his hands up to them and nodded, indicating he was fine, although he looked fairly battered.

"Come on," Ox announced to Vaughn. "We'll drive you home."

"I'm fine," Vaughn informed him while catching his breath, then stumbled to the bar. "I have to take my horse home."

"You're in no condition to ride," Moose reminded him.

"Especially that demon," Ox muttered.

As Vaughn leaned on the bar, now directly alongside Sky, she eyed his slightly battered profile. He was one tough son-of-a-bitch, making him even more intimidating and possibly a little sexy. In her sympathetic mood, Sky slid her glass of whiskey closer to him. Vaughn cast a sideways glance at her, nodded, and accepted the drink. He drained it in one swallow, returned the glass to the bar, and then placed his hand on her leg to balance himself as he straightened. Sky cast a sideways glance at Vaughn, but he wasn't even aware of his unintended touch, so she decided not to 'poke the bear'. Once he collected himself, she watched Vaughn leave the bar with his two friends, only a step behind. Dixie and Marlon approached only a moment later and looked around the bar, dumfounded.

"What the hell was that about?" Dixie asked.

"I doubt anyone's going to ask," Sky muttered as she ordered another glass of whiskey.

§

One hour and several drinks later, Sky finally joined her friends on the dance floor. She messed up just about every move in the line dance, but they were laughing too hard even to care. Everything that happened during that hour was a massive blur. But when she found herself slow dancing with Jerry and unable to remember how she got there, Sky suddenly realized the extent of her intoxication. She knew she sometimes became a little too 'affectionate' while drinking, and it was possible she'd sent Jerry the wrong message while they slow danced. She liked Jerry. Always had, just not in the romantic sense. Before she did anything stupid, Sky knew it was time to go home. It wasn't a long ride, but she feared passing out and falling off her horse if she didn't head out soon. Thankfully, the fresh, cool night air would help clear her head.

"Maybe you should drive home with us," Jerry suggested, expressing concern for her unusually drunken condition.

"I have Admiral," she reminded him. "Even if I can't find the trail, he can. He knows his way home better than I do."

"One of the guys can take Admiral back," Jerry informed her. "The wind picked up, and they're calling for storms tonight."

"We'll be fine, Jerry," she insisted. "Admiral likes to pull stunts with new riders. I wouldn't want anyone getting hurt attempting to ride him home."

Jerry glanced at Tom, Dixie, and Marlon for backup. All three frowned and shrugged, not willing to fight her on it.

Chapter 11

Sky rode her horse at a slow and steady walk along the dark, well-worn wooded trail on the trek home. Jerry had been right. It appeared as if a storm was brewing, so the forest was a lot darker and far breezier than usual. At least, she thought Jerry had said that. Maybe she was mistaken. Thankfully, the path was smooth and relatively flat. Sky wasn't afraid of riding at night and in the dark, but what she found mildly frightening was not remembering leaving the bar or even getting on her horse. There was even a moment where she wasn't sure what path she was riding on. On the bright side, she soon realized she was almost halfway home already. Her horse was used to the familiar trail, since they rode that way almost daily. She rode into a large field that would eventually lead to the trail back home.

Now that she was out in the open field, she could see lightning in the distance. It was definitely going to be one hell of a storm, but, thankfully, she'd be home long before that arrived. As she rode into the slightly sloped field, her horse snorted and jigged sideways, surprising her with the quick action. Despite not exactly seeing straight, Sky immediately saw what had her horse uptight. A man, barely upright, was kneeling in the pasture several yards away. Sky stopped her horse and stared at the man a moment, attempting to make sense of what she was seeing and even who she was seeing. Being drunk wasn't helping her focus at all. It was a bit of a blur. Even without his signature cowboy hat, she realized it was Vaughn kneeling in the field with no sign of his spicy horse, Diablo, to be found.

Sky considered staying near the woods and avoiding Vaughn, but she realized he had been thrown from his horse, and he might have been injured. She couldn't remember when he left the bar, but it had to be at least an hour ago. She couldn't just leave him there. Sky groaned, disgusted with herself. Curse her drunken sense of pity. She reluctantly rode across the pasture and stopped several feet from the infamous man, who was now at her mercy. He sat on his feet, obviously drunk, and stared at her.

"Come to gloat?" Vaughn asked while looking up at her.

Sky frowned, spun her horse around, and extended her hand to him. "More like pity," she muttered.

Vaughn smirked while standing and placed his hat on his head. He then grasped her hand, put his foot in the stirrup, and attempted to mount the horse. With the first attempt, he nearly pulled her off Admiral. On his second attempt, he fell back to the ground and lay on his back laughing at himself. He finally groaned, pulled himself to his feet, and made his third attempt. Vaughn made it onto her horse behind her, nearly lost his balance, and almost took Sky off the other side with him. If she hadn't been equally drunk, keeping her own balance would have been easier. Vaughn again laughed, then clung to her on the horse in front of him.

"Christ, if we make it home without falling off, I'll be surprised," he announced with a chuckle close to her ear.

"Just mind your hands," she scoffed.

"Relax, darling," he announced, somewhat humored. "In my condition, I'm completely at your mercy, so you'd better watch your hands."

§

At a trot, it was only a ten-minute ride to Marcus's ranch from the field, and she could feel Vaughn's beard nuzzling the side of her face the entire way. Or maybe he was just trying to keep his balance. It was unclear. The flashes of lightning were getting closer, the wind had picked up dramatically, and she could now hear thunder rumbling loudly in the distance. Halfway to Marcus's farm, a light rain started. Vaughn chuckled, humored at something, and placed his hat on her head, possibly to keep her head dry. By the time the barn came into sight, it was pouring. Sky couldn't pick up the pace, especially riding double, so all three were drenched by the time they reached the massive barn. The big door on the barn was open, allowing them to ride directly into the tall, enormous aisle. Vaughn's saddled horse stood inside the barn, happily munching on a stray bale of hay and watching them.

Vaughn eyed his horse with disgust. "Traitor," he muttered.

He finally released Sky and dismounted by sliding down her horse's rump, laughing all the way. Surprisingly, he managed to stay on his feet when he hit the concrete floor, although he did hold onto the horse's tail for support. Thankfully, her horse didn't mind or react. Sky tossed Vaughn his hat before he headed for his saddled horse. She then turned around and rode back to the open barn door. Not only was it pouring outside, but she could hear thunder rumbling loudly and getting closer. It was only going to get worse.

"You're not actually going back out in that storm, are you?" Vaughn asked her as he unsaddled his horse.

"I don't have much choice," she remarked and frowned at the thought of being drenched the entire way home.

"Sure you do," Vaughn insisted while nearly stumbling over his saddle on the ground. "There are several empty stalls, and my apartment is above the barn. I've got plenty of room."

"I'm not sleeping with you, Vaughn," she informed him, somewhat curtly, while staring out at the pouring rain.

"I wasn't suggesting that, darling," he informed her matter-of-factly. "I'll take the sofa, you can have the bedroom." He then grinned. "Because I'm such a gentleman."

Even Vaughn had to laugh at his words. Sky glanced back at Vaughn and watched him lead his horse into one of the nearby stalls. Even sober, riding her horse during a thunderstorm was a bad idea. Add excessive wind and being drunk, and it was only asking for trouble.

"Fine," she reluctantly replied and dismounted her horse a little too quickly, immediately feeling dizzy from the action. She glared at Vaughn. "Just make sure you behave."

"Me?" he asked, then chuckled. "I'm the drunk one. You'd better make sure *you* behave. I don't want you molesting me in my sleep."

He obviously didn't realize she was drunk too, which actually worked in her favor. Let him believe that. It would make him mind his manners a little better. Sky managed to unsaddle her horse, while at least attempting a sober appearance, and put him in one of the vacant stalls. Vaughn gave both horses some hay, then smiled his usual devious smile and showed her to the staircase leading up to one of the loft apartments.

Chapter 12

While Vaughn stumbled across the room to retrieve some towels in the bathroom, Sky briefly looked around the loft apartment from her safe spot near the main door. She shouldn't have been surprised by the nicely appointed staff quarters above the barn, but she was. The apartment had a living room, a small kitchenette, a bathroom, and a bedroom. A nice added touch was the French doors leading to a small, private balcony. Marcus had an expensive barn with expensive horses, so naturally, he'd have nice staff quarters as well. The apartment was only one of four located above the two barns attached to either side of the indoor riding arena. The place apparently came furnished with expensive furniture, despite its inhabitants being the rugged cowboy types. The furnished living room came complete with a large screen television mounted on the wall, a small portable bar, and a work desk.

The kitchenette consisted of a full-sized refrigerator, a small counter with an equally small sink, a microwave oven, and a coffeemaker. A tiny island counter offered more counter space as well as counter seating for two. Vaughn returned with two towels and handed her one of them. Sky accepted the towel with some apprehension, then dried her hair. She gave a nod to the apartment.

"This is nice."

"Yeah, you should have seen how pissed Tony was that I got his loft apartment," Vaughn announced and chuckled.

"I saw how pissed Tony was," she reminded him, indicating his bruised face. "He tried to take it out of your ass."

"I assure you, he's mad at me for a hell of a lot more than just this apartment," Vaughn reported, seemingly amused. "Tony's about to be de-throned, but that's a secret." Vaughn winked at her. "I'll get you something dry to change into."

Vaughn was only gone a moment and soon returned with a t-shirt and a pair of shorts for her to change into. She saw little choice but to accept the change of clothing. She certainly didn't want to spend the next few hours in wet clothing. Sky went into the private bathroom to change and locked the door without a second thought. The bathroom was small and simple. There was a four-by-five-foot standing shower with glass doors, a toilet, and a sink with some counter space. For a single guy, particularly one of Marcus's goons, he kept his bathroom neat and clean. While changing, she could hear the storm raging outside with the rain beating heavily against the tin roof. Sky was momentarily lost in her thoughts, again remembering the night her parents died eight years ago this very night.

In her drunken condition, she had to wonder if there was some sort of cosmic irony at play. Sky frowned and attempted to suppress those feelings, concentrating on changing. She had a difficult time standing straight, everything slightly hazy, and her ears were ringing. Despite too much alcohol, she collected herself and managed a sober appearance as she returned to the living room. Vaughn, also in dry clothes, stood at the wet bar while pouring himself a drink, then indicated the whiskey bottle.

"Nightcap?" he asked, then snorted a laugh. "I'm pretty sure I took your drink at the bar, although I can't be sure." He cast a glance at her, then poured a second glass without waiting for her response. "Might ward off that chill of yours."

Sky wondered what he meant by 'warding off her chill' when she remembered that she'd removed her soaked bra. When she glanced down, she realized the thin t-shirt material revealed her perky nipples poking through. She subconsciously folded her arms across her chest to hide her 'chill'. Against her better judgment, she agreed to the double shot of whiskey. One drink to forget the horrible thoughts racing through her mind, and then she'd lock herself in Vaughn's bedroom to keep him honest. She accepted the glass and collapsed into the smaller chair not far from the sofa. Sky didn't trust Vaughn and knew better than to risk sitting where he could get too close. Vaughn collapsed onto the couch closest to her chair and groaned loudly.

"I'm going to feel that in the morning," he muttered, then sipped his drink. "I think I landed on my ass."

"Serves you right," she remarked. "Riding drunk at night with a storm approaching."

Oh, the irony of that remark! Look where she was after all her bad decisions while drinking!

"I thought you weren't going to gloat," he scoffed while casting a sideways glance at her.

"I never made that promise," she reminded him. "You expect too much from a horse that young and green."

"So you're going to gloat *and* give horse training advice?" he remarked as he raised a curious brow.

"Nope," she replied with a sigh and took a large swallow of whiskey. "You're too stubborn to listen to good advice. I wouldn't waste my time or breath."

"So being stubborn comes with a few perks, huh?" he teased with a chuckle. "Good to know."

Sky eyed him and the smirk on his face. He seemed so pleased with himself. "You're something else," she scoffed.

His grin widened as he held up his hand, revealing his fingers. "Acht, you don't get to nag me until you put a ring on my finger."

Sky stared at him a moment, surprised by the comment, then suddenly laughed. Somehow, she found that funny.

"Huh? You can smile," Vaughn remarked. "I may have misjudged you."

"In my defense," she announced. "You didn't make a very good first impression." She then considered the comment and shrugged. "Of course, I wasn't exactly impressed with your second and third impressions either."

"I'm an acquired taste," he informed her. "You're not ready for *this* particular vintage."

Sky couldn't keep from laughing again. Was he always so funny, or was it just because she was drunk? Or was it because he was drunk?

"You're probably right," Sky remarked.

She drained the remaining shot and set her glass on the coffee table, prepared to make a hasty departure for the bedroom. When she stood, Sky realized Vaughn was staring at her with a strange look on his face.

"I'm sorry," he remarked somewhat timidly.

Sky stared back at him from where she stood, slightly puzzled. She wondered what prompted that. Had he done something? She knew he hadn't spiked her drink because she watched him pour it.

"About what?" she finally asked.

"What I said in the arena on July 4th," he replied with a soft groan. "Like a true asshole, I put two and two together and came up with five."

"You're making no sense," she informed him, and that wasn't just because she was drunk. He was literally making no sense.

"My comment about Tony," he replied. "I've met Tony's girlfriends, and I guess I wanted to rub you the wrong way before you did it to me first. I didn't know you were actually his high school girlfriend. I didn't know he hurt you."

"Yeah, well, I don't like to dwell on *the good old days*," she remarked with a sigh. "And I'd like to forget about Tony."

"You and me both," he muttered, then downed his drink in one swallow.

Sky caught a glimpse of the scrapes on his knuckles and then glanced at the abrasions on his cheek, reminding her of Vaughn's earlier altercation with Tony. She suddenly felt bad about Tony hitting Vaughn. Sky approached the sofa apprehensively and sat facing him. Vaughn remained completely still, watching her, possibly curious about her agenda. Sky studied his scraped cheek a moment in silence before finally meeting his gaze.

"Even though Tony and I were a long time ago, and I really don't give two shits about him," she remarked, then smirked. "I sort of enjoyed watching you beat his ass."

Vaughn snorted a laugh and indicated his scraped knuckles before flexing them. "Not nearly as much as I enjoyed it," he replied.

Both laughed a little more than they should have at Tony's expense. Sky leaned on Vaughn's shoulder and continued to laugh. When she looked back at him, his face close to hers, he maintained his smile but was now silent.

"How pissed would he be if he knew you were in my apartment right now?" Vaughn asked.

Sky groaned and snorted a laugh. "So pissed," she replied. "He secretly seethes when his boss flirts with me."

Vaughn cocked his head and looked somewhat surprised. "Really?" he asked. "Why's that?"

Sky couldn't hold back her laugh. "Why?" she scoffed. "Because he couldn't have me. And if he couldn't have me, no one else should."

"You and Tony never--?" he asked, genuinely surprised.

"No, never," she insisted a bit loudly. "The boy never even made it to second base."

Vaughn was instantly humored and snorted a laugh. "That's interesting, because he honestly believes he's made it to third as well as catching a few foul balls."

"Well, Tony is a lying sack of shit," she casually informed him. "Although I really have no idea what you mean by 'foul balls'."

"I don't think I can have that conversation without a few more drinks," he remarked, then heaved himself off the sofa and stumbled to the portable bar.

Vaughn returned with the bottle of whiskey and poured each of them a glass before collapsing back onto the sofa, now a little closer to her than before. Sky picked up her glass and took a sip while Vaughn downed at least a shot's worth from his. He finally looked at her and grinned.

"I will tell you anything you want to know," Vaughn informed her, his grin cheapening. "Only if you tell me why Tony never made it to second base."

She eyed him suspiciously but maintained her humor because, well, she was drunk. "Why do you want to know about that? It was five years ago."

"Because Tony's a prick who brags about things, and I take a perverse pleasure in his misfortune," Vaughn replied.

Sky set her glass down on the coffee table, then sat back and hung on Vaughn's shoulder with her face close to his. She stared into his eyes while grinning almost slyly.

"If I'm going to share intimate details about anything with you, I want something more in return," she informed him.

Vaughn cocked his head and grinned like a schoolboy. "Name it," he quipped while hovering over her and moving his mouth closer to hers.

"I want to ride your horse," she replied a little too quickly.

Vaughn hesitated at the request, then quickly pulled away and began undoing his belt. "Deal!" he cried out. "Ride away!"

Sky cried out with surprise, immediately stopping him, and then laughed. "I meant your *actual* horse," she insisted.

Vaughn frowned and straightened. "You're no fun," he muttered, then resumed smiling and casually placed his hand on her thigh while groaning. "Fine, you can ride Diablo." His grin again increased. "Now, tell me why you rejected Tony."

Sky retrieved her drink, downed the rest of it, and sank against Vaughn, resting her head on his shoulder as she met his gaze.

"I was only eighteen and wasn't ready for that kind of relationship yet," Sky informed him, then shifted slightly. "I wanted to wait, and he was okay with it-- until he wasn't."

Vaughn stared into her eyes while maintaining a tiny smile. "I've heard rumors about your reputation around town, Sky," he informed her. "I wasn't really looking for a reason why you haven't had sex. I was just curious why you never let Tony get a little, well, *further*."

As she studied his face, his smile became more natural, and there was an unusual warmth behind his eyes. Or maybe she just thought that way because she was drunk. It had been so long since she'd even been semi-intimate with someone that she felt herself enjoying the physical closeness at that moment. Vaughn's rugged good looks didn't help repress those feelings either.

"I suppose I just wasn't ready," she again insisted. "Tony certainly wasn't the asshole that he is today, but he was still a little, well, aggressive even back then." She shuddered slightly while reflecting and seemed to make the connections while drunk that she could never make while sober. "It's like you with Diablo."

Vaughn was slightly taken aback and even chuckled. "How was it like me and Diablo with you and Tony?" he asked, almost humored.

"You could ride Diablo at a nice, easy trot, and he was fine," she reminded him. "But every time you tried to lope him, he'd want to gallop."

"That is true."

"Well, it was the same with Tony," she informed him. "If I let him get past a trot, he'd want to gallop."

Vaughn was silent for a moment, then nodded. "I get it," he replied. "The boy has no self-control. That hasn't changed either. If anything, his impulse control has gotten worse. He's like a little boy who was never told 'no' his entire life. Just a spoiled brat throwing a tantrum when he doesn't get his way."

Her eyes widened as she sat up straight. "Yes, exactly!" Sky's mind was reeling at how quickly he'd deduced that. He barely even knew Tony! "You're a lot smarter than I gave you credit."

"I wouldn't go that far," Vaughn assured her. "I mean, it's kind of natural when you think about it. Your father, a man you undoubtedly admired deeply, died when a teenage girl needs a father figure the most. Your uncle attempted to fill his shoes but had reservations about his new role in your life, leaving you to govern yourself throughout your teens and causing you to act the way you think would make your father the proudest."

Sky stared at Vaughn as he talked, a strange sort of epiphany exploding in her mind. The added alcohol increased the impact of his words.

"Then along comes Tony, the dick," Vaughn continued almost dramatically. "He's hyper-aggressive, and it makes you feel safe, so, naturally, you fall for him. Except his hormones overpower your feelings of sexual security. So rather than awakening your sexual desire, he represses it, leaving you uncertain of yourself and 'spooked' by men."

Sky maintained her stare, unable to respond. Vaughn finally turned his head and met her gaze, raising his brows.

"Am I close?" he asked.

"Why does everything you just said make so much sense?" she almost gasped, unable to wrap her drunken mind around it.

"I wasn't aware I was making any sense at all," he informed her, then chuckled. "I'm too drunk to know what the hell I'm saying." His smile then increased as his eyes swept over her before again meeting her gaze. "If you're *that* cold, I can turn the heat on."

Sky's heart pounded as she stared into his eyes, aware that he had again taken notice of her hardened nipples pronounced against the thin t-shirt. The longer she stared into his eyes, the more he smiled and seemed pleased. Sky gently took his hand in hers, caressed it a moment, and then guided it beneath the shirt she wore. Although somewhat surprised, Vaughn shut his eyes and groaned softly at where she placed his hand. He warmly fondled her, then opened his eyes and met her gaze as she leaned in closer to him while enjoying the warmth of his touch. Sky moved her mouth closer to his and then spoke softly.

"Take me to second base."

Vaughn immediately groaned and met her lips halfway, kissing her warmly yet passionately.

Chapter 13

Sky woke the following morning to sunlight poking in through the part in the curtains of the unfamiliar bedroom. She was dizzy from too much alcohol, and the room was spinning. Sky attempted to move, then realized she was anchored by an arm snuggly around her as a man's hand cupped her naked breast beneath the shirt she wore. Despite her disorientation and dizziness, she could distinctly feel a man's naked body pressed against her from behind. It took a moment, but Sky finally remembered being in Vaughn's apartment last night; therefore, the naked man nestled against her had to be Vaughn. She internally panicked as bits and pieces of her drunken, sex-fueled night came back to haunt her. No matter how much she wished it wasn't true, there was no denying she and Vaughn had sex. What was more disturbing was that, from the parts she did remember, she was the instigator. She couldn't believe she was saving herself all this time, and her first time was with someone like Vaughn.

Sky attempted to pull away from Vaughn without waking him by gently removing his hand from her breast and slipping out from under his arm. Vaughn groaned, then sighed and reestablished his hold on her. He woke, then warmly kissed her neck from behind and groaned.

"Last night was amazing," Vaughn muttered softly in her ear while kissing her along her neck and shoulder.

She was horrified when she heard those words spoken aloud. As Vaughn pressed against her, Sky could feel his arousal building. She abruptly pulled away from him despite his attempt to keep her from leaving.

"I have to get out of here," she gasped and sprang from the bed, immediately regretting the action. She held her pounding head and waited for the room to stop spinning.

Vaughn sat up, revealing all his naked glory for her to admire. Despite his undeniably toned and attractive physique along with several noticeable scars, Sky groaned and looked away.

"Can you just stay under the covers until I leave?" she snapped, then looked around. "Where are my clothes?"

"They're in the dryer," he replied somewhat sharply, then raised his brow. "A little late for modesty. Considering the many ways you violated me last night, I'd assume you're on a first-name basis with my pecker."

"Last night was a mistake," she informed him and cast a quick look at him while attempting to avoid looking at his exposed man parts. "I was drunk. It never should have happened."

Vaughn chuckled, humored. "*You* were drunk? You only had a double shot of whiskey," he reminded her. "I was the drunk one. You took advantage of me, remember?"

"No, I was drunk," she snapped back, barely holding back her outrage. "I was completely wasted when I left the bar last night."

Vaughn considered her comment and appeared genuinely surprised by the confession. "Really?" he remarked. "You hid it well, but I guess that would explain the wild sex."

Sky groaned and held her head. "I'd rather not hear any details," she snapped back. "Let me be blissfully ignorant about last night."

"There's no reason to stress over it," Vaughn remarked. "Although you were like a sailor on shore leave with that mouth."

Sky glared at him, now annoyed. "I'm allowed to be stressed over it. I was saving myself for someone special. Certainly not you. It is a big deal." She then looked around while becoming flustered. "Where is the dryer? I need my clothes."

"I'll get your clothes in a minute," Vaughn insisted while clinging to his knees close to his chest. "We need to discuss this first."

"No, we don't," she informed him.

"I think we do," he remarked, finally turning defensive. "You told me that it was your first time right before *you* jumped on *me*. When I asked if you were sure about it, you insisted you were more than okay with it."

"I was drunk," she loudly reminded him. "I'm not *okay* with it."

Vaughn groaned and rubbed his eyes, then looked back at her, even though she remained flustered and unable to meet his gaze.

"Maybe I'm not the 'special someone' you had in mind, but you had no regrets at the time," he reminded her. "Quite the opposite."

"You just don't get it," she remarked. "I didn't want my first time to be with someone as questionable as you, and I certainly didn't want it to be a drunken one-night stand."

Vaughn patted the bed beside him and appeared almost sympathetic. "It doesn't have to be a one-night stand," he insisted, then smiled reassuringly. "Come back to bed."

She glared at him, her eyes narrowing. "That's not funny," she scoffed.

"I wasn't trying to be," he remarked, then groaned. "Okay, you made a mistake. You can beat yourself up over it, or you can embrace it."

"You know what," she snapped. "You've had your fun. Go brag to all your sleazy friends about it. I'm sure they'll have a lot of fun with it, considering how many times they've tried to get into my pants and failed."

When Sky turned to leave, Vaughn bolted from the bed and cut her off halfway to the door. She avoided looking at him, as he was still very much naked, and involuntarily jumped when he placed his hands on her shoulders, forcing her to face him.

"I'm not bragging to anyone," he firmly announced with sincerity.

She finally met his gaze while insecurely rubbing her shoulders. "You're not?" she asked, then immediately snorted a laugh. "I'll believe that when I see it."

"If Marcus finds out I slept with you, he'll skin me alive," Vaughn informed her. "You're his little angel. He wants to be the one defiling you. You're expressly off limits."

It was possibly the first time anyone in Marcus's circle actually admitted what she'd speculated for so long.

"I assure you, it's in my best interest that no one knows, as much as it is in your best interest." He offered a mildly sympathetic look as he stared into her eyes. "Consider this. You're already in, you may as well be all-in."

"Nice sales pitch," she scoffed, then sneered at him. "Hard pass, thanks."

Chapter 14

One month later. Sky entered the mostly empty, quiet bank in the middle of town and paused a moment to look around. Dixie waved to Sky from behind the teller counter, then motioned her over. Sky smiled and approached her friend.

"We weren't meeting for lunch today, were we?" Dixie asked. "It's Wednesday. Ladies' night at the bar, in case you'd forgotten."

"No, I haven't forgotten," Sky replied with a tiny laugh. "The ranch hands keep reminding me and insisting they're buying me drinks tonight."

"Oh, you're actually drinking tonight?" Dixie asked, now enthused.

"No," Sky replied, then groaned. "I'm never getting drunk again. I've learned my lesson the hard way."

"You're no fun," Dixie teased.

"So I've been told," Sky muttered, then resumed her cheerful mood. She placed two deposit tickets on the counter. "Just running a few errands for Uncle Nash. A ranch deposit and one for Uncle Nash's personal finances."

Dixie accepted both tickets and processed them. "Yes, pay day is coming up for the guys," Dixie announced, then moved on to the second transaction. "Uncle Nash is moving a chunk of change from savings to checking. Is he planning a trip?"

"Yes, my aunt and uncle are going to the city for the weekend with Uncle Cyrus and Aunt Fran," Sky informed her. "They're visiting Uncle Carlton and Aunt Beth."

"That's right," Dixie remarked. "The boss said he was going to the city this weekend."

Sky sometimes forgot that her Uncle Cyrus was Dixie's boss at the bank. Dixie had only been working at the bank for a little under a year, so she didn't always associate the two. While Dixie gathered Sky's receipts, Sky glanced across the lobby and saw a familiar man enter.

"Uncle Carlton?" Sky gasped with surprise.

Carlton, Selma's brother and the middle child, was a solid five foot ten with a slightly more athletic build than his older brother. Handsome in his own right, Carlton had more of a baby face and sandy brown hair, which may or may not have been dyed to avoid being a ginger. As with all the children in their family, Carlton also had blue eyes.

"Sky!" Carlton cried out and met her halfway to the counter.

They exchanged a warm embrace before pulling away, both surprised to see the other.

"I wasn't expecting to see you here today," Sky informed him. "I thought everyone was going to meet you in the city this weekend."

"Those plans haven't changed," Carlton informed her with a humored chuckle. "I just drove out to visit with your Uncle Cyrus today. We have some business here in town before they drive out to the city for the weekend. Your Aunt Beth is staying in the city. She has to work and wants to straighten up for company."

His grin then increased. "Tell me you're coming along this time. Your Aunt Beth will be so excited."

"No, not this trip," she replied while managing a smile. The city was *not* her thing. "But tell her I said 'hi'."

"I most certainly will," Carlton replied, then looked at Dixie and indicated the back. "Is Cyrus in his office?"

"Yes, he's back there," Dixie replied. "His door is open, so he's not conducting business."

"Great," Carlton replied and again looked at Sky. "It's great seeing you, Sky. You have to come along on one of these visits."

"Or you and Aunt Beth can visit us at the ranch," Sky suggested.

Carlton managed a tiny chuckle. "She's allergic to grass, cattle, and bugs, but I'll mention it," he teased, then gave a cheerful wave before heading back to his brother's office.

"Is your aunt really allergic to grass, cattle, and bugs?" Dixie felt compelled to ask.

"No, just country air," Sky teased.

"Some people are built for the city, while others are bred for the country," Dixie informed her.

"That is very insightful, Dixie."

"I heard Marlon say it once," Dixie remarked, then grimaced. "Don't tell Marlon you caught me quoting him."

§

Later that evening, the energy level at the Lake House Bar suddenly increased, and it didn't take much to figure out Marcus's men were left off their leashes early on a Wednesday night. Vaughn, Ox, and Moose crossed the bar in a flurry of rowdy and somewhat crude behavior. They claimed their usual table near the back, which offered some privacy but also allowed the trio a view of the entire bar. Although most people avoided the three men as much as possible, the waitresses eagerly took care of them. They were often crude, but they were generous with the tips. With the entrance of Marcus's newest enforcers, several patrons immediately left, which only seemed to humor the rowdy men.

"Your boyfriend is here," Marlon informed Sky with noted disgust.

Sky didn't even bother looking at the back table, then muttered, "I wish you'd stop saying that."

Dixie cast a look at the disorderly table, wrinkled her nose, and glanced back at Sky. "Maybe we should go," she suggested. "With the way Vaughn's been acting around you lately, it's only a matter of time before he tries something."

"He's not going to do anything," Sky informed her friend.

"You need to stop challenging his authority," Marlon insisted. "Dixie is right. He's a powder keg, and he's just waiting to get you alone."

"He's not going to *do* anything," Sky again insisted. "He's just a loud-mouthed prick."

"Sky!" Vaughn cheerfully called from across the loud barroom, his voice easily carrying.

Sky groaned and glanced toward Vaughn's back table. He grinned, beckoned her to him, and then patted his lap. Sky gave him the middle finger and returned her attention to her friends. Ruby approached Sky and handed her a shot glass.

"From your boyfriend," Ruby announced dryly while indicating Vaughn.

Sky accepted the drink while shaking her head, somewhat disgusted at herself. She drank the shot and returned the glass to her tray before Ruby continued on her trip to the rowdy table. Vaughn and his crew were heard laughing at Sky's expense.

"Why do you even accept those shots?" Marlon asked. "It just encourages him."

"Actually," Sky remarked, matter-of-factly. "He's less annoying if I just accept the drink. If I'd refused it, he'd just bring it to me himself. Pick your battles carefully."

"You know," Dixie remarked, eyeing her friend. "Maybe he actually believes you're his girlfriend. You know, in some strange, twisted sort of way."

"He can believe anything he wants," Sky replied. "But that doesn't make it real."

"One more line dance," Marlon informed Sky while indicating Dixie. "And then we're leaving. That includes you."

"It's bad form giving in to him," Sky reminded him, then sighed. "But whatever makes you more comfortable."

Sky watched her two friends head onto the dance floor for the line dance, then stood while returning her attention to the poker game in progress. She was suddenly grabbed by the arm from behind and whirled around. Before she even realized what had happened, Vaughn already had her in his arms, pinned firmly against him, and grinned somewhat slyly.

"May I have this dance?" he asked.

Sky thrust her palm harshly against his shoulder, but it wasn't enough to even move him, let alone free her from his vicelike grip.

"I'll take that as a 'yes'," Vaughn replied and spun her around and onto the dance floor.

Sky saw several men within the barroom suddenly tense as they watched. They appeared ready to pounce on Vaughn if she caused a scene. She already knew how the scene would unfold, and it wouldn't be pretty. She gave in and reluctantly slow danced with the overly enthusiastic man, even though the current music was fast country line dancing.

"See," he announced cheerfully while holding her close as they slow danced. "You can be agreeable."

"You need to stop sneaking up on me," she snarled while glaring into his eyes. "It may not end so well for you."

Vaughn maintained his smile. "Seems to be working out pretty good so far," he replied without taking his eyes off hers. "Let's see. I bought you a drink, and we've had our slow dance. The only thing left is for me to take you home for an incredible night of unadulterated passion." His cheap smile never faltered. "Be forewarned, anything longer than an hour of foreplay comes out of our quality, after sex, cuddle time."

"You're a sick man, Vaughn," she informed him. "I suggest you seek professional help."

"Do you have any idea what professionals charge?" Vaughn demanded. "I'd have to skip the foreplay and the cuddling and get right to it." He then winked at her. "And, darling, I like to cuddle."

She stared into his eyes with little reaction. "If you want to keep your testicles, you'd better get your hand off my ass."

Vaughn chuckled and moved his hand back to her waist. "You're so feisty," he announced while moving his mouth closer to hers. "I look forward to violating you three ways to Sunday."

When the slow song ended, Vaughn released her and warmly kissed the back of her hand.

"Catch you later, darling," he announced, then winked before walking away.

Sky groaned, then walked back to her table, where her friends immediately joined her. Both cast glances at the rowdy table before returning their attention to Sky.

"Something needs to be done about that man," Dixie informed her friend. "He can't keep treating you that way."

Sky glanced at Vaughn's table and caught him staring at her with what could only be described as lust in his eyes. She showed no reaction, then looked back at her concerned friends.

"He's just having a little fun at my expense," Sky informed them. "He's not going to *do* anything. There's nothing to worry about. He tries anything stupid, and Marcus deals with him. I need you guys to trust me and stop worrying about him."

"We hear you," Marlon reported, then shifted uncomfortably, "but it's difficult believing it's all just fun for him. The man is going to hurt you seriously one day."

"You've been saying that about Tony for years," Sky reminded him. "Tony got bored and doesn't even give me a second glance anymore. Vaughn will eventually get bored, too. You just need to give it some time."

"Still," Marlon announced. "Maybe we should spend a little more time at the ranch and less time here. We can grill steaks and play horseshoes with the guys. It'll be less stressful."

"I have to agree with Marlon," Dixie remarked. "You have a thousand acres to hide on. What are we doing here? Get some of the ranch hands together for a BBQ with a bonfire, and it'll be like a party."

"Should probably invite a few women, though," Marlon remarked, while sinking into thought. "Too many men."

"If I agree to a BBQ sometime in the near future, will you guys give it a rest?" Sky asked.

Dixie and Marlon considered the question, then nodded with a little too much enthusiasm. Perhaps that was their master plan all along.

§

Sky left the bar with her friends less than half an hour later. While her friends approached their car, Sky headed to the nearby hitching post and untied her horse. There were several other horses tied to the post, all belonging to men who lived close to the bar. Sky glanced across the tied horses and noticed that Vaughn still chose to ride Diablo, apparently not learning his lesson regarding the green horse. As she untied her horse from the hitching post, she saw her Uncle Carlton's car parked not far from the horses near the back. She didn't remember seeing her Uncle Carlton in the bar, but she also hadn't been looking for him either. She'd heard whispers between her Uncle Nash and Aunt Selma in the past about Uncle Carlton's obsession with poker. Perhaps he was playing poker, and she just didn't notice him. When it came down to it, he was an adult and could do what he wanted.

After Sky mounted her horse and headed for the wooded trail on the other end of the parking lot, she looked back and saw her friends waiting in their car until she made it safely into the woods before pulling out. She appreciated them making sure she reached the edge of the woods without incident. Despite their worries, Sky only had a twenty-minute ride to get home, and her horse was accustomed to riding in the dark on familiar trails. Sky and her horse were only a few minutes away from the bar when she thought she heard something behind her. Sky stopped her horse and looked around, but didn't see or hear anything unusual. Admiral didn't seem particularly concerned either. She considered it only a moment and then continued on her journey.

§

Gus was slouched on the sofa, having fallen asleep while watching television. The glow from the TV was the only light within his small studio apartment above the feed store. The open concept and high vaulted ceiling with natural wooden beams made the place appear far roomier than it actually was. The original barn wood was still in place on the walls and floors, although it had been refinished. Each area was defined by the large throw rugs contained within. Something woke Gus, rousing him from his light slumber. He drowsily looked around, not sure what he'd heard. When he didn't see anything, he assumed it was something outside, possibly in the alleyway. Crime in their town was almost non-existent, but that didn't pertain to the stray cats fighting over female company. The competition usually ended with the toppling of garbage cans.

Gus stood, stretched his cramped back, and shuffled toward his bed on the other side of the studio. When he heard a floorboard creak just behind him, he suddenly stopped and spun around. He appeared startled and somewhat confused.

"What are you doing--?"

Gus was suddenly shoved backward, knocking him off his feet. He had no sooner hit the floor when he was struck on the head with a baseball bat.

Chapter 15

The following morning, Sky hurried downstairs to the kitchen with her new camera in hand while fiddling with it. Her aunt and uncle were already seated at the table, having breakfast. Both looked up as she reached the bottom of the stairs.

"You're late for breakfast," her aunt insisted and was about to stand.

"Nothing for me this morning," she announced. "I'm already late. The ranch hands have probably started without me."

"Yeah, I kind of think they have other things to do than pose for your cowboy calendar," her uncle remarked, lightly mocking her with a smile.

"Funny," she quipped, then patted his shoulder as she passed him at the table. "I'm glad you're spending the weekend in the city. It'll give me a chance to miss your wit."

Selma hid her humored grin and then looked at Sky. "You should come with us to the city," she pleaded. "It'll be fun. I'm sure your Aunt Beth would love to see you."

"Thanks, but I'm good," Sky replied a little too cheerfully. "I kind of like the idea of having the house to myself for a few days. I heard we're going to have some spectacular thunderstorms, too. I'm hoping to get some really great shots with my new camera."

"What's with you and thunderstorms?" Selma remarked, then shook her head. "It's a little morbid, don't you think?"

Sky shrugged, then grinned. "I can't help it," she announced. "I'm fascinated with powerful forces and the raw beauty of nature."

"Just make sure while you're admiring the 'raw beauty of nature' that you're not out riding your horse in it," Nash threatened.

Sky managed a tiny laugh, humored that her uncle would even feel he had to remind her. "I know better, Uncle Nash," she insisted. "I really have to go." She was about to leave, then hesitated and looked back at her Aunt Selma. "Oh, by the way. I thought I saw Uncle Carlton's car at the bar last night. Wasn't he supposed to be heading back to the city yesterday afternoon?"

Selma tensed slightly, then frowned. "He stopped off at the bar, did he?"

"I'm pretty sure it was his car," Sky informed her. "But I didn't actually see him."

Selma maintained her frown as she shook her head. "Any time he visits, it seems it's always when he's having some sort of disagreement with Beth," she remarked. "I hope they're not fighting again. It's going to make for an awkward visit, if they are."

"It's time for him to admit he has a gambling problem," Nash muttered, somewhat disgusted.

"I think he might have stopped in for the nightly poker game," Sky informed her uncle. "That could be why I didn't see him." She frowned and shook her head. "I hope he doesn't divorce Aunt Beth. I actually like her."

"Certainly better than his first wife," Nash reported.

"Okay," Selma huffed with a sigh. "Let's not gossip about Carlton. Whatever he's going through, he needs our support." She then offered a slightly tense smile. "I'll talk to him and Beth during our visit. Make sure everything is okay with them."

§

Sky rode her horse at a leisurely trot across the pasture filled with steer and wranglers on horseback. She loosely held the reins in her left hand while holding her professional-grade camera steady in both hands. She took several pictures of the guys working with the cattle. The men went about their business, although occasionally hamming it up for the camera. She took photos of the calves, scenery, and plenty of action shots. Once she had enough pictures for the morning, Jerry and Tom joined her, wanting to see the highlights of their morning work. She showed them her favorite, which was one of the wranglers with his back to the camera while taking a leak on one of the trees. Both men had a good chuckle.

"Remind me never to take a piss while you're around," Tom remarked while grinning.

"Better that than the one where you fell off your horse," Jerry reminded him.

"Like you've never fallen off your horse," Tom scoffed at his friend.

"I have," Jerry replied. "Just never because I was scratching my ass."

"I wasn't scratching my ass," Tom insisted defensively, then straightened in his saddle. "I was pulling my drawers out of my ass."

"Yeah, that's much better," Jerry muttered.

Sky hid her smile while keeping her eyes on the photos she'd taken. She loved listening to Jerry and Tom banter. They were quite good at it, like an old married couple. She finally stowed her camera in her saddlebag and returned her attention to the ranch hands.

"Maybe try using fabric softener," Jerry informed Tom, as the conversation about Tom's briefs continued.

Sky leaned on her saddle horn and watched the guys continue their debate as if it were some serious conversation. In recent weeks, she formed a deeper connection with the guys, gaining a new perspective. Finally standing up to town bullies had increased her confidence, and it felt good. When she returned from her own thoughts, Sky realized Jerry and Tom were staring at her with befuddled looks.

"Are you back with us?" Tom asked, appearing almost offended that she hadn't been paying attention to their 'insightful' conversation.

"You've been zoning out a lot lately," Jerry remarked. "Are you concerned about staying home alone the entire weekend? You could always come with us to the rodeo."

Sky smiled and chuckled at the offer. "I appreciate the offer, but I'm looking forward to having the entire weekend alone for a change," she informed him.

"If you'd like, I could ask the new guys to check on you once or twice a day," Jerry announced.

"No, that's not necessary," she insisted. "They're going to be camping out in the far pasture with the herd the entire weekend. I wouldn't want them to make that journey. Besides, it's not necessary." Jerry was about to speak when Sky interrupted him. "Really, it's not necessary, and I don't want anyone checking in on me."

Jerry nodded while forcing a smile. "Okay, but if you have any problems, radio the guys in the south forty."

"I'll do that."

Sky decided it was time to take her leave before she was drawn into a debate about staying home alone for a few days while her aunt and uncle were in the city.

"I'll catch up with you later this afternoon," Sky announced, then waved and rode off.

Jerry and Tom returned the wave and watched her ride off toward the woods. As Sky entered the trail in the woods, she slowed her horse to a walk and took in the scenic beauty. She loved her morning rides when everything seemed so peaceful. Sky took some forest pictures and even saw some wildlife. Mornings were the best for photography. Then in the evening, around sunset, she'd find even more great shots. Sky eventually looked at her watch, frowned at the time, and then headed toward the nearby stream. She had to ride through the six-inch deep water for several yards before finding her usual, secluded spot. It was a small clearing near a large boulder and a good place to tie her horse to a nearby tree.

Despite the stream, that particular area of the woods was untraveled, indicated by the lack of any sort of trail, which was why she rode through the water. There was plenty of access to the stream from easily traveled paths, so she knew none of the ranch hands would ride to her secluded spot, giving her all the privacy she needed. Sky dismounted and took several pictures of the stream, the woods, and even her horse by the boulder. It was her favorite spot to think and, at times, daydream. She turned when she heard something rustling around in the woods. Even though there was nothing there, she listened a moment and continued to scan the area. When nothing moved, she resumed looking for the ideal scenic shots, although she now remained alert to the sounds around her.

Her horse suddenly let out a low snicker, catching her attention. She looked back at her tied horse.

Rather than indicating something was out there, her horse was looking at her.

"You're too nosy for your own good, Admiral," she informed the horse matter-of-factly, then continued toward the stream.

Sky saw something on one of the rocks near the water. She squinted at the object, then held up her camera and zoomed in on it to get a better look. A black cowboy hat on the rock came into focus. She snapped a picture, then hesitated as concern swept over her. She was suddenly grabbed around the waist from behind. Sky released her camera that only fell as far as the strap around her neck allowed, and struggled to free herself from the constrictive hold. There was a low, familiar male chuckle close to her ear.

"You should really be more aware of your surroundings," Vaughn's unmistakable voice chuckled in her ear. "A pretty little girl out here all by herself. No telling what sort of perverts you'll run into."

Vaughn refused to release her, presumably getting some sick pleasure from the way she struggled against him.

"Get your hands off me," she snarled.

Vaughn eyed the neckline of her tank top as he leaned over her shoulder. "Hmm," he groaned softly near her ear. "You went braless for me. I like it."

Vaughn gracefully spun her around and pulled her off her feet and against him with his hand beneath her jean-clad buttocks. She gasped at the sharp action and braced her hands against his chest while staring into his devious eyes. He wore a playful grin while caressing her backside.

"I'll bet you aren't wearing any panties, either," he announced with a chuckle.

Sky stared into his eyes with anger and loathing. "Put me down," she snarled.

Vaughn maintained his devious smile but released her. Sky jumped back a step while glaring at him, then immediately checked her camera.

"If you broke my camera, you're buying me a new one," she scoffed, then walked past him toward the boulder and her horse.

Vaughn casually turned and followed her while maintaining his cheap grin. She paused by her horse and placed the camera in its protective case before stowing it in the saddlebag.

"Put on the wide-angle lens, and you can take some great nude pictures of me," Vaughn informed her.

Sky buckled the saddlebag while keeping her back to him. "Have I ever told you how much I hate you?" she snarled.

Vaughn placed his arms around her waist and shoulder while pressing against her from behind. "At least once a day," he replied while maneuvering his mouth past her ponytail and aggressively kissing the back of her neck as his hands mildly groped her.

Sky placed her hands over his and shut her eyes while enjoying the sensation of his hot tongue against her neck and his hands caressing her body.

"Did you remember the sleeping bag?" she muttered almost reluctantly.

He pulled his mouth away from her neck and chuckled. "Of course I did," Vaughn replied, then released her.

Sky turned and watched Vaughn head around the boulder to where his horse was tied. He removed the sleeping bag from the back of the saddle and untied it as he approached her. He swiftly rolled it open across the ground, then struggled to balance on one foot while removing his cowboy boot.

"Boots off, huh?" she remarked as she stepped onto the sleeping bag.

"Sorry to disappoint you, darling," Vaughn announced while grinning. "No quickie today." He stepped on the sleeping bag as he moved closer to her. His eyes and hands settled on the tank top she wore without a bra. "When you don't wear a bra, I know that's code for the extended ravishing."

Sky groaned with disgust before taking a step back and removing her boots. "I really need my head examined," she muttered.

She had no sooner taken off her boots when Vaughn pulled her into his arms and against him. His hands eagerly traveled her body.

"I'd prefer it if you didn't get professional help," Vaughn teased and immediately unbuckled the belt on her jeans. "I like it when you degrade yourself, slumping with me."

Vaughn slid her jeans off her hips and buttocks and immediately placed both hands on her bare backside. He groaned as his finger lightly traced the strap of the lacy thong.

"Oh, you wore the black lacy thong this time," Vaughn announced. "You must really be wound this morning. I knew I should have been more attentive to your needs last night."

"I wish you talked less," she remarked as she unbuttoned his shirt.

"Sorry," he announced while maintaining his grin. "You know how much I enjoy calling out each play, *blow-by-blow--*" He pressed his pelvis sharply against hers with a grunt. "--if you will."

Sky slipped him out of his shirt and admired his toned and mildly scarred chest while running her hands over his body. Without hesitation, she eagerly unbuckled his belt. Vaughn grinned and held his hands up, giving her unobstructed access.

"Oh, I love when you get rough with me," he announced as she pulled down his pants.

Sky grabbed the bulge contained within his boxer briefs and momentarily met his gaze. "Stop talking," she ordered.

Vaughn grunted from her quick action, then grinned. "Yes, ma'am."

He grabbed her by the back of the neck and aggressively kissed her before practically tackling her to the sleeping bag.

Chapter 16

"That was amazing," Vaughn groaned loudly as he collapsed onto the sleeping bag while attempting to catch his breath with a permanent smile on his face. "I think I died for a brief moment there."

Sky fell onto her back alongside him and was unable to move. Riding Vaughn was like riding a wild stallion. He didn't give up until she had nothing left. Sky wasn't sure how long she lay there, unable to move, before finally glancing at the silent, motionless man alongside her. Vaughn appeared to be asleep. As she studied him, she kept asking herself what the hell she was doing. When she attempted to sit up, he rolled onto his side and placed his arm around her, holding her down on the sleeping bag.

"In a hurry," he remarked with a slight chuckle in his tone. "I thought we'd enjoy the scenery before round two."

"Yeah, not happening," she groaned and removed his arm with some effort.

Sky was finally able to sit up and search for her clothing. Vaughn didn't bother moving from where he comfortably rested, still panting, and watched as she slipped into her tank top. He finally sat up, placing his cowboy hat on his head and his arms around his knees. He then watched her with a satisfied grin on his face.

"You enjoyed that, admit it," he teased.

"Fuck you," she scoffed.

"You can turn it on and off so fast," he announced while maintaining his grin. "I like that psycho button of yours. Keeps me guessing."

"Sex time is over," she informed him as she slipped into her jeans.

Vaughn didn't bother reaching for his clothes and continued to watch her. "You know what I heard?" he remarked.

"Don't care," she replied while standing to finish pulling up her pants. She then sat back down on the sleeping bag to pull on her boots.

"I heard Auntie and Uncle are going away for a few days," he announced.

"Yeah, so?" she scoffed without looking at him and not giving the comment much thought.

"So?" he gasped, then laughed. "So, I'm thinking I come over, and we have a little bed sex."

"You're not coming over," Sky informed him while pulling on her boots.

"You can't tell me you wouldn't love a little bed sex for a change," he remarked. "Remember the last time we had bed sex?"

"Yeah," she scoffed. "A month ago, when I got drunk and you took advantage of me."

"We were both drunk, and *you* seduced *me*," he reminded her. "You were like a demon. A very *horny* demon." He groaned softly while reflecting on their first time together, then looked back at her. "I need to get you drunk so we can relive that moment. I may not survive, but what a way to go."

"It'd probably be the easiest way to get rid of you," she muttered.

"Then I can come over?"

"No," she snapped back and finally glared at him. He was still completely naked except for the cowboy hat. It was one of those images where she again wished she could take a picture. "You're not coming to my house. I don't want you in my house and certainly not in my bed. I'd rather just keep this as it is. Quickies here and there." She pulled on her second boot. "Remember, we're only here to scratch each other's itches. No woman in her right mind would ever touch you, and since you took my virginity, you're all I've got."

"I love it when you say those things out loud," he remarked slyly. "If you say it again, I might be ready for round two."

"There is no round two, and you're not coming to my house," she scoffed.

Vaughn groaned and shook his head, disappointed by her response. As she was about to stand, he caught her hand, stopping her. She immediately pulled her hand from him and shot him a death glare.

"I'll make you a little deal," he remarked cheerfully despite her reaction.

"No deals," she snarled.

"I'll show up at your house tomorrow night around eight o'clock," he informed her. "You can decide then if you want to let me in. If you slam the door in my face, I'll go home." He then raised his brows. "If you invite me in, it's game on."

"I won't even be opening the door," she informed him.

"You're going to be so horny, you'll practically ravish me on the porch," he replied.

"You're so full of yourself," she scoffed.

"Yeah, well, remember that when you're riding home," he informed her. "When your ass is slapping the saddle, you're going to be thinking of me." She wasn't humored, but that didn't stop him from continuing. "If you're so confident about rejecting me, you won't care if I show up at your door. All you have to do is slam the door in my face."

"Fine," she snarled. "I look forward to bruising your ego with such a brutal rejection."

"Fair enough," he replied and winked at her. "Tomorrow evening at eight."

"Be warned," Sky scoffed in response. "If you don't keep your end of the bargain and leave, I'll fill your ass with buckshot."

Vaughn chuckled lowly, humored at her response. "See you then."

Sky shook her head then sprang to her feet, leaving the naked man, wearing only his cowboy hat, sitting on the sleeping bag.

§

After returning home later that morning, Sky unsaddled her horse and turned him loose in the pasture. She then glanced at her watch as she hurried to the house with her camera in hand. She had just enough time for a quick shower before meeting Dixie, who would be taking her lunch break. Curse Vaughn and his desire for a long, drawn-out sex-ploit rather than his usual morning quickie. She didn't want to have lunch with Dixie smelling like cattle, let alone smelling like Vaughn. Between his musky cologne and his musky deodorant, his scent attached itself to her like black mold. She sometimes wondered if he did it on purpose, as if marking his territory. As Sky hurried into the house, she yanked off her boots and immediately headed up the stairs to her room, grabbing a change of clothes before darting into the bathroom.

Sky stripped out of her horse and steer scented jeans, carelessly tossing them into the basket near the door, then removed her lacy thong underwear that again reminded her of her morning rendezvous with *that man*. She cast her lacy thong panties onto the pile of clothes, disgusted with herself, then jumped into the hot shower. She didn't want to be late, but she felt an overwhelming need to sanitize her entire body. Every time she hooked up with Vaughn, she felt the same regret afterward. Each time, she was reminded how she had refused to have sex with Tony because she wanted to wait, yet here she was, letting a man like Vaughn violate her practically every day for the last month or so. Who was she kidding? Most times, it was more than once a day. What made the entire thing far worse? Vaughn wasn't entirely wrong about their hook-ups. Most of the time, he just needed to show up, and she was good to go.

On rare occasions, when she wasn't in the mood to deal with him, he just needed to kiss or caress her, and she was once again fulfilling his needs. Her inability to control her sexual desire around him almost made her physically ill. She knew the kind of man he was, yet she freely handed her body to him, catering to his every whim like his private plaything. He could be gentle, and he could be aggressive. When he was sexually aggressive, it sometimes frightened her, yet she never discouraged it. There were even times she actually *encouraged* it. Despite she often professed her hatred for him, she always showed up each time without fail. Sky wanted to believe Vaughn was somehow coercing her so she wouldn't feel as guilty, but she often did little things like going braless and wearing thong panties to get a more aggressive response from him.

Sky turned off the shower, drying her hair and body in more of a hurry. She'd taken too long in the shower and would now be pressed for time. As she changed into a pair of clean underwear and bra, she looked at herself in the steamy mirror. To her horror,

Vaughn had given her a hickie that was visible above her bra. She groaned in disgust. She hated it when he did that, and she knew he often did it on purpose, once again marking his territory. And, even though neither of them told anyone about their hook-ups, Vaughn liked to push the envelope now and again, as he sometimes did with things he said in the bar. Sky looked at her watch, groaned at the time, and finished dressing a little faster.

Chapter 17

Sky drove her Jeep into town only a few minutes before noon and would arrive at the diner with a minute to spare. As she passed through town, there seemed to be quite a buzz around the feed store. The sheriff's blazer was nearby, as well as an ambulance. Sky then recognized one of her ranch trucks parked in front of Gus's store. Concern for her ranch hands swept over her, and she zipped into the first parking spot she found. As she got out of her Jeep, she saw the crowd outside the feed store appeared to be waiting for something, possibly indicating that a fight had broken out. Sky whipped out her cell phone and pressed Dixie's phone number to tell her she'd be a few minutes late. She immediately heard the familiar ringtone from nearby. Dixie was only a couple of feet from her, standing among the crowd. Sky disconnected the call and hurried closer to her friend.

"What's happening?" Sky asked.

Dixie shook her head. "Some trouble at the store," she remarked. "Sheriff Burke went inside."

Sky then saw Jerry and Tom closer to the front. She nudged Dixie, then made her way through the small crowd to her men, with Dixie only a few steps behind.

"Jerry," Sky announced while touching his arm to get his attention. "What's happening?"

"Some sort of accident," Jerry reported while shaking his head. "The shop was still closed when we stopped by this morning. We came back later this morning, and he still hadn't opened. No one could reach Gus, so Sheriff Burke was called to check inside."

Tom shook his head as he stared at the closed door, with Deputy Rhodes standing guard out front. Deputy Rhodes was a shorter man, possibly in his early twenties, with slightly longer hair and a baby face. He was lean and not very imposing, even in uniform and wearing a gun holster.

"Some sort of forklift mishap," Tom continued. "Or so they say."

Sky stared at the feed store with a look of horror. "Is Gus okay?"

"Deputy Rhodes isn't sharing any information," Tom replied. "Big surprise."

The door opened, and two ambulance workers exited the building with the stretcher containing a black body bag. There were several gasps from those gathered outside. Sky and Dixie gasped as well. Deputy Rhodes attempted to disperse the crowd, but most refused to leave, demanding to know what had happened. Sheriff Burke finally stepped outside and shut the door behind him.

"Sorry, folks," Sheriff Burke announced. "The feed store is closed for the foreseeable future."

"What happened?" one woman from the crowd called out.

"Forklift accident," Sheriff Burke replied. "A couple of pallets must have slipped when Gus was lifting them. Unfortunate accident."

"Accident, my ass," Ron muttered not far from Sky, Dixie, and the ranch hands. As he turned, Ron eyed the four. "Gus told me Marcus's men were harassing him about selling the feed store yesterday afternoon. Ironic that he suddenly has an *accident* the next morning."

"Do you really think Marcus would go that far to acquire the feed store?" Dixie whispered, haunted at the thought.

Ron raised his brow and eyed the young woman. "When I told him no several months back, he'd sent his men to *persuade* me. That night, the brakes on my truck failed, and I crashed into a telephone pole."

Sky and her friends exchanged looks.

§

Sky's Jeep and the ranch pickup truck pulled up to the diner a little after twelve o'clock that afternoon. Sky and Dixie got out of the Jeep and eyed Marcus's expensive town car parked out front. There was no mistaking Marcus's vehicle. It was overpriced and impractical for a farming community that contained mostly woods and back roads.

"What do you suppose he's doing here?" Dixie muttered. "He never eats at the diner."

Tom and Jerry approached Sky's Jeep and eyed Marcus's town car as well.

"Well, that can't be good," Tom muttered.

Despite knowing Marcus and his men were probably in the diner, all four headed for the entrance anyway. Jerry smiled and politely opened the door for Sky and Dixie. Before they could pass through the door, Roscoe and Foster barged out the open door and plowed into Jerry, just about knocking him off his feet.

"Watch where you're going, dickhead," Roscoe snarled at Jerry.

"What the fuck is your problem?" Jerry scoffed back in response.

"Are you threatening me?" Roscoe shouted back while turning and immediately stepped closer to Jerry, attempting to grab his jacket.

Jerry blocked his hands and shoved him backward. Sky and Dixie gasped in horror. Although Jerry was in the right, it wasn't wise to provoke one of Marcus's men. Roscoe sneered and threw his fist at Jerry's face. Jerry blocked the punch and delivered two fast, hard hits to Roscoe's gut and face. Foster lunged for Jerry to defend his friend, but Tom stepped in his path and shoved him back.

"Back off," Tom snarled at Foster.

Without warning, Foster took a swing at Tom, which he seemed to anticipate. Sky and Dixie groaned and watched the four men pommel each other. Tony suddenly appeared from the diner and stepped in to gang up on Jerry. Sky leapt in front of Tony and thrust her palm into his large chest, stopping him with the surprising action. He glared at her with his fist clenched and carefully considered his next move. Her eyes were locked on his.

"Try it," she snarled at the man and found herself quoting her father. "It'll be your last mistake."

As Tony backed away from Sky, she could see the anger in his eyes, but he knew better. If he hit her, the off-limit rancher's daughter, a woman, and Marcus's favorite girl, it would be asking for the full weight of the town to crash down around him. Sky knew she'd be playing that card eventually, and she had been saving it for just such an occasion.

"Enough," Tony cried out to his men, then motioned them to the trucks. "Let's go."

Roscoe and Foster both had gotten their asses kicked and wanted to settle the score with the ranch hands, but Tony called the shots. They reluctantly joined Tony and headed for their truck. Marcus hurried from the diner, approached Sky, and glanced around before looking her over.

"What happened?" Marcus asked her with surprise and possible alarm as he scanned her face. "Did one of my men hurt you?"

"No," Sky replied, managing a tiny smile. "Just a misunderstanding."

"Oh, thank God," Marcus announced with a relieved sigh, then turned unusually stern. "I'll talk to my men. Make sure there aren't any further *misunderstandings.*"

"I'd appreciate that," Sky replied, although it wasn't going to end well for any of them.

"Tell Jasmine to put your lunch on my tab," Marcus announced, then offered a polite smile. "It's the least I can do."

Sky nodded, then watched Marcus head for his town car. Jerry and Tom brushed the dirt from their clothes while keeping a watchful eye on the truck and car as they departed.

Jerry then shot a look at Sky, turning almost angry. "What the hell were you thinking?" he demanded. "Tony could have broken your face with one punch."

"He never would have done it," Sky informed him. "Marcus has a weak spot for me."

"And a hard one," Tom muttered while shaking his head. "That was stupid, Sky."

"I wasn't going to let them gang up on the two of you," Sky informed them. "One-on-one is a fair fight. They don't fight fair."

"Could this day get any worse?" Dixie muttered and then ushered them inside.

The four took a table near the back and hadn't even settled in when Jasmine approached their table with two coffee mugs and the coffeepot. As she silently filled the two mugs for the ranch hands, everyone took note of her unusual quietness.

"Everything okay?" Sky asked Jasmine.

Jasmine frowned and shook her head. "Marcus made me an offer on the diner," she remarked with a sigh. "One I couldn't refuse."

"Couldn't because it was that good?" Tom asked, then cocked his head. "Or couldn't because you were threatened?"

"Don't ask questions that you already know the answers to," Jasmine remarked with little emotion. "I'll be back with your iced tea."

All four exchanged looks.

"Notice a pattern?" Dixie muttered.

Marlon hurried across the diner and approached their table. He didn't seem too surprised to see Jerry and Tom with them.

"Did you hear what happened to Gus?" Marlon asked while pulling an extra chair up to the table.

"Did you hear what happened to Jasmine?" Tom muttered.

"What happened to Jasmine?" Marlon asked, then looked behind him at the diner owner and waitress. "She seems fine to me."

Chapter 18

After lunch, Dixie, Marlon, and the ranch hands went back to work while Sky headed to the general store. She didn't need anything, but she wanted a chance to talk with Ron in private. She roamed the aisles while Ron rang up some customers. Once they were alone, she approached the check-out counter and casually leaned on it.

"Did you hear about Jasmine selling the diner to Marcus?" Sky asked the older man.

"Yeah, I heard," Ron replied dryly. "That spread around town pretty fast. I guess she didn't want to end up like Gus."

"You seem pretty convinced it wasn't an accident," Sky remarked. "Did you notice anything strange about the feed store this morning? I know he usually opens an hour earlier than you, but did you see or hear anything unusual?"

"No, but I probably wouldn't have," Ron remarked, then leaned closer to her across the counter. "Gossip around town says Gus had his *accident* last night after he closed. Well, he closes an hour before me, and he's almost always back in his upstairs apartment by the time I'm closing. I also know for a fact that he doesn't run the forklift after he closes. No reason to." He then met her gaze. "With the way Sheriff Burke described the accident, I would have heard something from my apartment above the shop, but I didn't hear anything." He then hesitated and reconsidered his comment. "However, something did wake me around midnight. Sounded like thunder. I thought nothing of it and went back to bed."

"There weren't any thunderstorms last night," she informed him. "I've been actively watching for them ever since I bought my new nighttime camera equipment."

"I was convinced there wasn't either," Ron remarked. "Between you and me, I think one of Marcus's stooges came back to the feed store last night, busted into his apartment upstairs, and staged that accident."

"Maybe the city coroner--?"

"There won't be any city coroner," Ron informed her somewhat sternly. "The county coroner investigated it. He's good friends with Marcus and Sheriff Burke."

"Are you serious?" Sky gasped.

"Yep, and I'd be willing to bet money his body will be *accidentally* cremated within twenty-four hours," Ron remarked.

Sky shook her head while staring at Ron with horror in her eyes. "How can they get away with that?" she demanded.

"Marcus owns many people," Ron informed her. "And he surrounds himself with dangerous men who don't mind getting their hands dirty for the right price."

Sky's thoughts strayed to Vaughn. She knew he wasn't a Boy Scout, but she never really thought about what he actually did for Marcus. Stable security was the happy version.

"So there's nothing we can do about any of this?" Sky demanded. "He's just going to buy out everyone at bargain basement prices, and no one dares stand up to him in fear of losing their life."

"Pretty much," Ron replied with a defeated sigh. "I guess the best we can hope for is someone reporting his illegal activities to the FBI and them actually busting him for it. But with the law in his hip pocket, he'd be tipped off before they'd get within a mile of him."

"I wasn't even aware of his basement gambling operation until I noticed the secret doorway," Sky remarked.

"It's not in the basement," Ron informed her. "There are no basements by the lake. It's upstairs on the second floor."

"Really?" Sky asked with surprise.

"Yep," Ron replied. "Checked it out myself one time. Gambling and prostitution."

"I'm surprised he doesn't sell drugs," Sky muttered.

"I'm sure that's at one of his other buildings," Ron muttered. "You can get a bunch of people to go along with gambling and prostitution, but when you get into drugs and other things, the average person sours on it."

"Interesting," Sky remarked while sinking into thought.

"Sky," Ron announced sternly and boldly, forcing her to look at him. "I know you're not thinking about checking into his illegal gambling activity."

"What?" she demanded, almost offended. "Why can't I check it out? Is the casino 'boys' only or something?"

"Well, no," Ron remarked, then fidgeted slightly. "But you're sort of Marcus's sainted girl. It may not be in your best interest to let him see you as 'tainted' or corrupt."

"What difference would that make?"

"Well, if he lowers his opinion of you, he might consider corrupting you in other ways," Ron remarked, then raised his brows for added effect.

Sky rolled her eyes, understanding what he wasn't saying. She wasn't sure which was worse. Being thought of as a virgin or people finding out that Vaughn was the one who tainted her. She decided she was going to stick with being a virgin. Admitting the other part was more than she could bear.

Chapter 19

Later that evening, Sky walked across the moderately crowded Lake House Bar with Jerry by her side. Thursday was half-price wine cooler night, which was basically an extension of ladies' night and consistently drew a good crowd. However, Jerry seemed tense this particular night while looking around.

"This is a bad idea," Jerry muttered as they approached the bar. "I don't know how you talked me into this."

"I didn't," Sky informed him. "I asked you how to get into the casino. You're the one who insisted on coming along."

"I wasn't about to let you go alone," Jerry informed her. "I was only ever inside once, and I didn't care for the experience."

"Why's that?"

"The place is crawling with prostitutes," Jerry informed her.

"And that's a problem?" she asked while eyeing him with a hint of mockery.

"It's more of a 'who' problem," Jerry replied while fidgeting. "Let's just say you might recognize some of the faces."

Sky shot a look at him and raised her brows. "Really?"

"Yeah," Jerry replied, seeming slightly squeamish. "And it becomes extremely uncomfortable when you'd previously asked someone out and were shot down, only to find out she's available by the hour. A real ego buster."

"I can see how that might make things awkward," Sky muttered.

"And the other girls must be bused in or something," Jerry insisted while shaking his head. "Real high-end girls and at high-end prices. Women I'd never seen around town."

"How do you know they get high-end prices?" she questioned while glancing at him almost suspiciously. "Did you actually ask?"

"I was curious," he replied with a shrug, then turned somewhat defensive. "Hey, I'm a good boy. I wouldn't do that sort of thing." He then shifted uncomfortably. "My mother would kill me."

Sky chuckled while hiding her smile. She loved that her macho wranglers still feared their mothers. It was endearing.

"Wait near the entrance," Jerry announced. "I'll get the bartender to buzz me in. I'd rather he didn't see you asking to get in. He might question it."

Sky did as Jerry requested, although she didn't understand the big deal. She then glanced at the bar and saw him talking to the bartender, Randy. As Jerry approached the nearly concealed door, she heard a faint buzzing sound. Jerry opened the door, and Sky slipped in behind him.

§

Sky and Jerry walked along the small, bland corridor toward the stairs where one of Marcus's men waited. The man guarding the door eyed Jerry while briefly glancing at Sky.

"What's she doing here?" the man almost demanded.

"My bankroll," Jerry informed him, then raised his own arrogant brow. "Problem with that?"

The man again eyed Sky, frowned, and then nodded them toward the stairs. Sky linked onto Jerry's arm as they headed up the steps.

"Nicely handled," she announced while grinning.

"He's one of Marcus's clueless goons," Jerry informed her. "No freethinking for that one."

They reached the top of the stairs, where another guard stood outside the only door to the second floor. He saw them, didn't even comment, and opened the door for them. As they entered the casino, which encompassed most of the second floor, Sky looked around in amazement. She couldn't believe the extent of Marcus's little gambling venture. Although not a legitimate casino nice, it came close.

"Wow, this is quite the operation," she muttered, then noticed the abundance of sexy women. "So where is the brothel?"

"Apparently, there are some bedrooms on the third floor," Jerry remarked, then turned almost defensive. "Not that I'd know for sure. I'm guessing through the door at the far end of the room. When I was here, I noticed a lot of women escorting men through that door." He drew a deep breath and scanned the room. "What would you like to play first?"

"I've never even been to a legitimate casino," she informed him. "You may have to give me a guided tour of the games."

"Okay," Jerry replied and patted her hand on his arm as they walked past the rows of table games filled with people.

There were several tables of blackjack, craps, roulette, and an abundance of video poker and reel slot machines. Jerry explained each game to her as they passed.

"What do you recommend?" she asked.

"For you? Roulette," he replied. "For me, blackjack or craps."

Sky removed a wad of cash from her pocket and handed him several hundred dollars. "Show me what you've got," she announced while grinning.

Jerry laughed and accepted the money. "I should take you out on a date more often." He then found a spot at the craps table and placed his bet.

While Jerry played, Sky remained glued to his side, glancing around the room at the familiar faces and some she'd never seen before. To her surprise, she saw Vaughn across the room by the bar. More surprising was the high-end hooker cozying up to him. She was seductively hanging on his shoulder and smiled while speaking close to his ear. Candy was a slender, attractive woman in her early twenties with long blonde hair and big brown eyes. She wore excessive amounts of make-up, a revealing dress, and daringly high heels. Vaughn was grinning at whatever she said. Sky felt her stomach suddenly tie in knots. She shouldn't have been surprised, but for some reason, she was. Sky knew she was only *entertaining* Vaughn because she had an itch that needed scratching, and she had already been invested in him, but seeing him with a high-end prostitute made her suddenly feel cheap.

Sky had heard rumors that Marcus's men had their pick of the girls attending his parties. Supposedly, his men got laid for free, but she never really thought much about it until now. She certainly wasn't jealous, but she couldn't deny she was disgusted with him and herself. When Vaughn placed his arm around the woman's waist, in what could only be described as a sensual manner, and guided her across the room, Sky felt sick to her stomach. She decided to focus her attention on Jerry at the craps table instead. He seemed to be winning, although she couldn't be sure. Without warning, a man at the nearby blackjack table jumped from his chair and lunged across the table while yelling at the dealer. A lot of attention was focused on the angry man. Vaughn, Ox, and Moose crossed the room looking like gladiators on a mission, swooping in on the irate man. Vaughn glared at the man and said something Sky couldn't hear.

The man turned violent and swung at Vaughn. Vaughn blocked the man's fist and then punched him twice in the face, knocking him to the floor. Sky rarely saw that side of Vaughn. Of course, most days, she rarely saw Vaughn with his clothes on.

"Get him out of here," Vaughn bellowed to his men loud enough for half the room to hear.

Moose and Ox grabbed the man by an arm each and hoisted him to his feet. The man continued his tirade, but Moose and Ox didn't give him much room to protest as they shoved him toward the exit. As Vaughn turned, his eyes fell upon Sky. Surprisingly, he didn't even flinch when he saw her and continued on his way. He seemed to suddenly pick up his pace as he crossed the room back toward the bar. Sky followed his movements to the same sexily dressed prostitute, who was talking to one of Marcus's men. Vaughn didn't slow his pace while heading toward them. He suddenly grabbed the man by the arm, twisted it behind his back, and slammed him face down on the bar top, rattling the entire bar. Vaughn leaned over the writhing man and said something to him that no one seemed to hear. He released the man and shoved him toward another door in the back.

"That's one nasty man," Jerry informed Sky, having followed her gaze. "I heard he actually beat the shit out of Tony. Can you imagine?"

"I'd rather not think about Vaughn," Sky muttered, fidgeting internally.

"That's smart," Jerry replied and resumed his craps game.

When he pressed a large bet, a roll of the dice won him a hefty amount of money. Sky couldn't say she understood what had happened, but the entire table seemed excited as everyone was paid. Jerry cried out, high-fived the man next to him, and then turned to Sky, hugging her. She laughed and returned the quick embrace before pulling away and eyeing his stack of chips.

"I assume that was good," Sky remarked.

"Good?" Jerry asked, then laughed. "I just quadrupled your money."

"I've seen enough," she informed him, once again losing her enthusiasm. "Maybe you should cash out so we can get out of here."

"Yeah, sure," Jerry replied. "If you're ready."

Sky managed a tiny smile and nodded. "Yeah, I've seen enough," she replied.

"Okay, give me a minute to cash out at the cage," he announced and scooped up his chips. "I'll be right back."

Sky walked across the room and headed toward the exit. At the same time, Moose and Ox entered the casino while laughing and joking about the man they had just *showed out*.

"Vaughn's going soft," Moose remarked. "A year ago, he would have broken the guy's jaw."

"He's more tolerable when he gets laid regularly," Ox insisted while grinning. "Apparently, Candy has one hell of a sex drive."

"I doubt she's his girlfriend," Moose remarked. "Vaughn was never very good at sharing. He's certainly not dating a hooker."

"I use the term 'girlfriend' loosely," Ox informed him as they crossed the room, getting further away. "Whatever she's doing, it's working."

Sky felt unusually angry, and she wasn't even sure why. Vaughn wasn't her boyfriend; not by a long shot. Mostly, she couldn't even stand the guy, but thinking about him with a prostitute was eating away at her. Between their morning and sunset 'engagements', when did Vaughn have time for another woman? Jerry approached her while grinning and handed her the wad of cash.

"Congratulations," Jerry announced cheerfully.

"Just give me my original bankroll," she informed him. "You're the one who played and won."

"Are you sure?"

"Yeah, of course," she replied, then managed a smile. "You only came here because you felt you had to."

"Not entirely true," he remarked, then shrugged and handed her the original money she'd given him, then pocketed the rest. "But I suppose I can use it when you finally agree to let me take you on a real date."

Sky eyed him, then smiled and laughed. "Let's go, cowboy."

Chapter 20

Friday morning. Sky skipped her usual morning routine with the ranch hands as well as her morning rendezvous with Vaughn. After what she saw at the gambling parlor last night, she wanted nothing to do with Vaughn. When she didn't show up, he'd get the message loud and clear. Sky couldn't deny she had some anxiety about her decision. Clearly, getting on Vaughn's bad side could come with its own concerns, but she was willing to take that risk. She never should have become involved with him after their initial oopsy anyway. Sky wasn't even sure why it seemed like a good idea at the time. Still, there was no telling how he'd handle rejection or if he'd even accept it. Rather than meet with Vaughn, she drove into town and arrived at the general store shortly after Ron opened for the day. Ron appeared surprised to see her so early.

"Well, good morning, Sky," Ron announced, somewhat cheerful despite how bad yesterday had been. "What brings you by my shop so early and on a Friday?"

"Purely a social visit," she informed him, and stopped at the check-out counter.

"Aren't your aunt and uncle leaving for the city this weekend?"

Sky eyed him and raised a curious brow. "Does everyone in town know about that?" she practically demanded.

"It's a small town," Ron informed her with a chuckle. "And your aunt has been boasting about this weekend all week. From what I heard, it kind of sounds like your uncle is less enthusiastic."

"Well, my aunt knows how to spend money," Sky remarked. "Uncle Nash can afford it, but he's gotten used to a less extravagant lifestyle."

"I feel for him," Ron replied, then offered a tiny smile. "Somehow, I think there's a less social reason for your visit. What's going on?"

"One of the ranch hands took me to the bar's gambling parlor last night," she informed him.

Ron groaned and shook his head. "I told you to let it go, Sky," he insisted. "There's nothing you can do about Marcus, and getting involved in his dirty dealings could be hazardous to your health."

"People I know and care about are having their lives destroyed," she informed him. "When am I supposed to do something? After he comes for me and my family?"

"You're pretty safe," Ron informed her.

"Yeah, until I'm not," she snapped back. "Something has to be done. Marcus needs to be exposed and put behind bars."

"He'd have his goons put us in the ground long before we ever exposed him," Ron remarked. "Take my advice and let it go. You'll live longer."

"What would it take to get the FBI out here and raid his place?" Sky asked.

Ron groaned and shook his head. "That's quite literally doing the opposite of letting it go, Sky," he reminded her.

"Ron, please."

He drew a deep breath and straightened. "You'd need proof of illicit activity."

"I saw it with my own eyes."

"That'd be enough if we were talking about murder," Ron informed her. "We discussed this before. Going through the proper channels involves Sheriff Burke. He warns Marcus, fingers you as a snitch, and you get a one-way ticket to the desert."

"So we'd need evidence that Sheriff Burke is on Marcus's payroll?"

"Yes, but you'll never get close enough to Burke to implicate him," Ron announced. "He'll bury you if he even *suspects* you're up to something."

"Okay, so first we need proof of Sheriff Burke's corruption," she remarked.

"You're only hearing half of what I'm saying," Ron reported, then turned stern. "Do yourself a favor, Sky. Go with your aunt and uncle this weekend. Get away for a while. You need to clear your head and start worrying about yourself."

"Ron--"

"No," he announced, waving his hands. "It's not up for discussion. No more talk of suicide."

Sky frowned and glanced toward the large front window. She saw a familiar truck pull up and suddenly groaned. "Speak of the devil," she muttered. "Here come some of his goons now." She then nodded across the shop. "I'll be in the women's health aisle, hiding out among the tampons. It's the safest aisle and the last one they'd go down."

"Smart move," Ron replied.

Sky darted for the third aisle, which held feminine products, just past the condoms. She heard the doorbell jingle as the men entered, accompanied by their usual flurry of loud talking and joking. When she heard Vaughn's voice, she glanced at her watch. She thought it was too early for him to be in town, but if he rode to their usual morning spot and discovered she wasn't there, he had plenty of time to ride back to the stable and drive to town.

"Just try and stay out of trouble while I'm gone," Vaughn announced to his men as Sky heard them crossing the store and entering the next aisle over.

"So where are you taking her?" Moose asked with a low chuckle.

"I was thinking about that riverboat hotel and casino," Vaughn replied. "Any place where she can wear fancy dresses, look like a lady, and not smell like horses or cattle. Six weeks of farm girls in this town is about all I can handle." He then chuckled. "There are only so many ponytails and cowgirl boots a guy can stomach."

Sky made a face and touched her hair, pulled back in its usual ponytail. He was talking about her! She knew they were hooking up out of convenience, but she thought he was at least *moderately* attracted to her. Apparently not.

"You should probably stock up on the essentials," Ox insisted.

Ox appeared at the opposite end of the aisle that Sky occupied. He didn't even seem to notice her and pulled two boxes of condoms from the rack. Vaughn and Moose then appeared within the aisle as well. It wasn't as if Sky could make a hasty getaway at that point. It would look suspicious. Instead, she grabbed the closest box to her and pretended to look at it, hoping they wouldn't notice her.

"We've got glow in the dark and ribbed for her pleasure," Ox announced while proudly holding up a box in each hand. "And they even have your size. Micro penis."

"You're going to be the first man in history to die choking on condoms," Vaughn scoffed to his friend.

Moose suddenly cleared his throat, and all three men were unusually quiet. Sky knew they were looking at her and felt compelled to look back. Sure enough, they were staring at her. Moose managed a tiny smile at her.

"Sorry about that," Moose remarked to her, sounding surprisingly sincere.

Vaughn suddenly grinned and waved off Moose. "It's just Sky," he announced. "She's practically one of the boys." He met Sky's gaze with a cheap smile, then held up each box. "What do you think, darling? Glow in the dark or ribbed for her pleasure?"

Sky stared at him without emotion. "If you have to ask, I already feel sorry for the poor girl," she remarked.

Despite the insult, Vaughn chuckled along with his men.

"Well, if anyone knows how to disappoint a woman, it's Vaughn," Ox announced.

Vaughn backhanded Ox in the groin just hard enough to make him gasp and clutch himself. He then slapped both boxes against Moose's chest and grinned as he sauntered up to Sky, his smile never faltering. He stopped and hovered over her.

"You're in town kind of early," Vaughn announced while standing a little too close and met her gaze. "Shouldn't you be out for your morning *ride* right about now?"

Sky stared at his grin and wanted to wipe that smug smile from his face. She kept her hostility in check and smiled through gritted teeth.

"I had better things to do," she informed him. "And running into you wasn't one of them."

"Ouch," Vaughn announced loudly while chuckling. "That felt personal."

"Maybe you're just overly sensitive," she remarked without taking her eyes off his. "Now, if you'll excuse me, I need to take my ponytail and cowgirl boots back home."

Sky replaced the box on the shelf and walked past Vaughn toward Ox and Moose at the opposite end of the aisle. She eyed the men, who had obviously heard her comment.

"Gentlemen," she announced as she passed them. She then smiled and waved to Ron. "See you later, Ron."

Chapter 21

With her aunt and uncle gone by noon, Sky was excited to have the house to herself. Her uncle gave all the ranch hands the weekend off, except the two new guys, who would camp out with the herd far from the house. Naturally, the ranch hands graciously accepted the time off, planning a trip out of town to partake in a rodeo. At least Sky didn't need to worry about any of them stopping by and checking on her. Sky decided she'd spend her time downloading all the pictures she'd recently taken onto her laptop, finding the ones she liked best, and making prints for her photo albums. That evening, she planned on watching some scary movies, taking a long bath in her aunt's whirlpool tub, and getting a couple of hours' sleep before the thunderstorms that were supposed to be rolling in after midnight. While she looked at the pictures on her computer, she had a glass of whiskey to celebrate her alone time and relax. The first glass went down easily, so she had a second. She couldn't deny that the tingling in her toes felt good, maybe a little too good.

Unfortunately, her thoughts strayed to Vaughn and their ongoing, intense, and all-too-frequent sexual relationship over the last month. She needed to wipe those thoughts from her mind. That was over. She wouldn't give him the satisfaction any longer. A little before seven o'clock, Sky went upstairs and soaked in her aunt's whirlpool tub. Unfortunately, while naked and up to her neck in scented bath water, her thoughts once again strayed to Vaughn. Even though there would have been no way in hell she'd invite him to her house for a sleepover, she was a little annoyed that he tossed her over for some high-priced hooker. A lot of men in town, decent men, had asked her out over the years. Any one of them would be thrilled to have Vaughn's arrangement with her. Of course, maybe prostitutes were more Vaughn's speed. He certainly wasn't someone she should lose sleep over. Still, his remarks about small-town country girls stung.

Didn't she mean anything to him? No! She wasn't going to think about Vaughn anymore tonight. He made his decision to run off with a hooker for the weekend, and that was fine by her. No more morning hook-ups with that man! She was finally free of him. Once she dried off, she slipped into her tank top and sleep shorts, went downstairs, and had another glass of whiskey. Sky tried to relax but found herself pacing the kitchen, cursing Vaughn for running off with some hooker. It was ridiculous! Was it possible she meant absolutely nothing to him? Granted, she had nothing to compare him with, but he seemed *very* pleased with her, well, sexual performance. No! She needed to forget about that and just relax. Maybe another drink or two. That would take her mind off the prick!

A little before eight o'clock, there was a knock on the kitchen door, startling her. Sky hadn't been expecting anyone, and her heart was now pounding from the surprise and too much alcohol. It wasn't as if people just happened upon her farmhouse in the middle of nowhere. She cautiously approached the door and opened it to find Vaughn standing on the porch with a sly and devious grin on his face. Sky stared at him with a strange mix of astonishment and disbelief. Despite all the anger and frustration she'd felt toward him just a moment ago, her drunken mind and sexual desire joined forces and swiftly overtook any rational thought. Sky just about leapt onto him, throwing her arms around his neck and her legs around his hips, and kissed him with urgency. Vaughn groaned and returned the kiss while holding her tightly against him with his right arm. He then placed his left arm beneath her buttocks, maneuvered inside the kitchen, and swiftly kicked the door shut behind him.

"I knew you'd invite me in," he moaned as he just about tackled her onto the nearby table, dropping the bag he'd been holding, and aggressively kissed her neck. "And you smell so good!"

"You wanted me drunk," she gasped while pawing at him, enjoying his assault on her neck and gripping his hips with her legs. "Well, I'm drunk."

"Oh, you started without me?" he teased with a throaty chuckle between kisses.

Vaughn's mouth eagerly sought her lips, and he kissed her with such aggression that it made her head spin. While she attempted to keep up with his wildly passionate kiss, he thrust his hips against her, practically moving the table and nearly driving her insane. He quickly broke off the kiss and pulled back just far enough to meet her gaze while his strong arms kept her tightly pinned between his body and the table.

"Is it okay if I have a drink or two and catch up with you?" he asked between shallow breaths and his rising anticipation.

Sky groaned her response while indicating the nearby whiskey bottle. While Vaughn took a healthy swig from the bottle, Sky resumed pawing his body in a clumsy attempt to hurriedly undress him. She couldn't believe how badly she wanted him! She didn't even care if it was right there on the kitchen table! Vaughn just about dropped the bottle, reacting to her hand groping him, and grabbed her by the back of the neck, kissing her with surprising aggression. He broke off the kiss just as quickly and resumed kissing her neck while practically panting with excitement.

"Let's go upstairs," he murmured with his lips against her neck. "I want to take a shower with you, okay?"

"I'd like that!"

"Oh, I love you drunk," he groaned while pulling away from her before grabbing his bag and the bottle of whiskey.

Without warning, Vaughn swept her off her feet and into his arms. Sky let out a tiny, startled scream as her head and the room spun in response to the swift action. As Vaughn carried her up the back stairs like an enemy invader, Sky giggled uncontrollably.

§

Sky woke to the sound of thunder loudly cracking outside her open bedroom window as the dark room lit up with the flash of lightning. Her head was spinning as she attempted to look around the room while moderately disoriented. She recognized her bedroom, although she wasn't sure how she got there or any of the events leading up to it. When she couldn't move, she realized she was anchored against Vaughn, who held her from behind tightly against him. She groaned lowly, realizing that she'd invited Vaughn into her house *and* into her bed even after she swore she wouldn't. Sky had a difficult time remembering what had happened, but she soon discovered that her right wrist was bound to the bedpost with a pink, fuzzy handcuff. Not surprisingly, she felt oddly sore. Naturally, it was her own fault. She'd invited a gremlin into her home, and now she was paying the price for it. She barely moved when Vaughn groaned and reestablished his hold on her.

"Oh, you're awake," he announced while pressing against her, already fully aroused. "Three times a charm, eh?"

"Three?" she muttered while still feeling dizzy from the alcohol.

"Yeah, that time in the shower counts," he informed her, then rolled her over and cuffed her free wrist to the other bedpost. "I loved the way you screamed my name."

Before she could even comprehend what he'd said or the position she was now in, he was already doing things her body couldn't resist. The next hour was an assault on her senses as Vaughn pleasured her six ways from Sunday, as he often promised he would. Although she knew she should protest, everything he did felt amazing, making her writhe against the handcuffs that kept her restrained against the bed. She couldn't seem to control herself as she groaned and cried out his name while her head continued to spin from the lingering effects of the alcohol. When he finally released her from the handcuffs, Sky was completely exhausted and could do little more than close her eyes and pant softly.

"You aren't going to pass out on me, are you?" Vaughn asked while caressing her body.

Sky managed a tiny grin and chuckled without opening her eyes. "No, I'm fine," she replied, despite almost not knowing where she was anymore.

"That's what I like to hear," he groaned softly while moving on top of her.

Sky immediately clung to him as his body meshed against hers and groaned softly in his ear. She clung to his shoulders, enjoying the rhythm of his body moving against hers.

Chapter 22

Sky woke the following morning well after sunrise. She had a pounding headache, and her entire body seemed to hurt. She felt someone pressed against her from behind and attempted to eye the arms securely wrapped around her. Sky made an effort to free herself from the strong arms, but they seemed to tighten even more.

"I have to pee," she announced.

The arms immediately released her, and she just about jumped out of bed. She instantly regretted the action and had to catch her balance or risk falling to the floor. Sky stumbled into the bathroom, unable to piece together what had happened last night. She barely remembered entering the bathroom, almost sure she was still drunk all these hours later. Once she finished, she returned to her bed and stared at Vaughn sleeping peacefully beneath the covers. He looked severely rumpled, even more so than the bed. There was a mostly empty bottle of whiskey on the bedside table, but Sky was sure it was at least half full yesterday evening. To her surprise and possible horror, she saw fuzzy pink handcuffs hanging from the headboard. They certainly weren't hers, and she had no idea where they came from.

Sky didn't want to return to bed, but the world was spinning too fast, and she needed to get off her feet. She collapsed onto the bed and was immediately ensnared within Vaughn's arms. He sighed while nuzzling her, then kissed her shoulder.

"Good morning," he announced somewhat cheerfully while cuddling her. "What an amazing night."

"Really?" she muttered. "Because I don't remember it."

He chuckled and nuzzled her chest, kissing her cleavage above the neckline of her tank top. "I'll give you the highlights after brunch," Vaughn replied.

"Are those fuzzy pink handcuffs on my bedpost?" she asked.

Vaughn chuckled close to her ear. "You must have been drunker than I thought," he remarked.

"Where did they come from?" she asked with a little more insistence.

"I brought them with me," he replied, now kissing her shoulder. "Remember? While we were in the shower, I told you I visited an adult store yesterday afternoon." He chuckled deviously. "Dropped a bundle, but it was well worth it."

Sky groaned and shut her eyes. "Please don't tell me anymore. I don't want to know."

"I'm going to grab a shower and then start brunch," he informed her. "You should take that bath. You have to be sore after last night."

"Yeah, kind of," she muttered.

Vaughn climbed out of bed with a little too much enthusiasm. "Don't worry," he announced. "I've got you covered. I also bought three different kinds of lube at the adult store. I'm sure it'll be enough to get us through the weekend."

When his words finally registered, Sky was about to comment, but Vaughn was already strolling toward the bathroom. She watched his naked backside as it disappeared through the doorway, although he didn't shut the door. Sky groaned softly and held her throbbing head.

"He's never going to leave," she muttered.

§

Sky took an extra-long bath in her aunt's whirlpool tub and even found one of her special, expensive bath bombs. When her aunt and uncle moved into one of the spare bedrooms after her parents' death, they remodeled the bathroom to match the one Selma had when they lived back in the city. Although it seemed like an excessive remodel, Sky couldn't deny she enjoyed the large, deep jetted tub. The entire bathroom was elegant, from its large standing shower encased in glass to the dual marble vanities. It was the fanciest and brightest room in the whole house. As Sky lingered while soaking in the tub, she hoped Vaughn would grow bored waiting for her and eventually leave. When she changed and headed downstairs, she found Vaughn in the kitchen. Sky wasn't surprised that he hadn't gone, but she had been hopeful.

Although she wasn't surprised by Vaughn's presence, the lifelike dildo on the kitchen counter did take her by surprise. Vaughn saw her, smiled, and placed a filled plate in the microwave.

"If I had known you were taking one of *those* baths, I would have joined you," he announced while placing a mug of tea in front of her.

With some astonishment, she pointed at the dildo on the counter. "What is *that* doing in here?"

Vaughn eyed the adult toy and shrugged as the microwave dinged. He removed the plate with a dishrag and set it in front of her.

"Careful, the plate's hot," he announced, then put the second plate in the microwave. "I guess we left that down here after our little exploit on the kitchen table while we were reheating our Chinese food."

Sky eyed the table with surprise and just about gasped. They had an exploit on the kitchen table? When did that happen? That was only one of many questions racing through her mind.

He chuckled at her reaction. "Relax, I washed the toy and sanitized the part of the table that I had you bent over," Vaughn informed her.

The rest of his comment then struck her. "When the hell did we get Chinese food?" she just about demanded.

"I brought it with me," he reminded her. "You may be a little fuzzy on that part, considering you barely let me get in the door before jumping on me."

"I know I didn't do that."

"Oh, but you did," he announced, then grinned and winked. "You little vixen."

She eyed him without touching her breakfast. "What time are you leaving?" Sky almost demanded.

Vaughn smiled and chuckled. "After breakfast," he replied.

Sky was relieved to hear that.

"Monday morning," he cheerfully added. "Don't worry. I'll be gone long before your aunt and uncle return."

She stared at him with surprise and some shock. "You're not staying over one more night, let alone two," she informed him.

"That's not what you said last night," he insisted. "You told me I could stay until Monday morning as long as I 'put out'."

She eyed him with some surprise. "I seriously doubt I said that."

"But you did," he casually insisted. "I remember it clearly. I was handcuffed to the bed, and you were bouncing off of me like I was a trampoline. That's when you asked me to stay until Monday."

"I know I didn't say that," she insisted, then sank into thought. She wasn't sure she could dispute the part about her bouncing on him like a trampoline.

"No take-backs." Vaughn got his own breakfast plate and sat beside her at the table, where he eagerly dug into his eggs. "If I knew I was staying until Monday, I would have bought the waterproof sheets and the sensual massage oils."

"You're not staying until Monday," she snapped back.

"You promised we'd play naked twister," he reminded her. "And when are we going to watch our porn flick?"

"What porn flick?" she demanded.

He stared at her with surprise. "The one we made last night." Vaughn laughed, then groaned. "We definitely want to watch that together."

"You filmed us?"

"No, you did," he replied. "Of course, you used my cell phone, so technically it's my video."

"You're going to delete that."

"I will," he replied. "Just as soon as we watch it together."

"I will smash your phone," she snarled.

"Won't do much good," Vaughn informed her. "Everything is uploaded to the cloud."

Sky stared at him with surprise. "Are you blackmailing me?"

"No, of course not," he insisted. "I'll delete the video as soon as we watch it. How is that blackmail?"

"Fine," she snarled. "Let's watch it now."

"Over breakfast?" he asked, surprised. "That's just plain gross." Vaughn's smile returned. "We'll watch it tomorrow night. Tonight is naked twister."

"You really need to cut back on whatever testosterone enhancer you're taking," she informed him.

"I'm not on anything like that," he casually replied, then winked at her. "All Marines are supercharged naturally, darling. That's why we're Marines."

Sky's head was still spinning, and she was having a tough time processing everything he was saying. She finally glared at him and cocked her head.

"I thought you were going away for the weekend with that girl," she announced.

"What girl?" he asked with surprise.

"The one you were discussing with your boys yesterday," she snapped. "You know, the one who wears dresses and doesn't wear her hair in ponytails or smell like horses."

Vaughn stared at her a moment with a strange look and an odd smile. "There's no other girl," he insisted. "I just told the guys that when they pressed me for details about my weekend away. I had to tell them something." He leaned closer while grinning. "And full disclosure, I like that you smell like horses, and I love ponytails."

"What about that girl in the gambling hall?" she insisted. "The one I saw you cozying up to."

He didn't seem to understand the question, then suddenly smiled. "Oh, Candy," Vaughn announced, then laughed. "She's a nice girl and a great sport. She's been seeing this guy that she doesn't want anyone to know about, so she and I came up with this arrangement. We let everyone think something is going on between us, so no one questions our *actual* sex partners. I dropped her off in the city yesterday afternoon at some fancy hotel. Everyone saw us leave together. That way she's with her boyfriend, and I'm here with my girlfriend." He grinned. "Pretty sweet deal, huh?"

Sky again glared at him. "I'm *not* your girlfriend," she snarled.

"Those hickies on your tatas say otherwise," Vaughn remarked matter-of-factly, then took a sip of his coffee.

Sky pulled her shirt away from her chest and attempted to peer down at her chest.

Vaughn leaned back in his chair and eyed her somewhat sternly. "Now, let's discuss Jerry."

"Jerry?" she asked with some surprise.

Vaughn leaned on the table and stared into her eyes with a somewhat commanding look. "I don't know what's between the two of you," he remarked. "But I don't intend to share you with another man."

"Jerry and I--"

"No," he announced firmly without taking his eyes off her. "Like it or not, we're exclusive. I don't fuck around on you, and you don't fuck around on me. It's that simple."

"He and I are friends," she informed him. "Nothing more. Most of my friends are guys."

"I can deal with you having guy friends," Vaughn replied. "Just as long as they don't have access to my *toys*. Those are my terms." He cocked his head and raised his brows almost commandingly. "Do you agree to those terms?"

Sky couldn't seem to look away as he stared into her eyes. She felt a strange, dull ache deep inside her, possibly the remnants of their wild night together. Her body suddenly ached for him, and she didn't even know why.

"Yes, I agree to those terms," she replied, somehow unable to refuse him.

Vaughn groaned while grinning. "We're going to have a great weekend," he announced, almost overjoyed. "Like a mini honeymoon."

As she stared at him a moment longer, she felt her cheeks redden at the dirty thoughts going through her head.

"Okay," Sky replied somewhat softly. "You can stay until Monday morning."

Chapter 23

Sky entered the house from the barn early that afternoon and saw Vaughn vacuuming the living room carpets. It seemed almost bizarre that he didn't even seem bothered by doing housework. She hated to admit it, but the house looked cleaner than when she had cleaned it. The large living room had refinished hardwood flooring with several large area rugs throughout. The old, tall windows allowed plenty of light to flood the room, keeping it bright despite the darkness of the wood. A gorgeous antique 1901 Steinway Rosewood Grand piano occupied the back corner beneath its own area rug and was the showpiece of the room. There were several sitting areas with large sofas and antique chairs. A large stone fireplace with a gorgeous wooden hearth had a painting of her grandparents above it. Being the formal living room, there wasn't a television. That was in the smaller family room.

Sky noticed one of her many private photo albums, which she had created over the years, on the large coffee table. Her photo albums, all in matching leather covers, were kept in a bookcase in her bedroom, which meant Vaughn must have brought one downstairs with him since she knew it hadn't been down here earlier. When Vaughn saw her, he shut off the vacuum and gave her his full attention.

"They're calling for severe storms again tonight," he informed her. "The horses should probably stay in again."

"I heard," she replied. "The stalls are ready."

"I'm thawing some steaks for dinner," Vaughn reported. "I should be able to grill them before the storm arrives."

Sky stared at Vaughn for a long moment in silent disbelief. "Who are you?" she just about demanded.

"What do you mean?"

"You turn into June Cleaver while I was in the barn?"

His arrogant smile returned. "Why? You miss the surly bastard you've come to love?"

"I just never would have imagined you cooking and cleaning without a loaded gun to your head," she remarked.

"My momma raised me right," Vaughn announced. "I'm not an animal." A sly grin suddenly crossed his face, which was followed by a wink. "Well, except maybe during mating season."

"Okay, now you sound more like you," she muttered. "I'm going upstairs to shower."

"Want me to wash your back?"

"No, I would rather you didn't," she announced. "My entire body hurts from whatever it was you did to me last night."

"Hey, my pecker is a little tender too, but you don't hear me complaining."

"Well, at least we're on the same page with that," she remarked.

"I know," he replied with a soft sigh. "It's a good thing I bought all that lube. We're going to need it tonight."

Sky was about to comment when Vaughn switched on the vacuum and continued cleaning the carpet. She watched him a moment longer, oddly fascinated and perhaps a little turned on. The most feared man in town was vacuuming her house, and she couldn't deny it was pretty sexy.

§

As Sky walked down the stairs after taking her shower, she heard a sound she hadn't heard in years. Beautiful piano music echoed throughout the living room. She reached the bottom of the stairs and listened to the romantic ballad. Sky paused in the living room archway and peered across the room, where Vaughn sat behind the piano, playing the love song. Sky was momentarily transformed back to her childhood when her mother's piano music filled the house. She wasn't sure how long she stood there, listening to the piano that hadn't been touched in eight years sounding exactly how she remembered it. Sky finally made her way across the living room and approached the piano bench. She sat on the bench alongside Vaughn and listened to him play. Although he looked at her, he didn't let her presence interrupt his playing.

"I haven't played in years," he informed her. "Reminds me of my childhood."

"Yeah, me too," Sky replied softly. "My mother loved playing piano. She always wanted me to learn, but I was too much of a tomboy. I guess I kind of regret that now."

"You got off easy," Vaughn informed her while continuing with the romantic song. "My mother was a piano instructor in her free time. My brother and I had to play or there'd be hell to pay."

Sky studied his profile and the grin he wore and somehow couldn't look away. He must have realized she was staring at him and turned his head just enough to meet her gaze, although not allowing it to interfere with his playing. Sky placed her hand on his face and eagerly kissed him. Her own actions surprised her, causing her to pull back with some embarrassment, but it was too late. He stopped playing, gathered her in his arms, and kissed her passionately and aggressively. Vaughn just about tackled her against the keys, creating a hideous sound from the piano, before taking her to the floor.

§

The storms rolled in just after Vaughn finished cooking the steaks on the grill, and the power went out shortly after that. Fortunately, power outages during storms were a common occurrence, and Sky kept plenty of candles and kerosene lamps on hand for such an occasion. Although not intended, Vaughn and Sky ate dinner at the cozy kitchen table by romantic candlelight. Despite feeling the romance, Sky was almost twice as suspicious, possibly of her own feelings.

"So," Vaughn announced while grinning. "This is kind of romantic, don't you think? Mother nature provides."

Sky stared at him a moment, then cocked her head. "Why are you being so nice?" she just about demanded. "This feels like some sort of crazy lab experiment."

"What do you mean?" he asked as if he had no idea what she was talking about.

"Usually, I can barely tolerate you long enough for you to zip your pants," she remarked. "We should have killed each other by now."

"I'm saving that for the bedroom," he announced while suggestively raising his brows.

"You're loud, obnoxious, and mean," she scoffed. Her eyes then narrowed as she squinted at him. "Why are you being so nice?"

"You know, there's more to me than just a scary man," Vaughn informed her, matter-of-factly. "I like puppies and kittens, rom-coms, and sappy commercials. It's not all stomping on Tokyo, slashing college co-eds by the lake, and sliding stiff ones into sexy cowgirls."

"Honestly, I can't even tell when you're being serious," she remarked while shaking her head, defeated.

Vaughn groaned and leaned across the table while looking into her eyes. "It's a job, Sky," he announced. "My boss pays me to be the big, bad wolf, which means I occasionally need to huff and puff, and sometimes blow the house down." He leaned back in his chair. "You're the closest thing I've had to a girlfriend in a long time. You kind of matter to me. More than just a great piece of ass."

"Better than average sex aside, you don't even know me," she informed him.

"Better than average?" he demanded, now offended. "I dare you to find one guy who gets you off two and three times the way I do. I put in a lot of overtime keeping you satisfied. More importantly, you were a virgin the first time I boned you, and you admitted under extreme duress that I'm still the only one banging you. So you'd better step up that praise to the best you've ever had, little girl."

"I hate when you call me little girl," she scoffed.

"And I hate that you treat our wild lover romps like cheap toilet sex," he snapped back. "I could find a hundred women in bars to do that."

"Convenient and accessible," she reminded him. "Those were your words after you conned your way into my pants the second time."

"I hardly conned you, darling," he remarked. "You were looking for a rematch less than twenty-four hours later. *You* sought *me* out."

"And you wanted quick and easy," she huffed. "That's how you sold it."

"Okay," he groaned and rubbed his eyes. "I don't want to get into an argument about it. Let's just say you're right and move on."

"That's smart," she replied.

They listened to the storm rage on outside as they finished their meal. Vaughn wiped his mouth on his napkin, set it on the table, then looked at her and smiled.

"Might be a good time to get those storm pictures you wanted," he announced. "Add some more photos to your storm collection albums."

"Yes, I noticed you've perused your way through my albums," she remarked, then eyed him and made a face. "Lots and lots of horses, cattle, cowboys, and scenery, I know."

"Yeah, but much more than that," he remarked while studying her. "Considering how seriously you take your photography, I'm sure you know that."

Sky studied him a moment, a little surprised that someone like Vaughn would 'get it' when even her aunt didn't. She shifted almost uncomfortably.

"Well, I've been told quite often that I waste too much time taking pictures of 'nothing'," she remarked somewhat bitterly.

Vaughn grinned and chuckled lowly. "Let me guess," he announced. "Words of wisdom from the career shopper."

Sky hid her smile and avoided looking at Vaughn for fear of laughing. "No comment."

Vaughn shifted in his chair and then sat forward while maintaining his grin. "I'd bet money she has at least twenty pairs of shoes with purses to match," he remarked.

"Well, you wouldn't be wrong."

"I think you can go ahead and ignore whatever advice she gives you," Vaughn reported, then offered a pleasant smile. "We could sit on the porch and enjoy the storm while you take all the storm photos you want."

His suggestion made her smile, even if it was unnecessary.

"Actually, I have a special motion sensor camera I recently bought already set up in the attic," she informed him. "It takes photo bursts whenever it detects movement. It's probably taken a thousand pictures already since yesterday evening."

"I wouldn't mind seeing those photos," he reported. "Although I hope it has a good battery pack. No power, remember?"

"Enough to get through the night," she replied with a tiny shrug.

"Well, we still don't have any power," Vaughn remarked with a sigh. "So dishes will have to wait." Vaughn then met her gaze across the candlelit table. "There's really only one thing left to do on a night like this."

"Sleep?"

"I was actually thinking erotic massage," he remarked.

Sky stared at him for a brief moment, mildly suspicious of his suggestion. "Who's giving and who's getting?"

"Oh, I'm giving and you're getting, trust me," he replied with a sly grin.

Sky studied him and the devilish look on his face while considering his words. She finally groaned, giving in to the temptation.

"You'd better have a lot of lube," Sky softly threatened.

Vaughn's grin increased. "Enough to keep you happy until Monday morning, I promise."

Chapter 24

Around two o'clock in the morning, Vaughn was nestled against Sky from behind with a firm grip around her while both slept peacefully. There were several half-burnt, extinguished candles around the room, clothing strewn across the floor, and a bottle of lube on the nightstand. The pink, fuzzy handcuffs still hung from each of the bedposts like badges of honor. Vaughn suddenly stirred and lifted his head, looking around the room with some disorientation. The bedside clock was now flashing twelve o'clock.

"Everything okay?" Sky muttered, seeming too exhausted even to open her eyes.

Vaughn groaned and returned his head to the pillow, then resumed nuzzling her. "Power's back on," he replied.

They could hear the rain pouring outside through the open window and distant thunder rumbling, but the worst of the storm was possibly over. Vaughn affectionately kissed Sky's neck.

"If you're up for another round, don't expect me to be awake for it," she muttered into her pillow.

He chuckled near her ear. "Not a problem," Vaughn teased. "You weren't awake for the last round."

Her eyes popped open for only a moment. "I guess that explains the erotic dreams I had."

Vaughn warmly kissed her neck. "I'm going downstairs for a glass of water," he informed her. "You want anything?"

"Sleep."

"Okay," he replied close to her ear, then chuckled. "I'll try not to wake you when I slip it in."

Sky wasn't sure why, but that made her smile, although she was grateful he didn't see it. Vaughn crawled out of bed, slipped into his boxer briefs, and headed out of the bedroom. Sky fell back to sleep almost instantly, and the erotic dreams continued. The distant yet loud sound of shattering glass abruptly woke her. Sky lifted her head and looked around the dimly lit room. Vaughn hadn't returned yet, and the bedside clock, annoyingly, still flashed twelve o'clock. She wasn't sure how long he had been gone or what had woken her. It was possible the sound even came from within her dream. She then heard a faint thud from somewhere inside the house.

"Vaughn?"

If he were downstairs, he certainly wouldn't hear her. Sky jumped out of bed and slipped into her discarded tank top and sleep shorts. She was about to leave the room when she heard another thump from downstairs. Any thump loud enough for her to hear upstairs couldn't be good. Sky hesitated, then darted to her bed and pressed on the base of the headboard, which revealed a hidden compartment containing a sawed-off shotgun. She removed the weapon and hurried from the room. As she headed into the second floor hallway, she swore she heard someone on the front stairs, but there was a loud thump from the back stairs, indicating someone was in the kitchen. Sky quietly walked along the second floor hallway with the shotgun snug in her arms and her finger near the trigger.

Sky crept down the back stairs and paused just inside the dark kitchen, wondering why Vaughn would be in the dark, especially since the lights would have been on when the power had gone out. She reached around the corner and flipped the switch, brightening the kitchen. To her horror, the kitchen was ransacked, and there was broken glass and blood everywhere, with no sign of Vaughn. She looked across the room to the wall phone near the hallway door, then darted across the kitchen and picked up the receiver. She was about to call the sheriff when she heard someone thundering down the back stairs. Sky gasped, dropped the phone, and aimed the shotgun. Vaughn appeared at the bottom of the stairs in just his boxer briefs with a semiautomatic in his right hand and a kitchen knife in his left. When he saw her with the shotgun, he cried out and ducked.

"It's me!" he shouted while holding up his gun and knife where he crouched close to the floor.

Sky released the breath she'd been holding and lowered the shotgun. "Jesus, Vaughn," she gasped. "What happened?"

Vaughn relaxed and straightened, carelessly tossing the bloodied knife onto the kitchen table. "Someone broke into the house," he informed her, then ushered her toward him.

Sky hurried across the kitchen, mindful of the broken glass, and approached him by the stairs. He was panting heavily as he pulled her into his arms, holding her close.

"I chased him upstairs and caught him in your bedroom," he informed her. "Thankfully, you weren't there. We fought, but he got away. I thought he came down the back stairs, but he must have gone down the front stairs instead."

Sky then noticed the blood running down his left shoulder from what appeared to be a knife gash. His freely bleeding cut explained some of the blood spread out across her kitchen. She then saw his slightly battered face and the blood on the corner of his mouth.

"You're hurt," she gasped with concern and pulled away, attempting to check his injury.

"I'm fine," he muttered, then tucked his gun down the waistband of his boxer briefs before looking around the disastrous kitchen. "Thankfully, most of the blood around here is his."

"You got him?" Sky gasped.

"Yeah, I injured him," Vaughn replied. "I gave him a decent gash on his arm and side down here and stabbed him in his calf upstairs in your room. That's when he took off."

"We need to call the sheriff and let him know, then get you to the hospital," she insisted while grabbing a clean dishtowel and placing it to his bleeding shoulder before hurrying for the kitchen phone.

Vaughn caught her arm and pulled her back to his side. "No," he announced in a stern tone. "I need a minute to figure this out."

"What's there to figure out?" she gasped, somewhat surprised. "Someone broke into my house and attacked you."

"Yeah, a little convenient, don't you think?" he remarked.

Sky stared at him a moment, not understanding his logic. "Everyone knew my aunt and uncle were going away for the weekend," she informed Vaughn. "The intruder probably took advantage of them being gone."

"Yeah, and everyone also knew you'd be home alone," he informed her while raising an arrogant brow. "If robbery was the motive, why not case the place and wait until you went out for a ride or into town for a few hours?" He frowned and shook his head. "No, instead, they broke in when they *knew* you'd be at home, supposedly alone, and at your most vulnerable."

Sky stared at him for a moment, then concern swept over her. "Are you suggesting they were *hoping* I'd be alone?"

"Well, there's that," he replied, then eyed her. "Or it's possible someone knew I was here, making me the intended target."

"That sounds more logical," she insisted without hesitation. "There are plenty of people who want a piece of you."

"Maybe so, but there are also quite a few men who want a piece of your virgin ass as well," he reminded her.

Sky was a bit surprised by his response, then brushed it aside. "Either way, we need to call the sheriff," she insisted. "Because you injured the guy, he might be able to catch him."

Vaughn removed the dishtowel from his injury and cringed slightly, but remained in thought. "Yes, you need to call the sheriff," he finally admitted. "But no one can know I was here."

"What? Why?" she asked with surprise.

"Marcus will kill me," he replied matter-of-factly while staring into her eyes. "I've gone to great lengths to cover up our rendezvous and to give Candy a cover story for her weekend getaway. If it's discovered I was here the entire weekend, Candy and I are both in trouble." He eyed her almost sternly. "No one can know I was here."

Sky couldn't deny she was uncomfortable with keeping that secret in light of what had just happened, but she couldn't exactly throw Vaughn under the bus either.

"Okay," she finally announced, her defeat evident as she met his gaze. "But the intruder knows you were here. What about him?"

"He didn't get a good look at me any more than I got a look at him," Vaughn informed her. "If he spreads any gossip about you having overnight male company, he'll be giving himself away. And, believe me, the last thing he wants is me learning his identity."

Sky drew a deep breath, then sighed. "Okay. What do you want me to do?"

"Lock yourself in your room, and give me a thirty-minute head start before you call the sheriff," he informed her. "I'll almost be back to the stables by then."

"What about your horse?" she asked. "If you left town in your car, won't they have noticed your horse was missing?"

"No, I informed the guys I was leaving Diablo out in the big pasture before I left," he replied with little concern. "And I hid my Jeep after I dropped off Candy. It'll be fine. I have all my steps covered."

His cover story had Sky a little unnerved. He wasn't kidding. He'd gone to great lengths to keep his lie intact. A tiny part of her wondered if there was more to the break-in than he was telling her. Was it possible he actually knew the intruder? Maybe it was one of his own men, Ox or Moose. If he had lied to them as well, the break-in may have had more to do with him than anything else.

"What if the sheriff asks about the blood?" she asked. "Some of that is yours."

"Tell him the truth. The blood was there when you came downstairs," he replied while tossing the dishtowel over his shoulder and grabbing the discarded butcher knife. As he thoroughly washed the knife, he continued with instructions. "Let the sheriff think two intruders turned on each other. They're not going to swab the house for a home invader's DNA out here in fucking Mayberry."

Once he dried the knife, he replaced it to the butcher's block with the rest of the set.

"Well, that's good," she remarked somewhat firmly while snatching the towel from his shoulder and reapplying it to his freely bleeding wound. "Because they'd find your DNA just about everywhere." She then eyed him, now tense. "What if the guy comes back after you're gone?"

"I doubt he will, but that's why I want you to lock yourself in your room," he insisted and resumed holding the towel over his injury so she didn't have to worry about it. "If he comes back, you have the shotgun. Just don't leave your room until the sheriff gets here." He indicated the back stairs. "I'll walk you to your room and grab my things."

Once they reached her room, Sky crudely patched Vaughn's cut shoulder. Thankfully, his injury wasn't too severe. She then tossed the bloodied dish towel into a plastic bag and hid it in her closet. While Vaughn dressed and threw some things into his bag, Sky cleaned up what little blood there was in her room from the continuation of his altercation with the intruder. It was a little bizarre that the intruder didn't leave as much blood in her room. Perhaps Vaughn only nicked the man in the leg. She wouldn't let the sheriff know that the intruder made it upstairs and needed to hide any evidence of it, if they were to believe it had been two intruders turning on each other. Keeping the sheriff out of her room altogether was the best course of action. Since neither of them could find her cell phone, Vaughn handed her the cordless phone from her nightstand.

"I need to saddle my horse," he informed her. "When you see me ride away, give me thirty minutes before calling the sheriff."

"Be careful," she announced. "You don't know if he's waiting outside for you."

Vaughn smiled warmly and touched her face. "It's nice that you're worried about me," he remarked. "But I'll be fine." He kissed her affectionately on the lips, then pulled away and met her gaze. "Thanks for letting me stay." He kissed her again, then left the room, locking the door behind him.

Sky sank against the window seat and thought about everything that had happened. She hated that she didn't trust Vaughn, but he didn't give her much reason to trust him. Sadly, she knew what kind of man he was. Yet, somewhere over the last two days, she'd come to know a different version of the town's most feared man. The entire thing left her confused and with a massive headache.

Chapter 25

Deputy Rhodes arrived at the house less than ten minutes after Sky placed the phone call. Despite being a small town, the few law enforcement officials they had were efficient when needed. Well, when it didn't involve Marcus and his minions. Once the deputy arrived, Sky watched him attempt to collect evidence, but it was apparent he didn't have a clue where to start. When he removed his cell phone to take photos of the crime scene, Sky stepped in. Photography was her thing, and she could take crime scene photos far better than he could. While she took pictures of everything broken, smeared, or spattered in the kitchen, Rhodes placed broken shards of bloodied glass into plastic baggies; baggies that Sky had provided. At least Deputy Rhodes was moderately sympathetic about what happened. She was grateful it hadn't been Sheriff Burke on call. He'd undoubtedly feel the need to search her underwear drawer for evidence.

Other than the most basic questions, Deputy Rhodes didn't ask her much, although he kept asking if she had seen the men who broke into her house. It seemed odd that he kept asking that over and over, as if he didn't believe her the first half a dozen times she said she hadn't. Wouldn't he think she'd tell him who it was if she had known? Despite not being part of his job, Sky watched as Deputy Rhodes nailed boards across the broken window on the kitchen door so she'd be able to lock her house until the door was repaired or replaced. Once the ranch hands returned from their weekend away, they'd have the door replaced that same afternoon. Each one of them was a handyman by trade.

"I just don't understand," Sky remarked as she watched Rhodes secure her door. "Why would someone break into the house at night? Wouldn't they realize I'd be here?"

She couldn't deny Vaughn had an excellent point about that. She'd leave the house for hours at a time every day, leaving the home empty and, most times, unlocked. Had the intruder been counting on her being home? Was she a target? Was Vaughn the target?

"I don't know," Rhodes replied while kneeling on the floor alongside the door with a hammer in his hand. "We don't get a lot of break-ins around here." He seemed to consider his comment. "I mean, I suppose a stranger could have broken in, but it's not as if your place is located along the road."

"If it had been a stranger, he would have had to travel down our long driveway before even reaching the house," she remarked.

"And risk being seen or heard by you," Rhodes replied. "Everyone knew your aunt and uncle were going away for the weekend, but I can't imagine anyone in town desperate enough to come all the way out here to break into your house. Everyone in town knows you have an armory of shotguns, rifles, and handguns."

Deputy Rhodes finally stood and set the hammer on the nearby counter.

"That should hold until you can have the door replaced," Rhodes informed her. "Maybe one without single-pane glass so close to the lock."

"Thank you, Deputy Rhodes," she replied, her voice trailing off with a slight sigh of defeat.

§

Since it was nearly four o'clock in the morning by the time Deputy Rhodes left her house, Sky didn't bother going back to sleep. She couldn't have slept if she wanted to. Against Deputy Rhodes' suggestion, she didn't call her aunt and uncle. Why ruin their weekend? Naturally, Sky was a little on edge and kept the shotgun close by her side until the sun came up. She had spent most of the early morning hours picking up the remnants from the adult store Vaughn had left scattered about her bedroom and stuffed the many toys, handcuffs, and lube into the unmarked plastic bag they came in. The store receipt was still in the bag along with the receipt from the Chinese restaurant. Both the store and restaurant were halfway between the city and town. Out of curiosity, Sky glanced at the adult store receipt and gasped at what Vaughn had spent on sex toys. His credit card got almost as much of a workout as she had. She stuffed the receipts into the bag and stashed the adult items where they wouldn't easily be spotted by anyone poking their noses in her room.

Around seven o'clock that morning, Sky finally called Dixie and told her about the break-in. Like a true friend, Dixie was at her doorstep within thirty minutes and gladly helped her clean the mess in the kitchen.

"I can't believe someone broke into your house," Dixie remarked while helping Sky sweep up the last of the broken glass. "While you were upstairs sleeping, no less!"

"I guess they took off when they heard me pumping the shotgun," Sky easily lied.

The sawed-off shotgun Sky kept hidden in her room wasn't a pump-action but rather a Weatherby Orion twelve-gauge over-under.

"Did they steal anything?"

"I don't think they got that far," Sky remarked, then sighed and looked around. "According to Deputy Rhodes, there must have been two intruders who turned on each other and got into a fight, which is probably what I heard."

"Thank God for that," Dixie announced while remaining tense. "That had to be scary. Want me to stay with you tonight?"

"Are you sure it's no trouble?" Sky asked while cringing at the thought. "The ranch hands have the weekend off, and I'd hate to call them back early to babysit me."

"Of course, I don't mind," Dixie insisted. "I'd love any excuse to get out of my parents' house for an overnight." There was an awkward moment of silence before she continued with the current conversation. "Honestly, I thought you would have invited me over for the entire weekend."

"I thought about it," Sky remarked, then frowned. "But I'm glad I didn't. You didn't need to be here for my little home invasion."

"Why *didn't* you invite me?" Dixie finally asked, eyeing her almost suspiciously. "You don't have some secret boyfriend you don't want me to know about, do you?"

Sky tensed and felt her heart just about stop at her friend's speculation and the accuracy of it. However, she wouldn't classify Vaughn as a boyfriend. She then let out a slightly nervous laugh.

"No, you know me better than that," Sky remarked, then was suddenly reminded of her two-day sex-a-thon with Vaughn.

Before Vaughn invited himself over for the weekend, she really just wanted to have the house to herself and concentrate on her photography. Sky thought up the next best plausible reason for excluding Dixie, which was actually the truth.

"I wanted to do some night photography," Sky announced. "I bought that new camera that takes amazing night photos, and I wanted to get some pictures of the storms."

The words no sooner left her lips when she remembered her camera equipment in the attic. The camera had been set on automatic photo burst with a motion detector! She might have gotten a picture of the man who broke into her house! She wanted to scream out her new revelation, but she couldn't share that information with Dixie. Dixie would want to view the pictures with her, which would clearly show Vaughn's arrival and departure as well. She'd have to wait to investigate until Dixie went home for her overnight bag.

Chapter 26

After lunch, Dixie went home to pack her overnight bag, which would give Sky almost an hour before her friend returned. As soon as Dixie drove down the driveway, Sky ran upstairs to the attic and headed for her camera equipment, which was positioned on a tripod in front of the small attic window. It would be too hot in the attic to view the hundreds of pictures saved to the large memory file, so she took the camera with her to her bedroom. Sky made herself comfortable on the window seat, attached her new night vision camera to her laptop, and downloaded all the photos. She was able to browse through the thumbnails, which were all time-stamped, making it easier to pick through them. She started with the pictures after midnight, early Sunday morning, which was approximately two hours before the intruders broke into the house.

Unfortunately, with the angle she had set the camera to capture the storm across the horizon, she didn't have a view of the front or back door. There were a few wildlife shots after the rain started, but then it was mostly pictures of lightning. Some were even quite spectacular. She ignored those photos for now and continued onward to the two o'clock in the morning mark. There weren't many photos until two-thirty. A photo burst revealed a man dressed in black running into the woods near the driveway. There could have been a car parked at the end of her massively long driveway, hidden from the view of passersby. She zoomed in on each of the five photos depicting the man, but none showed his face, as he was running away. The larger the picture became, the more it was distorted. There only appeared to be photos of him leaving. Since she didn't see any of him approaching the house, it must've meant he came through the woods out of the camera's view to reach the kitchen door.

Although Vaughn seemed to think there was only one intruder, that didn't mean there weren't two or more, and anyone leaving through the broken kitchen door might not show up on the photos at all. The next series of photo bursts was Vaughn riding away on his horse, heading into the field for the path that would take him back to Marcus's farm. Sky slammed her laptop lid shut with disgust. She had an actual picture of the intruder fleeing, but she couldn't see his face. Nothing else from the backside view was enough to identify the man either. Sky leaned against the wall of the window seat and groaned in disgust. She then heard a ding from her cell phone. Sky looked around for her phone, which she hadn't seen since Friday night. When she heard another ding, Sky sprang from her seat and searched for her phone. When it dinged a third time, she peered under the bed.

Sky saw her phone on the floor beneath her bed, near the headboard. It must have been near her pillow Friday night and fallen through the space in the headboard. Sky reached under the bed, feeling for the cell phone. Her arms were almost too short to reach. She felt something other than her phone, hesitated, and then pulled her hand back. When she saw the lifelike penis vibrator, she grimaced and cast it aside. She thought she had cleaned up all the paraphernalia Vaughn had left behind. Apparently, that one had slipped through the crack along with her cell phone. She again reached under the bed and finally grabbed her phone. Sky sat on the floor and checked the text messages that had just come through. To her surprise, the texts were from Vaughn. He'd sent her a selfie of them huddled close together on her bed and smiling. She knew they were both drunk, and possibly naked, when the picture was taken, but she couldn't deny it was a nice picture. Well, if she could digitally alter the pink fuzzy handcuffs hanging from the bedpost behind them.

The second was a video. When she tapped the play button, the X-rated video she'd filmed while Vaughn had her bent over the kitchen table started playing. Although there wasn't much to see, she took the video of her drunken, smiling face, then panned to the side, showing Vaughn holding onto her hips while slamming hard against her. He saw the phone aimed at him, then grinned and winked. Thankfully, the video ended there, but it was enough to make her cringe. Sky pressed the button for the video options, then hesitated with her finger hovering over the 'delete' button. She considered it a moment, then changed her mind.

Another text message came through and read, "Can I come over and play with you?"

Sky managed a tiny laugh, then responded with, "Sorry, Dixie is spending the night."

The typing bubble showed up, then Vaughn's response came back. "Threesome?" There were several question marks and a winking emoji.

Sky snorted a laugh, then took a picture of her middle finger and sent it to him. She waited several minutes for a response. When the response came back, she stared at an aroused dick pic.

Following the photo, Vaughn texted, "Thinking of you!" There was a winking emoji after it.

Sky took a picture of the discarded vibrator and sent it to him with the caption, "You've been replaced."

Vaughn immediately sent an image of his right hand with the caption, "So have you!"

Sky laughed and again looked at the picture he'd sent of them together, which made her smile. Her heart suddenly sank. What was she doing? She couldn't possibly think they could have an actual relationship. Even a meaningless fling with a man like Vaughn was risky. There was no telling what sort of skeletons he had hiding in his closet. Another selfie came through. This one was of Vaughn grinning with her barn behind him in the background. She realized it had to be taken in the woods, not far from her house.

The text message beneath the photo read, "I'll be spending the night at this romantic inn. Please visit after lights out."

Sky felt her heart skip a beat. How could a man like that be so damned cute? She couldn't help but smile and, against her better judgement, sent a 'thumbs up' emoji.

Another message from Vaughn immediately came through and read, "Bring snacks! Hungry. Might eat my horse!"

Sky then realized that Vaughn had been hiding out in the woods since leaving her house, as he couldn't go home until after he picked up Candy in the city on Monday morning. She couldn't say she understood what he was up to, particularly with Candy, but she wasn't going to let him starve either.

Sky typed her response. "Will put a cooler with food in the barn."

Sky then sprang to her feet and hurried from her room. If she were quick, she could probably throw some things in a cooler and get it out to the barn before Dixie returned.

§

Fifteen minutes later, Sky hurried across the driveway with two medium-sized coolers. One had drinks and the other had an assortment of sandwiches and some junk food. Dixie still hadn't returned, so she was in the clear. Sky entered the barn, set the coolers down near the tack room, and looked around. The barn had ten standard stalls, each with a barred rolling door on either side of the concrete aisle. There was one wash stall and the large tack room that held almost forty western saddles and bridles, as well as other tack and grooming items. The cattle ranch had thirty horses, but ten of them were kept in a smaller barn closer to the bunkhouse, making it easier for the ranch hands to saddle them in the morning. Sky was suddenly grabbed from behind, forcing her to scream with surprise before Vaughn spun her around and pulled her into his arms.

"Looks like Dixie is a no-show," Vaughn announced, then kissed her somewhat aggressively while caressing her body.

She briefly returned the kiss, then broke it off and glared at him. "Don't sneak up on me like that," she scolded and smacked his shoulder. He yelped, as it was his injured shoulder. "Especially after last night. You nearly gave me a heart attack!"

"Sorry," he replied as his hands continued to travel her body while he held her close. "I missed you."

"You just saw me less than twelve hours ago," she reminded him.

"So?" he teased, then moved closer and kissed her neck. "I can still miss you."

Sky affectionately ran her fingers through his hair while he warmly kissed her neck. The last two days seemed to change the dynamic of their relationship, and she wasn't sure that was a good thing. She didn't need to get attached to him. No matter what he said or how he acted, she knew it was just his playful way of luring her in to fulfill his own sexual needs. Sky didn't know how to say no, and if she wasn't careful, he would break her heart. Her own admission suddenly frightened her. Did she actually have feelings for Vaughn that went beyond physical ones? Dixie's car was heard pulling up the driveway long before it would pass by the barn. Sky pulled away from Vaughn and patted his chest.

"Try to keep it down out here," she informed him. "And I'll try to keep Dixie on the back patio."

"Just keep her out of the barn," Vaughn remarked, then indicated the horse wash block. "I need a shower."

"You're going to shower in the horse's wash stall?" she asked while raising a clever brow.

"Well, yeah," he replied. "I haven't showered since that erotic massage. I'm smelly and crusty."

"Too much information."

"You asked."

"No, I didn't," she replied, then eyed him. "Do you have a towel?"

"No, but I'll air dry."

"Seriously?"

He grinned, taunting her. "Yeah, upstairs," Vaughn replied while pointing up. "In the hay loft. Naked and thinking of you." He raised his brows suggestively and pulled her into his arms. "You sneaking out when the other campers fall asleep?" His grin increased. "Take a little roll in the hay with me?"

Sky heard Dixie's car door shut and knew she was running out of time. She patted his chest and then kissed him quickly on the lips. "Yes, I'll sneak out after Dixie falls asleep."

Vaughn groaned and kissed her quickly but passionately. "I'll be waiting for you in the hay loft."

Chapter 27

Later that afternoon, Sky and Dixie sat on the porch, drinking iced tea and talking about everything but the break-in. Despite the good time they were having, Sky was aware that Vaughn was hiding out in the barn, possibly naked in the loft. As long as he didn't make any noise, Dixie wouldn't have any reason to go into the barn. She planned to feed the horses later in the evening, when she could convince Dixie to do something inside. It wasn't just finding Vaughn in the barn, but his horse was also inside and would be easily recognized.

"I know the bunkhouse is about five hundred yards from the house, but it seems so quiet around here," Dixie remarked, then eyed her friend, clearly fishing for confirmation of a secret boyfriend. "Did *all* the guys leave for the weekend?"

"There's a rodeo in the next county over," Sky informed her friend. "All of them except the two new guys went to that. Took some horses too. I just hope they all return in one piece."

"Oh, we should have gone to that," Dixie remarked, then practically pouted. "I wish you had said something sooner. That sounds like fun."

"I don't mind going for a few hours, but I can't do all-day events like they do," Sky replied. "It gets to be too much."

"The pictures would be amazing though," Dixie added.

"I'd have to be right up against the fence to get any good shots," Sky reminded her, then frowned. "Eating a lot of dust. Honestly, I prefer being here with the whole house to myself. I love my aunt and uncle, don't get me wrong, but sometimes I just want a little peace and quiet."

"How much noise do they really make?" Dixie asked with a humored laugh.

"When Uncle Nash is doing the books and paying bills, he makes a lot of noise," Sky informed her. "If the account isn't to the penny, he curses and thumps around until he finds the error." She allowed a soft groan to escape. "And Aunt Selma--?" Sky rolled her eyes and groaned. "She's always pushing fashion magazines under my nose, showing me dresses I should buy, and picking out curtains for her new house in the city that she doesn't have yet. Then Uncle Nash gets on her case about her credit card purchases. It's a whole thing."

"He's a bit of a penny pincher, isn't he?" Dixie remarked. "Like Scrooge McDuck."

Sky chuckled at the comment. "He can be a bit tight with his wallet," she replied, "but Aunt Selma does have expensive taste."

"I guess with all their money, they can afford it," Dixie insisted.

"I wouldn't know," Sky replied with all honesty. "I don't ask him about his finances, and he doesn't usually offer."

They heard a car on the extensive, dirt driveway long before they could see it, interrupting their conversation. Both watched and waited for the vehicle to appear around the last bend. Sky was a bit surprised when she saw the sheriff's blazer with Marcus's car just behind it. Sky and Dixie exchanged bewildered looks.

"I wonder what that's about?" Dixie muttered but didn't bother getting up.

Sky was wondering the same thing as she stood and approached the porch steps while watching both vehicles park in front of the house. Sheriff Burke walked up to the porch with Marcus and Tony only a few steps behind him.

"Sheriff," Sky announced almost politely before cocking her head. "Is there something I can do for you?"

Sky was internally twitching, wondering if they somehow got wind that Vaughn was hiding in her barn, although she wasn't sure how she even came to that conclusion.

"Just following up on your earlier break-in," Sheriff Burke replied.

Was Sheriff Burke doing actual police work? Marcus walked past the sheriff and up the porch steps to greet Sky. He took both her hands in his and kissed her cheeks.

"Are you okay, Sky?" Marcus asked while gazing into her eyes. "Sheriff Burke just informed me of your ordeal last night. You should have called me. I would have sent some of the guys over to patrol your property."

"Completely unnecessary," Sky insisted while delicately pulling her hands from his.

The thought of Marcus's men patrolling her property was enough to give her a mild panic attack. Not only were they probably worse than the intruder, but they'd sniff Vaughn out almost immediately.

"Apart from a little broken glass, they didn't even take anything," she informed him.

Sky's eyes strayed to Tony and the brainless goon image he'd gotten down pat. He somehow seemed void of all emotions after years of working for Marcus. In high school, he was affectionate and, at times, even charming. Nowhere near as charming as Vaughn. Probably not as brave either. As her thoughts strayed to Vaughn tackling an intruder wearing only his boxer briefs, she had to hide her smile. It must have been one hell of a shock for the intruder.

"And there were two of them?" Marcus asked, now interested.

"I guess so," Sky replied, keeping with the lie. "There was quite the ruckus in the kitchen. One of them must have injured the other because there was some blood on the floor, wall, and countertop. Honestly, I missed whatever happened."

"Thank God for that," Marcus announced, then guided her toward the love seat rocking chair.

Sky was compelled to sit down, with Marcus taking the spot alongside her, although turned partially sideways, facing her.

"I could send a few of my men over to keep an eye on the place tonight," Marcus again insisted.

"No, I'm fine," Sky protested. "I have Dixie with me this evening, and I'm sure Marlon will be along later tonight after he gets off work. We'll be fine."

Dixie eyed Sky somewhat suspiciously about Marlon joining them. That wasn't part of their evening plans.

"Do you mind if I have a look around the kitchen?" Sheriff Burke asked, surprising Sky.

"Look for what?" she asked. "Dixie and I cleaned everything up this morning. There's nothing to see but a boarded-up door."

"I asked Sheriff Burke to check things out," Marcus insisted. "Indulge me. I just want to make sure you're safe."

Sky reluctantly gave in and nodded to the front door. She watched Sheriff Burke enter her house and immediately felt uneasy about it. She didn't like the sheriff, and she certainly didn't want him invading her private space. While Sheriff Burke checked out the kitchen and living room, Marcus clung to Sky's hand and talked to her as if she were a helpless child, believing she needed comforting. If she had, it wouldn't be from him. Even Dixie had a difficult time sitting through the show, squirming in her rocking chair. When Tony started making his way toward the barn, Sky internally panicked. She just about shot up from her seat and stared after Tony.

"Hey," Sky snarled, catching his attention. "No one invited you to snoop around my property."

Marcus appeared slightly embarrassed as he stood and looked at Tony as well. Tony eyed his boss, then walked back to the car and leaned against the driver's side. Sky collected her emotions, then looked at Marcus and managed a smile.

"Sorry," she remarked, now fidgeting. "I guess I'm still a little on edge from this morning."

"You don't have to explain yourself," Marcus insisted, then offered a knowing smile. "I know you're not Tony's biggest fan."

"That doesn't help," she muttered.

Sheriff Burke returned from the house and offered a polite smile to Sky and Dixie. "Everything seems secure," he announced. "Deputy Rhodes did a nice patch job."

Marcus again took Sky's hands and held them affectionately. "If you need anything at all, just call me," he insisted.

"Thank you, Marcus," Sky replied while attempting to keep her repulsion for the man buried deep inside.

Sheriff Burke tipped his cowboy hat and then followed Marcus from the porch. Sky leaned against the porch post and watched as both cars turned and headed back down her driveway.

"You don't think it was Tony who broke into your house, do you?" Dixie asked, surprising Sky.

Sky turned and looked at her friend, then snorted a laugh. "He may be a lot of things, but I don't think he'd be bold enough to break into my house," she insisted. "He knows I'd shoot him on principle alone."

Chapter 28

Just before sunrise, Sky woke in the hay loft and stared across the rib vaulted ceiling, which was partially filled with second-cutting hay. The rest of the hay was kept in the larger hay barn, separate from the horse barn. Sky had slept on her back within the old sleeping bag while Vaughn clung to her. She glanced at Vaughn while he slept. He had strands of hay and hay particles within his slightly mussed hair and beard. As she studied him while he slept, she kept wondering how she ended up here, naked, in Vaughn's arms. It was so foreign, yet so familiar. When she stirred, he nuzzled her and groaned softly.

"You're not leaving already, are you?" he asked softly, near her ear, then kissed her warmly on her bare shoulder.

"I have to get back inside before Dixie wakes up," Sky insisted, then turned onto her side while propped up on her elbow and met his gaze. "And you need to get out of here before sunrise, if you don't want to get caught."

He groaned softly and rolled onto his back. "No, I don't want to get caught," Vaughn muttered, briefly glanced at his watch, and then met her gaze while grinning slyly. "But if it was just my ass I had to worry about, I think I'd reconsider." He grasped her hand and affectionately kissed it before holding it against his bare chest. "I'm addicted to you, Sky."

Sky stared into his eyes and saw the sincerity behind his words. She may have been drunk the night she gave away her virginity, but, as she stared at him, she suddenly understood why she did it. Without words, Sky slid on top of him, straddled his hips, and sat up while caressing his chest with both hands. Vaughn grinned, pleased with the way she initiated intimacy.

§

After their aggressive lovemaking, Vaughn kissed Sky's neck and shoulder before she finally pulled away and collapsed onto the sleeping bag alongside him. Sky only rested a moment before sitting up, frantic about the time.

"I really need to go," she insisted before casting a quick look at him. "And so do you."

Vaughn released a loud sigh, then sat up behind her and affectionately kissed her bare shoulder. "I don't want to," he remarked.

"Too bad," she informed him as she slipped into her jeans. "I can meet you later. My aunt and uncle will be home this afternoon, and they'll want to have a family dinner. Maybe after dinner? Our usual sunset ride?"

"I have to run to the city and pick up Candy, but I should be back later this afternoon." Vaughn again kissed her shoulder and seemed pleased. "But I'll gladly meet you in our usual spot around sunset," he replied, then caught her face and kissed her quickly but passionately on the lips.

Sky hid her smile and then finished dressing. Once she pulled on her boots, she kissed him quickly and then headed down the loft ladder to the barn below. Since she was out in the barn already, she fed the horses before heading out the main barn door just before sunrise. She was a bit surprised when she saw Dixie sitting on the porch railing, impatiently staring at the barn. Dixie then glanced at her watch as Sky approached.

"What are you doing up so early?" Sky asked while remaining almost casual.

Dixie raised a curious brow. "I could ask you the same thing."

"I was feeding the horses," Sky informed her as she walked onto the porch.

"For five hours?" Dixie asked in a somewhat arrogant tone.

Sky stopped halfway to the door and eyed her friend. "Five hours?"

"I heard you go out to the barn at midnight," Dixie informed her.

"Yeah, I sometimes check on the horses in the middle of the night, if I hear something," Sky replied, then cocked her head. "It's not unusual."

"Nice try," Dixie announced while standing. "I waited. You never came back in."

Sky stared at her friend and was suddenly at a loss for words. "You must be mistaken."

Dixie chuckled and shook her head, now grinning. "No, I'm not mistaken," she insisted, then turned giddy. "You're seeing someone!"

"What?" Sky gasped in surprise.

"You met one of the guys in the barn," Dixie announced enthusiastically. "I crept out there a few minutes ago, and I clearly heard you getting it on with someone in the hay loft. You can't deny it because I *know* what I heard." She then casually looked around.

"And since there aren't any cars, it has to be one of the ranch hands. So, spill it. Who are you seeing?"

Sky stared at her friend with her mouth hanging open. Dixie heard her and Vaughn, not so quietly, getting it on in the loft. It would be impossible to deny she had met a man in the barn, but she didn't know what to say.

"Come on, Sky," Dixie just about whined while maintaining her grin. "Tell me." She then cocked her head and grinned. "It's Jerry, isn't it?"

"I, uh," Sky fumbled, then saw Vaughn riding his horse out the main barn door.

When Vaughn saw her with Dixie on the porch, he swiftly backed the horse up and back into the barn, vanishing from sight.

Sky attempted a smile and nervously laughed. "I, uh, probably shouldn't say," she insisted. "We're not ready to tell people just yet." She opened the house door and ushered her friend inside.

"It is!" Dixie cried out while excitedly entering the house. "I knew it!"

Sky followed her friend into the house and shut the door behind them. Vaughn and Diablo peered out the barn door, saw it was clear, and galloped across the dirt driveway and into the nearby field.

§

It was a little past noon, which meant Nash and Selma would be home soon. Sky sat on the window seat in her room, staring at the picture of her and Vaughn on her cell phone. She'd never seen him smile like that. She'd never seen herself smile like that. She could still hear Vaughn's words in the hay loft.

"I'm addicted to you, Sky."

She shut her eyes and relived the sexual highlights from her erotic weekend. Even thinking about Vaughn created a dull ache deep within her. Sky softly cursed herself for actually developing feelings for Vaughn. She had to be insane! When she heard a car in the driveway, she looked out her bedroom window and saw her aunt and uncle's car traveling down the long, dirt driveway to the house. Sky reluctantly stood. She was happy they were home, but she was already nostalgic for Vaughn's sleepover. As she headed into the upstairs hallway, she heard her aunt calling for her with a little more enthusiasm than usual. Obviously, her Aunt Selma had something she wanted to share. Unfortunately, Sky wasn't looking forward to what she had to share about the break-in while they were away. She knew they would turn clingy and overbearing. Sky reluctantly headed down the front stairs, hearing her aunt calling to her from the kitchen.

"Sky?" Aunt Selma called out, now sounding alarmed. "She has to be here. Her Jeep is here and so is her horse."

"Maybe she's taking a bath or a nap," Nash remarked, then muttered under his breath. "I know I could use one or the other."

Sky entered the kitchen just as Selma was about to go up the back stairs. "Hey," she announced in her best cheerful tone. "How was the trip?"

Selma turned away from the stairs and looked at Sky, possibly startled by her sudden appearance, then appeared relieved.

"You didn't answer when I called," Selma announced while placing her hand to her chest. "I was worried something had happened."

"Well," Sky remarked while cringing with a tense smile. "I suppose you're not entirely wrong. How was the city?"

Nash eyed the boarded back door and pointed at it while looking back at Sky. "What happened here?" he asked.

"The city was fabulous, as always," Selma announced cheerfully. "I bought something for you." Her grin broadened as she handed Sky the velvet jewelry box. "I just know you'll love it."

"Aunt Selma, you didn't have to buy me anything," Sky announced, then eyed her aunt. "Except those bath bombs."

"I got you those, too."

"You're the best," Sky informed her aunt, then opened the box.

Sky stared at the gaudy citrine and emerald bracelet in fourteen-karat gold. She couldn't imagine where or when she'd wear such a colorful and expensive bracelet, in her aunt's taste, but Aunt Selma had a heart of gold.

"Oh, it's beautiful, Aunt Selma," Sky replied, then hugged her aunt. "I love it. Thank you!"

Selma glared at Nash and stuck her nose in the air. "I told you so," she announced, then turned her attention to Sky, growing giddy. "Go on. Try it on."

Sky removed the bracelet from the box and let her aunt clasp it for her.

"Oh, it looks even better on you than it did on me," Selma squealed.

"Well, feel free to borrow it anytime," Sky insisted and sincerely meant it.

"I was hoping you'd say that."

"So how was your weekend?" her Uncle Nash asked and again indicated the door. "And what happened to the door?"

Sky fidgeted while drawing a deep breath. "Well, there was an incident."

"What sort of incident?" Nash asked while cocking his head. "Did one of the steer get loose and break into the kitchen again?"

"No, but *someone* broke into the house," Sky reported while cringing.

"What?" Selma gasped and quickly turned motherly. "Are you alright, dear?"

"Yeah, I'm fine," Sky replied. "Fortunately, they didn't get around to stealing anything."

"They?" Nash gasped, then turned angry. "I hope you shot them. Please, tell me you shot them. I'll get the backhoe."

"Not exactly," Sky replied. "I guess they were a bit incompetent. They got into a brawl right here in the kitchen. Broke the glass cupboard doors and some glasses."

Selma looked around more closely and gasped. "Oh, I didn't even notice the missing glass on the cupboards."

"Thankfully, I heard them," Sky remarked. "I grabbed the shotgun, and the pumping sound must have scared them."

Nash eyed her and cocked his head, somewhat bewildered. "The Weatherby?"

"No," Sky replied, realizing her uncle knew his weapons. "The Browning in the closet."

Nash nodded, satisfied with her response.

"You must have been so frightened," Selma gasped while patting Sky's shoulder. "I should run you a bath."

"Actually, that was Saturday night," she replied, then smiled. "I'm fine now. Dixie stayed with me last night."

"I'll find those bastards and kill them," Nash snarled in rarely seen anger.

"Deputy Rhodes was out to the house and wrote up a report, but, honestly, I didn't even see them," Sky informed her uncle. "We may never know who they were."

"The bastards must have heard we were going away," Nash remarked, then looked at Sky. "Probably thought we were all going." He glared at Selma. "No more telling people our travel plans."

"Don't blame me," Selma bellowed.

"I'm not," Nash snapped back, clearly upset, and then attempted to collect his temper. "I'm sorry, dear. I didn't mean to yell at you. I just don't want to think of what could have happened if Sky didn't have the shotgun."

"Deputy Rhodes is on the lookout for anyone with new bruises and lacerations," Sky added. "There was quite a bit of blood on the floor. They must have gotten pretty rough with each other."

"We need an alarm system," Selma announced.

"We're not getting an alarm system," Nash scoffed. "We don't live in the city. We just need a big dog."

"I'd love a corgi," Selma remarked.

Nash glared at his wife. "In what world is a corgi big?" He then held his hand mid-thigh. "I said a *big* dog."

"Oh, no," Selma remarked and shook her head. "I don't want a big dog. They slobber."

Sky suddenly felt as if she were stuck in a nightmare. With the way her uncle was snapping at Selma, her aunt obviously spent a small fortune on their trip. He was often cranky when they got back from a trip to the city and again after the credit card bill arrived. Sky wished she could tell them that Vaughn was the only reason nothing was stolen and why she was okay. Honestly, Vaughn was the only security they needed.

§

After a relaxing family meal together on the back patio, Sky excused herself for her usual sunset horseback ride. Before she had a chance to sneak away, her aunt followed her into the kitchen. Selma had a strange grin on her face all afternoon, and Sky was growing suspicious.

"Can we have a little girl talk?" Selma asked, then nodded to the porch. "Without your uncle."

Sky paused by the island counter and eyed her aunt almost suspiciously. "Uh, sure," she replied. "What's on your mind?"

"I sort of ran into Dixie today at the bank," Selma announced, immediately making Sky uneasy. Her grin increased. "She accidentally let it slip that she didn't think you were alone this weekend."

Sky stared at Aunt Selma for a long moment without breaking character, waiting out her aunt. Selma maintained her grin.

"*Are* you seeing someone?"

"Dixie was just jumping to her own conclusions," Sky insisted. "She believes what she wants to believe. There wasn't any boyfriend."

Selma didn't seem convinced, and by the grin on her face, she wasn't about to let it go. "Come on, you can tell me," she insisted, then turned almost giddy. "It's Jerry, isn't it? That's why you take so many sunset rides. You're meeting Jerry somewhere for a little romantic rendezvous."

"Aunt Selma," Sky groaned softly. "I'm not secretly dating Jerry, and there's no mystery man."

"You can tell me," Selma insisted. "I'll be happy for you, I promise."

"Good night, Aunt Selma," she announced, then headed out of the kitchen.

§

During the nice, leisurely ride, Sky had time to reflect. Although she often got tiny goosebumps thinking about Vaughn's aggressive lovemaking, tonight felt different. She was excited to see him. These new feelings were somewhat concerning. She couldn't get her mind off him. The more she thought about it, the more she realized Vaughn was often on her mind even before this past weekend. She thought about him when deciding what to wear, whenever she shaved her legs, and how she looked, despite wearing her hair in a ponytail. As she entered the woods, she was suddenly conscious of her appearance and quickly pulled the hair tie from her hair. She gave her hair a quick, flirty toss while envisioning Vaughn riding up on his mighty steed. Her heart skipped a beat, and a dull ache swept through her entire body. Sky hoped he remembered the sleeping bag, because she wanted him tonight more than ever.

When she reached their usual spot, she wasn't surprised that she didn't see him. He enjoyed sneak attacks as a prelude to foreplay. She dismounted her horse, tied the reins to the usual tree branch, and then walked through the woods a little way. The forest was filled with evening woodland sounds, but she didn't hear Vaughn's horse. Sometimes she didn't. He could be sneaky. After fifteen minutes of roaming the woods not far from her horse, she realized Vaughn wasn't waiting to pounce on her. She looked around for any sign of him, but she didn't see him. When half an hour had passed and no Vaughn, she started pacing. He didn't forget; he never forgot, and he was *never* late. However, Marcus might have had him working hard since he had the entire weekend off. She checked her phone for any missed messages, as she sometimes put her phone on 'do not disturb' when riding and would forget to turn it back on. However, there were no missed messages.

After an hour had passed, and Vaughn didn't show up, Sky wasn't sure if she was mad or concerned. She decided to send him a cryptic text.

It simply read, "Were you out here messing with the cattle again?"

If anyone happened to see his phone, they wouldn't think anything of the message she sent him. She waited, but there was no response. It was puzzling, to say the least. Sky finally got back on her horse and headed through the darkened woods for home.

Chapter 29

Tuesday morning. Sky woke and immediately grabbed her cell phone from the nightstand. There was still no response to her text message. She sat up in bed and sank into thought. Maybe something happened to him. If whoever broke into the house on Saturday night was actually after Vaughn, it was possible they came back and finished the job. Of course, there was another, less sinister but more heart-wrenching explanation. Given his reputation and who he worked for, Vaughn might have been playing her the entire time. Perhaps his weekend plans with Candy were real but had fallen through, and she was his backup sex toy. Was he a master manipulator? Had he been using her and had simply grown bored? Could their sex fueled weekend have just been a long con to get even with her for embarrassing him the first time they'd met? Thinking about the many possibilities was starting to make her physically ill.

Until she had definitive answers, Sky decided to stick to her usual routine. She took a quick shower and went for her morning ride. Right on schedule, she showed up at her secluded stream location for her regular morning *appointment* with Vaughn. Although she was a little disappointed and a lot concerned, she wasn't exactly surprised when he didn't show up. She waited nearly half an hour before giving up and heading back home.

§

Just before lunchtime, Sky drove to Bear Creek. Going to town seemed like the quickest way to find answers through local gossip. Sky entered the general store and saw Ron behind the counter reading the morning paper. She knew she couldn't just come right out and ask if he'd seen or heard anything about Vaughn, but she could do a little fishing. One way or another, she needed to know if she should be angry or concerned about him.

"Hey, Ron," she announced, attempting to sound cheerful as she approached the checkout counter. "Did I miss anything this weekend?"

"You're asking me?" Ron asked with surprise while staring at her as he pushed the paper aside, then turned concerned. "I heard you had a break-in at your place over the weekend. Are you okay? What happened?"

Sky retold her rehearsed lie about possibly two intruders getting into a fight while breaking into her home and scaring them off with the shotgun. As she told her story, she leaned against the counter, maintaining a position that allowed her a view of the street.

"So, besides gossip about me," Sky announced and eagerly cocked her head. "What else have you heard? Anything interesting?"

"Nothing new," Ron informed her. "It was pretty quiet in town yesterday."

"Oh?" she asked, then built on the conversation. "Any particular reason for that?"

"Marcus's men didn't come around," Ron informed her. "Kind of odd for a Monday, but I doubt anyone was complaining."

When she didn't learn anything new at the general store, she headed to the diner for a late breakfast or an early lunch. Jasmine was always good for local gossip, since she heard almost everything. Instead of sitting at a table, Sky chose a counter seat so she could hear everything that went on over the weekend from gossiping locals. If you wanted gossip, the counter offered the best seats in the house.

"By yourself today?" Jasmine asked Sky as she poured her a cup of hot tea.

"Yeah, I missed yesterday," Sky casually replied. "My aunt and uncle came back home from their trip to the city, so I spent the day with them."

Jasmine leaned on the counter, appearing both interested and concerned. "I heard you had some trouble out your way," she remarked. "What happened?"

Sky wanted to get gossip, not share it. But when in Rome. She again retold her rehearsed story. Real gossip would have been the part about Vaughn being there and stopping the intruder in only his underwear. Sky must have been in the diner, gossiping with Jasmine, for over an hour without spotting any of Marcus's goons.

"Seems pretty quiet around here today," Sky remarked to Jasmine. "Did I miss something?"

"No, I don't think so," Jasmine replied while straightening. "Our second drama-free morning. None of Marcus's men were around yesterday, and I haven't seen any this morning either. Kind of odd, but I'm not complaining."

"Yes, Ron said the exact same thing," Sky remarked, then fished for a few more details. "Any idea why that is?"

"Not really," Jasmine replied, then casually shrugged. "The last time his men pulled a 'no show' for a few days, they were lying low after some scandalous incident outside of our town limits. I guess it's Marcus's form of damage control or maybe a time-out for the guys."

Sky sank into thought. "That's an interesting theory."

There was a long list of things Marcus's men could have done to earn them a time-out, but considering what they'd been allowed to get away with over the years, it had to be something beyond their usual thuggery. For a brief moment, Sky wondered what she was doing. Did one sex-filled weekend with Vaughn suddenly absolve him, at least in her mind, of all his wrongdoings? She should have been happy to be rid of him. Why couldn't she convince herself of that? While she was momentarily lost in her own world, she heard someone enter the diner. Sky nearly gave herself whiplash turning her head to see who had entered while her heart skipped a beat in anticipation of Vaughn. She was slightly disappointed when she saw her Uncle Cyrus instead.

Cyrus nodded a greeting to Jasmine, who held up a large take-out bag. As he approached the counter, he saw Sky and immediately beamed with delight.

"Sky," Cyrus announced and leaned against the counter near her. "This isn't your usual lunch date with Dixie. She's going to be disappointed she missed you."

Jasmine placed the take-out bag on the counter and accepted Cyrus's credit card.

"Looks like you have her covered," Sky remarked, indicating the bag.

"Yeah, I wasn't in yesterday, so they didn't get their Monday morning donuts," he informed her. "I thought they'd eat me alive. Lunch today was the least I could do."

"I'd never even consider taking donuts to the guys," Sky reported. "They're already heavily caffeinated. I can't imagine adding sugar on top of that."

"I've seen those guys go through pots of coffee in the morning," Cyrus remarked, shaking his head. "I can only imagine how wired they must be."

"Did you spend Sunday night in the city with Aunt Selma and Uncle Nash?" Sky asked. "I thought you usually came home on Sunday evenings so you wouldn't miss work on Monday."

Cyrus groaned and shook his head. "It's a long story," he remarked, then considered the question and shrugged. "Well, maybe not long but a little complicated."

"Well, now I have to know," Sky announced, now curious.

Cyrus frowned and shifted with some discomfort. "Your Uncle Carlton and Aunt Beth were having a *disagreement*," he remarked. "Well, maybe several of them."

Sky frowned and nodded. "Yeah, Aunt Selma may have mentioned it," she replied.

"It made for an awkward weekend," Cyrus informed her. "I thought it was best to remove Carlton from the situation for a while and give everyone a little space. Although I kind of felt bad for your Uncle Nash, us abandoning him like that. But he found his own entertainment. I heard he cleaned up at the race track, so I guess it all worked out for him. I don't even know what time he rolled in on Sunday morning."

"He went to the race track?" Sky asked, surprised to hear. "I didn't think Uncle Nash even liked horse racing."

"After getting roped into shopping all day Saturday afternoon with three women, I suppose he needed to blow off a little steam," Cyrus replied, somewhat sympathetically. When Jasmine returned with his credit card, he offered a sly grin at Sky. "Maybe he didn't tell your Aunt Selma that part, so you might want to keep that between us."

"I'd never rat out Uncle Nash," she reminded him.

Cyrus picked up this bag of take-out and smiled. "If I value my life, I'd better get this food to the ladies while it's still hot. See you later, kitten."

Sky watched her Uncle Cyrus leave, then sank into thought. She didn't even think her Uncle Nash liked horse racing, let alone enough to stay gone so long at a track. Understandably, Selma, Beth, and Fran were probably too much for him to handle all by himself, but she just couldn't see him at a race track.

Chapter 30

Sky hung around town a while longer without a single sighting of Marcus's men. Under normal circumstances, she'd be happy that they were absent. Where were they? What was going on? Did it have something to do with Vaughn's 'no show' last night and again this morning? She periodically checked her phone, but there were still no messages. She finally went back home and arrived in time to pick up the mail at the end of the lane. As Sky headed back to her Jeep, she eyed a padded envelope that had been sent priority overnight mail. It was addressed to her, which was always exciting, even though she had no idea what she had ordered. Most times, packages arrived for her aunt. Sky jumped into her Jeep and eyed the handwritten return address. It came from a company called "Virtual Visions". The 'Vs' were written in big, bold letters, which seemed odd.

Something then occurred to her. Sky didn't bother putting her Jeep into drive and, instead, opened the thick envelope. Two carefully bubble-wrapped cell phones fell onto her lap. She stared at the cell phones with some confusion. Sky unwrapped the first one and pressed the 'on' button. The display came on, revealing Vaughn's horse as the front screen. Sky's heart pounded faster as she stared at Vaughn's cell phone. Unfortunately, it was password-protected, preventing her from accessing it. Who and why would someone mail Vaughn's cell phone to her? She looked inside the envelope for any kind of note, but there wasn't one. Sky then eyed the second cell phone. Whose cell phone was that? She unwrapped the cell phone and saw a small handwritten note attached to it. It simply read, 'Hold onto these for me. Tell no one! V."

Sky felt horror sweep through her. With some apprehension, she pressed the 'on' button on the second phone. When the screen came on, she saw Candy and another woman dressed up in their 'evening clothes' sitting on top of the casino bar together. Sky felt her heart pounding now. Why did Vaughn send her Candy's cell phone? Each scenario sounded worse than the last. She rewrapped each phone and stuffed them back inside the envelope. Sky sat in the driveway for a long moment, thinking about what had possibly happened, and she was suddenly scared. Vaughn was a no-show last night, was nowhere to be found today, and he'd sent her his cell phone via priority mail. Whatever happened to him yesterday couldn't be good.

§

Sky skipped lunch with her aunt and uncle, since she'd already eaten, and hung out in the barn with Jerry while he trimmed and re-shod some of the horses' hooves. With Jerry being a jack-of-all-trades, it helped keep costs down, and the farm ran more efficiently. Sky was often his shoeing buddy, streamlining the process by lending a hand where she could. She leaned against the wall and stared at the concrete aisle longer than she should have, eventually catching Jerry's attention.

"Is everything okay?" Jerry finally asked after he was done rasping the nail heads, finishing three out of four hooves on the current horse.

Sky looked at him as he stood up straight. Jerry was always one of her favorite ranch hands, and she often felt she could tell him just about anything until now. Since Vaughn torpedoed his way into her life, she confided less with her friend. How could she share that part of her life with him? No one could know about her and Vaughn. Initially, she was just embarrassed about it. Now, it was just, well, complicated.

"I was in town today," she informed him, trying to skirt her way around the issue. There was a chance Jerry or one of the guys might have heard something more than she had. "It was unusually *quiet.*"

"Yeah, so I've heard," Jerry remarked and moved to the last back hoof. He loosened the nails on the old shoe before pulling it off. "It was kind of nice, for a change."

Sky watched as Jerry trimmed the horse's back hoof. "Actually, it made me a little nervous," she remarked. "Like the calm before the storm."

Jerry rasped the hoof with the large file, then let the horse drop its foot, giving both of them a much-needed break. He rested his arm on the horse's rump and eyed her.

"Let's face it," Jerry announced. "With Marcus's men, it's always the calm before the storm. Whatever they're up to, though, I doubt it'll spill over onto our ranch. There's nothing to worry about."

Jerry picked up the discarded shoe and pulled out the old nails. Sky then watched as he rhythmically banged the shoe back into shape on the anvil. Once he was satisfied that the shoe was even, he paused and looked back at Sky.

"Something's bothering you," he announced. "Instead of tiptoeing around it, why don't you just be direct with me?"

Sky stared at him a moment, uncertain how to respond, then smirked. "In case you haven't noticed, I'm a woman. I don't know how to be direct."

Jerry snorted a laugh, then grabbed some shoe nails and returned to the horse's bare back hoof. He picked up the hoof and tacked on the horseshoe with ease and precision.

"Does any of this have to do with the rumors going around about you and me?" he asked while focusing his attention on clipping the ends of the horseshoe nails.

Sky twitched and subconsciously straightened. Although Jerry hadn't been looking at her, he must have noticed her movement from his bent-over position. His head tilted slightly, eyeing her, before resuming with the shoe.

"I'll take that as a 'yes'," he remarked before rasping the nails of any sharp edges.

Jerry released the horse's foot and again rested his arm on the horse's rump.

"Want to tell me about it?" he asked. "What's really going on? And how did I get involved?"

Sky knew she couldn't deny the rumors going around, but she couldn't tell Jerry the truth either. Too much was at stake.

"There is someone," she replied in a soft, timid tone. "It's *complicated*."

"Given you're too smart to go back with Tony again," Jerry announced. "I'm assuming it has to be Vaughn."

Sky tried her best to hide her reaction, but she knew her shock at hearing him say that aloud was a huge tell to someone who played poker as well as Jerry had. The color rapidly rising to her cheeks wasn't helping either.

"Why would you--?" She attempted to deny it, but could barely get the words out. "Why would you think that?"

Jerry studied her for a moment in silence, making her mildly uncomfortable. "Because I saw the way he'd look at you across the bar," he casually replied. "The first time was obviously lust. After that, it was somehow different. Like a stallion keeping an eye on his mare."

"Well, you're wrong," she easily lied while fidgeting slightly, needing to shut Jerry's theory down as fast as possible. "But that doesn't--"

"He always left the bar fifteen minutes after you," Jerry informed her. "And it always took you thirty minutes longer to get home than it usually did." He shrugged, then raised his brows. "Yeah, I timed you once or twice."

Sky's expression dropped at his admission. He thought she was hooking up with Vaughn and somehow kept it to himself?

"A few times on your morning rides, you'd go braless," he continued. "You tried to cover it with your jacket, but it's something guys notice. Most evenings you'd go out for a ride looking shower fresh and then come back somewhat disheveled."

Sky fidgeted, now tense, and felt the color in her cheeks. She must have been every shade of red. "All the guys noticed this?" she sheepishly asked.

Jerry shook his head. "No, just me," he informed her. "And I wouldn't share that sort of gossip with anyone for any reason. Not even with Tom. I care about you, Sky. I wouldn't betray you like that." He held his breath a moment while staring at her. "I just have to know. Why him? Why Vaughn?"

Sky groaned softly as she paced the aisle. "A drunken mistake," she replied timidly, then hesitated before blurting out the entire ugly truth. "He was my first, and it was a drunken mistake. It's not as if I could take it back or even remember much about it. But since I couldn't deny to myself that it did happen, I decided to go 'all-in'. See what I'd missed the first time, so it wouldn't drive me crazy. I only meant to meet him once." Sky held her breath then briefly met Jerry's gaze. "Unfortunately, I found out I actually enjoyed it." She cringed at what she was admitting. "*A lot.*"

"Yeah, that happens with sex," Jerry muttered and again shook his head, bewildered. "But still. Why Vaughn?"

She considered the question a moment before reflecting back on their first few times together. "When we were alone together," she informed him. "He became this whole other person. Passionate and, oftentimes, submissive."

"Submissive?" Jerry questioned, then snorted a laugh. "Vaughn?"

"Yes, believe it or not," she replied. "Quite often, in the beginning." Sky reflected back on her first few times with Vaughn. It then finally clicked. She now understood how she had reached this point in time. "He wanted me comfortable at a lope before we galloped."

Jerry eyed her somewhat suspiciously. "I'm afraid you lost me with that one," he remarked.

Sky snapped out of her thoughts and smiled with more confidence. "Whenever we were alone, I got to see this different side to him," she informed him. "And I suppose I wanted to hang on to that."

"Fair enough," Jerry replied, then sighed. "I just hope you don't end up getting hurt. You've seen both sides of him. Good and bad. Eventually, you're going to find out which guy he really is, and I don't think you're going to like what you find."

Jerry wasn't wrong, and she was already thinking those thoughts. For now, she needed to let things play out a bit longer.

"So you won't tell anyone?" she asked while cringing.

Jerry managed a tiny smile and opened his arms to her. Sky moved into his arms and clung to him in a warm embrace.

"I'm here for you, Sky," he whispered in her ear, holding her. "I don't have to like your choices, but I'll always defend you no matter what."

Sky clung to Jerry and allowed her emotions to surface for a brief moment. She wanted to ask him for his help with the whole situation, but she didn't feel comfortable doing so at that moment. Just then, they heard a tiny gasp. Jerry and Sky pulled apart in time to see Selma standing in the barn doorway, looking slightly embarrassed. Her smile immediately increased as she backed away.

"I'm sorry," Selma announced, unable to hide her lustful grin. "I didn't mean to interrupt. Continue. By all means, continue."

Before Sky could say anything, Selma backed away from the barn entrance and even took time to close the large door behind her, giving them some privacy. Sky groaned and shook her head.

"And this is how rumors start," she muttered.

"Well, better she thinks it's with me than knowing the truth," Jerry replied. "The last thing we want is for her to gossip with Marcus about it. That wouldn't be in anyone's best interest."

"You're not wrong."

Chapter 31

That evening, Sky still hadn't heard from Vaughn, and since she had his cell phone, it almost seemed as if she wouldn't. She was worried, but there wasn't anything she could do. Well, there was one thing. She saddled her horse and rode to the bar. When she arrived, she looked for Vaughn's horse at the hitching post. Although there were a few horses tied to the rail, none were Vaughn's. When she entered the bar, she immediately looked around. Keeping with the theme of the day, none of Marcus's goons were anywhere to be found. What did it mean? Since she was alone, she sat at the bar. Although she wasn't exactly friends with the bartender, they had spoken plenty of times in the past, and he knew who she was.

"This place is quiet," Sky announced, using her tried and true line from that morning.

"It's always dead on Tuesdays," Randy informed her, then appeared curious. "I heard you had some trouble at your place over the weekend. What happened?"

Sky internally groaned. She retold the story of her Saturday night break-in so many times, she was sick of it. But it was nice to know so many people in town enjoyed gossiping about her. She had just finished telling her harrowing story of survival when Ox and Moose entered the bar. Sky's heart pounded faster as she waited with anticipation. When she realized Vaughn wasn't with them, her heart sank. Why? Where was he? She watched Vaughn's men out of the corner of her eye as they took their usual table near the back. Neither man was in his typical jovial mood, having entered without the usual fanfare. That couldn't be good. Her heart was racing as she considered what she should do--what she *needed* to do.

Sky took a deep breath, slid off her barstool, and crossed the room toward the back table. She couldn't deny that her heart was pounding and her body twitching at the mere thought of approaching either man, but she needed answers. Ox and Moose saw her coming and immediately stared at her, making her somewhat self-conscious. She couldn't let them intimidate her. She needed to talk to the hardened men, but she had to remain in character.

"Where's the other one?" she asked, attempting to use her usual sarcastic tone. Unfortunately, it sounded forced, causing her to cringe internally.

"Sorry, sweetheart," Moose announced with little emotion and even less warmth. "You'll have to buy your own drinks tonight."

"I'm perfectly capable of buying my own drinks, thank you," she replied, then raised a cocky brow. "Where's Vaughn?"

"Why?" Ox asked with even less compassion, if that were possible.

"I have a bone to pick with him," she announced sternly. Then, before they could question her, she quickly added, "It's personal."

"He's not here," Ox informed her while maintaining direct and chilling eye contact with her. "Why don't you just give me the message, and I'll see that he gets it."

"Okay, if you insist," Sky announced in a firm tone, then scrolled through her phone, attempting to keep her hands from shaking while doing so. Drastic times called for drastic measures. She turned her phone toward the two men and showed them Vaughn's dick pic.

"Jesus!" Moose cried out, showing emotion for the first time, and immediately looked away.

Ox nearly spit out his beer before tearing his eyes from the image.

Sky returned the cell phone to her pocket and smirked. "When you see him, tell him I want to talk to him," she snarled in a commanding tone. "He can either talk to me, or I can talk to Marcus. The choice is his."

She composed herself, then returned to the bar where she sat perched on her barstool and waited while watching the two men out of the corner of her eye. Since she had left their table, they seemed to be debating something quite heatedly. Revealing that picture might be embarrassing for Vaughn, but its crudeness was still in character for him. When both men got up, she thought she would surely get some answers. Instead of approaching her at the bar, they tossed some money on the table and left without finishing their beer. Since they could have just called him, Sky was discouraged. Even though Vaughn didn't have his cell phone, she was certain they had alternate means of contacting him. She waited a little longer, hoping for their return. When nothing happened, she finished her drink and left, calling it a day.

§

Discouraged, Sky rode her horse away from the Lake House Bar and passed through the woods toward the first field. She no sooner entered the clearing when she saw Vaughn on his horse across the meadow just outside the woods on Marcus's property. Sky sighed with relief and sent her horse into a gallop across the field to greet him. As she got closer, she realized it wasn't Vaughn but Moose wearing a similar black hat and sitting on Diablo. She pulled her horse to a sliding stop several feet away and stared at the stern-looking man. She was angry, frightened, and confused. For a moment, she didn't know which emotion she should lead with.

"You thought I was Vaughn, didn't you?" Moose announced with a strange look on his face.

"Well, you're on his horse," she snapped back, attempting to cover for her actions.

Out of the corner of her eye, she saw Ox riding toward her from the opposite direction, essentially boxing her in. It felt a little like an ambush, but she wasn't prepared to bolt just yet. She came for answers, and maybe now she'd get them. Of course, perhaps they intended to kill her instead. And here she was without her shotgun.

"How many people would run *to* Vaughn?" Moose remarked, then cocked his head while studying her. "Makes me curious. Is there something going on between you and Vaughn?"

"No, of course not," Sky scoffed and went 'all-in' with anger as her emotion of choice in this particular situation. Despite her cheeks turning red and possibly giving her away, she doubled down. "And I resent you even asking that sort of question."

"I'll bet you do," Ox muttered, keeping his eyes on her.

The way the two men stared at her from both sides slightly unnerved her, but she tried to maintain her composure. Moose shifted on Vaughn's horse while scratching his chin.

"Don't get the wrong impression," Moose announced while locking eyes with her, "but I'm pretty sure that was actually Vaughn's dick in that picture you shared. We served in the Marines together, and that scar on his thigh was the one I stitched up for him."

"Yes, and I told you that's what I wanted to talk to him about," she snarled in response. "I guess you actually believe me then. So where is he?"

Moose and Ox continued to stare at her as if privy to some inside information they weren't quite willing to share, and it made her nervous. For a moment, she was almost positive they were going to kill her and leave her for coyote cuisine.

"You know, Vaughn may be a lot of things," Moose informed her. "But he'd never send something like that unless it was consensual. There's something you're not telling me."

"And there's a whole hell of a lot you're not telling me," she snapped back, turning a little more hostile than she probably should have. "I'm getting tired of asking. Where is he?"

Moose and Ox exchanged looks, as if secretly communicating without words, then returned their attention to her.

"How long has Vaughn been seeing you behind Marcus's back?" Moose finally asked.

The bluntness of his question took her by surprise. She hadn't actually been prepared for it, although maybe she should have been.

"First off, no one is seeing me behind Marcus's back," she snapped hotly. "Marcus doesn't own me. There's nothing between me and Marcus, and I don't need his permission to *see* anyone." She cocked her head and gave Moose an arrogant look. "And there's nothing between me and Vaughn except his dirty mind."

"Yeah, sure," Ox announced with a humored, throaty laugh. "Whatever you say."

"I have to admit, you with Vaughn is a lot more convincing than Candy and Vaughn," Moose informed her.

"And I'm telling you--"

"Let's just cut the crap, okay?" Ox bellowed, startling Sky with his outburst.

Moose held up his hand, effectively silencing Ox, without taking his eyes off Sky. "I'm going to lay it all out for you, Sky. Vaughn is in a lot of trouble," he informed her. "And we just want to help him."

Sky felt her heart pounding faster at Moose's words. "What sort of trouble?" she just about gasped before realizing how it sounded, and attempted to collect her emotions.

Moose smirked and pointed at her. "That right there," he remarked with obvious satisfaction. "Your concern tells me everything I need to know."

Sky checked her emotions and went with anger instead. "How about *you* cut the crap and tell me what happened?" she snarled.

Ox eyed Moose, while pointing at Sky. "I like her," he remarked. "She's feisty."

"Vaughn's being questioned in Candy's murder," Moose replied while gauging her reaction.

Sky couldn't hide her surprise and the gasp that escaped. "What? Candy's dead?"

"Yeah," Ox replied with an arrogant nod. "And Vaughn was supposedly with her."

"He took her away for a romantic weekend, and now she's dead," Moose informed her. "He's the prime suspect."

"I-I don't believe that," she remarked while shaking her head. "He wouldn't kill her."

"Of course he wouldn't," Moose replied.

"But he booked the hotel room and drove her to the hotel," Ox informed her while raising a cocky brow. "Now, he suddenly can't account for his whereabouts for the entire weekend, so he doesn't have an alibi."

Sky stared at Ox and realized he was insinuating that she knew where he was on the weekend and could provide him with an alibi.

"I guess the real question is, what do you know, and how do you intend to help?" Moose just about demanded.

"I don't know what I can do," she remarked while lost in her own thoughts, then met Moose's gaze. "I need to talk to him."

"Well, Detective Garland isn't going to let that happen," Moose informed her. "I need you to be honest with me, Sky." His look was stern and serious. "Did Vaughn send you anything?"

Her heart nearly stopped as she stared back at him. "Send me anything?" she asked, her surprise somewhat genuine. "What would he have sent me?"

Her mind was suddenly racing. Were they responsible for Candy's murder? Had either of them broken into her house and gotten the surprise of their life when they ran into Vaughn? Did they know more about the package than they were willing to admit? She wasn't sure she could actually trust either of them, despite how much they seemed to know. Maybe they knew so much because they were behind everything.

"We want to help Vaughn," Ox informed her. "But to do that, you need to trust us."

Sky eyed both men while a thousand scenarios ran through her mind, then finally shook her head. She wanted to trust them, but she couldn't stop wondering why Vaughn didn't send the phones to either of his 'friends'. If he didn't trust them, she probably shouldn't either.

"He didn't send me anything," she informed them, then raked her trembling fingers through her hair. "I-I have to go."

She turned her horse and raced away as fast as she could. Thankfully, neither man followed her.

§

Once Sky got home, she unsaddled her horse and set him free in the pasture, then hurried into the house, somehow afraid Vaughn's so-called friends would get the drop on her. She didn't know if she could trust them. Were they even on his side? Should she be on Vaughn's side? Could Vaughn have murdered Candy the morning he went to pick her up? Maybe he killed her on the afternoon he dropped her off. Sky was so confused. She barely talked to her aunt and uncle before heading upstairs and locking herself in her room. She paced the room for several minutes while attempting to sort things out and calm her spiking anxiety. She hated that she even cried a little, but she was beyond frustrated. Vaughn wouldn't kill Candy. Would he? Sky hurried to her closet, removed the envelope containing the two cell phones, and looked around her room. She needed a better hiding place.

Sky wasn't sure why Vaughn had Candy's cell phone, but he sent it to her for a reason. For safekeeping. But safekeeping from whom? For now, she'd hide the phones and worry about the rest later. Fortunately for her, her house was a treasure trove of fantastic hiding places, both big and small. Sky removed several boxes from her closet, unearthing a small, folded stepstool. She opened up the stepstool, positioning it within the closet, and climbed up to the third and top step. She pushed open a hidden panel and pulled down a small rope ladder attached to the ceiling beyond the opening. Sky found a flashlight and then grabbed the envelope containing the two cell phones before climbing the rope ladder.

She sat inside the crawlspace and shone the light around the small area. The area was only six foot by six foot and no more than four feet tall, with even less height near the outer wall. There were treasures from her childhood, including her mother's jewelry box and various items with sentimental value, within the small space. Sky crawled across the small area and stuffed the envelope inside a box filled with old framed photos and her father's old rodeo trophies. She tossed an old blanket over the box for added measure. Sky took a moment to collect her emotions, just enough to keep from crying, and then climbed back down the ladder and onto the stepstool. She returned the flimsy rope ladder to the crawlspace and replaced the panel.

Once the piece of wood was in place, it was almost impossible to see the hidden opening. Sky returned the stepstool and the boxes to their original place within the closet and resumed pacing her room. She didn't know what to do next. Pacing seemed to be the only thing to relax her, so she continued to pace while her thoughts ran rampant. It was going to be a long, sleepless night.

Chapter 32

Wednesday morning, Sky continued with her usual routine, although she skipped photographing the ranch hands with the herd that particular morning and opted for an extended horseback ride instead. She rode to the edge of Marcus's property just far enough to take in a sweeping eyeful of the massive stables in the distance. Even from that distance, she could see Vaughn's horse grazing in the pasture. Despite his horse still being at the stable, Sky rode in the direction of their usual rendezvous in the woods. Perhaps Vaughn was released from custody or posted bail and chose to take a different horse to meet her. Since she rarely rode from the direction of Marcus's estate to her favorite secluded spot in the woods, Sky took a trail she seldom traveled. She was certain it was the path Vaughn rode when he met her by the stream, as it was a more direct trail for him.

As she rode along the lightly traveled path, she noticed fresh hoofprints in some of the softer ground. Sky easily recognized the hoofprints belonging to a horse from Marcus's ranch. Since his saddle horses weren't used heavily on rugged terrain, his regular horses were without horseshoes, whereas all of her horses, being ridden on all sorts of terrain, wore shoes. Only his racehorses had shoes. Sky felt her heart skip a beat. It was possible that Vaughn took another horse and was waiting for her at their usual meeting location. She glanced at her watch, realizing she'd be late, if that were the case, and picked up the pace. As she trotted Admiral along the trail, she kept her eyes on the fresh hoofprints that went in both directions. They had to be from yesterday or today, that was certain.

Admiral suddenly snorted, alerting her to something close by. Usually, it was just a deer or a fox, but she remained focused on her surroundings, just in case. Admiral again snorted with his ears pricked forward and stepped sideways, avoiding going forward until he identified what he saw. Sky then saw it too. There was something large spread out on the trail up ahead. She encouraged her horse onward. Although he obliged her request, his head remained high, and some defiant snorting was involved. As they got closer, Admiral again sidestepped and lowered his head slightly to have a better look. Sky was now able to identify what was across the path as well. To her horror, it was a man!

"Vaughn!" she gasped and sprang off her horse, leaving the reins over Admiral's neck.

As she ran toward the fallen, motionless man, Admiral snorted, conveying his concern, but felt compelled to follow her. As a ranch horse, it was kind of his job. When Sky got closer, despite the man being face down, she immediately realized he wasn't big enough to be Vaughn. She slowed her approach, hesitated a moment, and crouched alongside the man. She knew better than to move someone after a fall unless they said they're okay. Any severe neck or spinal injury could cause paralysis with the slightest movement. Sky immediately recognized the man from his profile. It was Marcus's racehorse trainer, Hammond.

"Hammond?" she gasped while reaching out and gently touching his shoulder. "Hammond?"

When he didn't respond, she placed her fingers on his neck and checked for a pulse. Her heart skipped a beat as she attempted a different location on his neck. Sky's heart suddenly pounded hard and loud. He was dead! She sprang upward, spooking her horse, which had silently crept up behind her and was peering over her shoulder. Admiral bolted a couple of steps but didn't go far. Sky immediately removed her cell phone and called the sheriff's department. Thankfully, there weren't too many places on either ranch where she couldn't get cell service. Just a few years ago, that wasn't the case. Back then, they had to carry high-tech, two-way radios.

§

Sky paced the quiet, secluded area several yards away from Marcus's dead horse trainer while her horse stood patiently alongside her, watching her. Admiral suddenly lifted his head, and his ears pivoted like highly tuned antennas. He snickered softly, telling her everything she needed to know. Sky looked down the path and saw Jerry and Tom riding along the trail from the opposite direction. Both stopped their horses when they saw the dead man, who remained untouched while face down on the path. Both men looked equally horrified at the scene. Sky walked through the woods to avoid getting too close to the body, then reentered the path, joining her men on the side closest to her property. Both men dismounted but couldn't take their eyes off the dead man.

"What the hell happened?" Tom bellowed, his eyes wide at the sight.

"I'm assuming he was thrown," Sky informed Tom, then nervously shook her head. "But I wasn't about to turn him over and examine the body. That's the sheriff's job."

"Who is he? One of Marcus's men?" Jerry asked. "I don't recognize him."

"It's Hammond," Sky informed him. "Marcus's new racehorse trainer. He'd been working at the farm for over a month now."

"Did you call Nash?" Tom asked while whipping out his cell phone.

"No," Sky replied and commanded him with a look. "And neither are you. He and Aunt Selma went to the city for an afternoon matinee and dinner. They don't need to be disturbed over an accident that wasn't even on our property."

"Do you have any idea how close we are to the property line?" Tom demanded while pointing. "There's a dead man practically on our ranch. Nash would want to know."

"And you can tell him," Sky insisted. "When he gets back from the city tonight."

It was then they heard the distinct sound of four-wheelers approaching from the direction of Marcus's ranch. Sky was slightly puzzled by the sound until she saw the vehicles appear on the trail. Sheriff Burke and Deputy Rhodes were on borrowed four-wheelers following Tony, Roscoe, and Foster on their own ATVs. Marcus's men were equally shocked when they saw the motionless man and attempted to dart in for a closer look. Sheriff Burke stopped them and forced them back.

"We need to have a look first," Burke insisted. "Have to make sure it was an accident."

"Of course it was an accident," Roscoe scoffed, somewhat offended. "He was outside training some of the horses earlier this morning and suddenly vanished."

"We found the horse he was training, fully tacked, outside the barn, grazing on grass," Tony informed the sheriff. "When we found the horse, we were looking for him all over the estate but couldn't find him anywhere."

"Did you ride out looking for him?" Sheriff Burke asked.

"Well, no," Roscoe reported with a slightly dumbfounded look. "Why would we? He was training on the track. It's completely fenced in."

"Although," Tony began, then hesitated. "The gate was open. I suppose something could have happened from the time he opened the gate until we found his horse."

Burke nodded, then eyed Deputy Rhodes. "Let's turn him over," Burke announced to his deputy. "Nice and easy."

The sheriff and deputy crouched alongside the dead man and gently rolled him onto his back. His face and chest were visibly battered and bloodied. Sky gasped with surprise and some horror at the sight. Jerry grabbed her around the shoulder and pulled her against his chest to tear her eyes away from the horrific sight. Hammond's face was mostly mangled with clear evidence of multiple skull fractures. Judging by the lumps under his shirt, he clearly had several broken ribs as well. Sky managed to pull away from Jerry, compelled to have another look. She'd never seen that sort of damage before from a riding fall. Rhodes had already straightened and took a step back while Sheriff Burke remained crouched over the body. Burke pointed at a thrown horseshoe on the ground that had been beneath the body. It contained traces of blood from Hammond's face on it.

"Looks like he got tossed," Sheriff Burke insisted. "Maybe got caught in the reins or stirrup and ended up trampled or thrashed to death." He shook his head and grimaced at the sight. "Must have taken one hell of a beating."

"That's the shoe from the horse he'd been training," Tony informed the sheriff. "The horse was missing a front shoe when we found it."

"Front shoe?" Sheriff Burke asked and again looked at the man's mangled face. "It's obvious then that he'd fallen off or gotten off. The horse panicked and reared up, thrashing down on him with its front hooves." Burke straightened and eyed Marcus's three men. "I'd like to have a look at that horse, just to confirm the shoe came off him."

Sky stared at Hammond's mangled, bloodied body while a thousand thoughts and images played out in her mind. She wanted to speak, but she stopped herself. Sky quickly moved into Jerry's arms and shivered slightly while clinging to him.

"Sheriff," she announced. "Do you need me for anything else? I'd really like to go now."

Sheriff Burke glanced at Sky and shook his head. "No, I don't need to ask you anything else," he replied. "It was clearly an accident."

"I have a question," Tony scoffed, surprising everyone. He folded his arms across his chest while glaring at Sky. "What were you doing on Marcus's property in the first place?"

Sky glared back at Tony while attempting to pull away from Jerry's arms. She felt her hostility building, and it showed.

"I was riding," she snapped back at Tony. "Marcus gave me permission to ride on his land." She then gave him an arrogant once-over. "The bigger question is, what was a track trainer doing riding a racehorse out in the woods?"

Although Tony wouldn't admit it, she got him with that one. Most of the thoroughbreds were young, high-strung, and barely knew more than 'run as fast as you can'. Hammond had no business riding a horse like that outside of the arena, let alone into the woods, particularly by himself.

"It's obvious something spooked the horse," Roscoe offered. "Busted through the gate and took off with Hammond."

"I'd think a horse trainer would know how to stop a runaway horse," Sky scoffed in response. "Stopping a runaway horse is basic horsemanship 101." She demonstrated a single rein stop to drive home her point.

All eyes were now on Roscoe, waiting for a rebuttal, but obviously, he didn't have one. Deputy Rhodes then looked at Sheriff Burke in silent question. Burke was obviously uncomfortable since Marcus supplemented his income.

"We should probably take a look at that gate too," Burke replied. "Make sure his death was purely accidental."

A crackling sound came from Burke's radio on his utility belt. "Sheriff Burke," the voice announced. "This is the ambulance driver. We're at Marcus's estate. What's your twenty?"

Burke removed his radio and placed it to his mouth. "We'll bring the body to you," he replied. "Hold position."

With that, Sky, Jerry, and Tom mounted their horses and headed back for their own ranch. All three were unusually quiet despite what they'd just witnessed. They were almost halfway back when Sky finally felt compelled to speak.

"It wasn't an accident," Sky finally announced.

Both men looked at her with some surprise. "What?" Tom asked. "How do you know that?"

"There were a couple of sets of fresh hoofprints in the soft soil," she informed them. "All of them came from unshod horses."

"Are you sure?" Jerry asked.

Sky nodded with conviction. "Someone beat Hammond to death, then placed a shoe from the racehorse he'd been riding under his body for the sheriff to find. Horse without a shoe, bloody shoe under the bludgeoned body equals an accidental death."

"I'd say we should report what you saw," Tom muttered. "But say that in front of the wrong person, and you get a target on your back."

"Exactly," Sky replied.

Chapter 33

After her ordeal with Hammond's *accident* and dealing with the "Abbott and Costello" of crime fighting, Sky finally returned home. She took an extended shower, changed, and went to town for a late breakfast by herself. The diner was once again quiet, which was almost unnerving. Needing some company after the morning she had had, Sky sat at the counter, where Jasmine served her tea.

"Had you heard the latest?" Jasmine asked while leaning on the counter.

Sky eyed Jasmine with some surprise. There was no possible way she'd already heard about Hammond's death.

"I don't think so," Sky replied while suspiciously studying the diner's former owner.

"A woman who worked for Marcus was found murdered in a city hotel room," Jasmine remarked, then raised her brows. "Apparently, she went away for the weekend with Vaughn, and now the city homicide detective is questioning him in her death."

Hearing someone else report the tragic news of Candy's death made it seem more real somehow. Sky shifted uncomfortably and pretended this was the first she'd heard.

"That's awful," Sky replied, acting surprised, although the devastation on her face was real. "Have they arrested him?"

"I don't know," Jasmine replied and shrugged. "I just heard they were questioning him."

Sky resisted the urge to sink too far into her own thoughts. It might look suspicious. She just had so many questions. When Jasmine continued speaking, Sky snapped back into reality.

"Honestly," Jasmine announced. "I prefer him over Tony. Kind of a shame."

"Yeah," Sky replied and again allowed her thoughts to stray. She tried to shake Vaughn from her thoughts and keep up appearances. "Do you know who she was? Are they saying how and when this woman died?"

"I guess she worked for one of his other companies, not someone from here in town," Jasmine remarked, then raised her brows. "They found her late Monday morning in Vaughn's hotel room, strangled to death in the bathtub."

Sky stared at Jasmine with a slightly sickened look. The last time she'd seen Vaughn was when he left her barn on Monday morning. He was on his way to the city to pick up Candy. If that's when she died, he could have done it.

"I can't imagine Vaughn doing that," Sky whispered almost to herself, then pushed her teacup away. "I'm sorry, Jasmine. I lost my appetite. Cancel my order."

Jasmine immediately straightened and grimaced. "I'm sorry, Sky," she announced sympathetically. "I shouldn't have told you that. This is a restaurant. I wasn't thinking."

"No, it's okay, Jasmine," Sky replied while standing, then tossed some money onto the counter. "I should get back home anyway."

§

Sky still felt ill as she drove her Jeep through town on her way home. When she spotted a familiar truck, Sky suddenly gasped and made a sharp turn, pulling into the feed store parking lot. To her surprise, Vaughn was loading bags of grain and specialty feed onto the back of his pickup truck. Sky's heart was pounding hard and fast as she parked her Jeep a few yards from his vehicle and got out. She was unable to take her eyes off Vaughn, almost as if she'd seen a ghost. It seemed like a lifetime since she'd last seen him. When he saw her, he immediately looked away without acknowledging her. Sky stood by her Jeep for several minutes and watched as Vaughn resumed stacking bags onto the truck bed.

"If you're here to stomp on my balls, Sky, you'll need to take a number," Vaughn announced loudly and boldly to her while only briefly looking at her.

Sky drew a deep breath, then folded her arms across her chest while casually approaching him on the opposite side of the truck.

"Yeah, I already heard," she announced. "Word travels fast in a small town."

Sky leaned on the truck bed and watched him as he continued to stack grain. He eyed her several times without lingering.

"They're watching me, Sky," he announced softly before turning back for another bag. "You need to keep your distance from me for now. Marcus has me on house arrest until things blow over." He frowned, somewhat disgusted. "I'm officially the stable boy."

Sky rounded the truck and hopped on the tailgate, purposely putting herself in his way. Vaughn straightened with a bag of feed and glared at her.

"Do you mind?" he demanded, but revealed his concern with his eyes.

"I have no problem hitting a man while he's down," Sky announced boldly for anyone who might be listening, then spoke softly. "I need to know. Were you with me when Candy was killed?"

Vaughn's arrogance seemed to return as he took a step toward her while removing his gloves. He hovered over her and stared her down with his best intimidating look.

"I've got places to be, darling," he announced. "Are you going to move or must I move you?" Vaughn cocked his head and grinned. "Might be more fun if you resist."

Sky maintained her glare and didn't respond.

Vaughn didn't back down and hovered over her, moving in close. "She was killed sometime Saturday night," he whispered before immediately slipping back into his bad boy persona.

Despite the tragic death of Candy, Sky was suddenly relieved. Vaughn didn't do it! He couldn't have!

"I'm your alibi, Vaughn," she announced just loud enough for him to hear. "I can account for your every move from Friday night to early Sunday morning. You were with me all night Saturday."

"I know," Vaughn replied softly and managed a tiny lustful grin. "I remember. I was handcuffed to your bed."

"I can clear you," she insisted.

"No," he announced firmly and straightened while giving her a stern look. "They don't have any evidence against me. The hotel security cameras show me checking in with Candy and then her going alone with the bellman to the room. The security cameras prove I never went up to the room, and I didn't come back until late Monday morning to pick her up. When I arrived on Monday, I tried her cell phone, but she didn't answer. The front desk clerk told me she checked out, and he even called the room. When there wasn't any answer, I left."

"But the cell phones--?"

"That's a long story," he muttered.

"This can all be resolved if I just tell the truth," she insisted. "Why are you fighting me on it?"

Vaughn groaned while hovering over her for appearances and shook his head. "Best case scenario," he remarked. "Marcus kills me for defiling his little angel."

"I'm not *his* angel," she snarled in anger.

"Yeah, well, I certainly can't tell him that you're my little devil," Vaughn remarked. "The less happy version has some not-so-friendly men questioning my deception with Candy. Then, what got her killed comes after me."

"What if that already happened?" Sky asked.

He appeared puzzled. "What do you mean?"

"What if the man who broke into my house Saturday night was after you?" she asked. "What if he killed Candy, realized you hadn't been with her, and then came after you at my ranch?"

"It's possible. There would have been enough time between the time she was killed and when your house was broken into," Vaughn replied, then eyed her, his look turning stern. "You need to keep your distance, Sky. No one can know about us, and don't let anyone find those phones."

"The phones are safe," she reassured him. "Our secret? Not so much. I think Moose and Ox suspect something. Moose kind of played me by riding your horse and waiting for my reaction."

"I wouldn't worry about him. Moose isn't exactly bright," Vaughn remarked.

Sky studied him a moment while he continued stacking grain. There was more on her mind than just Candy.

"Did you hear about Hammond?" she asked.

"Yeah, I heard about it," Vaughn muttered, then shook his head without looking at her. "I heard the idiot took one of the racehorses out for a trail ride and got thrown."

"Well, he may have been thrown, but that wasn't what killed him," she remarked. "He was trampled to death."

Vaughn hesitated briefly but still didn't look at her. "I guess our gossip grapevine isn't as accurate as the one here in town," he replied.

"There's more to it," Sky informed him, causing him to meet her gaze briefly. "They found the horse's lost shoe under his trampled body, but there weren't any shod hoofprints anywhere leading up to and around his body."

Vaughn suddenly froze with a heavy bag in his arms and looked at Sky. "Are you sure?" he asked.

"Positive," she replied. "The only fresh hoofprints were from an unshod horse."

He tossed the bag into the truck bed and again pretended to ignore her. "How do you know that?" he asked.

"I'm the one who found Hammond," she informed him.

Vaughn shot upright and eyed her with a mixed look of surprise and concern. "You didn't tell anyone else about this, did you?"

"No, just Jerry and Tom."

"Good," he announced firmly and quickly resumed his work. "If Hammond didn't actually have an accident, you don't want anyone thinking you suspect anything else."

"So I should just let it go?"

"Yes," he scoffed as he tossed another bag into the truck near her and finally met her gaze. "You'll live longer. You need to go now." Vaughn hovered over her and doubled down on his arrogant smirk. "I'm going to need you to hit me."

"What?" she asked with surprise.

He maintained his cocky grin. "If you ever cared about me, Sky, you'll do it." His smile mocked her. "If someone's watching, they need to see you angry with me. Come on. One right across the kisser. Don't be shy. Give it your best shot."

Sky sneered her annoyance and sprang up from the tailgate. "I'm kind of pissed at you anyway," she huffed, then slapped him across the face.

Vaughn was momentarily surprised, then felt his cheek while eyeing her, although his arrogant smile didn't fade. "I knew you liked me," he remarked, then winked at her.

"I hope you and your right hand will be happy together," she scoffed loudly, then stormed off.

"You'll come around," he called after her and chuckled.

Roscoe and Foster approached the truck from the feed store and watched Sky jump into her Jeep and then burn out of the parking spot.

"What was that about?" Roscoe asked.

"She wants me," Vaughn replied while maintaining his grin.

"Keep dreaming," Foster muttered.

"Fuck you," Vaughn scoffed, then slammed the tailgate shut.

Chapter 34

Friday evening. Sky sat on the window seat in her bedroom and stared at the picture of her and Vaughn on her cell phone. Part of her missed being with him while the rational part of her wondered if he was capable of killing someone. Although she knew he couldn't have killed Candy, if he was telling the truth about the time of death, that didn't mean he wasn't a bad man. He worked for Marcus, and Marcus hired bad men to do his bidding. Hammond's gruesome death then crossed her mind. She would never get that image of his mangled, broken face from her thoughts. Vaughn insisted she let it go, but she was certain Hammond didn't die at the hooves of some expensive racehorse. The more she thought about it, the more she was positive he was killed elsewhere and dumped on the wooded trail along with the discarded horseshoe.

There'd be no proving what happened, even if she had more evidence than hoofprints in the mud. Sheriff Burke wasn't going to investigate, especially if someone from Marcus's ranch was involved. Sky cast her phone aside and groaned in disgust before looking at the clock. It was only going on seven o'clock, officially making it the longest day of her life. There was a light knocking on her door right before it opened. Her Uncle Nash poked his head inside and met her gaze with a smile.

"Jerry and Tom are already saddling the horses in the barn," Nash informed her while grinning like a schoolboy at recess. "Are you coming?"

Sky smiled at her uncle as she snatched her phone and sprang to her feet. "You at the bar with me and the guys?" she remarked, then laughed. "I wouldn't miss tonight for the world."

"Well, don't get too excited," her uncle announced. "We're not staying past ten."

"That's fine by me," Sky replied and joined him. "It's been one of those days."

"Finding Hammond's trainer like that," Nash remarked, then shook his head. "That had to be traumatic. You might want to consider steering clear of his property." Her uncle frowned as they headed into the hallway. "People seem to have a lot of accidents around his place."

Sky cast a quick look at her uncle, noting his frown. He wasn't just saying that tongue in cheek. He, too, had his doubts about Marcus and his dealings. Sky decided to heed Vaughn's warning and keep any concerns regarding Hammond's accident to herself for now. They headed downstairs together and just about ran into her Aunt Selma, who appeared flustered while frantically looking for something. Selma eyed them as she continued her search.

"I thought you two were out in the barn already," Selma remarked, then paused to look around the hallway.

"Lose something?" Nash asked with a curious look.

"I would have sworn I set my book down on the hall table," Selma remarked, then groaned and shook her head. "My book club is at eight, and I lost my damned book."

"Did you look in the kitchen?" Nash asked while raising his brow. "I saw you cramming when you were making dinner."

Selma glared at him, lacking humor in response to the comment. "I wasn't *cramming*," she reported. "I was *skimming*. You know I have trouble remembering names. I want to know what I'm talking about at my book club."

Nash folded his arms across his chest and raised a cocky brow. "You and I both know you didn't finish that book," he announced. "Your bookmark hasn't moved from the halfway point all week."

Selma groaned and shook her head. "With our weekend in the city and everything that happened when we got back, I just didn't have the time," she insisted, then appeared disgusted. "That's it. I'm not going to book club tonight."

"You say that every week," Nash reminded her, then guided her to the kitchen. "Do what you always do. Read the dialogue of the last few chapters. No one will know you didn't read the entire book."

Sky shook her head while leaving the house, then paused on the porch and stared at the barn. She couldn't shake the memory from sunrise on Monday morning when she woke up with Vaughn in the hay loft. It was the last time she was in his arms, and she missed that. She missed his kiss. She missed his touch. Oh, how she missed his touch! Uncle Nash joined her on the porch, although she didn't react when he appeared.

"Everything okay?" he asked, transforming her back into the here and now. "You've been preoccupied ever since we've been back."

Sky put on her happy face and tried to appear upbeat for her uncle's sake. He didn't get out much, and she wanted him to have a good time.

"Yeah, I'm fine," she insisted, then nodded to the house. "Did Aunt Selma find her book?"

"Yep, in the kitchen right where I thought it'd be," he remarked, then shook his head. "I convinced her to go to her book club tonight, but I think she should give it up. She doesn't even like any of the women in that club, and she has hated each book they've chosen to read since day one." He groaned softly. "I'll never understand women."

"Yeah, me either," Sky remarked as they headed to the barn.

Nash cast a look at her, then grinned while hugging her to his side. "You're a piece of work, you know that?"

"Yeah, back at you, Uncle Nash."

§

The Lake House Bar was moderately crowded by the time Sky, Nash, Jerry, and Tom arrived. More people would show up well past nine o'clock. The four secured a table and were almost immediately greeted by Ruby. While she took their order, Sky saw Moose and Ox at their usual table near the back. Her heart pounded with anticipation, but she didn't see Vaughn anywhere. She had hoped he was in the bathroom, but that didn't appear to be the case. Moose and Ox seemed to be in equally foul moods, which wasn't typical for them, particularly on a Friday night. Moose locked eyes with Sky across the room, and she suddenly felt a cold chill run down her spine. They were supposed to be Vaughn's friends, but Vaughn didn't seem to trust them. At least, he didn't trust them enough to send them the cell phones or reveal his relationship with her. Sky decided to mind her own business and noted the schoolboy grin on her uncle's face.

"I see someone's happy to be out," Sky teased her uncle.

Nash grinned and held up his mug of beer. "I like getting out once in a while for a boy's night," he informed her, then hesitated. "Well, you know what I mean."

Sky laughed along with Jerry and Tom. "I know you don't mean any disrespect toward Aunt Selma," she assured him. "I get it. She enjoys her froo-froo things, and sometimes you don't want to be, well, froo-froo."

"Well said," her uncle announced while chuckling and clinking his glass to hers. "An entire weekend in the city with your aunt is just, well, exhausting." Nash groaned and rolled his eyes. "I never want to see another *boutique* shop again. It was one big shopping excursion."

"I ran into Uncle Cyrus," Sky informed him. "He mentioned that he felt bad that they abandoned you on the all-day shopping trip."

"And after they promised they wouldn't," Nash reported while shaking his head. "They stole me away for a game the first night, but when the wives mentioned shopping Saturday afternoon, they disappeared on me. Saving their own hides, I suppose." He stared into Sky's eyes. "An entire afternoon of non-stop shopping and giggling with Selma, Fran, and Beth." He leaned closer to her and stared into her eyes, his expression serious. "I've seen hell, Sky, and it wasn't pretty."

Sky and Nash chuckled a moment at her three aunts' expenses. She then remembered what she'd been told and turned serious.

"Uncle Cyrus told me on Tuesday that he needed to get Uncle Carlton away from Aunt Beth for a while over the weekend," she informed him. "Apparently, they were having some sort of lovers' spat." Sky cringed slightly as she studied her uncle. "I guess you forgot to mention that when you gave me the highlights from the weekend."

Nash groaned and rolled his eyes. "Yeah, sure," he muttered. "That was just their cover story. I overheard Carlton mention a new strip club that opened up across town. I think that's where they spent the entire evening. Not really my thing, which is probably why they didn't invite me."

"Strippers cost money," Tom remarked, essentially calling Nash cheap, then chuckled into his whiskey glass.

Nash cast an evil glare at Tom, but the ranch hand didn't care. He then looked back at Sky. "They probably didn't trust me not to rat them out," her uncle remarked, then waved her off. "I've always been a bit of an outsider with them."

Sky was slightly disappointed to think her Uncle Cyrus lied to her about why they ditched Uncle Nash. Honestly, lying was more of an Uncle Carlton thing. More disappointing was their feeling the need to run off to a strip club.

"And they wonder why they're both on their second wives," Sky muttered.

"I suppose things aren't going so great with wife number two for either of them either," Nash informed her. "So maybe there was an ounce of honesty to what Cyrus told you. Over the weekend, I heard a lot of complaining from both sides." He then considered the comment. "I wonder if Selma would have joined in if I hadn't been with them."

"Oh, come on," Sky announced and clung to his arm. "You're a great husband. Aunt Selma has it good."

"She wants to move back to the city," Nash reminded her while frowning. "I know she's not as happy as she used to be. Maybe not with me, but with our living arrangements."

Sky felt bad for her uncle's situation and was about to speak when he held up his hand as if reading her mind.

"No," Nash insisted firmly, not allowing her to say what he knew was coming. "Don't even start. Two more years. We'll survive two more years. Don't even bring it up."

Chapter 35

An hour later, Sky danced to some slow songs with Jerry, Tom, and her Uncle Nash. It was actually a nice evening out, even if her uncle was getting a little more than buzzed. Possibly why he wanted to leave at ten. They couldn't let him get drunk and expect him to stay on his horse the entire ride home. It was almost nine-thirty when Tony, Foster, and Roscoe entered the bar with their usual rowdy energy. Sky and Uncle Nash had just returned to their table from their slow dance and saw the insufferable men passing through like royalty. Ox and Moose also didn't seem happy to see the three men, who sat down at their table with them. Whatever Tony said instantly annoyed the two quiet men, but neither man responded. Sky cast glances at their table several times, trying to piece everything together. If Vaughn were on house arrest, Marcus probably would have reassigned more responsibilities to Tony, which would have made Tony very happy. The man enjoyed his power.

Sky attempted to put everything from her mind, but it wasn't easy. Since they would soon be leaving, Sky wanted to visit the little cowgirl's room one more time. When she stood and headed toward the bathroom, she noticed Moose was already gone from his table. As Sky entered the back hallway and approached the bathrooms, Moose suddenly appeared from the men's room and took two quick steps toward her, startling her and causing her to jump. He only partially faced her, avoiding direct eye contact.

"Come to Marcus's party tomorrow night," Moose announced while showing no emotion.

Sky stared at the large, intimidating man's profile. "I beg your pardon?"

"You heard me," Moose announced, briefly glancing at her as he started to pass her. "It's important that you attend. You didn't hear it from me."

Moose then continued past her without further comment. Sky watched him head back into the bar and considered his words before heading into the ladies' room. Once she finished in the bathroom, Sky returned to her table in time to witness Moose and Ox in a standoff with Tony, Roscoe, and Foster. Ox attempted to rein in Moose while Foster tried to calm Tony. Moose and Ox finally grabbed their jackets, threw some money on the table, and left the bar. Thankfully, it was time for them to go as well. Sky didn't want to be around for tonight's episode of the "Three Stooges". As they stood to leave, Ruby approached their table to gather some of their empty bottles. Sky caught a glimpse of the young woman's mascara partially streaking down her face as she attempted to hide her tears.

"Are you okay?" Sky asked, not sure if she'd missed something while in the ladies' room.

Ruby managed a tiny smile and sniffed while piling the empty bottles on her tray. "Just Tony," she remarked softly. "Karma once again biting me in the ass, I suppose."

Sky hesitated and watched Ruby walk away from their table and toward the bar. Nash frowned and guided Sky in the same direction that would take them to the front door.

"Let it go, Sky," Nash whispered, close to her ear. "She destroyed your friendship years ago. It's her mess now."

Sky followed Jerry and Tom toward the bar with Uncle Nash only a step behind her, bringing up the rear. As the guys turned to the right and headed for the front door, Sky caught a glimpse of Tony stepping into Ruby's path. He grabbed her around the waist and pulled her against him, toppling her entire tray of empty bottles. The sound of clattering bottles and breaking glass always silenced the room for a brief moment, and the spectacle received several looks, although most weren't about to get involved because it was Tony. Something suddenly snapped in Sky. Maybe it was a fleeting memory of her past friendship with Ruby or her frustration with the entire Vaughn situation, but Sky veered left while picking up speed. Without missing a beat, she grabbed Tony by the shirt collar with both hands without slowing her momentum at all and nearly took him down onto the table behind him.

The moment he lost his footing, Sky leapt away from him so she wouldn't go down with him. Tony struck the table before catching his balance, then took an aggressive step for Sky with his fists clenched. Jerry and Tom were suddenly behind her, ready to defend her to the death, if necessary. At that moment, nearly every chair in the bar suddenly screeched against the wooden floor. Tony and his two goons froze in place and looked around the almost silent bar. Just about every man had their venomous gaze on Tony with clenched fists, almost daring him to touch Sky. Tony and his men appeared slightly baffled by the death stares they were receiving, as so few ever stood up to them in the past. Behind the bar, Randy shifted looks, almost as surprised as they were, and despite being in Marcus's back pocket, he, too, glared at the three men.

"I think you fellas need to leave," Randy announced to Tony and his men.

Tony shot a look at the bartender with a mix of surprise and rage. "Are you serious?" he demanded. "If Marcus hears about--"

"If Marcus hears about *this*--" Randy reminded him while indicating his altercation with Sky, who hadn't even flinched at the threat, "--it might be your ass you need to worry about."

Tony only thought about it for a moment before grabbing his jacket from the table and storming out of the bar. Roscoe and Foster briefly hesitated before hurrying after him. As the door shut behind the last of them, a round of chuckles, a few clinking beer bottles, and a round of applause followed. Ruby sheepishly met Sky's gaze and offered a tiny, thankful smile. There was a time not so long ago when Sky hated Ruby, but there was also a time before that when she loved her like a sister. At the moment, she felt sorry for her former friend. For as much as Sky had hated her for betraying her friendship, it was possible Ruby hated herself more. Maybe it was in that moment that Ruby realized she needed to forgive herself because Sky had already forgiven her.

§

The return ride home took longer than usual, as her uncle was drunk more than buzzed. He managed to stay on the horse, but they had to ride at a walk the entire way. Jerry and Tom thought Nash's condition was funny, but Sky knew her aunt wouldn't appreciate him coming home drunk. If they were lucky, they'd beat her aunt home, and she could get Nash into bed before she saw him in his current condition. Her aunt wasn't necessarily a prude, but her uncle tended to morph into a less refined man when he drank. Selma didn't appreciate that side of Nash. Truth be told, he was less sophisticated than he led on, and the longer he hung out at the ranch, the more it showed. Jerry eyed Sky several times as they rode along the field toward the woods and the trail back home.

"What were you thinking back there?" Jerry finally asked, essentially scolding her. "That could have gone very badly with Tony."

"What was he going to do?" Sky demanded. "Hit me in front of my uncle and two of my fiercest ranch hands?"

"He certainly seemed to be considering it," Jerry reminded her. "You don't even like Ruby. I just don't get it."

"I also don't hate Ruby," Sky informed him. "Well, not for a long time. I mean, I did, once upon a time." She frowned and shook her head. "Something in me just snapped tonight. The disrespect toward Ruby. Tony's 'no one can touch me' attitude." Sky sank into her own thoughts for a moment. "Maybe it's partly my fault."

"What do you mean by 'partly your fault'?" Jerry asked, somewhat surprised. "That she slept with your boyfriend?"

"No, not that," Sky groaned, then shrugged. "My family name still means something to the people in town. People treat me differently. Even Marcus treats me differently."

"Marcus wants to get in your pants," Jerry muttered. He then reconsidered his comment and shrugged. "Actually, a lot of guys in town want to get into your pants."

Sky glared at Jerry, not amused. He saw her look and chuckled.

"Sorry, that's the alcohol talking."

"No one stood up for Ruby when Tony harassed her, but they were willing to risk Tony's wrath by standing up for me," Sky informed him. "When I ended my friendship with Ruby, a lot of people in town turned on her as well. Picking my side, so to speak. Maybe I needed to be the bigger person."

"Sky, she was your best friend, and she screwed around with your boyfriend," Jerry reminded her. "That's why they took your side. You had and still have every right to hate her for that."

"I know," she replied. "I'm not denying that, but there was never any closure between us. She tried to apologize, but I wouldn't hear her out."

"Yeah, she apologized because she got caught screwing your boyfriend," Jerry scoffed.

"I wish you'd stop saying that."

"I have to," Jerry insisted. "Because you seem to be forgetting what she did to you."

"Yes, she betrayed me," Sky agreed. "What she did was far worse than Tony's betrayal because she was my best friend, but Tony was already walking on the path toward the dark side by then. He was even getting aggressive with me. Maybe it wasn't as easy for her to refuse him. He was already frustrated with me for refusing his advances. She may have been an easier target."

"When you put it that way, it does sound sad," he replied, but quickly brushed it aside. "But it doesn't really change the end result any. Her betrayal broke you. I was there. I saw it happen." He managed a tiny smile. "I don't want to see you hurt like that ever again."

"You're sweet, Jerry."

"Yeah, I'm also a little drunk and can't control my mouth," he remarked.

§

When the four riders arrived at the house, Jerry and Tom led the horses to the barn, while Sky ushered her uncle into the house. Her aunt would probably be gone until eleven, so Sky still had time to get him into bed before she got back. The moment she opened the kitchen door, Sky knew something was wrong. She turned on the lights and immediately saw the broken lock. A few of the kitchen drawers were partially open and appeared to have been ransacked. Nash noticed it only a second after she did. Both cautiously approached the living room and peered inside. Oddly enough, it wouldn't be the first time one of the steer found its way inside and trashed the place. To their surprise and horror, many items were scattered around the room, systematically ransacked.

Nash pushed Sky toward the closer front door. "Go to the barn with Jerry and Tom," he insisted. "Call the sheriff."

Horror crossed her face while staring at her uncle. "Oh, no," she gasped and shook her head. "I'm not leaving you in here by yourself. What if it's that guy from last weekend? He'll kill you!"

Nash approached the hall closet beneath the main stairs and opened the door, revealing a large gun safe. "I'll be fine," he insisted. "Go."

Sky ran to the door and threw it open as her uncle opened the gun safe. "Jerry! Tom!" she cried out, then returned to her uncle and the open safe.

Nash removed a .357 Magnum and eyed her. "I told you to leave," he snarled.

"No," she snapped back and removed a semiautomatic, then cocked it. "I'm not leaving you in here alone. You're drunk."

"Not anymore," Nash muttered.

Jerry and Tom ran into the house through the rarely used front door, stopped, and immediately looked around.

"What's wrong?" they asked in unison, then saw the condition of the living room.

Without hesitation, both men joined Sky and Nash by the gun safe and removed handguns as well. One thing was certain. The boys knew their way around weapons.

"Jerry, you go with Sky and check upstairs," Nash announced, then motioned to the living room. "Tom and I will search downstairs."

Jerry led Sky up the stairs, gun in hand, while cautiously checking the corners, but they didn't see anyone in the second floor hallway. As they continued past the bedrooms, they saw each one had been ransacked as well. Sky's heart was now pounding, and she was in a hurry to reach her room. As Jerry entered her room, she followed him. Her heart sank when she saw things scattered across her bedroom. Sky's drawers were partway open, and her clothing was tossed haphazardly about the floor. The closet door was also open, and it was apparent someone had torn through it. She saw the bag from the adult store was open and cast aside, but the contents remained contained within the bag. She was grateful Jerry didn't see what was in that bag.

Sky moved closer to the open closet and peered inside. The panel in the ceiling hadn't been disturbed. Even her uncle didn't know about that hiding spot. Some random person tearing through the room certainly wouldn't find it, but there was a small part of her that wondered if the burglars had been looking for the cell phones. What were the chances of their remote farmhouse being burglarized twice in one week? Sky looked at her dresser as she approached Jerry, who eyed the smashed television that was still mounted to the wall.

"I guess they were a little pissed when they couldn't get the television off the wall," Jerry muttered in disgust.

Sky looked at the open and empty bracelet box on her dresser and frowned. "They stole the bracelet my aunt bought for me," she muttered, then looked at her open jewelry box. "Got my grandmother's pearl necklace and my mother's engagement ring too." She sneered in anger and kicked the dresser. "Son-of-a-bitch!"

"I'm sorry, Sky," Jerry replied softly.

They continued onward to her aunt and uncle's bedroom, only to find more of the same. Their room received the same treatment. Sky immediately noticed her aunt's jewelry box open and empty on the bed with a few cheaper pieces scattered across the comforter. They took the good pieces and left the junk.

"Sky?" Nash was heard calling from the back stairs. "Jerry?"

"Up here," Jerry called out.

Nash entered his room, paused, and looked around. He groaned, approached the larger dresser, and rooted through it before shaking his head.

"Damn it," he muttered with disgust. "They took my locked box with all my cash." Nash then saw the jewelry box and groaned. "All Selma's jewelry." Nash sat on the bed and ran his fingers aggressively through his hair. "The bastards."

They suddenly heard Selma's scream from downstairs.

Nash sighed with defeat and looked at Sky. "Your aunt's home," he announced with little emotion.

Chapter 36

It was late Saturday morning by the time Sky and Nash got up and met in the kitchen to start breakfast. After Sheriff Burke left last night, no one was able to sleep. Sky, Nash, and Selma spent several hours cleaning up the mess in their rooms while Jerry and Tom fixed the broken lock on the back door and straightened the kitchen. Both ranch hands and their pump-action shotguns then spent the night as added protection. They refused to leave Sky, Selma, and Nash alone. Tom, their front line of defense, slept on the downstairs sofa with his shotgun, while Jerry slept in one of the spare bedrooms upstairs as their second line of defense. Although weary herself, Sky glanced at her uncle several times, not used to him being so quiet in the morning. Maybe he was just tired too, but she doubted that was the reason.

"Are you okay, Uncle Nash?" she finally asked.

He looked at her, almost startled by the break in the silence. Nash then managed a tiny, reassuring smile.

"Yes, of course," he replied, then appeared sympathetic. "Are you?"

"Feeling a little vulnerable and a lot pissed," she informed him, "but, yeah, I'm fine otherwise."

"Yeah, I know that feeling," Nash muttered, then managed a tiny smile. "Your aunt had a rough night. It might be best if we didn't talk about the break-in this morning."

Tom shuffled into the kitchen with his shotgun, having smelled the coffee, followed by Jerry appearing on the back stairs with his twelve-gauge. Coffee was the number one smell that motivated the men. The second was the smell of bacon. Nash and Sky placed several platters on the table while the guys helped themselves to some coffee. Their table looked like a gangster's paradise. Several cups of coffee, two shotguns, and two semiautomatics.

"After breakfast," Jerry announced, then indicated the crudely fixed back door. "We'll get another door and get that replaced by this afternoon."

"I'm thinking a nice new security system too," Tom muttered.

"It had to be the same guy," Nash insisted. "Kind of brazen, though, don't you think?"

"I doubt the thief was working alone," Jerry remarked. "And it's obvious they were casing the place. They had to know when everyone had left. Too many trucks parked outside to assume the house was empty."

Sky shivered slightly and then joined the men at the table. She sipped her tea but wasn't very hungry. Last night was a little too familiar for her comfort.

"That's a creepy thought," she muttered into her tea mug. "Thinking those guys were out there, hiding within the woods, watching us and waiting for us to leave."

"Could it have been Tony and his goons?" Nash asked, now concerned. "Payback for what happened in the bar."

"No," Jerry insisted. "We left a few minutes after they did. What happened here took time and a little bit of planning."

All four were suddenly alerted to voices in the hallway. Jerry and Tom grabbed their shotguns and sprang to their feet, aiming their weapons at the doorway only a second before Uncle Cyrus and Aunt Fran appeared. Both cried out, leapt back, and put their hands in the air.

"It's just us!" Cyrus cried out. "We knocked on the front door and called, but no one answered."

Jerry and Tom groaned as they lowered their weapons, then returned to their seats at the table. Cyrus and Fran relaxed as well, although they were now slightly rattled. No one really used the front door anymore, which, oddly enough, should have been locked. Most people came through the back kitchen door, which was technically closer to the barn.

"We came over as soon as Selma called this morning," Cyrus informed them, then looked around. "Where is she?"

"Getting dressed, I suppose," Nash replied.

"We thought you might need help cleaning or straightening," Fran remarked.

"We cleaned most of the mess last night," Nash informed them. "None of us could sleep."

Selma came down the back stairs, saw her brother, and immediately ran to him while holding back her sobs. Cyrus held her a moment while she thanked him for coming. She finally pulled away from her brother and then hugged Fran.

"I'll get you some coffee," Fran insisted and crossed the kitchen.

"Carlton said you should call him if you needed more help with repairs and cleaning," Cyrus remarked to Selma.

"No, we're good," Selma replied while offering a warm and pleasant smile. "Just a little rattled, that's all." She then indicated the table. "Have some breakfast with us. There appears to be plenty. Nash cooks when he's stressed."

§

After breakfast, Nash went with Jerry and Tom to the closest home and garden store to find a replacement door, which was nearly an hour away. They left Cyrus and Fran with Sky and Selma to keep them company. Sky went out to the barn while Selma and Fran cleaned up after breakfast. The horses were receiving a late breakfast, but they had plenty of pasture to keep them occupied until she got there. Sky had just finished filling the large water tub when she heard a car in the driveway. She rounded the barn and saw Marcus's car pull up to the house. As he got out of the vehicle, Sky was thankful that he hadn't seen her. The sight of him after everything that happened last night at the bar and in their home made her skin crawl. Was it possible he was somehow responsible? Doubtful. It wasn't as if he'd made any offers to buy their ranch. Did she believe his men might have broken into the house in retaliation for what happened last night? Or maybe for something else? She wasn't ruling that out.

Selma, Cyrus, and Fran greeted Marcus at the front door and invited him inside. On the bright side, Tony wasn't with him for a change. Sky wasn't sure how she would have felt about that. She was just angry enough to take another shot at him, and that wasn't in her best interest right now. She decided to play it smart and hide out in the barn until Marcus left. Admiral stood outside the back door watching her and waiting, possibly thinking they would be going for a late morning ride. It was unusual that they didn't go out for their morning ride. Sky brought her horse into the aisle through the back barn door and let him munch on some hay while she brushed him, in no particular hurry. Had she been smart, she would have saddled her horse and taken off while Marcus was inside with Selma, but Admiral still needed time to digest his morning grain.

Twenty minutes later, Sky was considering her options. She wasn't sure if she should risk peeking out the main door to the house to see if Marcus had left or just saddle her horse and take off for the woods. When Admiral lifted his head from his hay and looked toward the main door, Sky realized she ran out of options. She looked back and wasn't surprised when she saw Marcus approaching. She knew she should have escaped when she had the chance right after he arrived. Sky managed a smile but went for her saddle pad, hoping to send a clear message that she was going riding.

"Hey, Sky," Marcus announced as he paused near her. "How are you holding up?"

"I'm okay," she replied, then returned for her saddle. She swiftly tossed the saddle onto her horse's back and began cinching it. "We weren't home when they broke in. Could have been worse, I suppose."

She could feel Marcus hovering as she tightened the girth, but she refused to look back at him, not wanting to prolong the conversation.

"Sheriff Burke is putting a priority on your break-in," Marcus informed her. "That's the second time someone broke into your house. The bastard needs to be found."

"I won't argue that," she replied, then found Admiral's bridle. "Jerry thinks the thieves were casing the house, waiting for us to leave before making their move. Kind of a bold move, considering all the open land around us."

"You think it's someone from town?" Marcus asked.

"Don't you?" she quipped, casting a quick look at him.

"I guess that would explain a lot," he replied.

Admiral just about took the bit out of her hand, as if he too wanted to get going. Sky threw the reins around the horse's neck before finally looking at Marcus.

"I'd better get my ride in," she remarked. "Or I won't get home in time to get ready for your party tonight."

Marcus appeared surprised, then seemed pleased. "You're coming to my party?"

"Aunt Selma needs to get out of the house and get her mind off of last night," Sky informed him. "I won't have to twist her arm too much."

"I'm glad to hear you're coming," Marcus replied, pleased with her response, satisfying him. "I'll see you tonight then."

Sky swiftly mounted her horse, then looked at Marcus while forcing a smile. "I'll see you then," she announced, and then rode at a leisurely walk from the barn.

Once she was outside the barn, Sky sent her horse into a lope and headed for the woods. She just wanted to get away from Marcus for now. Whether she would have to deal with him later tonight was a problem for another time. At least at his party, there would be more than one hundred guests to occupy his time. Whenever he caught her alone, it made her very uncomfortable.

Chapter 37

After taking her shower later that day, Sky approached her aunt's bedroom and found Selma sitting on the bed, organizing her jewelry box. She looked disgusted as she tossed pieces into the box, practically in tears.

"Aunt Selma?"

Selma sniffed, wiped her eyes, and looked at Sky while attempting a smile. "Sky," she announced almost pleasantly. "Did you make a list of everything that was missing for the insurance company?"

"Yeah," Sky replied timidly. "I guess I didn't have much they wanted."

Selma snorted a laugh and tossed a ring into the jewelry box. "All my mother's jewelry," she scoffed. "Gone."

"They took my mother's engagement ring and my grandmother's pearl necklace, too," Sky remarked timidly.

Selma looked at Sky, offered a sympathetic smile, then stood and hugged her. "I guess this is the part where we're grateful it was just material things," she muttered with a sigh. "Sadly, I really like my material things."

Sky returned the hug and managed a tiny, uneasy laugh as she pulled away. "Yeah," she replied, then ran her fingers through her still-damp hair. "I wonder if it was the same guys. Maybe they came back to finish the job."

Selma snorted a laugh and flopped back onto the bed with her scattered jewelry. "You really think they'd come back after you scared them off the first time with the shotgun?" she asked, then eyed Sky. "How would they know you weren't here? Your Jeep was here." She managed an uneasy laugh. "Hell, Jerry's truck was here, too. You'd think they'd assume someone was home."

"Yeah, I suppose there were quite a few vehicles parked outside the house," Sky remarked while deep in thought.

Burglars wouldn't know they took the horses out that evening to the bar. Although people they knew would. She now had more questions than answers. Either someone was watching the house, or it was someone who was aware of her aunt's Friday evening book club and had noticed Sky and Nash at the bar. The cell phones again crossed her mind. It might have been someone looking for the cell phones, and they just robbed the place so it wouldn't raise suspicions. Whatever Vaughn had gotten himself into, whoever was looking for those cell phones must have known he was at her house last weekend. Somehow, it all seemed to come back to Candy's murder.

"I think I'm going to take a long bath and turn in early," Selma muttered while tossing another piece of jewelry into the box.

"Tonight is Marcus's party," Sky reminded her.

Selma looked up at Sky with some surprise. "Oh, I don't think I want to go to that," she muttered.

"Why not?" Sky asked and then indicated the room. "There's nothing left to steal, and it would do us all some good to get out of the house and stop thinking about this."

"Us?" Selma asked with some surprise, then cocked her head as a smile crossed her face. "Are you thinking about going?"

Sky held her breath a moment, then offered a tiny smile. "Why not?" she replied, then sighed. "I need to get out of here just as much as you."

Selma considered it for a moment, then became almost enthusiastic. "You know," she announced. "That's actually a good idea. I'm going to take a bath and think about what I'm going to wear while you tell your Uncle Nash he's going to that party with us."

"Me?" Sky asked with some surprise. "Why do I get to tell him?"

"Because it'll sound better coming from you, and I won't have to hear him moan about it," Selma announced somewhat cheerfully.

§

While deciding which dress to borrow from her Aunt Selma, Sky was cautiously optimistic. Moose summoning her to attend the party could be an extremely good thing or a very bad thing. She didn't see much middle ground. Hopefully, the request from Moose came through Vaughn. She wanted to see him badly enough that she was willing to take the gamble. That she wondered if she was gambling with her life should have been enough to deter her, but it wasn't. She couldn't kid herself about who and what Marcus really was. He was an evil man, but was he the kind of man who had people killed? She wasn't sure. That she couldn't answer 'no' was a bit frightening as far as Vaughn went. She knew very little about his past, except that he had served in the Marines, a fact verified by his tattoo and battle scars. He'd mentioned serving with the Marines a few times, but he never went into great detail. Other than that, she knew very little about him.

Once she was dressed, Sky looked at herself in the full-length mirror. She wore a low-cut, thin-strapped, black evening dress that was both form-fitting and moderately revealing, featuring a long slit up the side. And, although it looked similar to the one she wore on the Fourth of July, it was actually a completely different dress. Add a pair of strapless high heels, a smidge of eyeliner, a bit of lipstick, and her black, lacy thong underwear, and the outfit was complete. It was very rare for her to wear her hair down outside the house. Most of the time, when she was outside, she was working with her horse, which required her to wear her hair up. Her heart raced while staring at herself in the mirror. She dressed with one mission in mind. Seducing Vaughn.

Sky again wondered how she got to this point. How did she go from hating Vaughn to selling her soul just to see him? What if Vaughn hadn't requested to see her? What about that more sinister scenario? She needed to hope for the best yet prepare for the worst. She hurried to her bed and pressed on the base of the headboard, which revealed the hidden shotgun. She reached up and under the headboard above the shotgun and removed a pearl-handled, two-shot derringer. Sky checked the chamber, snapped it closed, and then tucked it down the cleavage of her dress. It took a few adjustments, but she finally got it positioned just right so that it was completely hidden and wouldn't fall out. That didn't mean it was entirely comfortable, but that wasn't the important thing right now.

§

Even though she took longer than usual getting ready for Marcus's party, Sky still beat her aunt downstairs. She waited on the porch, alternating between pacing and sitting on the railing. She had been so preoccupied with thoughts of what tonight would bring that she hadn't even realized Jerry had approached the house. He stopped on the steps and whistled at her. Sky saw him ogling her and met his gaze. A sly grin crossed his face.

"Can I assume you're not all dressed up for Marcus?" Jerry remarked.

Sky remained tense but attempted a smile. "I don't know what I'm doing," she informed him.

"You're hoping to run into a certain cowboy, aren't you?"

"I'd like to get some answers," she remarked. "Not sure I will, though."

"Be careful, Sky," Jerry warned her. "I don't want to see you get hurt."

"I'm already hurt," Sky replied. "Now, I need closure."

"Well, then, good luck."

Chapter 38

Every party at Marcus's house was the same with only minor menu changes, but this time was different. Sky felt her heart pounding with anticipation from the moment she entered Marcus's house. She hated how badly she wanted to see Vaughn. She hated that she missed him as much as she did. He was bad for her. Common sense screamed for her to listen, but her heart ached at the thought of seeing him. Shortly after they entered the ballroom, Marcus was quick to greet them with compliments and his ever-so-famous cheek kisses. Sky barely heard the conversation between her aunt and Marcus. She was too busy nonchalantly scanning the room for Moose. He was the one who requested she show up, and it was time to find out why. For a man who should have been easily spotted, she couldn't seem to find him in the sea of well-dressed men and women.

"Don't you agree, Sky?" Aunt Selma announced, pulling Sky back into the present.

Sky hated to admit she hadn't heard any of the conversation, but she couldn't exactly fake it either. She had no idea what she would be agreeing to. Even worse, she hadn't even noticed that her Uncle Nash had vanished on them.

"I'm sorry," Sky replied while smiling with some embarrassment. "I thought I recognized one of the women over there. What were you saying?"

Selma managed a tiny, tense laugh while returning her attention to Marcus. "You have to forgive Sky," she remarked. "Last night still has both of us a little out of sorts. None of us got much sleep. And who would?" She shook her head. "A couple of the wranglers were camped out in the living room with shotguns all night. That's enough to make anyone uneasy."

"I can understand how that might make you uncomfortable," Marcus replied, glancing between the two women. "Sheriff Burke and Deputy Rhodes try their best, but they can't be everywhere. I'd feel much better if a few of my men patrolled your house for a couple of weeks."

Sky felt her heart just about leap from her chest at the suggestion. There was no way in hell! Before she could protest or even speak her mind, Selma answered for her.

"I appreciate the offer, Marcus," Selma replied. "But I wouldn't feel right, and Nash would absolutely hate the idea. We have more than enough wranglers to keep a couple of them posted until we get proper security equipment installed."

Sky was a bit surprised that her aunt actually turned down the offer. Selma was a huge Marcus fan. It seemed odd that she'd turn down anything he offered. Sky realized how bad that thought sounded right after thinking it. Not that her aunt was infatuated with the man. It then dawned on her. If Selma believed she was secretly dating Jerry, did that mean she'd stop pushing Marcus on her? Was it possible that her aunt *approved* of Jerry? It sounded almost too impossible to believe. While staring at nothing in particular, Sky's eyes strayed past a handsome man across the room. So handsome, he deserved a second look. Sky was stunned to see Vaughn, dressed in an expensive suit, looking the part of an aristocrat, and talking with a small group of men and women. She stared at Vaughn in stunned disbelief. She never thought she'd see him in a suit. Her heart pounded in response. Vaughn was now a whole other level of sexy, and she couldn't take her eyes off him. When his gaze fell upon her, he barely gave her a second glance and continued his conversation with those around him.

Sky suddenly felt stupid. She had gone all out just for him, and he didn't even acknowledge her! When Tony approached, Sky's hostility spiked. He was the last person she wanted to see at the worst possible time. Tony met her gaze, secretly loathing her with his eyes. Apparently, the feeling was mutual.

"Marcus," Tony announced without emotion. "Your friend arrived."

"Oh, yes, of course," Marcus announced, then smiled at Sky and Selma. "Forgive me. I've been trying to snare a potential business associate for over a week now. I'll check on you a little later."

As Marcus left with Tony, one of Selma's book club friends approached. The two women practically squealed with delight and greeted each other with fake cheek kisses. Ironically, Aunt Selma had mentioned numerous times how fake she thought that woman was, yet they were acting like best friends. As the two women squawked about nothing of interest, Sky finally spotted Moose and Ox talking with another man. She barely excused herself from her aunt and her friend and made her way across the room, working her way closer to Vaughn's right and left-hand men. She didn't want to approach Moose while he was talking to Ox and another man. She still wasn't sure why he had asked her there, but she made sure Moose saw her before approaching a secluded end of the large buffet table.

Sky secured a glass of champagne from a passing waiter and looked over the buffet spread even though she wasn't the least bit hungry. Her stomach was already in knots, and being ignored by Vaughn didn't exactly help. For now, she just needed to distance herself from others in hopes that Moose would seek her out. At least he was more responsive than Vaughn had been. Only a moment passed when Moose made his way closer to her and picked at the appetizers near her without making it seem as if he was seeking her out.

"A few minutes before eight, be waiting at the side hallway door across from the bar," Moose informed her.

Without further comment, he popped another appetizer in his mouth and walked away. Sky eyed him almost suspiciously, but he wasn't waiting around for a Q&A session. Sky glanced at the grandfather clock. It was now seven-thirty, and she was somewhat uncertain whether to put blind faith in a man named Moose. There was no telling what he was up to, but she didn't really seem to have much choice. She finished her champagne and made her way closer to the bar. Sky glanced around the crowded room but didn't see Vaughn anywhere. She frowned while remaining mindful of the time. Surprisingly, she no longer saw Moose or Ox either. She had a bad feeling about this, but did as she was instructed. Two minutes before eight, the lights suddenly went out, and there were several screams.

Sky looked around the nearly dark room, which was only lit by the little moonlight that shone in through the wall of glass from outside. Sky was suddenly grabbed by the arm and pulled out the doorway just as the emergency lights came on. Vaughn pulled Sky through the dimly lit hallway and to a door near the back. She hurried to keep up with Vaughn's long, fast strides in her less-than-stable high heels. Moose and Ox stood just outside the now-open door.

"Thirty minutes before the lights come back on," Ox informed Vaughn. "Another fifteen minutes beyond that before the interior cameras reboot and come back online."

"Got it," Vaughn announced while pulling Sky through the doorway.

Ox shut the door behind them, and both men casually stood before the door as if having a conversation. Vaughn stopped Sky within the dimly lit, personal gym, spun her around and into his arms, and kissed her passionately with added aggression. Sky immediately returned the kiss and just about climbed his body. He caught her beneath her buttocks and tackled her to the nearby leather sofa.

"You wore the thong," he groaned while aggressively pulling up her dress between them. "I knew it."

"Those guys won't come in, will they?" she asked between kisses.

"No," he replied while working his way down her neck to her cleavage as his breathing became heavy. "But they'll probably listen."

"Then I'll try to keep it down," she announced while writhing beneath him.

Vaughn hesitated, then removed the derringer from her cleavage. He eyed the weapon and then looked back at her.

"Oh, that's such a turn-on," he announced and tossed the weapon aside before resuming his assault on her cleavage.

Despite skipping foreplay and both being mostly dressed, Sky enjoyed every blissful moment from the squeaking of the leather cushion beneath her crinkled dress to the way Vaughn gripped her shoulders, holding her in place. The sofa had way too much give and had a slight trampoline effect. Sky attempted to keep quiet but dug her nails into Vaughn's buttocks instead. He felt so good, and she missed him so much. Vaughn finally collapsed on top of her and attempted to catch his breath. He then cupped her face in his hand and warmly kissed her.

"Oh, I missed you, Sky," he whispered and kissed her again.

Sky opened her eyes and met his gaze along with his warm smile. "I missed you too," she whispered and then eagerly kissed him.

Chapter 39

Sky adjusted the hemline of her dress while Vaughn tucked his shirt into his dress pants. Sky then looked around the mostly dark room, somewhat baffled.

"Have you seen my underwear?"

Vaughn squinted and looked around the floor. "Too dark," he responded, then grinned. "You'll just have to go without panties."

Sky groaned that he found that amusing. Or possibly a turn-on. It wouldn't be funny for whoever found them in the morning. She located her derringer and replaced it in her cleavage with some adjustments. Vaughn eyed the action and grinned while sitting on the nearby weight bench to admire her silhouette within the dim lighting.

"I like that," he announced, indicating the gun. "A little *booby* trap."

"I wasn't sure I could trust your friend, Moose," she informed him while slipping into her strapless shoes.

Vaughn straightened on the weight bench and eagerly patted his lap. "Sit," he announced. "Let's talk."

Sky smiled and sat on his lap while clinging to his neck. "Okay, talk."

"I heard about the break-in," Vaughn remarked as his look turned serious. "That worries me. Are you sure you're okay? What did they take?"

"I'm fine," she insisted, touched by his concern. "They only got a few pieces of jewelry and some other items to make it look good."

He studied her a moment, then cocked his head. "You think they were looking for something else?" Vaughn asked with concern.

"Yes, I think so," she replied, then groaned while frowning. "I think it was the same guy who broke in Saturday night. If so, he knows you were there, and he knows about us."

"I've been stuck on house arrest the last few days after the homicide detective released me," Vaughn informed her. "If it were any of the guys on Marcus's payroll here at the house, they're doing a great job of keeping it a secret."

"What's the endgame here, Vaughn?" she asked, defeated. "Something has to give. I'm almost certain that someone broke into my house because of you, because of us. It's only going to get worse until he finds what he's looking for."

Vaughn looked at his watch and groaned. "Fifteen minutes," he informed her, then met her gaze. "I'll tell you the honest truth about everything." He hesitated a moment, then drew a deep breath before continuing. "About six months ago, there was a man named Sebastian, who was working for Marcus. Candy and Sebastian became rather close, and then Marcus had him killed. What Marcus didn't know was that Candy witnessed her boyfriend's murder. Out of desperation, Candy redialed the last person who called Sebastian's cell phone moments after he was killed." Vaughn drew a deep breath. "That man was me. Sebastian was my brother."

Sky stared at Vaughn in stunned silence.

"With Candy's help, my former military buddies and I secured jobs with Marcus," Vaughn informed her. "Together, the four of us have been gathering intel on Marcus, his operations, and his entire network of enablers. We finally had enough evidence to take to the FBI. Candy was supposed to meet a federal agent last weekend, but someone must have figured out what she was up to and silenced her." He sighed softly and buried his face in her hair. "I couldn't go with her to the feds, but that's a complicated story for another time."

"Since we don't have time for your complicated back story, I'll let it slide for now," Sky remarked while attempting to look into his eyes through the dim lighting. "Tell me about the cell phones. How did you end up with Candy's cell phone if you hadn't seen her since Friday afternoon?"

"It wasn't Candy's cell phone," Vaughn informed her. "It was Sebastian's. He had some of Marcus's dirty dealings documented on his phone, but we needed the big things so Marcus would never get out of jail. She asked me to hold onto it in case something went wrong with the FBI." Vaughn shrugged. "Well, something went wrong. When the hotel told me she had checked out, I knew something had happened to her, and I would be questioned, so I mailed my phone and my brother's phone to you for safekeeping. I certainly couldn't mail them to Moose or Ox and risk someone else here at the mansion opening their mail. You were the only other person I trusted." He groaned and rubbed his eyes. "I'm sorry, Sky. I never should have gotten you involved, but I just couldn't keep my pecker in my pants."

"It wasn't entirely your fault," she reminded him. "We were both drunk."

"Yes, but I still made a conscious decision to seek you out even before that," he informed her. "I was supposed to establish Candy as my love interest so we could meet without scrutiny." He drew a deep breath and hesitated before meeting her gaze. "From the moment I started in Marcus's employment, I knew I was playing Russian roulette. I've been in situations with the Marines where death felt inevitable." Vaughn stared into her eyes. "Whenever you were around, it was like an emotional stress release. And then, after our drunken night together, I felt almost renewed. Every time we got together, I found new strength and focus to do what needed to be done."

Vaughn groaned and looked away, stranded in his own thoughts. He finally came back to life and focused his attention on her.

"It was more than just sex," he insisted. "Being with you gave me purpose and the will to go on even when I knew my days were numbered." Vaughn shut his eyes. "We were careful, so I thought, and you certainly weren't going to tell anyone about us. I thought you'd be safe." He finally looked at her. "Then I got greedy and went all-in. I just couldn't pass up spending the entire weekend with you, and now you're involved."

"Yes, I'm involved," Sky announced with a sigh. "In for a penny; in for a pound. I should have a say in my own fate." She raised an arrogant brow. "I think we should clear your name in Candy's murder and force the hand of the men responsible."

"That's reckless."

"Seems to be our theme," she remarked, then placed her hand on his face and gently caressed it while staring into his eyes. "You can tell the city homicide detective and Marcus that you and Candy pretended to be involved because you both had secret lovers. She never told you who she was seeing, but you suspect he was someone of importance, or maybe he was a married man. Someone she couldn't risk being caught seeing."

Vaughn considered the ruse and nodded. "I see where you're going with this," he remarked. "If Marcus suspected she was ratting him out, he'll be less likely to think I was involved." He stared at her for a long moment, then raised a curious brow. "But how will you convince the homicide detective that we really were together and that you're not just lying to protect me? No one saw us together except the man who broke into your house. There's no real proof that you're telling the truth."

"That's not entirely true," she informed him. "While you were playing stable boy, I had a lot of time to reflect."

"You think you can prove it to the homicide detective?" he asked with surprise.

There was a light tapping on the door. "Hey," Moose announced through the door. "Wrap it up in there. Five minutes."

As they stood, Vaughn again pulled Sky into his arms and held her.

"Are you sure you want to do this?" he asked with some apprehension as he caressed her backside. "It's going to kill your reputation."

"Let me worry about my reputation," Sky announced before turning concerned. "Can you keep Marcus from killing you?"

Vaughn drew a deep breath and offered his best arrogant smile. "Foreshadowing blackmail."

"You just made that up."

"Yeah, kind of," Vaughn announced with some humor. "If I joke around that Marcus will probably kill me, and I'm waiting to have an 'accident', it could make Marcus just uncomfortable enough to rethink it."

"You're a bit psychotic, you know that?" she remarked while walking toward the door.

Vaughn chuckled as he followed her. "You're just figuring that out now?"

Chapter 40

It was a little after two in the morning, and the Lake House Bar had officially closed for the night, although a few patrons still lingered, finishing their last drinks. Just because the bar was closed, that didn't affect the upstairs casino and the even further upstairs brothel. The flux of people, primarily young men, leaving through the 'employees only' door was almost criminal. Ruby was still cleaning up the tables after those who had already left, while the bartender took care of those remaining at the bar. She brought a tray full of empty beer bottles to the bar, then removed her apron.

"I'm hitting the little girls' room," Ruby informed Randy.

He nodded and removed the empty bottles from her tray as she headed for the back hallway. Ruby was about to enter the bathroom when she heard a man's panic-filled voice just beyond the open back door. The name 'Winchester' caught her attention. Ruby took a couple of quick, quiet steps closer to the partially open door and listened a moment.

§

A few minutes later, Ruby hurried from the bathroom area and rushed past the bar for the front door with her cell phone in her hand. She didn't even speak to the bartender, who watched her leave without a word.

"Ruby--?" he called after her, but she didn't respond.

Ruby rushed onto the front porch of the bar with her cell phone to her ear. "Pick up," she whispered into the phone.

When the voicemail picked up, she disconnected the call and immediately pressed a different button. The phone on the other end rang several times before it was finally answered.

"Hello?" came Nash's weary voice.

"Nash, it's Ruby," she announced into the phone with panic in her voice as she hurried to her car near the area by the hitching posts, where only a few horses remained tied.

"Ruby?" Nash responded with surprise as his voice came to life. "What's going on?"

"I need to talk to you," Ruby insisted. "I overheard something here at the bar that I need to tell you. It's urgent. I'm heading to your farm now."

"Urgent?" Nash responded from the other end. "What did you hear at the bar at this hour?"

Ruby fumbled in her pockets for her car keys, nearly dropping her phone. The keys fell from her hands.

"Shit," she gasped.

"Ruby?" Nash cried out over the phone. "Are you okay?"

"Just my car keys," Ruby remarked, then crouched down, snatching them from the ground, and straightened.

"Stay there," Nash announced through the phone. "I'm on my way."

"No," she replied. "I should come to you. It's not safe--"

As Ruby opened her car door, a shadow fell over her. She spun around with a startled gasp, then cried out. Her cell phone fell from her hand and struck the ground.

"Ruby?" Nash cried out over the phone with concern. "What happened? Are you okay?"

A booted foot suddenly stomped on the phone, effectively ending the call.

§

Only ten minutes later, Sky's Jeep flew recklessly into the bar's parking lot and came to a screeching halt near Ruby's car. Sky, Nash, and Jerry jumped from the Jeep, witnessing the gut-wrenching sight alongside Ruby's car. All three ran to the scene where Ox stood near Moose, who kneeled over the young, unresponsive woman on the ground with his hands pressed against her.

"Moose--" Ox muttered a possible warning.

Moose looked up as the three approached. His blood-covered hands were firmly pressed against Ruby's shoulder and her side as blood seeped between his fingers. She had fresh bruise marks on her face and blood trickling from a laceration on her temple.

"What happened?" Sky demanded, horror in her eyes at the scene as she abruptly stopped.

Randy hurried from the main entrance, his cell phone pressed against his ear and a clean bar rag in hand.

"The ambulance is on its way," Randy announced, then handed Ox the fresh rag before backing away, staring in horror at Ruby on the ground.

Ox joined Moose on the ground alongside the injured, unconscious woman and placed the new rag on her shoulder wound, swiftly applying pressure to help control the bleeding.

"What happened?" Sky again cried out while quickly moving to Ruby's side, once the shock had worn off.

"I don't know," Moose informed her, looking up briefly. "We came out of the bar, and she was already on the ground."

"She ran outside right after using the restroom," the bartender informed her. "She hadn't even finished cleaning up or even clocked out yet. Something had her fired up."

Sky stared at Ruby's pale, freshly bruised face and the minor laceration on the corner of her mouth. Someone had obviously hit her in the face, maybe more than once, struck her on the head, and then stabbed her twice. It had to have been a fast, brutal attack, taking only a minute or two. Sky timidly took Ruby's seemingly lifeless hand in hers and checked for a pulse. She was obviously still alive, or Moose wouldn't be holding pressure on her wounds, but Sky had to know for sure.

"Yes, she called me," Nash remarked, then eyed Moose and Ox with some skepticism. "I guess the two of you left at the right time, huh?"

Moose glared at Nash from his position over Ruby's bleeding, battered body while Ox appeared ready to pounce on the man for what he was possibly insinuating.

"We came out only a minute or two before you arrived," Moose snarled, then shifted his eyes at the bartender. "We have witnesses."

Sky knew how 'witnesses' were in her little town, especially where Marcus may or may not be involved. She thought she trusted them after what Vaughn told her, but now she wasn't so sure. Why had Ruby called the ranch after two in the morning? She had called Sky's phone seconds before she called Nash. Ruby hadn't called Sky or her family in five years. It wasn't a coincidence.

"Ox came back inside only a few seconds after they went out and had me call for an ambulance," Randy informed them, confirming their alibi. Again, not that alibies were worth much in a corrupt town like theirs.

They could hear the ambulance sirens in the distance, growing closer, while the flashing lights glowed against the trees, lighting the way. Sky gently squeezed Ruby's hand.

"Ruby," Sky whispered while leaning over her. "I'm here. What happened?"

The young woman didn't respond or even indicate that she could hear her. As the ambulance pulled into the lot, its siren wailing loudly, Ruby gently squeezed Sky's hand.

Chapter 41

Monday morning. Sky sat in the city homicide detective's dated office, decorated with old baseball memorabilia from years past, while awaiting the detective's return. Sky remained stranded in her thoughts as she sat alone with only the sounds from the bullpen beyond the closed door. Sky couldn't get her mind off what happened with Ruby last night outside the bar. It kept her awake the rest of the night. What had Ruby so riled that made her reach out after five years at two in the morning? What was so important that she immediately called Nash when she couldn't reach her? What did she see or hear that got her violently beaten and stabbed? It had to involve Sky or her family; otherwise, why call them? The bartender alibied Moose and Ox, the two men who seemed to be Vaughn's friends and appeared to be helping Ruby, but did that really mean anything? Things weren't always as they appeared.

Had they been the reason Ruby called in the middle of the night in the first place? Had they attempted to kill her, and Randy covered for them? Her former friend was currently stable but in critical condition. The next few hours and days would be touch-and-go. Of course, Sheriff Burke was calling it an unfortunate mugging. People didn't get mugged in their little hick burg. Her thoughts then strayed back to Hammond's horseback riding accident. And what about Gus? There seemed to be a whole lot of people having a whole lot of accidents lately. Detective Garland finally entered the office with a cup of coffee and shut the door behind him. He briefly glanced at Sky as he rounded the desk, then collapsed into his chair across from her. Detective Garland was in his late forties to early fifties, with dark, curly hair, but surprisingly, little gray. He was neatly dressed and clean-shaven but a little out of shape, possibly due to working in a smaller city with a lower crime rate. Detective Garland leaned back in his chair and studied Sky for a long moment.

"I appreciate you coming forward, Ms. Winchester," Garland announced while studying her with a look that conveyed his doubt. "But your word alone may not be enough. This is a murder investigation, and as a love interest, you can see why your testimony may not carry much weight without proof, especially considering he allegedly murdered his *other* love interest."

"I know," Sky replied while maintaining a strange sense of calm.

When there was a knock on the office door, Detective Garland leaned back in his chair and looked past Sky.

"Come in."

The door opened, and Vaughn entered. He immediately noticed Sky in the chair before the desk and groaned.

"What are you doing here, Sky?" Vaughn just about demanded. "I told you to stay out of this."

"Have a seat, Vaughn," the detective announced somewhat sternly. "I want to hear what she has to say." He then looked at Sky. "Keep this in mind, Ms. Winchester, if I find out you're lying, you'll be charged." The detective then indicated Vaughn. "He's not worth going to jail over."

"Actually, Detective Garland, I'm aware of Vaughn's questionable lifestyle and his rather deplorable traits," Sky remarked.

Vaughn cast a disapproving look at her. "That's uncalled for," he remarked, then eyed the detective. "And my record speaks for itself. I've never served any jail time."

Detective Garland picked up a folder and skimmed through it while peering through his bifocals. "Drunk and disorderly. Assault and battery." He then lifted his eyes above his glasses and glared at Vaughn. "Public urination."

"I had a bad night," Vaughn insisted.

"In front of a nun," Garland added.

"For the record, *he* wasn't a nun," Vaughn insisted. "He was returning from a Halloween party."

Detective Garland tossed the file onto his desk and leaned back in his chair again. "I won't even get into your military record. That reads like a war novel."

"Well, it was the Marines, and I was active duty," Vaughn reminded him. "Breaking things comes with the territory. It's not only expected but also encouraged."

"You punched your CO in the mouth," Garland scoffed.

"It was his fault for not ducking," Vaughn insisted. "Bars in Budapest can be very dangerous, and punching him in the mouth did save his ass. That's also in the report."

Sky watched the two men locking eyes across the desk. It was possible this could go on for hours. She finally cleared her throat and effectively ended their staring contest. Sky smiled at Detective Garland.

"If we could get back to the reason for my visit," Sky announced, but didn't bother waiting for permission to continue. "Vaughn is very much aware that our current relationship is the result of a drunken mistake and that it has continued out of, shall we say, *convenience.*"

The detective eyed the frown on Vaughn's face and snorted a laugh. "She's got you pegged." He looked back at Sky. "Okay. Let's have this 'so-called' proof that Vaughn was with you that Saturday night when the young lady was murdered."

"That Friday afternoon, Vaughn drove Candy to the city and checked her into the hotel," Sky informed the detective. "I assume you have security cameras that show him entering the lobby, but not going up to the room at any point."

"Correct," the detective replied.

"You also have documentation from his credit card provider that he bought gas, Chinese food, and made purchases at an adult store later that same afternoon," she informed him.

"Also correct," Detective Garland replied, then cocked his head. "Are you, at any point, going to tell me something I don't already know?"

Sky opened a large envelope she had sitting on her lap and removed copies of the Chinese food receipt and the adult store receipt.

"These are the receipts he left at my house," she informed him.

Garland eyed the copies of the receipts through his bifocals and shrugged. "That's not proof they were at your house, nor that he was there Friday night," he informed her.

"No, it's not," she replied.

"I'm not really sure you're actually helping, Sky," Vaughn informed her while slouching in his chair.

Sky removed a stack of photos from the envelope, stood, and placed them on the detective's desk. "I'm an amateur photographer," she informed the detective. "Friday and Saturday night, I had my new nighttime camera equipment set up in my attic to capture the thunderstorms we were having those nights. You can check the weather reports to verify the storms on those particular nights."

Vaughn appeared interested and suddenly straightened. "The motion detection camera with photo bursts?" he asked.

"Yes," Sky replied and showed the detective the photos. "Here's one timestamped seven-fifty-five Friday evening."

The photo was of Vaughn on his horse with his overnight bag across his back and full saddlebags across the back of the saddle. Vaughn now stood and eyed the photos as well. A grin crossed his face, and he chuckled.

"Oh, my God," Vaughn announced, now humored as he collapsed back in the chair. "That's priceless."

Sky revealed another set of photos, stamped ten minutes later, that showed Vaughn leaving the barn and heading toward the house with a bag of Chinese food, an unmarked plastic bag, and his overnight bag. The detective was also interested now.

"Okay," the detective replied. "Now you have my attention. I just hope you have some sort of proof for Saturday night, because that's the night she was killed."

"I'm getting there," she informed him. "This is a prelude to his alibi. Right now, I'm just showing you that our, uh, *relationship* is real."

"It proves he visited you," Garland remarked. "I'll give you that. Proving an actual relationship might be a little harder."

Sky smiled and nodded as she removed her cell phone. "Got that covered too," she informed him.

Vaughn eyed her almost suspiciously, wondering what she was up to. She found what she was looking for and turned it over to the detective, revealing the picture of her and Vaughn.

"This is Friday night," she announced and zoomed in on the picture.

Just behind her and Vaughn was the pair of fuzzy pink handcuffs hanging from the bedpost.

"That's my bed," she informed the detective. "And that's one of the items Vaughn bought at the adult store listed on the receipt."

Vaughn now stared at Sky as horror suddenly crossed his face. "Don't do it, Sky," Vaughn warned her.

Sky ignored Vaughn and showed the detective a video. It was the X-rated one she filmed while bent over the kitchen table. Even though nothing could be seen, it was obvious that Vaughn was servicing her from behind. Vaughn heard some of the sounds and covered his eyes.

"He didn't need to see that," Vaughn muttered.

The detective squirmed slightly and waved her off. "Okay, I get the point," he announced. "You were in a relationship. Moving on."

Sky returned to the photos on his desk. "This right here," she announced and pointed at the picture, "is about thirty minutes after an intruder broke into my house late Saturday night, early Sunday morning. Note the time stamp on the photo."

Vaughn now stood and looked at the photo as well, but was disappointed that he couldn't see the guy's face. She showed the detective the pictures after the incident.

"And these are of Vaughn leaving my house after he chased off the intruder," she informed the detective. "He needed to leave before the deputy showed up. If it were found out we've been secretly having an affair, his boss would fire him *or worse*."

"Why do you think that?" the detective asked.

"Because Marcus has a thing for me, and I'm off-limits to everyone," she replied, then raised an arrogant brow. "There's nothing between Marcus and me, but that doesn't matter to him."

There were more photos of Vaughn riding away from the farm. Sky then produced a copy of the police report from that night, as well as photos she had taken for Deputy Rhodes.

"Vaughn fought with the intruder before chasing him away," Sky informed the detective. "Both Vaughn and the intruder were hurt in the process. I have the bloodstained dishrag at home, and Deputy Rhodes collected blood samples from the scene. You'll find some of that blood is Vaughn's." She then looked at Vaughn. "Show him your injury."

Vaughn eyed the detective, who raised his brow as if waiting. Vaughn groaned, then removed his jacket and then his shirt. The detective eyed the week-old cut along his left shoulder, which was healing, although it was still fresh and undeniably so. Once he was satisfied, Vaughn put his shirt back on. Sky then indicated the time stamp on the photo of Vaughn leaving early Sunday morning, and then the time of the police report.

"That's proof that Vaughn couldn't have been in your city murdering Candy," she announced. "Proof that he was at my house."

The detective sorted through the photos and studied the police report. "It does seem conclusive," he remarked. "I suppose there's a slight chance he still could have made it to the city in time to make the window, but not very likely."

"Then let me clinch the deal," Sky announced, returned to her phone, and then handed it to him. "These are my text messages, all time-stamped, to Vaughn Sunday morning and his corresponding texts. One has my barn in the background."

Vaughn suddenly gasped and shot up from his chair. "No, don't show him--"

The detective suddenly groaned and placed the phone face down on the desk. "Okay, I believe you," he announced, then waved the cell phone away. "Just get that away from me."

Sky removed her phone from the desk and smiled almost smugly at Vaughn. He glared at her through squinting eyes.

"You just had to go there," he muttered.

Sky smiled sweetly. "Just removing all shadow of doubt," she insisted.

"I'll just need both of you to sign sworn statements that you were together during the specified time, and I'll see that he's cleared of any suspicion in the young woman's death," the detective announced. "Just give me a few minutes to type up your statement and bleach my eyeballs."

"Thank you, Detective Garland," Sky announced.

"I know you're not allowed to discuss the murder investigation," Vaughn remarked while leaning forward, "but did the security cameras really not show anyone entering Candy's hotel room?"

"Just maid service Saturday morning and room service Saturday night," the detective replied. "No one else went in, and she never came out. We questioned housekeeping. Candy was alive when she freshened the room." He then hesitated. "There wasn't, however, any record of her ordering room service, and the man with the cart avoided the cameras."

"So that's her killer," Vaughn remarked.

"More than likely."

"What time was room service in her room?" Vaughn then asked.

"Approximately nine o'clock that evening," the detective replied.

"Strange, don't you think?" Vaughn remarked.

"What's strange?"

"That she never left the room after she checked in Friday afternoon, but she wasn't killed until Saturday night," Vaughn replied. "You'd think she would have met someone or at least gone out for something to eat."

"And she didn't even order the room service," Sky remarked. "She was in that room for over thirty hours and never went for anything to eat. Apparently, she never even thought about it."

"She was in good spirits when I dropped her off," Vaughn informed the detective. "What possible reason would she have to starve herself?"

"It made more sense when we thought she was depressed," Detective Garland remarked while eyeing Vaughn. "I don't have any reason to doubt you when you say she wasn't." He then nodded. "It wouldn't hurt to dig a little deeper into the room connecting to hers. Maybe the person in the connecting room was this mysterious boyfriend you mentioned."

Sky knew there wasn't a mysterious boyfriend, but the person in the connecting room might have been her contact with the FBI. Or someone posing as her contact.

"If I can help in any way, Detective," Vaughn announced. "Just ask."

"Yeah, sure," Detective Garland muttered. "Just try to stay out of my hair."

Sky then considered something else and eyed the detective. "Detective Garland," she announced. "Who in my town will know that Vaughn was with me on Saturday night?"

"Just your local sheriff," Garland replied and appeared curious. "Why?"

"I just want to know who's responsible when the gossip starts, that's all," Sky replied with a tiny smile.

Chapter 42

Vaughn drove his truck along the back road that eventually passed the ranch driveway. Sky remained lost in her own world most of the drive back and was relatively quiet. Vaughn glanced at her in the passenger seat several times before finally speaking.

"Moose and Ox didn't attack Ruby," Vaughn assured her, finally breaking the silence. "If you trust me, you can trust them."

Sky finally snapped out of her thoughts and glanced at Vaughn while shifting uncomfortably. "I believe they're telling the truth about what happened," she replied, then frowned. "But I don't think Uncle Nash is all that certain, though."

"Well, Uncle Nash doesn't trust me either," he informed her. "Moose and Ox would pass through the gates of hell for me, and I'd do the same for them. Despite our current *relationship* with Marcus, we're not as bad as we pretend to be. The only reason Moose and Ox are even here is because I asked for their help."

Sky offered a tiny smile and nodded. "I know," she replied. "But the urgency of Ruby's call has me troubled. Whatever the reason, it was something that someone was willing to kill her over."

"And it possibly involved you or your family ranch," Vaughn added, then nodded. "I agree, and that's why you need a little added protection. Fortunately, for you, my services are rather cheap and only a little bit kinky."

Sky cast a look at him and smirked. "I'll bet," she muttered.

Vaughn added a tiny chuckle and then turned serious again. "So, how do you want to play this? Do I drop you off at the end of your driveway, just as I did when I picked you up this morning? Or do I take you to your front door?"

"Do we want to wait and see if Sheriff Burke spreads the rumor first?" Sky asked.

"He's definitely telling Marcus the juicy gossip about us," Vaughn informed her. "In the time it took us to drive back from the city, Marcus probably already knows."

"Then we need to get it out there," she insisted. "We should make the first move."

"I agree," Vaughn replied before groaning softly. "Give me a fighting chance to live past tonight." He then eyed her. "How do you want to play this?"

"Big and loud."

Vaughn suddenly grinned. "Just my speed," he teased.

"Monday night at the bar," Sky remarked while frowning. "Not exactly the biggest audience."

"It'll have to do," Vaughn insisted, then turned down her driveway. "First, we need to have an uncomfortable conversation with your aunt and uncle."

"Then we'll ask our friends to meet us at the bar and make it public there," she added.

Vaughn drove up to the house and stopped his truck alongside Sky's Jeep. He shut off his vehicle and turned to face her.

"Don't take this the wrong way," Vaughn announced in an oddly serious tone. "But being that I'm rather fond of breathing, I came up with a plan that I think will help me in my quest to continue breathing a little while longer."

"Okay," Sky remarked, eyeing him somewhat suspiciously as she turned in her seat to face him. "What's your plan?"

He drew a deep breath while staring into her eyes. "I think you should tell everyone you're pregnant," Vaughn replied.

Sky stared at Vaughn with a shocked look. "What?" she practically gasped.

"Don't get all bent out of shape," he announced in an attempt to calm her. "It's a good reason why we're suddenly going public with it. It makes sense. And because I knocked you up--" He produced a diamond engagement ring. "We also got engaged."

Sky stared at the surprisingly stunning, antique diamond engagement ring, then looked back at Vaughn.

"You're out of your mind!" she cried out. "I don't want to tell people we're engaged, and I certainly don't want to lie about being pregnant!"

"It's the perfect ruse," he insisted. "This is my ass, Sky. I lost my private apartment above the barn, and I'm now living in gen-pop alongside men who may want to off me." He indicated the diamond engagement ring. "My grandmother's engagement ring is my key to moving out of gen-pop and into your bedroom, where it's safe."

Sky's eyes suddenly narrowed. "Don't lie to me," she scoffed while giving him a quick once-over. "We both know that's your pecker talking."

Vaughn groaned and rolled his eyes. "Not *just* my pecker," he insisted, then hid his smile. "Sleeping in your bed is just an added bonus." He then pleaded with his eyes, looking more like a whipped puppy. "You know Marcus will want my pecker on a silver platter, and you don't want me losing my pecker, do you?"

Sky rolled her eyes and groaned loudly. "You really are a prick," she scoffed.

Vaughn grinned. "Is that 'yes'?" he asked, then grabbed her left hand. "I'm taking that as 'yes'." He slipped the ring on her finger, then immediately leaned forward and kissed her quickly on the lips. "You and the baby have made me so very happy."

Before she could comment, Vaughn jumped out of the truck. Sky was once again left wondering what she had done.

§

Nash and Selma sat on the other side of the coffee table in the living room from Sky and Vaughn, staring at them with matching expressions of shock and dismay.

Vaughn seemed tense and leaned closer to Sky. "Maybe we should have skipped the part about me knocking you up," he muttered to her.

Sky glared at Vaughn and sneered. "You think?" She held her breath and looked back at her aunt and uncle. "I can understand your shock, but I wish you'd say something."

"Would 'I'm getting the shotgun' qualify?" Nash asked in an oddly calm tone.

"Oh, boy," Vaughn muttered.

Selma attempted a smile and patted Nash's hand. "Deep breaths, dear," she announced while maintaining her stare at Vaughn. Selma finally looked at Sky. "You know, you don't have to get married. You don't even have to have the baby."

Vaughn's eyes narrowed while glaring at Sky's aunt.

Sky saw the look on Vaughn's face and immediately caressed his leg before he could speak. "Let it go, Vaughn," she whispered.

Vaughn immediately pulled himself together, grasped her hand, and affectionately kissed it. Sky couldn't deny she enjoyed that a little too much. She met his gaze and smiled before finally looking back at her aunt and uncle.

"I know this is a lot for you to take in," Sky announced, gentle but firm. "But this decision is between Vaughn and me. We're happy with our choices, and I hope, in time, you'll come to accept it and be happy for us."

"I'm going to need some time and a few glasses of whiskey," Nash reported dryly.

"We'll support you, Sky," her aunt announced, managing a weak smile. "What's the short-term plan? Will your friend be moving in?"

"Yes," Sky replied.

"When?" Nash muttered.

"Tonight," Sky informed him. "He'll bring his horse and some things over tonight, and then he'll bring the rest over later in the week."

"The rest?" Vaughn asked Sky, then grinned. "You mean my duffel bag?"

Nash sneered, apparently not humored by Vaughn or his vagrant lifestyle.

"Can I assume he won't need a guestroom?" Selma asked with a loud sigh.

"No, he doesn't need a guestroom," Sky replied and received an affectionate hand squeeze from Vaughn, who was grinning a little too much.

Selma stood with a defeated sigh. "I should probably get something out for dinner."

"We're actually having dinner at the Lake House Bar tonight," Sky informed her. "We're meeting our friends and sharing the good news."

Nash snorted a laugh.

Vaughn glared at her uncle, not amused. "You may not approve of me, but that's my baby she's carrying," Vaughn informed him. "Show a little respect."

Sky watched her uncle silently stand and leave the room without further confrontation.

Selma gently cleared her throat and managed a smile. "I'll talk to him," she announced, then hurried after Nash.

Sky turned toward Vaughn on the sofa and gave him a stern and serious look. "You'd better go to the stable and get your horse before my aunt calls Marcus and starts gossiping," she informed him.

Vaughn nodded, then kissed her quickly but warmly on the lips. "I'll be back in less than an hour."

Chapter 43

Early Monday evening. Sky entered the Lake House Bar alone and saw Dixie and Marlon already seated at their usual table in the less-than-busy room. Mondays were never crowded, particularly during the dinner hour. Sky joined her friends and immediately felt the same awkwardness she felt when they broke the news to her aunt and uncle. Dixie and Marlon were going to be just as shocked and possibly more disappointed. Sky fidgeted while eyeing her friends, thinking about how she would explain it to them in the least 'shock and awe' way.

"There's something I need to tell you, and it's going to be a bit of a shock," Sky informed them while shifting in her chair.

Dixie suddenly grinned and leaned across the table. "Does it have something to do with a certain new man in your life?"

Sky stared at her friend with some surprise. "You heard already?"

Vaughn, Moose, and Ox entered the bar in their usual rowdy manner. All three were in great spirits, possibly due to Vaughn being cleared of Candy's murder and no longer being on house arrest. Sky immediately tensed when she saw them. She thought she had more time. Vaughn approached their table and flopped into the vacant seat beside Sky while Moose and Ox continued to their usual table in the back. Dixie and Marlon frowned at Vaughn's presence but refrained from commenting. Vaughn grinned and moved his chair closer to Sky's, then placed his arm over her shoulder. He eyed her friends, then looked back at Sky.

"By the outpouring of love I'm feeling, I guess you didn't tell them yet," Vaughn remarked.

"Tell us what?" Marlon asked, now skeptical and somewhat concerned.

Dixie's eyes widened as she stared at her friend with something resembling horror. "No," she gasped, then pointed at Vaughn. "Him?"

"I'm sorry I didn't tell you, Dixie," Sky informed her friend. "But it was *complicated.*"

"And it's not complicated now?" Marlon practically demanded.

"Actually, now it's more complicated," Sky muttered, then held her breath and cringed at the lie she needed to spread. "I'm pregnant."

Vaughn grinned and proudly held up Sky's left hand, revealing the engagement ring.

Dixie gasped while staring at the ring, then suddenly cried out with excitement. "You're getting married?"

Marlon looked at his sister with his mouth hanging open in astonishment at her sudden giddiness over the diamond ring. Sky nodded and stared at her friend, sharing the same bewildered look as Marlon. Dixie again cried out, jumped up from her seat, and happily hugged Sky.

"I'm so happy for you!"

"You are?" Sky and Marlon asked in unison.

Dixie returned to her seat but remained sitting on the edge. "Yeah, of course," she replied. "I am going to be your maid of honor, right?"

"Well--?" Sky looked back at Vaughn.

Vaughn suddenly grinned. "Hey, if you want a traditional wedding, we'll have a traditional wedding," he announced. "Just not in a church. I'll probably burst into flames."

"Vaughn," Moose called out from across the room. "You coming?"

All four looked across the room at Vaughn's usual table, which was now two tables pushed together. Vaughn gave his men a thumbs-up, then looked at Sky and her friends.

"Mind if we switch tables?" Vaughn asked, almost respectfully.

Dixie and Marlon exchanged apprehensive looks, then reluctantly collected their drinks and followed Vaughn and Sky to the back table. Sky knew exactly how her friends were feeling. It was strange sitting at the back table. It felt like a whole other world, and there was no doubt that the gossip was about to start. Of course, that's why they came to the bar. Dixie fidgeted before finally leaning closer to Sky for a private conversation.

"So it wasn't Jerry I heard you with in the hay loft?" Dixie asked, being sure she was only loud enough for Sky to hear.

"No, that was Vaughn," Sky admitted as the color rose to her cheeks.

Dixie seemed to consider the response, then nodded before glancing back at Sky. "Would you mind if I asked Jerry out?"

Sky looked at Dixie with some surprise. "You like Jerry?"

"Well, yeah," Dixie replied almost shyly with a slightly lustful smile. "Kind of. Well, a lot." She then groaned. "Jerry is so hot."

"Why didn't you say something before?" Sky asked. "Of course I don't mind. Why would I? We're just friends. I told you that."

"I wasn't sure, and I didn't want to get in your way," Dixie informed her with a tiny shrug. "I just always assumed there was something between you two, but you were just taking your time. I mean, come on! Jerry is so hot!"

Sky couldn't help but laugh. "By all means, go for it," she replied. "I'd love to see you two together. You both deserve happiness."

Dixie was pleased with the response and practically bounced in her seat. "It is *so* on," she announced.

§

Less than an hour later, the entire bar knew about Sky and Vaughn's relationship, while Dixie and Marlon warmed up to their new position among the rank and file. Moose challenged Marlon to a game of eight-ball, where the two had a lot of fun trash-talking each other while they played. Dixie, on the other hand, somehow ended up sitting alongside Ox and filing his fingernails after shaming him for chewing them 'like a barbarian'. He fought her a little on the manicure, but despite his ability to overpower the much smaller woman, he finally gave in. They ended up talking about their childhood over the manicure. Vaughn kept his arm securely over Sky's shoulder, holding her against his side as they both watched the manicure in stunned silence.

"You're seeing this, right?" Vaughn muttered without taking his eyes off Ox and Dixie.

"Yeah, I'm seeing it," Sky remarked. "It's like some twisted tale of 'Beauty and the Beast'."

Vaughn chuckled at the comment, catching Ox's attention. Ox looked up at him, met his gaze while indicating Dixie, and then mouthed, "She's so cute!"

Vaughn groaned and buried his face in Sky's hair. "I can't watch this," he muttered. "If she leaves with him, I'll probably puke."

"I'm pretty sure she's not leaving with him," Sky insisted. "She wants to go out with Jerry."

Vaughn lifted his head and eyed her profile, then grinned. "I prefer that hook-up," he announced. "It'll keep Jerry's mind and pecker off you."

Sky was about to scold him for the crude assumption when he pulled her to her feet.

"I think it's time for our first official boyfriend-girlfriend dance," he insisted as the slow song played, then guided her to the dance floor.

As he spun her into his arms, if there was any doubt about Sky and Vaughn together, that doubt faded when they slow danced. Vaughn held Sky close to him and affectionately caressed her body while nuzzling her neck. Perhaps he was doing it mostly for show, but she couldn't deny she was enjoying it.

Sky pulled back and met his gaze with a warm smile. "This is nice," she announced.

"Yes, it is," Vaughn replied while grinning. "Seems like just yesterday I was corrupting your morals. The forbidden rancher's daughter, Sky Winchester. After I met you, the guys laughed at me for even thinking about pursuing you."

"Well, yeah. I kicked you in the groin, remember?" she reminded him. "You should have been a little turned off."

"You'd think, but I don't give up that easily," Vaughn remarked with a humored grin. "Hard to believe a week or so later you were in my bed, giggling at my pecker." He chuckled and shook his head. "Honestly, you were like a kid at an amusement park. The virgin Sky Winchester giggling and playing with my tinker toy." He sighed while staring into her eyes with the most sincere smile she'd ever seen from him. "That was possibly the greatest night of my life. I still can't believe a woman like you letting me anywhere near her."

"Well, the alcohol had a little something to do with that," she reminded him.

"Not every day thereafter," he insisted. "And I'm certainly not that charming."

"Eh, you kind of are," Sky remarked while hiding her smile.

Vaughn grinned, leaned closer to her, and kissed her warmly on the lips. He pulled back, met her gaze, and laughed.

"Our first public kiss," he remarked. "That felt almost dirty."

Sky laughed while clinging to him, lightly caressing his chest. "Yes, it did."

Vaughn leaned down and kissed her again, this time with a little more aggression. Sky returned the kiss, then broke it off when his hands began traveling her body.

"Down boy," she announced while hiding her enthusiasm. "We have all night. You're sleeping over, remember?"

Vaughn groaned at the comment and pulled her a little closer. "Oh, I remember," he replied.

There was a loud commotion within the bar, catching their attention. Both looked across the room just in time to see Tony shoving Roscoe and Foster away from him while yelling profanities.

"What do you suppose that's about?" Sky asked, unable to take her eyes off the scene across the bar.

When Tony's gaze shifted to the dance floor, Vaughn groaned lowly.

"If I had to guess," Vaughn remarked almost casually. "I'd say Tony heard about our engagement and doesn't approve."

Sky internally panicked and looked back across the room in time to see Tony pull away from his men and charge onto the dance floor for them. Vaughn swiftly spun Sky behind him, attempting to shield her from Tony's aggressive approach.

"Don't do anything stupid--" Vaughn began, but was interrupted when Tony stopped in front of him and swung his fist at Vaughn's face.

Vaughn blocked Tony's fist and retaliated by punching him in the gut. Sky immediately backed up, shocked by Tony's aggressiveness and wanting to give Vaughn room to defend himself. Tony didn't appreciate the gut punch and struck back, hitting Vaughn in the ribs. Vaughn grunted from the hit and almost doubled over, but used the opportunity to ram his elbow into Tony's sternum. Tony clutched his chest and stumbled back a step from the surprisingly hard hit. Roscoe and Foster darted across the dance floor to defend Tony, but were plowed down by Ox, resembling a linebacker defending the football from the opposing team. By the time Moose and his pool stick made it to the dance floor, Ox was already back on his feet and staring at the writhing men. When Tony straightened from the crushing blow to his chest, Vaughn was already swinging his fist, striking Tony across the cheek. Tony stumbled backward, tripped over his men, and crashed to the floor with them.

As Vaughn took a step back, prepared to end the fight there, half the men in the barroom jumped up from their chairs and ran onto the dance floor, screaming and yelling at Tony and his men.

"Get out of here!" the men shouted. "You're not welcome here!"

Sky slid into Vaughn's arms and assessed him for any injuries, but he was too busy grinning and chuckling at the locals berating Tony and his men. Moose and Ox seemed a little surprised when the locals chased the three men from the barroom. They'd apparently had enough of Tony's thuggery and picked Vaughn as their horse to back in that particular race. As the three men were chased from the bar, the rest of the customers cheered and applauded.

"And so the revolution begins," Vaughn teased with a chuckle.

Sky pulled just far enough away from Vaughn to meet his gaze with her own somewhat dumbfounded one.

"That escalated fast," Sky remarked. "What did you do to piss off Tony?"

Vaughn eyed her and raised a slightly humored brow. "You, Sky," he replied. "I *did* you."

"Be serious," she scoffed. "We broke up five years ago."

"There's no statute of limitations on jealousy," he reminded her.

"He's not jealous of me," Sky insisted. "That was definitely about you."

"Yeah," Vaughn replied while nodding. "Me with you. Face it, Sky. The guy never got over you." He then offered a tiny smile and shrugged. "And I can't blame him. I doubt I'd ever get over you, and I'm not a sociopath like Tony."

"I still say it's not about me," Sky insisted. "But either way, you seriously need to watch your back around Tony."

"Way ahead of you, darling."

Chapter 44

As the sun rose, Sky woke to Vaughn pressed against her from behind, his arm anchored securely around her. She couldn't deny that it felt wonderful waking up to him holding her tight. She moved only slightly, which must have woken him. He lightly nibbled on her shoulder and groaned softly close to her ear.

"I'm enjoying being engaged," he announced warmly, chuckling while pressing against her with his early morning enthusiasm. "It's so *respectable*."

Sky giggled while caressing his arm around her. "Careful, Vaughn," she announced. "You're starting to believe your own lies."

"You seriously underestimate the lengths I'll go to perpetuate my lies," he remarked while kissing her neck. "A year from now, you're going to wake up in bed next to me, wondering how I got you to marry me."

"If you intend to ravish me, you'd better do it," she informed him. "As usual, your talking is killing the mood."

"Sorry, darling," he announced, then quickly kissed her shoulder before sitting up in bed. "I don't even have time for a quickie."

Sky turned over in bed and stared at him, somewhat stunned, and watched as he got up. "Seriously?"

Vaughn looked back at her and snorted a laugh. "I work, remember?" he announced. "I have enough time for a five-minute shower, put on some clothes, and saddle my horse. It's a thirty-minute ride to Marcus's stable from here, if I book it. And I don't even get coffee out of the deal."

Sky studied him a moment and considered his comment. "What if I made you coffee while you showered and drove you to Marcus's farm?" she countered, raising a curious brow. "Would you have five minutes then?"

Vaughn eyed her, then groaned, slipped out of his boxer briefs, and jumped back under the covers. "Deal!" he cried out.

As he practically jumped on her, Sky screamed and then laughed.

"You're such a naughty, horny girl," he announced while kissing her neck as he worked his way down to her chest. "I'm giving you the full-Vaughn experience tonight."

Sky giggled, then screamed. "Oh, my God, you're evil!" She again laughed. "I love it!"

§

A few minutes later, Sky hurried down the back stairs to find coffee already brewing despite the early hour. Her Uncle Nash sat in his chair at the table while holding his head. He looked hungover, but Sky knew he hadn't been drinking. At least, she didn't think he'd been drinking.

"Good morning," Sky chirped.

"I'm glad you think so," Nash muttered.

Sky glanced at her uncle, then searched for a travel mug. "Everything okay?" she asked.

Nash groaned and lifted his head. "Yes, everything is fine," he muttered in possibly the most sarcastic tone as the coffee finished brewing.

Sky filled the travel mug with coffee and then poured hot water into her uncle's tea mug. She set his tea on the table before him.

"I guess you're still upset about Vaughn, huh?" Sky asked.

"No," he announced almost calmly. "But I can do without the 'full-Vaughn experience', if it's not asking too much."

Sky tensed, then glanced at her uncle and the sideways glare she received. Sky suddenly cringed.

"You heard that?"

"Even the neighbors heard that," Nash reported sternly.

"We don't have any neighbors."

"My point," he scoffed.

Sky felt her cheeks redden as she grimaced. "Sorry."

Nash caught her hand, forced her to sit at the table with him, and looked into her eyes. "Do you love him, Sky?" he asked. "You don't need to get married just because you're pregnant."

Sky smiled warmly at her uncle and squeezed his hand. "I'm not pregnant," she whispered. "But that's just between you and me."

"You lied to him about being pregnant?" Nash gasped. "Why?"

"No, *he* lied about me being pregnant," she informed him. "It's really complicated, Uncle Nash. Please don't tell Aunt Selma. She gossips with his boss, and it'll create problems. I can't really explain right now, but I will. I promise."

Nash groaned a sigh of relief and shut his eyes. "Thank God," he whispered, then met her gaze. "I won't say anything to your aunt. If you really want to be with this guy, I'll try to support you, but just be careful."

"I'm not the one who needs to be careful," Sky remarked. "Marcus seems to think he owns me, and he might not be happy with Vaughn when he learns of our relationship. I'm worried about his welfare."

"Well, make an honest man out of him," Nash announced sternly while straightening proudly.

"What do you mean?"

"If he loves you and wants to marry you, offer him a job here at the ranch," Nash informed her. "It'll be a pay cut, I'm sure, but he'll probably live longer. We can always use more help."

"I'll keep that in mind," she announced, feeling rather proud of her uncle at that moment. She then heard Vaughn on the back stairs. "That's him. I promised him a ride to the stables."

"Yes," Nash groaned, leaning back in his chair. "I heard your counteroffer."

Sky groaned with some embarrassment. When Vaughn appeared in the kitchen, Sky sprang to her feet.

"I told you to keep it down," Vaughn reminded her and shook his head while smirking. "Now you went and pissed off the neighbors."

Sky handed Vaughn the travel mug. "Let's get you to work on time," she announced. "We can talk on the way." She then looked at her uncle. "Will you be here when I get back?"

"No," her uncle replied. "I'm meeting with my new accountant in the city this morning. Apparently, the one I had the last couple of years decided to run off with his business partner's wife."

"Hmm, scandalous," Sky remarked.

"Yes, the firm has been working overtime trying to sort out his clients' financial affairs before the end of the third quarter," Nash informed her with a defeated sigh. "So I won't be home until dinnertime."

"I guess I'm on my own for lunch then," Sky remarked.

"Selma will be here," Nash informed her.

"No, she's having lunch with some friends," Sky reminded him.

Nash considered it, then nodded. "Yes, of course," he replied with little enthusiasm. "The clucking hen club."

"See you later," Sky announced to her uncle, then headed for the kitchen door.

Vaughn grinned at Nash while following Sky. "Later, Uncle Nash," he announced as he left the kitchen.

§

Sky and Vaughn had no sooner gotten in the Jeep when Vaughn glanced at her while sipping his coffee.

"Was your uncle mad?" Vaughn asked.

"He wasn't too happy about what he heard through the walls."

"That's all on you," Vaughn remarked, somewhat humored, and shook his head. "I told you to keep it down."

"I guess he wasn't too mad, though," Sky remarked as she drove down the long ranch driveway. "When I told him that Marcus would probably take out his anger on you, he said I should offer you a job on the ranch."

Vaughn eyed her and raised a curious brow. "Really?" he asked with surprise, then looked back out the windshield as he sipped his coffee. "What does it pay? And does it include 'quickie' breaks with the rancher's niece?"

Sky snorted a laugh and shook her head. "I didn't ask, but I suspect Jerry would be your boss so--"

"Jerry--" Vaughn remarked, groaning.

"Yeah."

"That would be an interesting work situation," Vaughn remarked. "I'd go from working for a man who wants to kill me for banging his fantasy girl to working for another man who wants to kill me for banging his fantasy girl."

"Jerry and I are just friends," she reminded him with a groan.

"Doesn't mean he doesn't want to bang you," Vaughn announced with little emotion.

"Jealous?"

"Yep."

Sky cast a look at Vaughn's profile, surprised by the admission.

He met her gaze and smiled. "What? You think I'd bother denying it?" he replied.

"I don't understand why you'd be jealous," she muttered.

"Why wouldn't I be jealous?" he asked while glancing at her. "He's good-looking and an all-around Boy Scout. The only thing I bring to this relationship is a sensational sexual appetite and a pecker that never sleeps." Vaughn frowned and rested his head against the headrest. "The only reason you even let me in your bed is because I'm the one who happened to defile you and took your virginity. We both know I'm pretty much the bottom of the barrel as far as boyfriends go. You could do so much better and probably should."

"Did I give you decaffeinated coffee?" she suddenly asked while casting strange looks at him. "What's with you?"

"Nothing," he muttered. "Just a good stiff dose of reality slapping me in the face."

Sky stopped the Jeep at the end of Marcus's lane, threw it into park, and then turned in her seat to face him.

"What's going on?" she demanded.

Vaughn groaned softly, then turned to face her and stared into her eyes. "I conned my way into your life, Sky," he announced, clearly annoyed with himself. "I pursued you, orchestrated every meeting we've ever had, and happily fucked you three ways to Sunday despite knowing you pretty much hated me."

"Where's the part where you tell me something I don't already know?" she asked.

"Don't you get it, Sky?" Vaughn practically demanded. "Do you even see what's happening? You're *never* getting rid of me."

"Yeah, I kind of guessed that," she remarked, then threw the Jeep into drive. "You're going to be late for work. We'll talk about all of the above when you get home."

Vaughn stared at her profile in stunned silence as she drove up to the stables. Sky put the Jeep into park and turned to face him again.

"Are you packing up the rest of your things after work?" she asked.

He continued to stare at her. "Uh, yeah," Vaughn replied and attempted to snap out of his thoughts. "My truck is here, so I can drive back to your place when I'm finished." He then cocked his head while giving her a strange look. "You aren't bothered by anything I just said?"

Sky chuckled, amused by the question. "Everything you said, I already knew," she informed him. "It's as if every silent argument I've ever had in my head just came out of your mouth." She then considered the question. "Sure, I have questions about your past, but we'll eventually discuss that."

Vaughn shook his head in disbelief. "You actually kind of scare me," he remarked. "Something's not right with you. I know I'm not *that* charming."

Sky leaned across the seat, kissed him warmly on the lips, and then pulled away to meet his bewildered gaze.

"Have a nice day at work," she announced. "And watch your back."

"Uh, okay," he replied, then opened the door while seeming a bit dazed by her lack of reaction to his confession.

"Don't forget your coffee," she announced cheerfully.

Vaughn smiled awkwardly, then removed his travel mug from the holder. "Uh, see you tonight."

"Dinner is at six," she informed him, then turned stern. "If you're going to be late--call."

Vaughn forced a smile and nodded. Sky couldn't help but laugh at the puzzled look on Vaughn's face. It was probably a little cruel, but she enjoyed seeing him squirm.

Chapter 45

Sky had only been gone for twenty minutes, since it wasn't a far drive to and from Marcus's house. By the time she got home, her uncle was already gone, as promised, but her aunt was up and puttering around the kitchen, making breakfast. Selma glanced at Sky as she crossed the kitchen for the teakettle.

"I'm surprised you're up so early," Selma remarked while making French toast. "Did you want some breakfast?"

"Only if it's no trouble," Sky reported, then poured a cup of coffee for her aunt. "I'm sorry if I woke you this morning."

Selma cast a look at Sky over her shoulder while flipping the French toast on the griddle. "You're always up early," she remarked. "Honestly, I don't even hear you get up anymore."

Sky glanced at her aunt almost suspiciously. "Uncle Nash said I woke him," she reported.

Aunt Selma groaned and rolled her cycs. "Considering how often he woke me with his tossing and turning, I'd say he deserved to be woken this morning," she remarked, then shook her head. "My

God, you're twenty-three! You were going to have overnight company eventually. I guess the thought of a man in your bed was a little too much for him. He forgets you're not a little girl anymore." She waved her off. "He'll get used to the idea."

Sky removed two plates from the cupboard. "So you didn't hear anything through the walls this morning?" she asked, now curious.

Selma placed French toast on each of their plates, then eyed Sky. "You mean like a bed creaking or groans of ecstasy?" her aunt asked.

It sounded even worse when she heard it from her aunt than when she heard it from her uncle. Sky cringed at what she must have heard.

"Something like that," she muttered.

Selma handed Sky one of the plates and met her gaze while smiling. "No, I didn't hear anything," she replied, then frowned. "Well, except your uncle moaning and groaning." Her aunt sat at the table. "Him, I wanted to hit."

Sky joined Selma at the table and picked at her French toast. She was relieved it wasn't nearly as loud as her uncle made it out to seem.

"I know neither of you are exactly happy with my choices--" Sky began, but didn't finish her thought.

Selma glanced at Sky and managed a tiny smile. "We owe you an apology, Sky," she remarked. "The news was a bit shocking. I mean, we didn't think you were seeing anyone, and when we did, we sort of thought it might be Jerry. So, of course, we were shocked."

"I never led you on about Jerry," Sky insisted. "That was a rumor everyone wanted to run with. I denied it, remember?"

"You're probably right," Selma remarked, then sighed. "What I'm trying to say is, it was a lot to take in, but we trust your judgment."

"Really?"

Selma laughed softly and shook her head, meeting Sky's gaze with a hint of humor. "I get it," she announced. "He's very handsome and a bit of a bad boy. We've all been attracted to one of them in our lives. Even me. As long as he treats you well, which is the only real concern we have with a man like that, we support your decision."

"I won't deny his bad boy reputation," Sky remarked while eating her French toast. "But I honestly think he's trying to be a better man."

"What about that business with the murdered woman?" Selma then asked.

"Oh, that," Sky remarked somewhat timidly. "I thought that gossip had already passed around town. I think she was having an affair with some married man, and Vaughn let everyone believe they were a couple to keep the guy's wife from finding out." It was a reasonable lie. "Vaughn only went along with it because he didn't want anyone to know he was secretly seeing me."

"But Vaughn was questioned in her death," Selma reminded her.

Honestly, Sky thought her aunt would be the first one up on all the latest gossip. Even Dixie heard the entire story by the time she met with her last night. Admitting it aloud to her aunt was a bit uncomfortable.

"Vaughn was with me the entire weekend you and Uncle Nash were away," Sky timidly replied. "I was his alibi."

Selma eyed her and appeared somewhat surprised. "But the break-in--?"

Sky drew a deep breath and held it. "Vaughn was here when it happened," she admitted. "He's the reason the intruder ran off. I guess the guy assumed I'd be home alone, which means he was probably local." She snorted a laugh. "If he were local, could you imagine his surprise to see Vaughn, of all people, strolling around our house in nothing but his boxer briefs in the middle of the night. I'm guessing that had to be short of terrifying."

Selma snorted a laugh. "I guess that would have been quite the surprise," she remarked. "So he couldn't identify either of them?"

"Well, it was probably only one guy, and he was wearing a mask," Sky replied. "Apparently, he was also armed with a hunting knife." She managed a tiny laugh. "It must have been something. A man with a hunting knife going up against an unarmed, half-naked man and still losing. To be honest, Aunt Selma, his reputation is not exaggerated. Probably scared the crap out of him when Vaughn got his hands on the butcher knife."

"I guess that story makes more sense than two men turning on each other," Selma remarked with a tiny smile.

"Well, we don't have to worry about that man anymore," Sky informed her aunt. "Once it gets around town that Vaughn is living here, I don't think we'll ever need to worry about that sort of thing again. I mean, the guy usually has a loaded gun close by. If he had had his gun that night, the intruder would probably have been killed."

"And I'd still have my jewelry," Selma muttered, then managed a smile. "Let's talk about something more cheerful."

"Like what?"

"Well, we could talk about the wedding," Selma announced, then grinned and placed her hand on Sky's. "Tell me you're having a big wedding. I'd love to help plan a wedding. Even if you wanted to have it here at the farm, it could still be amazing."

"We should probably wait for Vaughn to have that conversation," Sky informed her while hiding her uncomfortable smile. "Dixie is already pushing for a traditional wedding so she can be maid of honor. I'm probably outnumbered."

"Good," Selma announced cheerfully. "We'll discuss it at dinner." She took her dirty plate to the sink, then turned. "I'm going to take a long, hot bath before I get ready for my lunch engagement."

Sky stood and took her plate to the sink as well. "Where are you going for lunch?"

"A few of us ladies are going to Marcus's house to offer some interior decorating ideas for his front sitting room remodel," Selma announced while grinning. "It should be fun." She then shrugged. "Well, for us. I kind of feel bad for Marcus. He's going to be outnumbered five to one."

Sky contained her loathing at the mention of Marcus. "He'll survive," she remarked.

§

By the time Sky returned home from her ride around eleven o'clock, her aunt had already left. She decided to take a shower and then go to town for lunch at the diner. Perhaps she'd run into Dixie while on her lunch break. Once upstairs, she grabbed Vaughn's shirt that she'd slept in last night and headed into the bathroom, pulling the door partway closed. There was no need to close it all the way since she wasn't expecting anyone to return home. Although she didn't notice, her closet door slowly creaked open. Sky shed her clothes while letting the water run and then stepped inside the shower. After she washed her hair and body, she stood beneath the hot streams, enjoying the pulsating showerhead. She was off in her own world when she heard what sounded like the bathroom door creaking open. Sky's eyes opened, and she looked through the frosted glass to the partially open bathroom door. Was it her imagination, or did it seem to be open further than she remembered? Sky shut off the shower, grabbed her towel, and hastily wrapped it around her wet body. She opened the shower door, listened a moment, and heard a creak from deeper within the house.

Maybe she was paranoid, but she knew she hadn't locked the doors. No one in their town did, especially during the day, but she realized she probably should have after the last two break-ins. Sky barely dried off and was still wet as she slipped into Vaughn's large shirt that went halfway down her thighs. She cautiously left the bathroom and looked around her bedroom before heading into the upstairs hallway, listening for any unusual sounds. She heard another floorboard creak from downstairs. Sky quietly approached the hall closet, opened it, and removed the Browning pump-action shotgun from the back. She clutched the shotgun across her body in both hands and quietly approached the back stairs. As she made her way silently down the steps in her bare feet, she avoided each one that creaked, reaching the kitchen without incident.

Sky remained close to the bottom of the stairs and looked around the kitchen, but didn't see anything. She might have been just hearing things, or the house might have been groaning as it sometimes did, but she was a little on edge, and with good reason. When nothing moved or jumped out at her, she released a breath and lowered the shotgun. Just then, she heard a creak on the stairs behind her. Sky gasped and spun, but she was too late. Vaughn grabbed the shotgun, twisted it in such a way that she was forced to release it, and pulled her sharply against him with his free arm.

"Too slow," he teased while casting the shotgun onto the table with a clatter just before grabbing her behind the neck and kissing her somewhat aggressively.

Sky gasped with surprise and pushed against him, effectively breaking off the kiss but not releasing his hold. She stared at him as her heart pounded from the perceived threat. It actually took her a minute or longer to figure out it was just Vaughn.

"What the hell?" she cried out, then slammed her palms against his chest in fear more than anger. "You scared me half to death!"

"I'm sorry," he replied with a soft chuckle. "That wasn't my intention." Vaughn's free hand slid down her hip and easily slipped under the shirt covering her backside. His grin then increased. "Hmm, you're not wearing any panties." He then eyed the wet shirt clinging to her naked body. "And you're all wet. So sexy."

Sky attempted to relax in his arms, but he had given her a pretty decent scare. "I was in the shower," she informed him, conveying her irritation with him. "What are you doing home? Did you just come here to scare me to death?"

Vaughn chuckled while caressing her naked backside as he sized her up. "I decided to drop in for lunch," he announced somewhat seductively. "I'd heard you were *all* alone."

Sky considered the comment, then snorted a laugh while relaxing, placing her hands on his chest rather than pushing him away.

"You saw my Aunt Selma at Marcus's house and decided to pay me a visit, huh?" she remarked.

Vaughn again chuckled. "And Uncle Nash was going to the city so--" He swiftly hoisted her up onto the kitchen table and maneuvered between her legs, maintaining his closeness. "You could scream and no one would hear." Vaughn lunged for her neck and eagerly kissed her while running his hands along her hips and back beneath his shirt that she wore. "I guess I was too late to join you in the shower," he muttered between kisses while working his way down the neckline of the shirt.

Sky groaned and relaxed in his strong arms. "If you had surprised me in the shower, I probably would have dropped dead."

"Definitely don't want that," he mumbled while unbuttoning the first few buttons as he kissed his way down her chest.

"You aren't seriously going to defile me right here on the kitchen table, are you?"

"Oh, yeah," he groaned as he unbuckled his belt with one hand while holding her against him with the other, and his mouth moved along her cleavage. "I disarmed you fair and square. That makes you my prisoner for the next fifteen to twenty minutes."

Sky giggled softly, then groaned. "Do your worst, Vaughn."

Vaughn groaned and tackled her onto the table as she let out a playful scream.

Chapter 46

Sky remained slightly dizzy while leaning against the table for support as she watched Vaughn pull up his pants. Without finishing buckling his belt, he caught a glimpse of her stare and immediately pulled her into his arms. He held her against him while warmly kissing her neck.

"Why do you let me jump on you like that?" he gasped softly into her ear, although she could tell he was smiling.

"I like it when you go all primal," she remarked with a humored laugh. "I like satisfying you."

Vaughn groaned, then pulled back and met her gaze, not even attempting to hide his smile. "There are no words to describe how much I love you," he announced warmly.

Sky stared into his eyes and gently caressed his face. "Do you?" she asked softly while searching his cycs.

Vaughn snorted a laugh and just about crushed her in his arms. "I fell in love with you the first moment I saw you riding my horse in an evening dress," he remarked. "Instant rock hard boner."

Sky hid her smile and laughed.

"It's okay, you know," he announced somewhat seriously.

She immediately met his gaze, now curious what he meant.

"It's okay if you don't feel that way about me," Vaughn remarked. "I can wait. I'm extremely patient." His smile was warm and genuine. "I can wait as long as it takes."

Sky kissed him quickly but warmly on the lips, then searched his eyes, unable to control her grin. "I love you too," she replied softly before gently caressing his chest. "Actually, I'm happy you crashed into my life, even against my better judgment."

"If I worked here at the ranch, I'd bet I could meet you for lunch every day," he remarked while grinning as he caressed her body against his. "We could have little picnic lunches in quiet, secluded spots."

"Are you considering it?" she asked, enjoying the way he smiled at her.

"If I can work out a benefit package that includes you, I think I could take orders from Jerry," he remarked, then hesitated. "Although Moose and Ox would have to be part of the deal. We're kind of a package deal."

She gently patted his chest as her look turned serious. "Sorry," Sky announced. "I'm not having sex with all three of you. You're almost more than I can handle already."

Vaughn suddenly grinned and chuckled before kissing her quickly on the lips. "They'd both lose their peckers if they even look at you wrong," he informed her. "I don't share."

"I'm sure there's room for all three of you at the ranch," Sky replied cheerfully. "I'll talk to Uncle Nash. I'm sure we can work something out."

"Okay," he replied while grinning. "We'll sit down and talk about it with Uncle Nash." Vaughn glanced at the clock behind her and groaned. "But, right now, I still work for Marcus, and my executive lunch is just about over."

Sky kissed him quickly, then managed to pull out of his arms, although it was difficult.

"Why don't I make you a sandwich to go?" she asked. "Take what you want."

Vaughn again grabbed her and pulled her back into his arms. "Okay," he teased.

She laughed and once more wriggled out of his arms. "I'm being serious," she announced.

"I was, too," Vaughn remarked with a wink, then turned and pulled open the refrigerator door. "I can manage a sandwich." He pulled some lunchmeat from the drawer and grabbed a few condiments before turning to the kitchen table. He eyed the table, wrinkled his nose, and then turned to the counter. "Though you might want to sterilize the table."

Sky removed homemade bread from the breadbox and set it on the counter. "Are you sure you don't want me to make that for you?"

"No, I've got it," he replied, then briefly glanced at her. "If you really want to do me a favor, though, I need a lighter. Tony and his goons packed up my apartment when I was banished to gen-pop, and my silver lighter seemed to disappear. Big surprise. Moose is getting cranky that I keep borrowing his."

"There are matchbooks in the cupboard," she informed him, and reached for the cupboard in question.

"No, I need a lighter," he replied. "We're burning a bunch of shit this afternoon, and with the light wind, I'm less likely to burn myself with a lighter." He sighed with defeat. "Though it would be easier to beat the crap out of Tony and see if he has my lighter."

"I'd rather you didn't provoke him right now," she remarked. "Especially since we're trying to keep you alive." Sky hesitated, then patted his arm. "I know where there's a lighter." Her look then turned stern. "But you have to promise I'll get it back. It was my father's."

"I won't lose it, I promise," Vaughn announced, appearing pleased. "As long as you're okay with me borrowing it."

"Yeah, it's fine," she replied, waving him off. "It's in the gun safe in my parents' bedroom closet. I'll just be a minute."

"You're in luck, I have two," he teased, then took a bite from his sandwich.

§

Sky darted up the back stairs and hurried down the hall to her parents' old bedroom. She opened the door and hesitated for a moment before entering, taking a look around. It had been a while since she'd been in their room. Despite being cleaned semi-regularly, everything in the room remained as they had left it. Thankfully, the intruders barely touched her parents' old room. Maybe he, or they, realized there wouldn't be anything of value in there. The master bedroom was significantly larger than any of the other bedrooms, and it also featured a larger bathroom. A heavy, sculpted antique bedroom set was the crowning jewel of the room. There was a huge, walk-in closet, which housed the aforementioned gun vault. Sky finally crossed the room to the walk-in closet and entered. Immediately to the right was the large gun vault. She had to think about the combination for a moment, then swiftly opened it since it had been a while since she had been in it.

Once the safe was open, she found her father's gold-engraved lighter on the lower shelf near the handguns. Sky then hesitated and looked at a small wooden box on the floor of the gun vault. She didn't remember that being there before. She crouched down and removed the lid. The first thing she saw was the gaudy bracelet her aunt had bought for her. Her mind instantly reeled at the sight of the bracelet. Sky then looked at the other items in the box. She discovered her mother's diamond ring, her grandmother's pearl necklace, and all her aunt's jewelry scattered along the bottom of the box. Sky dropped the bracelet and picked up her mother's engagement ring. She hesitated only a moment before slipping it on her finger, then sprang up and ran from the room.

"Vaughn!" she cried out as she thundered down the hall toward the kitchen stairs. "Vaughn!"

Vaughn appeared halfway up the stairs with a semiautomatic in his hand and a look of concern on his face. Sky saw the gun and jumped back with a startled gasp.

"What happened?" Vaughn asked, ready to pounce. "What's wrong?"

She indicated that he should follow her. Vaughn ran up the steps after her and into her parents' bedroom. Sky hurried across the bedroom to the open safe and pointed at the wooden box inside. It was then she noticed her uncle's locked box on the lower shelf as well. Vaughn scanned the contents, looking bewildered, and shook his head.

"What am I looking at?" he finally asked while remaining on his guard.

"The jewelry," she insisted, then indicated the diamond ring on her right hand. "My mother's engagement ring. It's all of the jewelry that was stolen the other day." She indicated the open box. "It's all right there."

Vaughn took a moment to consider what she was telling him, then looked around the room, somewhat baffled.

"Are you telling me that all the jewelry that was stolen ended up in the gun vault in your parents' room?"

She nodded while attempting to control her breathing, racing heart, and trembling body. Vaughn looked around the room a moment while scratching his beard with the barrel of his gun as he attempted to sort it all out. He finally turned to face her with a strange, concerned look on his face.

"This is bad," Vaughn informed her. "This is *really* bad."

"If my aunt and uncle were behind the last break-in--?"

Vaughn nodded while frowning. "It means they also had something to do with the first break-in," he remarked and again sank into thought. "But your Uncle Nash wasn't the man I fought in the kitchen. He's much too short. The intruder was closer to my height, and he'd been injured. The man I injured would be limping, and I haven't seen any men with limps around town."

Sky shook her head and rubbed her chilled shoulders. "I can't believe they'd do something like this," she gasped. "To me." She couldn't take her eyes off his. "They *knew* I'd be home that weekend. Did they willfully send someone to rob the house knowing I'd be here alone?"

Vaughn pulled Sky into his arms and held her briefly, then moved away just as quickly, meeting her gaze.

"Does anyone else have the combination to that safe?" he asked. "Is it written down somewhere where anyone could find it?"

Sky frowned and shook her head. "No," she muttered. "The only people who have access to that combination are them and me."

Vaughn groaned and shook his head, still trying to sort it out in his head. "I get insurance fraud in bad times," he informed her. "But I was here when that man broke in." The look in his eyes was chilling. "I have no doubt you would have been in real danger had you been alone."

Sky slowly sat on the bed and stared blankly at the floor. "They weren't even concerned for my safety," she whispered, then looked back at him. "They've been like a mother and father to me. Would they really do that? Risk my life for a few pieces of jewelry and a few thousand dollars in cash?"

Vaughn tensed, then looked around and shook his head again. "I'm sorry, Sky." He closed the vault, spun the dial, and then extended his hand to her. "Come on," he ordered. "Let's go."

She placed her hand in his and quickly stood. "Go where?"

"You need to get dressed," he insisted while practically dragging her from the room. "And I need to make a few phone calls."

They headed down the hall to her bedroom so she could change.

Chapter 47

While Sky hurriedly dressed within the safety of her bedroom, Vaughn used her cell phone to call Ox at Marcus's estate.

"Hey, it's me," Vaughn announced into the phone while pacing Sky's room. "I need you to cover for me this afternoon. Something happened at Winchester Ranch, and I'm not leaving Sky alone." He paused near the window and looked outside while listening to his friend. "No, the two of you have to be there today, but stand by in case I need you."

Vaughn disconnected the call and returned the cell phone to her. Sky placed the phone in her pocket, rubbed her chilled arms, and stared at him.

"I'm not leaving you alone," Vaughn insisted. "While your aunt and uncle are gone, we need to come up with a plan of attack."

"Can we trust the sheriff?"

Vaughn frowned and considered the question. "We have no real proof of anything," he informed her. "Insurance fraud, sure, but there's no proof that the man who broke in the other weekend was the same one who broke in the other day. Your aunt is in good with Marcus, and you're no longer Marcus's virgin angel. It could go either way with Sheriff Burke, and I don't want to take that risk."

Vaughn paced her bedroom, then stopped and eyed her. "The jewelry and cash were already reported stolen," he reminded her. "I think you should take it and use it to get out from under your aunt and uncle's control. It's a bit of an inconvenience, but it's the safest bet."

Sky stared at him with a look of bewilderment. "Get out from under them?" she questioned the comment with some surprise.

"I know," he moaned and started pacing again. "You don't want to leave your horse, but we can work around that. I've been putting some money away for a while now. If the Jeep's in your name, we could probably get top dollar for it. We only really need one vehicle anyway. I'm sure we can financially make it work somehow and still keep both horses."

"What are you talking about?" Sky asked, now confused.

Vaughn drew a deep breath, met her gaze, and sighed. "We'll probably have to share an apartment with Moose and Ox for a while," he informed her. "At least, until we can figure out something more permanent, and I find another job."

Sky stared at him for a long moment, somewhat surprised by his assumptions, then shook her head. "Vaughn," she announced matter-of-factly. "The ranch is mine."

Vaughn eyed her with the same surprise. "What?" he asked, then shook his head. "That can't be. Marcus said your aunt and uncle owned the place."

"Well, he was mistaken," she informed him somewhat firmly as she folded her arms across her chest. "My parents left the ranch to me, their only child. It's being held in escrow until I turn twenty-five. My uncle runs the place, so I don't have to depend on the accountant to handle the day-to-day operations." She snorted a laugh and shook her head. "I'm not going anywhere."

Vaughn remained confused, then cocked his head somewhat suspiciously. "Is Marcus aware that you own the ranch?"

Sky shrugged with little interest. "It never came up in conversation," she replied. "I don't know what my aunt or uncle told him or anyone else, for that matter, but the ranch is one hundred percent mine."

Vaughn continued to stare at her, and she could almost see his mind working. His eyes suddenly narrowed.

"What happens to the ranch in the event of your death?" he demanded.

"I don't know," she replied, then shrugged. "I guess it's turned over to my closest living relative."

"Your aunt and uncle?"

Sky stared at him a moment and felt horror sweep over her. She slowly sat on her bed without taking her eyes off him.

"Are you suggesting they didn't hire that man to rob the house but *kill* me to get the ranch?" she gasped.

"How much is the ranch worth?" he asked.

Sky considered the question, then groaned and shut her eyes. "Son-of-a-bitch," she suddenly cried out while leaping from the bed and staring at him. "Millions."

Vaughn was slightly surprised by the response and raised his brows sharply. "That's a real problem," he remarked, then sank into thought. "And so is you getting married." He suddenly groaned and turned angry. "I'm their worst nightmare!"

"What do you mean?"

"If you get married and something happens to you, your husband inherits your estate, *not* them," he informed her. "They think we're getting married. Not only would I inherit instead of them, but I'm a major roadblock. It's a lot harder to kill you with me standing in the way." He shook his head. "Whether you own the ranch or not, we need to get you out of here. As long as they're your beneficiaries, your life is in danger."

"So I just need to change my will?" she insisted.

"Can you?" he asked. "I don't know enough about estates and trust funds." Vaughn considered it only a moment and shook his head. "I'm not risking it. You need to pack some things, grab all the cash from the gun vault, and we'll take a little trip for a few weeks. You can contact your accountant and a lawyer when we're safely away from here."

Sky considered what he was proposing, then nodded. "You're right. I think having time to think this through is a good thing," she replied. "If they're really worried about us getting married, they're certainly not going to waste much time finishing the job."

"My concern exactly," Vaughn muttered, then indicated her room. "Pack a bag and pick a destination. I'm going to run outside and grab a few things from my truck. You've got five minutes." He was about to leave, then hesitated. "I'm going to need my cell phone. I have contacts in there that we're going to need." He didn't wait for a response, but instead hurried from her bedroom.

Chapter 48

Immediately after Vaughn left her room, Sky bolted for her closet and wasted little time moving boxes. She placed the stepstool beneath the hidden ceiling panel, scaled the three steps, and pushed the panel aside. Sky then pulled the rope ladder down and swiftly climbed up it and into the secret compartment. She crawled across the small space and removed the envelope, which contained both cell phones. After she found Vaughn's cell phone, she was about to move back to the opening when she heard the creak of her bedroom door. Sky immediately tensed and listened for a moment. Had Vaughn returned for some reason? When he didn't call out, she felt panic sweep over her. What if it wasn't Vaughn at all? Sky shoved Vaughn's phone into her back pocket and looked around the stored items within the attic. She grabbed one of her father's bronze and marble rodeo trophies and held it by the top as she slid closer to the opening.

The light through the opening briefly disappeared, indicating someone stepped into the closet doorway. Sky coiled back, prepared to strike as she watched the opening, when she heard the familiar metallic creak of someone stepping onto the step stool. She listened as the person moved up to the second step. When she saw the top of a man's head appear, wearing a black cap, her heart nearly pounded from her chest. She momentarily froze, needing to be sure before she caved some man's head in. As the head rose through the opening, she could see he was clearly wearing a mask, and that was all she needed to know. As Sky swung downward with the marble trophy base, the man must have decided he was making a bad decision and descended from the opening. The statue clipped the man's head, but it was enough of a hit to knock him off the stepstool.

Sky needed to make a decision and make it quickly. She slid feet first through the opening, catching onto the rope ladder, and looked down at the closet floor. The man, dressed entirely in black and wearing a black mask, was kneeling on the floor while clutching his head. Sky clung to the rope and kicked out, striking him in the head. When he went down, she jumped to the floor, narrowly landing on him, and bolted from the closet. She slammed the closet door shut behind her, and for what it was worth, she grabbed the nearby chair, toppling it so it was wedged between the closet door and the dresser. There was a thump against the door, cracking the chair. She knew she only had precious seconds before he broke the chair and freed himself.

Sky bolted for her bed, hit the panel on the headboard, and grabbed the shotgun. As she spun with the weapon, the man again rammed the door, shattering the fragile, old chair. The intruder lunged from the closet and spun in time to see her with the sawed-off shotgun. As he cried out in horror and bolted for the open bedroom door, Sky pulled the trigger. There was a thunderous explosion as buckshot scattered across the room. The man bolted out the bedroom door, but a light spray of blood painting the doorframe told her she'd winged him.

§

Vaughn had just removed his duffel bag from the cab of his truck when he heard the shotgun blast from the second floor. He spun toward the house and saw a masked intruder standing on the porch, a revolver in his hand, prepared to shoot him in the back. Vaughn immediately threw himself to the ground and rolled under his truck, as a bullet struck the ground near where he had been standing. If it hadn't been for the shotgun blast, he would have been struck down where he stood. Despite limited room beneath the truck, Vaughn was able to draw his semiautomatic and aim it at the porch. Realizing he'd missed, the intruder was already retreating into the house. Vaughn rolled out from the opposite side under the truck and darted to the side of the house, knowing the man was probably standing just inside the doorway waiting to ambush him.

Vaughn ran around the side of the house while keeping low as he passed beneath the windows. Once he reached the patio, he hurried to the kitchen door and then cast his back alongside it. He drew a deep breath, then spun toward the door and kicked it in. He crouched low while aiming his weapon. There was no one waiting beyond the kitchen door. Vaughn entered the kitchen, looking around and listening for any sounds. The distinct sound of someone thundering down the back stairs was then heard. Vaughn darted across the kitchen, behind the table, so that he could watch both the kitchen entrance and the back stairs. As another masked intruder, bleeding from his shoulder, appeared at the bottom of the back stairs, Vaughn popped up with his weapon aimed.

"Freeze or I'll blow your fucking head off!" Vaughn shouted loud enough to rock the ceiling.

The intruder skidded to a stop and put his hands in the air, clearly startled by Vaughn and his weapon. Just then, the hallway door was thrown open, and the intruder who had been outside appeared in the doorway. Vaughn reacted the moment he heard the man bolting through the interior door and dove for cover as the intruder opened fire on him. Sky suddenly appeared at the bottom of the stairs with her shotgun already reloaded and in position. By the time the man at the interior kitchen door saw her, she was already squeezing the trigger. With a thunderous bang, the buckshot tore into his chest with enough force that he was thrown backward against the doorframe before falling face down onto the floor. The man at the bottom of the stairs had been just out of her line of sight, so she hadn't seen him, yet he was close enough to pull the shotgun from her hands.

Before she had even realized he'd disarmed her, he struck her in the shoulder with the stock and aimed the shotgun at her. Vaughn was suddenly alongside the intruder, his eyes cold as he pulled the trigger. The intruder's head snapped to the side from the close-range shot, and he dropped to the floor like a rag doll. Sky released the breath she'd been holding and placed her hand on her chest.

"Son-of-a-bitch!"

Vaughn leapt to the stairs alongside her and immediately checked her for injuries.

"Are you okay?" he gasped while looking over her as he brushed the hair back from her face.

She clutched his hand and nodded. "Yeah, just a little freaked out," Sky informed him. She then glanced across the kitchen at both dead men bleeding out on the floor. "Do you think it's them? The same guys who broke in before?"

"One way to find out," Vaughn informed her before snatching her discarded shotgun and handing it to her. "Stay here. Back to the wall. Eyes on all entrances."

Sky nodded and did as he instructed. Vaughn approached the closest man, the one he'd shot, and pulled his mask away from his face, but not past the massive gunshot wound to his temple. He frowned and shook his head.

"None of Marcus's men," he informed her, then moved to the side, giving Sky an unobstructed view of the dead man's partially exposed face. "Anyone you know?"

Horror swept over Sky as she stared at the dead man. "Uncle Carlton," she gasped, then immediately looked at the man she had shot by the hall entrance. The color immediately drained from her face, and her legs nearly buckled beneath her. She shook her head, not wanting to believe it, while choking on her words. "Selma has two brothers."

Vaughn looked at the second dead man across the kitchen and approached him. He lifted the man's mask, revealing his face, and then looked back at Sky for confirmation.

Sky stared at her Uncle Cyrus, the intruder she had shot in the chest. "That's her other brother," Sky informed him as her world seemed to implode. "My Uncle Cyrus."

Vaughn frowned and nodded. "Yeah, I'd seen him around town," he remarked, then hesitated. "And a regular at the Lake House Casino. Frequently visited the third floor too."

Sky sank against the wall by the stairs while staring at her dead Uncle Cyrus. She loved that man and always thought he loved her too. She pulled herself together, took a deep breath, and then looked at Vaughn.

"The third floor?"

"Female company by the hour," Vaughn explained as politely as possible. He then glanced back at Carlton. "Actually, I think I remember seeing that one with him once or twice."

"Uncle Carlton and Aunt Beth live in the city," Sky informed him while struggling with her emotions over the shocking revelation. She then lifted her head and met Vaughn's gaze. "Uncle Nash and Aunt Selma were with Uncle Cyrus visiting them in the city the weekend of the break-in. It must have been one of them." She then reconsidered. "Or both who broke in that Saturday night."

"Let's find out," Vaughn announced, then pulled Cyrus's pant leg up to his knee, but there weren't any marks. He then pulled up Cyrus's shirt to expose his ribs, revealing a mostly healed cut on his side. "There's one." Vaughn then approached Carlton and pulled up his pants leg to reveal a week-old, stitched wound on his calf. "And that's two." He straightened and looked at Sky. "I really thought there had only been one intruder that night, but I guess there were two."

"That almost certainly implicates my aunt and uncle," Sky informed him, now turning angry. "Those fucking bastards!" She shook her head as she leaned against the wall. "I can't believe they'd do that. I feel so stupid."

Vaughn approached her and pulled her into his arms, holding her close. "I'm sorry, Sky," he announced, then kissed the top of her head affectionately.

"They had to be in on it together, right?" she whispered. "My aunt and uncle must have paid her brothers to kill me for the ranch."

"It looks that way," Vaughn gently replied, then released her. "But there's one way to find out for sure." He gently cupped her face in his hand. "Want me to handle it myself?"

She stared into his eyes a moment, briefly considered it, and then shook her head. "No, I want to hear it for myself," she insisted, then held her breath. "What did you have in mind?"

Chapter 49

Sky paced a small section of the front porch not far from Vaughn while he leaned on the railing with her cell phone to his ear.

"You need to come back to the ranch right away, Nash," Vaughn announced into the phone in a serious yet solemn tone.

Nash's voice could be heard shouting through the cell phone. However, he sounded more upset than angry.

"Just get back here."

Despite the harsh words from Nash on the other end, Vaughn disconnected the call even though he was still talking. He then looked at Sky, who now turned to face him.

"He was already on his way home, so he'll be here in about thirty minutes, depending on how fast he drives," Vaughn informed her.

Sky groaned and raked trembling fingers through her mostly dry hair that she had never bothered to brush after her shower.

"I don't like this," she muttered.

"Neither do I," Vaughn remarked. "But it's the only way we'll know for certain."

She nodded, understanding his reasoning, then watched as Vaughn pressed another button and placed the cell phone to his ear. Sky couldn't keep herself from pacing once more.

"Selma," Vaughn announced into Sky's cell phone using the same drone voice he used on Nash. "You need to come back to the ranch right away." He paused and listened briefly. "Just get here." He then disconnected the call and placed the phone in his pocket. "Okay, your aunt will be here in less than ten minutes, I'm sure." He nodded to the door. "You'd better get inside."

Sky nodded, then quickly entered the house through the front door while Vaughn casually sat on the porch railing and patiently waited.

§

Moose patrolled the casino floor while carefully watching those gambling as well as those dealing cards. Although he maintained his usual demeanor, it was apparent that something was troubling him. Ox hurried across the floor and pulled Moose aside.

"Where the hell is Marcus?" Moose demanded while attempting to hide his emotions.

"Something came up," Ox muttered, looking around the gaming floor.

"What sort of something?" Moose demanded, now losing his patience.

"How the hell am I supposed to know?" Ox scoffed lowly. "We aren't exactly BFFs. He's the boss. He makes his own schedule. A carload of women arrived at his mansion this morning."

"Well, that explains a lot," Moose retorted.

"Older women," Ox informed him. "Not his usual Playboy bunny types. Sky's aunt was with them." He then considered his own words and snorted a laugh. "No wonder Vaughn took off for an early lunch. His girlfriend was home alone."

"Great," Moose muttered while secretly glancing at his watch for the third time. "Vaughn gets laid, and we get screwed."

Ox gave Moose a sideways glance. "Well, someone's grouchy this afternoon," he scoffed, then continued scanning the casino floor. "Vaughn was supposed to be here. If he felt it was important enough to ask me to cover for him, there had to be something far more important at the Winchester Ranch than just an afternoon delight."

Moose secretly glanced at his watch, then pretended to look around casually. "Shut up and get ready."

As if on command, there was a commotion at the main entrance. Moose and Ox barely looked at the door, showed no emotion, and had their hands in the air the very moment an entire SWAT team bolted through the door, swarming the whole casino floor. There were screams from women, particularly the prostitutes, and gasps from most of the men. A few even bolted for the back door. Moose and Ox remained motionless and without expression as they held their hands in the air.

"Vaughn owes us big time for this," Moose muttered, barely even acknowledging the chaos around them.

"I don't know what you're complaining about," Ox scoffed. "This was my day off. That prick owes me a beer."

Both men watched as Roscoe and Foster bolted for the back door. Roscoe made it out the door with one officer in pursuit, but Foster didn't make it ten feet before being tackled to the floor. Ox made a face from the excessively hard tackle.

"Oh, that's going to hurt in the morning," Ox muttered.

"Seriously," Moose remarked with his hands still in the air and shaking his head. "What's the point in running?"

"Without Marcus here, this raid was pointless," Ox insisted. "None of his men are going to roll over on him. His retirement plan sucks."

"Son-of-a-bitch," Moose groaned and threw his head back in anger, immediately concerning Ox.

"What?"

"I left my clothes in the dryer last night," Moose remarked. "Now, everything I own is going to be wrinkled until I rewash it."

"Nah," Ox casually replied, then shrugged. "You just need to put it on fluff for twenty minutes. Works every time."

Two officers approached Moose and Ox, shouting at them to turn around and place their hands on the nearby slot machines. Both men complied without saying a word. As the officer handcuffed Moose, he leaned over his shoulder.

"Damn it," the officer scoffed. "Where's Marcus? You said he'd be here."

"He was a no-show," Moose muttered, shifting his gaze around the room as everyone was being zip-tied or handcuffed.

"Well, that's great," the officer demanded. "A lot of good this little party will be without him."

"The casino security cameras will come up empty," Moose assured the officer. "But you'll find some good footage on a hidden camera behind the casino cage. There has to be something on there. I planted it a week ago."

"An entire week," the officer remarked, then nodded, seeming satisfied. "We'll check it out." He then indicated Ox with a slight nod. "Why the cast change? Where's your *other* partner in crime?"

"Getting laid," Moose muttered.

"You mean--?"

"No, not upstairs," Moose assured him, then smirked. "He has himself a legitimate girlfriend. She's got him whipped and everything."

"Convenient for him," the officer remarked. "You know the drill. We'll load the two of you into a squad car and release you once we're at the precinct."

"I'd appreciate that," Moose replied. "I have clothes in the dryer."

"Yeah," Ox remarked. "And the handcuffs are a little tight, too."

"Suck it up," the officer scoffed before ushering them toward the door.

Chapter 50

Only five minutes had passed since Vaughn had called Selma before her car was seen flying down the dirt driveway with Tony's truck directly behind it. That wasn't a good sign.

Vaughn groaned when he saw the familiar truck and straightened. "Great," he muttered.

Selma jumped out of the passenger side of her car while Marcus got out of the driver's side, urgently talking on his cell phone. Tony parked his truck next to the car and got out as well. Marcus seemed upset about his phone call, snapped at the person, and disconnected them. Tony eyed Marcus, silently questioning the call.

"The casino had several *visitors*," Marcus scoffed bitterly.

"And?"

"The house lost," Marcus replied while attempting to hold back his anger as they followed Selma.

Selma practically ran to the porch with a look of concern on her face, then saw the blood on Vaughn's shirt and immediately panicked.

"What happened?" Selma gasped.

"There was another break-in this afternoon," Vaughn informed her.

Marcus and Tony stared at the blood on his shirt, wearing matching looks of surprise and concern. Marcus's reaction was expected, but Tony, who rarely showed any emotion, seemed genuinely distressed. Selma gasped, but before she could ask any more questions, Vaughn turned and entered the house without further explanation. Selma looked back at Marcus, her eyes wide and full of horror, then hurried into the house after Vaughn. Marcus and Tony followed on her heels, keeping pace. Vaughn led them just far enough into the kitchen that only the closest sheet-covered body could be seen. Blood had already soaked through the sheet from the gaping chest wound.

"Oh, my God!" Selma cried out in horror. "Sky!" She immediately looked at Vaughn with a mix of sorrow and hate. "You killed her!" She spun and looked at Marcus, practically sobbing, and pointed at Vaughn. "He killed my niece!"

Marcus appeared somewhat baffled and again eyed the covered body. "I don't think that's Sky," he informed Selma. "Looks like a man."

Selma returned her attention to the dead person under the sheet and appeared to be searching for some explanation.

Vaughn studied Selma for a moment, then shook his head. "I mentioned a break-in, but I never mentioned Sky being home," he remarked. "Why would you assume she was dead?" He then pulled the sheet off the body, revealing her brother.

"Cyrus!" Selma gasped in genuine horror as she stared at her dead brother's buckshot-riddled chest. "Oh!"

She placed her hand over her mouth, unable to look away from the gruesome sight. She trembled slightly while staring at her brother, then lowered her hand and looked at Vaughn with something resembling shock.

"That's my brother," Selma gasped.

"Yes," Vaughn casually replied, then cocked his head. "Ironically, he has an old injury matching the one I gave to the intruder who broke into the house the other weekend." Vaughn's eyes narrowed as he glared at Selma. "I have to wonder how it was possible that Cyrus was breaking into your house while he was supposedly with you, visiting your other brother in the city."

Selma shook her head, then met Vaughn's gaze. "I can't believe he'd do something like that," she gasped, then looked back at Marcus. "I knew he was hard up for money. Gambling debts, you know. But I would never suspect he'd do something like this."

"Sure you would," Vaughn reported with little emotion. "Considering you're the one who put him up to it."

Selma shot a glare at Vaughn as her mouth fell open. "How dare you?" she cried out, clearly offended by the accusation.

"Before your brother showed up, Sky found all the stolen jewelry from this past Saturday's break-in within her father's gun vault," Vaughn informed her. "She said only three people have the combination to that safe."

There was an awkward pause as Selma's mind raced for something to say in her defense. Before she could think of a lie, Vaughn turned angry and accusing.

"You convinced your brothers to kill Sky so you could get your hands on the ranch," Vaughn lashed out. "Probably offered them some sort of split of the sale money."

"No," Selma gasped defensively, shaking her head as her eyes widened with horror. "I'd never do that. I'd never hurt Sky."

Marcus suddenly eyed Selma, surprised by what he'd just heard. "You told me the ranch belonged to you and Nash."

"Well, that's just the first of many lies," Vaughn scoffed to his employer, then looked back at Selma. "I suspect when Sky announced her engagement to me, you needed to act fast. If she married me, as her husband, I'd inherit her estate. You knew she'd be alone in the house this afternoon, so you called your brothers and told them they had to do it today before it was too late."

Selma continued to shake her head while staring at Vaughn in horror. "No, that's not true."

Vaughn then stood aside, allowing her a glimpse of the second sheet-covered body by the back stairs with a pool of blood on the floor surrounding the head.

"Well, I hate to break it to you, but before your other brother died," Vaughn remarked, then indicated the second body, "he confessed everything to me. I know you hired them to kill Sky."

Selma shook her head with her eyes wide in horror. "No, he didn't tell you that," she insisted, then looked at Marcus. "He's lying. He must have planned the whole thing." She then looked at Vaughn while turning angry and pointing at him. "You were here that night with Sky. You probably planned the whole thing. There weren't any intruders and certainly not my brothers. You made it all up to weasel your way into her bed and get her money." She again looked at Marcus. "He's a sick and twisted pervert. Handcuffing my niece to her bed with those pink fuzzy handcuffs!" She shot a look back at Vaughn, doubling down on her anger. "You're sick!"

Vaughn eyed her and cocked his head. "How did you know there were pink fuzzy handcuffs on the bedpost?" he asked.

Selma was set back by the question and stared at him, almost dumbfounded. "Sky told me," she insisted.

Vaughn shook his head. "No, she didn't," he replied. "She made me clean the house and stash everything because she said you would disapprove. She wouldn't have told you that. In fact, the only person who would have seen the handcuffs on her bedpost was the intruder I caught in her bedroom and then chased down the stairs. And, in the dim lighting, I doubt even he would have known the handcuffs were pink." Vaughn then raised his brows. "You found them, didn't you? When you were ransacking her room to make it look like a break-in. When you stole her jewelry."

"No," Selma insisted, although she was now less convincing, almost pouting. She shook her head, now concerned that her lies were falling apart. "Nash and I are well-off. I'd have no reason to kill Sky."

Nash stood in the hall doorway and stared at Selma with a stunned look on his face. "You wanted to kill my niece for her money?" Nash gasped, unable to take his eyes off her, and shook his head. "I can't believe you'd do that."

"I didn't," Selma gasped while looking at her husband and pleading with him. "It's not true."

"There was a time I may have believed you," Nash remarked, remaining stunned at what was unfolding. "But I just came from our new CPA after he audited our account. All our money, our life savings, and the money from the sale of our house in the city. It's all gone. You've been siphoning our savings over the last year or so. You've bankrupted us."

Selma stared at Nash for a long moment, then shook her head again. "No, I didn't do that," she insisted, searching for a credible lie. "It must have been Carlton. He must have stolen the money."

"You were bailing out your deadbeat brothers again," Nash insisted, turning stern. "Paying off their gambling debts."

"And their expensive women," Vaughn added, showing little emotion.

Marcus frowned, then sneered at Selma. "All while building up her own debt," he scoffed before looking at Nash. "She's been spending a lot of time in my casino, losing a lot of money. Surprisingly, she's always been able to pay the house back within a week."

Selma stared at Nash, Marcus, and Vaughn while attempting to come up with something convincing to talk her way out of it. Her look then turned angry and hateful, directing her hostility at Nash.

"Yeah, I spent *our* money," she shouted at her husband. "You made me move out here to the middle of nowhere. I gave up everything to support Sky and this godforsaken ranch. You said until she turned eighteen. Three years! Well, it's been eight long years! Now you want to wait another two? I hate this place! I hate the country, I hate the cattle, and I hate how you raised that girl like a boy! You uprooted my entire life so your sister's child could grow up wild and unladylike! I deserved much better than I've gotten these last eight years, so I took what I deserved!"

"You did it, didn't you?" Nash gasped with horror. His eyes then turned angry and hateful. "You tried to have my niece killed for her inheritance! My sister's daughter! My only living relative!"

"Yes," Selma screamed back at him. "I did it! I tried to make it work with her. I tried to make her into a lady, but she was too much like her father. She just wanted to play with horses and ride with the boys among those smelly cows. She's worth millions, and that's all she wanted to be?" Selma pointed demandingly at Nash. "And *you* encouraged it! It's because of you she sought out filth like him!" Selma gestured to Vaughn. "Filth like her father!"

"Okay," Vaughn muttered while cocking his head. "Filth is a bit strong."

"Shut up," Selma snarled at Vaughn. "She could have had Marcus, but you ruined that by corrupting her."

Vaughn shrugged. "I did do that," he remarked somewhat bluntly.

Marcus stared at Selma with surprise and shook his head. "You convinced your brothers to kill Sky?" he demanded. "You actually did that?"

"You should be thanking me," Selma launched back at Marcus. "She wasn't changing her mind about you. She was never going to be with you."

"I'd never condone killing her for that," Marcus snapped back in anger. "I'd never condone killing her for any reason! You don't kill people you love!"

Marcus's gun was suddenly in his hand and pointed at Selma's face. She saw the gun but barely had time to gasp as Marcus pulled the trigger without a second of hesitation. As the bullet tore into Selma's forehead, her head snapped back, and she dropped to the floor. Vaughn stared with surprise while Nash jumped back in horror. There was an oddly quiet moment as Marcus collected his emotions before looking at Vaughn and Nash. Vaughn tensed, as if half expecting to receive a bullet to the head himself. Marcus then lowered his weapon and replaced it in his shoulder holster.

"Selma was killed after she caught her brothers breaking into the house when they came to rob it," Marcus informed them in a stern tone. "That's the story." He eyed Nash, then Vaughn. "Everyone got that?"

Sky appeared at the bottom of the back stairs, clearly shocked while staring across the room at her dead aunt. Marcus, Tony, and Nash spotted Sky, but none commented. Vaughn drew a deep breath, groaned, and shook his head.

"Yeah, we got that," Vaughn muttered softly. "Did you get that?"

There was a brief moment of silence and confusion before the hall door and the patio door were suddenly thrown open by state police with their guns aimed at Marcus and Tony. Tony reacted swiftly and punched the closest officer before bolting from the kitchen for the hallway. One of the officers ran after Tony while Detective Garland approached Vaughn, eyed the dead woman, and shook his head.

"I honestly was not expecting that particular turn of events," Garland muttered, then looked back at Vaughn and nodded. "Yeah, we got all of it on tape, but my boss is not going to be very happy about all the wet stuff."

Marcus glared at Vaughn while the police officer had him over the table, handcuffing him. A second officer then removed Marcus's weapon from the hidden shoulder holster. As the first officer pulled Marcus back up, Marcus maintained his death glare at Vaughn.

"I won't forget this, Vaughn," Marcus informed him while somehow maintaining his composure. "You're going to pay for this."

"If you hadn't killed my brother, we wouldn't even be having this conversation," Vaughn casually informed him. "He'd be living in peace with Candy right now."

Marcus stared at him only a moment before quickly putting it together. "Sebastian--?" He snorted a laugh while shaking his head. "You might want to talk to Tony about that."

"Yeah, I know Tony pulled the trigger," Vaughn replied. "Candy witnessed the entire thing. But Tony was just the messenger. You were the one giving the orders."

There was a crackle from the first officer's utility belt. "The other one got away," the officer announced over the hand radio. "Blue pick-up truck that was parked out front. Officer in pursuit."

Marcus snorted a laugh, then grinned at Vaughn. "Looks like you'll be spending a lot of time looking over your shoulder the next few weeks," he announced somewhat gleefully. "Tony will be coming for you when you least expect it."

"And you'll be spending the rest of your life looking over your shoulder--" Vaughn replied, "--when Big Bubba visits you in the shower."

Marcus's expression dropped just enough to give Vaughn a little satisfaction before the officer guided his prisoner from the kitchen. Vaughn approached Sky, who clung to her Uncle Nash near the stairs. Nash met Vaughn's gaze, managed a tiny smile, and released his niece. Sky moved into Vaughn's arms and clung to him.

Chapter 51

Sky paced the front porch while Vaughn and Nash talked with Detective Garland and one of the state troopers. There were two ambulances and the coroner's van outside the house alongside several police vehicles. Some still had their emergency lights flashing, which didn't comfort Sky at all. Detective Garland was going to have enough paperwork to last him weeks while also explaining to his superiors how one man was able to escape, and the murderer was shot and killed by Marcus right under his nose. On the other hand, the detective got Marcus on an ironclad murder wrap, succeeding in arresting him where the FBI had failed during their raid. Sky couldn't relax while the coroner and some of his forensic pals spent what seemed like hours evaluating the scene in the kitchen.

When the medical examiner's staff and the ambulance crew finally wheeled out three stretchers containing body bags, Sky perked up. She was emotionally drained and just wanted a little peace and quiet. She really wanted to ride her horse, which always cleared her mind, but received flak from everyone. While Tony was still at large, they weren't letting Sky out of their sight until he was caught, killed, or confirmed far enough away to be no threat. Honestly, it was a bit silly. Tony had no reason to come after her. The entire incident had to do with Selma, Cyrus, and Carlton. Marcus pulled the trigger, inserting himself into the fray, which was the only reason he was arrested to begin with.

"We're going to keep a patrol car on Marcus's farm," Detective Garland informed Vaughn. "On the off chance that Tony tries to solicit help from some of the guys."

"But the feds arrested Roscoe and Foster at the casino," Vaughn reminded him. "They were really the only ones with enough loyalty to Tony to help him out."

"They got Foster," Garland corrected, then frowned. "Unfortunately, Roscoe got away." He snorted a tiny, uncomfortable laugh and shook his head. "Looks like none of us brought our A-game today."

"Speak for yourself," Vaughn remarked, instantly receiving a dirty look from Detective Garland. "My guys and I played our parts as promised."

Nash groaned and walked away, joining Sky on the far end of the porch. Before Garland could grumble his discontent with him, Vaughn moved on to the next subject.

"You want my advice?" Vaughn asked.

"Not really," Garland replied, hesitated, and then sighed. "What's your advice?"

"Have an undercover officer at the Lake House Bar," Vaughn announced. "Keep an eye out for Tony there."

"The bar and casino are closed until further notice," Garland informed him. "Per the FBI."

"You can still put a guy there," Vaughn insisted. "Tony is looking for an escape."

"In all reality, he's probably a hundred miles from here by now," Garland informed him.

Vaughn shook his head. "No, Tony's a killer and an asshole, but he's not stupid," he remarked. "If he wants to disappear for good, he needs to secure a bankroll."

"Sounds like he's stupid to me, if he does that," Garland replied. "He knows we'll be watching Marcus's farm."

"And that's why he'll go to the casino," Vaughn insisted.

"The feds cleaned the place out and locked it down," Garland reminded him. "There's no reason for him to go there."

"There's always a plan B, C, and D," Vaughn informed him. "I guarantee there's money hidden somewhere in that casino that the feds haven't found. Tony will be going for a secret stash."

"Are you sure about the casino?" Garland demanded.

"Not one hundred percent, no," Vaughn replied, then raised a brow. "But I can assure you that men in that position always have emergency funds stashed for a hasty getaway."

Detective Garland groaned and rubbed his eyes. "We're short on manpower," he remarked, then hesitated. "I need to keep a man here at the ranch and two at Marcus's estate. I can spare one officer on your whim."

"Are Moose and Ox out of cuffs?" Vaughn asked, now curious.

"The feds kept their deal and released them," Garland replied. "Why?"

"They can hang out in the casino for the night and keep an eye on things," Vaughn informed him. "In case Tony shows up."

"Fine," Garland replied with a sigh of defeat. "They're your boys, you get them there, and I'll ask the feds to let them inside."

Without hesitation, Vaughn removed his cell phone and pressed a button. "That won't be necessary," he replied. "They can find their own way in and not be seen doing it."

"Can I go now?" Detective Garland demanded, as if he were the one being detained.

Vaughn nodded. "Yeah, you're free to go," he replied and casually waved him off. "Just don't leave town."

When Vaughn flashed a smile, Detective Garland rolled his eyes and then headed off the porch, giving a general wave to Sky and Nash.

§

Eight o'clock that evening, Deputy Rhodes sat in his patrol car outside of Marcus's mansion. Although the outside lights lit up the mansion's exterior, the interior was mostly dark. Everything was locked up, and no one was home. It was the same at the barn, where a state trooper was also parked. The horses were tucked away in their stalls, but none of Marcus's employees, those who weren't arrested at the casino, were allowed to return to their quarters. Deputy Rhodes picked up his hand radio while groaning at the boring assignment.

"Deputy Rhodes checking in, Trooper Miller," Rhodes announced into his radio. "Still quiet, and now you can add 'dark' to that as well."

"Copy that," the trooper replied over his radio. "Quiet here, too. Did you know horses make a lot of noise in their stalls?"

Rhodes grinned and chuckled. "That's affirmative," he responded. "Go inside. You'll hear a lot more noise. Lots of pissing and pooping."

"I'll pass," the trooper replied with a chuckle. "Got to go myself."

"There's a bathroom just inside the big doors to the right," Deputy Rhodes informed him. "Across from the office."

"Copy that," the trooper replied. "Maintaining radio silence for the next two to three minutes. Over."

"Over and out, Trooper Miller," Rhodes announced, then looked at his watch.

A few minutes of complete silence passed, leaving Deputy Rhodes bored and tired when the faint sound of glass breaking caught him by surprise. He just about jumped from his car while placing his hand radio closer to his mouth.

"Trooper Miller," he announced into the radio. "I have breaking glass here at the mansion."

Rhodes listened for any sounds around the house for a moment, but didn't hear anything. Oddly enough, if a window had been broken, the alarm should have gone off. Rhodes hesitated, then looked at his hand radio with some bewilderment.

"Trooper Miller, do you copy?"

There was no response. Even if he was still in the bathroom, he shouldn't have turned his radio off. Rhodes returned the radio to his belt and removed his police revolver.

"Shit," Rhodes muttered softly and approached the house.

Before he reached the porch, a small light flashed within one of the lower rooms. Someone was definitely inside the house. Rhodes crept onto the porch while removing the house key he'd been given. He quietly unlocked the door and pushed it open, light from the vapor lights flooding the foyer. When nothing moved, he stepped into the foyer and glanced at the alarm control pad alongside the door. It was no longer set. Rhodes considered his options. He could trigger the alarm for backup and alert the intruder, giving him a chance to flee or investigate without backup and potentially catch him, but risk being ambushed. Deputy Rhodes crossed the foyer and looked down the massive grand hallway and then up the grand staircase, searching for any sign of the intruder. Just then, there was a disruption of the exterior lights, creating a shadow over him. Deputy Rhodes gasped and spun with his weapon aimed. Trooper Miller jumped, surprised by the gun pointed at him.

"Hey, it's me," Trooper Miller gasped, holding his gun in the air.

Rhodes lowered his weapon partway and indicated the house. "Someone broke a window and disabled the alarm."

Miller lowered his arms and gave him a slightly bewildered look. "Wouldn't breaking the window set off the alarm?" the trooper asked. "That doesn't really make sense."

Rhodes hesitated while staring at the trooper. "It does if whoever broke in had a key and disabled the alarm first," he remarked.

"Then why break a window?" Miller asked.

"To set a trap for us," Rhodes announced, then pulled the trooper against the nearby wall while taking shelter as well.

There was a thump from upstairs, alerting both officers to someone's presence. Both aimed their weapons and remained motionless for a moment.

"There's no way that wasn't intentional," Rhodes insisted. "Someone's messing with us."

"You mean, someone's hunting us," Miller muttered.

Both men eyed the alarm panel near the door, then exchanged looks. Rhodes nodded. Miller slid down the wall and pressed the panic button. Nothing happened.

"Oh, that is not good," Miller groaned, then reached for his hand radio. "Detective Garland, you copy?"

"Garland here," came the response.

"We have suspicious activity here at the mansion," Miller informed him. "The alarm has been disabled, and there's definitely someone inside. Second floor. Requesting backup."

Chapter 52

Within the dark, war-torn casino, it looked as if an earthquake had struck. The aftermath of the raid remained as it was, leaving chairs toppled, thousands of dollars' worth of casino chips scattered across the floor, poker cards everywhere, and full glasses still on the tables. The room was mostly dark, with only the glow of the red exit signs and the outside street light shining through the stained glass windows to brighten the room. Moose stood on the inside of the craps table wearing a green visor hat and holding the rattan dice stick while Ox stood at the far end of the table and shook the dice in his hand. He tossed the dice across the table, easily bouncing them off the backboard.

"Seven, front line winner!" Moose announced as he scooped up the dice with the stick, then slid them across the table to Ox. "Shooter wins again."

Moose then placed a small stack of chips alongside Ox's original bet. Ox gathered up the dice and shook them in one hand while studying the table.

"I'm hot tonight," Ox called out excitedly, then shook his head. "Why can't it go this way when it's real money?"

"Performance jitters?" Moose asked while cleverly raising his brows.

Ox glared at his friend. "You're real funny," he scoffed, then threw the dice across the table, striking the backboard, rolling another five and two.

"Seven, natural!" Moose called out.

Before he could scoop up the dice, they heard a car door slam. Both bolted across the casino floor, only a short distance to the rear exit door, and opened it just far enough to peer outside to the back of the building, not far from the lake. They watched as the unmarked police car sped away from its hidden position near the woods. Moose removed his radio and pressed the button.

"Moose to fuzz," he announced. "Where's the fire? Over."

"All units responding to a code three, ten-thirteen," the officer responded.

"Speak English, please," Moose scoffed into the radio.

"Officer needs immediate assistance," the officer replied more bluntly. "Break the speed limit and make some noise."

"Where?" Moose asked.

"Marcus's mansion," came the response.

Ox groaned and shook his head. "Sounds like we're missing all the excitement," he remarked, then headed back to the craps table. "Think anyone will miss this table? Maybe we can slide it into the back of my truck."

"You live in a studio apartment back home," Moose reminded him while reclaiming his dice stick. "Where the hell would you put it?"

"In my storage unit with my gun collection and my Rolling Stones albums," Ox casually replied with a shrug.

Moose eyed him with some surprise. "You have a storage unit for your guns?"

"Yeah," Ox replied, then appeared curious. "Don't you?"

"If I could afford a storage unit, I wouldn't be renting that postage-stamp-sized bedroom at my sister's house," Moose remarked. "I'd be living in the storage unit. I have to share a bathroom with my three psychotic little nephews, and one of them can't hit a porcelain target at close range."

"Yeah, well, neither can the guys working for Marcus," Ox reminded him.

"How do you have so much money?" Moose demanded while cocking his head. "We do the same jobs for the same pay."

"I don't pay ten thousand dollars a month for my mother to live in a luxury senior apartment building," Ox replied.

Moose glared at Ox, offended by the remark. "Where the hell else is she supposed to live?" he scoffed.

"Literally anywhere else," Ox informed him. "Hell, you could buy her a nice house for less than ten grand a month."

"But I wouldn't be there to take care of her," Moose informed him. "And my sister certainly isn't going to do it."

"Dude, your mother is only sixty years old," Ox proclaimed. "She's in better shape than I am. She can take care of herself."

Moose suddenly became alert and held up his hand, silencing Ox. Both listened a moment. They could hear someone on the metal fire stairs outside the emergency exit. Moose and Ox bolted in opposite directions, removing their guns from their hidden shoulder holsters, and hid behind banks of dark slot machines. A key was jiggled in the lock just before the door opened. Moose and Ox remained still and silent, wanting to see who was entering before assuming it was Tony. Instead of Tony, they saw Roscoe hurrying across the casino floor. Moose and Ox exchanged looks from their respective hiding places, signaling their intent to cover him. Before they could coordinate their attack, the interior door rattled and then opened. Both men ducked back into the darkness and remained hidden a moment longer.

Randy entered from the hallway and jumped when he saw Roscoe, who had now pulled his weapon, aiming it at him.

"Jesus," Randy cried out. "You scared the piss out of me, Roscoe! What took you so long?"

"I had to wait for the state trooper to fall asleep or take a piss," Roscoe announced. "Thankfully, Tony's little mansion invasion got them moving. I don't know how long they'll be gone on that witch hunt. Where's the money?"

Randy nodded across the room. "There's a compartment in the wall by the cage," he replied, then crossed the room to the opposite corner from Moose and Ox.

Roscoe followed the bartender to the far side of the casino cage, putting them out of Moose and Ox's line of sight. Moose darted past the slot machines and to the opposite end of the casino cage, crouching low to avoid being seen. Ox watched the bartender open the panel, revealing a small safe. He opened the safe and pulled out two locked bags filled with money. Roscoe removed an expensive leather laptop briefcase from his shoulder and opened it.

"How much is in there?" Roscoe asked while the bartender stuffed the money bags into the soft briefcase.

"Uh, about two hundred thousand, give or take," Randy replied.

"That's not a lot," Roscoe muttered.

"It's enough to get you and Tony someplace far away and tropical," Randy scoffed with some annoyance. "The more remote, the cheaper the living and fewer questions asked."

"It'll have to do," Roscoe replied with a sigh.

"Where is Tony?" Randy asked.

"Off doing his usual stupid Tony things," Roscoe scoffed. "And if he's not at the rendezvous at the agreed-upon time, I'm out of here with or without him."

"Don't let him hear you say that," Randy muttered while sliding the hidden panel back in place. "He'll find you and kill you for sure."

"Yeah, well, it's his petty need for revenge that's going to get him caught or killed," Roscoe scoffed with noted disgust. "Vaughn's not an easy target like Hammond was."

Moose and Ox exchanged concerned looks. Was Tony going after Vaughn? They had to warn him!

"Hammond?" Randy asked with surprise. "I thought that was a riding accident."

Roscoe snorted a laugh in mild disgust. "Funny how so many people who disagree with Tony have accidents, don't you think?" he remarked. "Foster and I found the baseball bat he used to beat Hammond to death. Even nailed a horseshoe to it just to make it look believable. Poor guy looked like roadkill after he was through with him."

"What did some horse trainer do to deserve such a brutal death?" Randy asked, almost horrified.

"After the Fourth of July party, he complained to Marcus about Tony's *other* dealings," Roscoe replied. "I tried to talk Hammond out of crossing Tony, but he wouldn't listen. Marcus reprimanded Tony for it, and he lost his cushy loft apartment to Vaughn."

"And that was enough to set off Tony?" Randy gasped.

"Doesn't take much," Roscoe replied, then snorted a soft laugh. "Honestly, I'm surprised Sky's lived as long as she has. With the way she talks to him, I thought he would have killed her a long time ago."

"Sky's a completely different story. Tony knows better," Randy remarked. "She's the rancher's daughter, you know."

Roscoe eyed him, somewhat puzzled. "Someday, I'd like to know why they call her that, and why it actually seems important to folks around here."

"You don't have time for that story," Randy insisted. "Let's just say, if her father were alive today, Tony wouldn't be."

Moose signaled Ox to take the back wall toward the interior exit so he could cut them off, while Moose darted behind one of the blackjack tables. As Roscoe and the bartender headed for the hallway entrance, Moose kept low in the table pit area, hiding behind various tables while following them. Before the two men reached the door, Ox stepped out from behind the last row of slot machines with his weapon aimed.

"I wouldn't mind hearing the story," Ox announced, startling both men.

Moose straightened from behind the roulette table, his gun aimed as well. "I think we all have time," he announced.

Randy placed his hands in the air with a defeated look on his face. Without warning, Roscoe darted to the opposite side of the room and behind a bank of slot machines, leaving the bartender stunned, where he now stood alone.

"Turn yourself in now, Roscoe," Moose announced while scanning the dark rows of slot machines.

A gunshot rang out and struck the table near Moose. He gasped and ducked behind the roulette table. When Ox shot at Roscoe near the bank of slot machines, Randy took advantage of the situation and leapt to the floor, rolling out of the way. Ox's shot ricocheted off the machine and nearly struck Moose, who glared at his friend.

"Sorry, my bad," Ox announced to Moose.

"Come on out, Roscoe," Moose again called out. "You're not getting far, and we're not letting you take that money to Tony. It's him we want, not you."

"Yeah, Moose," Roscoe called out from the darkness of the slot machines. "I'm not that stupid!"

"The feds only want Marcus, and the detective is only interested in Tony," Moose again called out. "You can make a deal with them." He hesitated. "Just like the deal Foster's making."

"Foster's cutting a deal?" Roscoe asked, sounding surprised.

"As we speak," Moose easily lied. "Of course, if you kill anyone while helping Tony escape, there won't be any deals. Stop letting Tony bully you into making poor decisions."

"How about a counteroffer?" Roscoe called out.

"I'm listening."

"You let me walk out of here, with the money, and I'll tell you where to find Tony," Roscoe announced. "Yeah, that deal works better for me and my social life. Prison sounds too, well, confining."

"Counter counteroffer," Moose responded. "You come out now, and I won't shoot you."

"I'll take my chances, but thanks," Roscoe replied, then fired another round at the roulette table.

"Ox!" Moose called out.

"Yep!"

"You got this?"

"Yep," Ox replied.

Roscoe was moderately confused by the coded conversation and attempted to peek around the corner of the slot machine to see what Ox was up to, but it was too dark. Moose fired a shot that nearly clipped Roscoe's ear. He leapt back to safety and touched his slightly singed hair. That was too close! Roscoe took a step back, deeper in the aisle, and suddenly struck something. When he spun around, he saw Ox towering over him, only inches away. Ox grabbed his wrist, slamming his hand with the gun against the slot machine, and forced him to drop the weapon. Despite being disarmed, Ox grabbed Roscoe by the throat and his thigh, hoisted him high into the air, and launched him across the open aisle. Roscoe crashed onto a blackjack table, collapsing it like a folding table, and crashed to the floor. Neither man seemed to care that the bartender bolted from the room. They hadn't been after him. Moose and Ox both approached Roscoe, where he writhed in pain among the busted blackjack table.

Roscoe looked up at Moose and Ox standing over him and groaned softly. "I'm ready to make a deal now."

Chapter 53

Winchester Ranch. The vapor light above the barn kept the large area around the house and barn brightly lit. A police cruiser was parked between the two buildings, with an officer positioned inside the vehicle, keeping the area safe until Tony was in custody or no longer a threat. Sky left the house through the front door and headed for the porch steps, when Vaughn ran out of the house after her. He cut her off on the steps and stood unusually close.

"Where are you going?" he demanded.

"Out to see my horse," Sky insisted with an impatient groan. "I miss him."

"And we discussed you not going anywhere alone for the next few days," Vaughn reminded her. "Tony is out there somewhere, and there's no telling if he's looking for revenge."

"If Tony wanted revenge against me, he would have done it a long time ago," Sky reminded him.

"I wasn't talking about revenge against you," Vaughn informed her. "Revenge against me. And revenge against me would be him harming you." His look turned commanding. "You don't go anywhere alone."

Sky frowned while shifting uncomfortably. "I understand your concern," she replied with a deep sigh, then rubbed her chilled arms. "It's been a long, horrible day. I'm just going a little stir crazy being stuck in the house. I can't stomach going into the kitchen, even after the thorough cleaning."

"And with good reason," Vaughn replied.

"I just want to check on the horses," Sky insisted. "It'd make me feel better."

"Jerry and Tom can check on the horses," Vaughn informed her, and gently guided her back into the house.

When they entered the house, they saw Jerry, Tom, and Nash standing in the hallway before the open gun safe, loading rifles.

"I want this house secured," Nash instructed the men. "The two of you need to alert the officer in the patrol car, then sweep the barn. Remain vigilant."

Jerry and Tom took their rifles and hurried out the front door. Vaughn and Sky watched with surprise and bewilderment.

"What's going on?" Vaughn asked.

"You left your phone on the coffee table," Nash informed him as he cocked the rifle he held in his hands. "Your friend, Moose, called. They have reason to believe Tony might be coming this way to kill you. The rest of the troopers and Deputy Rhodes are at Marcus's mansion in a shootout with some of his men who were looting the place. Tony may or may not be among them."

Vaughn groaned and held out his hand. Nash handed him the rifle without hesitation, then gave Sky a handgun, before grabbing his own weapon.

"We need to lock the house down," Nash insisted. "Sky and I will take the second floor." He then eyed Vaughn. "You can secure this floor."

Vaughn seemed hesitant. "Maybe I should stay with Sky," he remarked.

Nash suddenly glared at Vaughn and cocked his head. "Something you'd like to say?" he demanded. "You think I had something to do with Selma's plot to kill my niece?"

Vaughn seemed conflicted but didn't respond to Nash's angry questions.

"It's okay, Vaughn," Sky announced, then glanced at her uncle. "I trust Uncle Nash."

Vaughn found it difficult to take his eyes off Sky even as she headed up the stairs with her uncle bringing up the rear. Nash looked back at Vaughn with a sneer but didn't comment.

§

Jerry and Tom patrolled the barn aisle, checking in each of the empty horse stalls. Leaving the horses outside tonight seemed like a good idea. If something did happen, the horses wouldn't be defenseless while confined to their stalls. The ground floor was secure, but they still needed to check the loft, which was a little more dangerous. Anyone poking their head into the loft from the ladder risked having it blown off. Tom eyed the ladder and the great unknown at its top before motioning for Jerry to head up.

"You'd better get up there," Tom insisted.

Jerry eyed Tom while cocking his head. "Me? Why me?"

"Because I have seniority," Tom reminded him.

"You don't have seniority," Jerry scoffed. "I'm the ranch foreman, and I've been working here longer than you have. How can you possibly believe you have seniority?"

"Because," Tom replied. "I'm older." He then felt his shoulder while rotating it and cringing. "And I have terrible arthritis."

"Arthritis in the head," Jerry muttered before slinging his rifle over his shoulder and removing his revolver.

Jerry drew a deep, tense breath, then slowly and quietly scaled the ladder. Before reaching the top, he removed his cowboy hat and extended it above the hay loft floor. When no shots were fired, he continued his climb. Jerry aimed his weapon as he climbed from the ladder and scanned the hay loft. Although the two hundred bales of hay were packed close together, there was still room for someone to be hiding among them. He approached the neatly stacked hay and peered around the last bale. The opening at the end was empty. Jerry was relieved, then continued his sweep. The entire loft appeared clear, and nothing was disturbed.

"Clear!" Jerry called down as he approached the ladder.

He looked down before climbing onto the ladder and suddenly hesitated. Tom wasn't there.

"Tom?" Jerry called out, but there was no response.

Jerry looked around the first floor from his position on the ladder, but could only see the open aisle. None of the stalls, the wash stall, or the tack room was visible from his elevated vantage point.

"Shit," Jerry muttered, momentarily concerned about his safety as well as that of his friend.

He quietly scaled the ladder while keeping watch behind him until he reached the halfway point, then jumped the rest of the way, crouching low as soon as his feet hit the ground. Jerry moved against the nearby stall and scanned the barn interior. There were too many blind spots. He was exposed no matter what he did. Jerry kept his gun securely in his hand as he removed his cell phone. He pressed Tom's name and listened. Tom's phone was heard faintly ringing from one of the nearby stalls. Jerry tensed, knowing which direction he needed to go, and then disconnected the call. He immediately texted Nash regarding the barn situation. Before getting a response, Jerry silenced his phone. As he edged his way along the stalls, while keeping low, his cell phone vibrated in his hand. He looked at the caller ID, which displayed an unfamiliar number. On the second vibration, it stopped. There was little doubt it was the person who attacked Tom, attempting to use the same trick to get his location through his ringing phone.

Jerry replaced his phone in his jacket pocket and moved closer to the stall where Tom's phone had been heard within. He checked the area surrounding him before grabbing the stall door and throwing it open. He aimed his weapon inside and immediately saw Tom, unconscious and bleeding from his head, within the wood shavings on the stall floor. Jerry slipped into the stall and then hurried to his friend. He easily woke Tom, who seemed groggy as he looked around with disorientation.

"What happened?" Tom demanded.

"You were ambushed," Jerry informed him, then texted Nash about their situation.

Nash immediately texted him back, assuring him they'd be out to assist them. Jerry returned his phone to his pocket and helped Tom sit up within the stall. Unfortunately, his rifle was missing, but his attacker didn't bother looking for his handgun. It took Tom a moment or two to stand on his own and hold his gun.

"I'm okay," Tom insisted, then dabbed the blood on his temple, looked at it, and sneered. "Just a little pissed off."

"At least you're alive," Jerry insisted, then looked around the stall. "We need to get you back to the house, but we have to make sure the stalls are clear so we're not ambushed on our way out."

Tom nodded, instantly regretting the action. They left the stall, keeping their backs to each other, and slowly made their way down the aisle, checking for any signs of their attacker. They made it to the tack room with no sign of anyone. It was obvious they were, once again, alone in the barn. Jerry opened the barn door just far enough to peer outside, the vapor light giving ample lighting to see the entire area between the house and barn. His eyes then fell upon the police cruiser parked in the middle. The driver's side door was open with what appeared to be blood on the window, but the officer was gone.

"Oh, that's not good," Jerry muttered, then looked back at Tom, who again dabbed his finger in the blood on his temple.

"Jesus, I haven't bled this much since that stampede," Tom scoffed.

"We've got bigger problems," Jerry insisted and indicated the world beyond the barn door. "The police officer is missing, and there's blood on the cruiser window."

Tom suddenly chuckled, seeming amused. "Hey, do you remember that time we were branding calves, and I accidentally branded Colten's ass?" He laughed almost to the point of tears while Jerry gave him a slightly stunned look. "Singed his jeans clean through." His look turned serious. "To this day, he still has the Winchester brand on his ass."

Jerry continued staring at Tom. "Are you okay?" he asked.

"Of course," Tom replied a little too cheerfully. "Never better." He again touched the blood on his temple, then looked up at the ceiling, turning serious. "Damned roof must be leaking."

"We'd better get you to the house," Jerry muttered. "Get your head checked out."

"You know what your problem is?" Tom demanded, pointing his weapon at Jerry as if it were his finger. "You're wound too tight."

Jerry snatched the gun from Tom and gave him a stern look. "You have a concussion," he announced. "You should sit down before you fall down."

"What'd I tell you?" Tom demanded, now pointing his finger at him. "Wound too tight!" His attention immediately shifted to something in the corner of the wash stall. "Is that my rifle?"

"Do you think you can make it to the house?" Jerry asked.

Tom grabbed the nearby rifle, looked it over, and suddenly grinned. "It is! It's my rifle!"

"Tom," Jerry scolded a little louder, finally getting his friend's undivided attention. "Can you make it to the house?"

"Sure, I can. Five bucks says I can make it to the porch before you," Tom insisted. "On the count of three."

"How about we just walk?" Jerry remarked, then pulled the barn door open a little further.

A rifle blast was heard less than a second before the barn door splintered near Jerry's head. Jerry gasped and was about to duck when Tom tackled him to the barn aisle.

"We're under attack!" Tom shouted while using his body as a shield to cover Jerry. "Run, Jerry! I'll cover you!"

Jerry easily shoved Tom off him and kicked the barn door closed as a second shot was heard, echoing and splintering the wood. Jerry panted while staring at the closed door with two fresh bullet holes in it, then looked at Tom, who was now on his back. He again touched the blood on his temple, eyed the blood, and suddenly cried out.

"Christ! I've been hit!" Tom groaned and writhed around on the floor. "I knew this day was coming! Momma, I'm coming home!"

Chapter 54

Vaughn stood in the living room alongside the larger window and peered out at the barn while clutching his rifle. He could see the vacant police cruiser with its door standing open, with no sign of the officer or the shooter. Thundering footfalls were heard on the stairs before Nash and Sky appeared at the bottom of the steps.

"Stay down," Vaughn called out to them. "Turn those lights out!"

Nash and Sky kept close to the floor while heading for the few lights that were still on, shutting them off at the wall switch.

"Who's firing out there?" Nash asked while nervously clutching his gun.

"Your guess is as good as mine," Vaughn muttered while keeping his attention outside.

Nash's phone dinged with a new text message. He looked at his phone, then glanced across the room to Vaughn next to the window.

"Jerry said the shooting came from behind the squad car," Nash announced. "The officer is missing, but there's blood. Tom has a concussion and is out of his mind."

"What do we do?" Sky asked.

"I need someone to keep watch on that squad car out there," Vaughn insisted.

Nash darted to the side of the window with Vaughn.

"Keep your head down and stay out of his sight," Vaughn announced. "If you see anything, call Jerry right away."

"What are you going to do?" Nash asked as Vaughn moved away from the window.

Vaughn indicated the ceiling with a nod. "I'm going to the attic, taking a sniper's position," he replied, then held up his rifle. "I might be able to see the shooter and take him out."

As Vaughn approached Sky and the stairs, she eyed him with concern. "What do you want me to do?" she asked.

Vaughn kissed her quickly on the lips. "Keep your head down," he replied, then ran up the stairs, taking them two at a time.

Sky clutched her gun and moved into the living room archway so she could watch her uncle, the front door, and the main staircase. She could hear Vaughn's heavy footfalls running along the second floor hallway practically above her head.

"Son-of-a-bitch!" Nash suddenly cried out and threw his back beside the window as several shots were fired. The shots penetrated the large window, leaving holes without shattering the thick glass. The spontaneous attack and flurry of shots momentarily paralyzed Nash before horror swept over him. "Hell, no!"

Sky was baffled by her uncle's panic.

Nash suddenly ran for her while yelling, "Get down! Get down!"

Her first instinct was to stare at her panicking uncle, but then she focused her attention on the main entrance, almost certain someone must have been rushing the door while the shooter covered him. Nash nearly plowed into Sky, shoving her across the hall and to the stairs. In that instance, she briefly saw someone in the back hallway near the kitchen just before she crashed into the stairway banister. It was Tony! Sky grabbed the banister, catching her balance, and spun just in time to see Nash leap in front of her, aiming his weapon at Tony. Tony's gun fired first, winging Nash in the shoulder with an explosion of blood and dropping him to the floor. Sky gasped in horror, frightened for her uncle, as her hand subconsciously gripped the revolver a little tighter. Nash floundered while attempting to sit up and aiming his gun at Tony.

"Run, Sky!" Nash cried out as he fired two shots down the hallway.

Hearing his words, Sky recovered from her shock and bolted up the first few steps when she heard Tony return fire. Sky looked back in time to see her uncle clutch the side of his head, blood seeping between his fingers, as he hit the floor. Sky screamed in horror only a second before Tony came into view, possibly to finish off Nash. Sky cried out in an explosion of emotions and haphazardly fired two shots at Tony, missing him with both, before bolting up the stairs and to safety. As Sky thundered up the stairs, she could hear Tony on the steps not far behind her. Her heart was pounding, knowing he could shoot at her any second, and effectively ending her life with a single bullet to the back.

"Vaughn!" she screamed several times as she made her way to the second floor. "Vaughn!"

Sky ran down the hall for the attic stairs, hearing the thumping of Tony's boots on the hall floor getting closer. When she reached the attic stairs, Tony grabbed her ponytail, harshly yanking her back by her hair. He forcefully slung her across the hallway and into the wall near her bedroom doorway. Sky was momentarily stunned by the solid hit, losing her gun in the process, then slowly straightened while staring at the angry man with his gun aimed at her. At that moment, Sky had never been so frightened. She never believed Tony capable of killing her, but she was now confident he would. He shot Uncle Nash, who was probably dead, and he would almost certainly kill Vaughn. Something inside her suddenly snapped. Possibly the switch from flight to fight had been activated. Now, she was angry.

"Where's Vaughn?" Tony snarled.

Sky felt her adrenaline spiking, preparing for what she had to do and her possible death as a result. Just when she was about to react, the barrel of a semi-automatic was pressed against Tony's temple from the partially open attic door.

"Right here," Vaughn snarled.

Tony cast a sideways glance at Vaughn, standing in the attic doorway with the gun aimed at his head, and frowned.

"Drop the gun," Vaughn ordered. "Hands in the air."

Sky was instantly relieved, releasing the breath she had been holding. Tony frowned and tossed his gun to the floor, possibly accepting defeat, but that would have been too easy. Tony suddenly spun and knocked the weapon from Vaughn's hand. His victory was short-lived. Before he could take advantage of having disarmed the man, Vaughn punched him twice in the face, nearly driving him to his knees. As he jumped the last two steps from the attic stairway, Vaughn kicked Tony in the chest for good measure. Surprisingly, Tony came back to life and spun on his knees, throwing his fist at Vaughn's crotch. Vaughn subconsciously protected his soft target with a 'twist and cover' defensive maneuver, every man's go-to response to a groin hit. Tony's fist struck Vaughn in the thigh instead, causing a fair amount of pain, but not enough to disable him. Before Vaughn had a chance to recover and swing back, Tony leapt up from his crouched position and tackled Vaughn to the floor. Both men hit the floor with a loud thump and immediately threw punches.

Sky watched in horror as the two powerful men rolled around the floor, punching each other with anger and aggression. She knew she had to do something if Tony managed to overpower Vaughn. She looked around the floor and saw her discarded revolver. Sky practically pounced on her gun, grabbed it, and sprang back to her feet, aiming the weapon.

"Give it up, Tony!" Sky cried out. "Or I'll shoot you!"

She wasn't exactly surprised when her threat was ignored entirely. Tony shoved Vaughn off him and directly into Sky, knocking them both against the wall and crashing to the floor. Tony reclaimed his semiautomatic and aimed it at them. Vaughn was about to scramble to his feet when he saw Tony now had the gun aimed at Sky. Both were momentarily frozen, not willing to gamble on Tony's state of mind. He was going to pull the trigger, but neither was sure exactly when he would do it. Vaughn lowered himself to one knee in such a fashion that his body shielded Sky a little better. She knew Vaughn would take the bullet meant for her, and all she could think about was the horror of watching him die at Tony's hand. She'd been through too much with Vaughn just to watch him die.

"This is between you and me, Vaughn," Tony snarled loudly. "Don't involve Sky, and she won't get hurt."

It was then that Sky felt the discarded gun poking against her hip, where she half sat on it. Her heart was racing as she ran several scenarios and their potential outcomes through her mind.

"Fine," Vaughn announced. "Let her go then."

"Do you think I'm stupid?" Tony snarled.

"Well--?" Vaughn began.

"Shut up," Tony ordered, turning angry. "You've been a thorn in my fucking side since day one. I've dreamt about the day I would finally be allowed to kill you."

"Right back at you, Tony," Vaughn casually replied.

With Vaughn distracting Tony and blocking her from his view, Sky gently pulled the revolver free from beneath her hip.

"I told you to stay away from her," Tony shouted in anger. "But you didn't listen."

Sky slowly slipped the gun down the back of her pants, attempting to make as little movement as possible.

Tony suddenly glared at her past Vaughn. "Get your hands up, Sky," he snarled. "Don't make me shoot you."

Sky slowly put her hands in the air without taking her eyes off Tony and his weapon aimed at her. "You're going to anyway," she scoffed while slowly moving out from behind Vaughn.

"Sky, don't provoke the man with the gun," Vaughn muttered sternly. "Stay behind me."

"Stop moving," Tony shouted in anger while aggressively waving his weapon at her. "I *don't* want to kill you."

"Why not? My own aunt wanted me dead. I would have thought you'd be first in line," she remarked while moving onto her knees so she was now partially blocking Vaughn. "You've hated me for years. You certainly hated me enough to sleep with my best friend."

When Tony clenched his jaw, Sky knew she'd clearly struck a nerve. Vaughn was about to threaten her into silence when he saw the gun sticking out of her pants, almost directly in front of his right hand, which was now concealed by her body. If they were going to die, at least Vaughn would have a sporting chance to defend them.

"I didn't hate you," Tony snarled, revealing his bitterness. "I never hated you! And you broke up with me, remember?"

Vaughn slowly lowered his right arm, which was blocked from Tony's view, and placed his hand on the gun grip.

"With good reason," she snarled back. "From the moment you started working for Marcus, you turned into someone I didn't recognize."

"Marcus was paying more than I ever could have made anywhere else in this Godforsaken town," Tony launched hotly. "You refused to see it. Everything I did, I did for us!"

"Screwing Ruby was for 'us'?" Sky shot back, almost purposely engaging his venomous side, hoping to keep him distracted and perhaps buy Vaughn a little time.

"No, that was pure revenge," Tony scoffed as his eyes narrowed. "When I heard you were going to dump me, I decided to hurt you first. What better revenge than pressuring your best friend into sleeping with me? You dump me; I implode your friendship." He shrugged while sneering. "I get it. I wasn't good enough for you, and I could have lived with that." Tony's anger then increased as he turned his weapon on Vaughn, his eyes narrowing. "But then you turn around and fuck this asshole?"

"Oh, boy," Vaughn muttered while gently freeing the weapon from the back of Sky's pants.

"Is that why you hate him so much?" Sky suddenly demanded, drawing Tony's attention away from

Vaughn and back to her. "Because I gave him what I'd never give you?"

"Fuck, yeah," Tony snarled while shifting his gaze back on Vaughn as his finger tightened on the trigger.

"Down!" Vaughn shouted.

Sky immediately cast herself to the floor, shielding herself. Tony pulled the trigger, but Vaughn fired first, the large caliber slug ripping through Tony's chest with an expulsion of blood. Tony appeared surprised by the reversal, allowing the gun to fall from his hand, then gasped while sinking to his knees. He managed to clutch his bleeding chest for a moment while still staring at Vaughn.

"That was for my brother, Sebastian," Vaughn scoffed.

Tony's eyes widened a moment, realizing who Vaughn was and why he had really been there, before collapsing to the floor. Sky lowered her arms from over her head and slowly sat up without taking her eyes off Tony, now lying dead, as his blood quickly spread across the hall floor. She released the breath she'd been holding, then looked back at Vaughn as he finally lowered the gun and met her gaze. Sky gasped with relief and moved into his arms. He held her with a constricting, python-like grip while trembling slightly, having almost lost her. Vaughn finally loosened his grip and met her gaze.

"Were you trying to distract him or get me killed?" he questioned.

"The first one, I suppose," she replied.

"You suppose?" Vaughn gasped.

Sky only took a moment to recover from the intense moment before her eyes suddenly widened in horror, and she pulled away from him.

"Uncle Nash!" she cried out, sprang to her feet, and ran down the hallway.

Chapter 55

The well-lit area between the barn and the vacant police cruiser was eerily silent, indicating a stalemate of sorts. Neither party was willing to make the first move and start the ball rolling. A loud cowboy wail from the barn loft broke the silence. Tom clung to the rope attached to a pulley outside the loft, which was meant to raise hay to the second floor. He cried out while swinging back and forth on the rope with his rifle in his hand, firing shots into the air. The man behind the police car straightened to take his shot at Tom when a rifle blast rang out. The shooter took a precision shot to his head and fell back behind the vehicle. Jerry ran from the lower barn entrance, with his rifle prepared to fire again, and cautiously rounded the car. He aimed his weapon, then hesitated when he saw the dead police officer. It was the deputy assigned guard duty in the cruiser that they thought had been killed. Apparently, Tony made him a better offer. Tom cried out a little too cheerfully as he continued to swing from the rope.

"Jerry, you have to try this!" Tom cried out and again fired his rifle in the air.

Jerry looked back at Tom, then frowned and shook his head. He then heard a car in the driveway just out of view but approaching fast. Jerry took cover behind the police car and aimed his rifle down the driveway until the truck came into view. As the truck came to a screeching halt not far from the police cruiser, Moose and Ox jumped out with their weapons in hand.

Jerry relaxed, then looked back at the barn loft. "Our backup just arrived," he called out, but Tom was gone.

"Where's Vaughn?" Moose cried out. "Did he get my warning in time?"

"I'm not sure," Jerry informed him, then indicated the house. "We heard a lot of gunfire but couldn't reach them."

As Jerry, Moose, and Ox hurried to the house, Tom suddenly cried out while running like a maniac from the barn with his rifle in hand and charged for the house, screaming the entire way.

§

Sky sat on the second-to-last step on the stairs with her Uncle Nash while he held a cold, damp cloth to the bleeding graze wound on the side of his head.

"I thought for sure you were dead," Sky whispered to her uncle while fighting her tears.

"So did I," Nash reported, then cringed as Moose patched his shoulder wound.

"I can plug up the entry and exit holes," Moose informed Nash, but you should go to the hospital and get real stitches."

"Is it over?" Nash asked while looking at the others. "Tony's no longer a threat?"

"He's very much neutralized," Vaughn announced from where he stood, leaning against the stairs, then offered a tiny, sympathetic smile. "I'm sorry for being so suspicious of you, Nash."

"I guess that makes us even," Nash replied. "I was convinced you were still working for Marcus and thought you'd eventually turn on us."

Moose finished patching Nash's shoulder and then stood. "That's as good as my field training gets," he insisted. "The rest is up to the ER doctors."

Sky tugged on Nash's good arm. "We should get you and Tom to the hospital and have you both checked out," she announced.

"I'm fine," Tom insisted from where he stood near the front door, eating mayonnaise out of the jar with his fingers.

"I'll take them," Jerry announced with a sigh. "You should probably wait here for Deputy Rhodes. After his shootout at Marcus's mansion, he thinks he's Wyatt Earp, and I don't have the energy to deal with his enthusiasm after his shootout at the O.K. Corral. I'm sure he's going to want reports from the rest of you about Tony and Roscoe."

"Are you sure you don't want me to come along?" Sky asked Jerry.

"We'll be fine," Jerry replied.

§

Less than an hour later, Sky and Ox stood on the porch with Deputy Rhodes, retelling their account of what had happened at the casino and at Winchester Ranch over the last few hours. Moose and Vaughn sat on the far porch railing and enjoyed the night air while waiting to be questioned.

"We caught Randy assisting Roscoe's escape," Moose casually informed Vaughn.

"That's odd," Vaughn remarked, somewhat skeptical. "I didn't hear Ox mention the bartender in his statement to Deputy Rhodes."

"That's because we handled him 'in-house'," Moose replied.

Vaughn glanced at Moose and was now curious. "Oh? Is that so?" he asked. "What did he have to offer in return?"

"Did you ever hear Sky referred to as the 'rancher's daughter'?"

"On several occasions," Vaughn replied, then cocked his head. "Is it important?"

"Maybe," Moose replied, then shrugged. "Maybe not. The bartender told us there had been a rumor going around town many years ago about Sky's father. Many believe her father was a mafia kingpin."

Vaughn shot a look at Moose, appeared slightly surprised, and then snorted a laugh. "Are you serious?"

"That was the rumor," Moose replied.

"Well, the rumors were false," Vaughn informed him. "I learned that her father's family lived here for generations. They were all cattle ranchers. You don't just become a mafia kingpin overnight."

"Yeah, I knew the rumors were skewed," Moose replied, then met Vaughn's gaze. "But I had a theory of my own and made a few phone calls."

"Now, that sounds promising," Vaughn announced and eagerly moved in closer.

"During the ten years while Sky's father was *supposedly* in the Army, he was actually working as a CIA assassin."

Vaughn suddenly grinned and snorted a laugh. "Oh, that is priceless," he remarked. "So that's why they called her the 'rancher's daughter'. As a warning to tread lightly around the man's kid or else." He then hesitated and studied Moose a moment longer. "Do you think her father told her what he actually did during those ten years that he was supposedly in the Army?"

"Do you intend to tell her about your work with the CIA after your brief career in the Marines?" Moose asked.

Vaughn suddenly cringed. "Not if I can help it," he muttered. "Besides, there's not really much to tell. Most of it is considered classified anyway."

"Good point."

Chapter 56

The following morning, Detective Garland walked out of the hospital room and glanced at Sky, where she was standing in the corridor with a vase of pink and white lilies.

"Is she okay?" Sky asked.

"Yeah, she's fine," Detective Garland replied, then held up his cell phone. "She gave her statement, and it explains a lot."

"Oh?"

"I'll let you discuss it with her," Detective Garland informed her. "I want to get this typed up so she can sign it this afternoon."

"Is she being released then?" Sky asked.

"Not until she can make arrangements to stay with someone," he replied. "She can't take the stairs to her second floor apartment, and they want her on mostly bedrest. If she can't make other arrangements, she'll have to remain here."

Detective Garland gave a general wave and then headed down the hall. Sky drew a deep breath, pulled herself together, and then headed into the hospital room. Ruby was sitting up in bed with several monitors and tubes attached to the IV port taped to her arm. The marks on her face from the night of the attack were now heavily bruised. She looked rough and battered, but at least her color was better than it had been the last time Sky saw her. Ruby saw Sky and immediately shifted, being slightly uncomfortable, but forced a tiny smile.

"I, uh, wasn't expecting to see you," Ruby remarked somewhat timidly.

Sky placed the flowers in the vase on her bedside table, offered a tiny smile, and sat in the chair next to her bed.

"You look a lot better than the last time I saw you," Sky informed her. "I hear you're going to make a full recovery."

Ruby gingerly rubbed her side. "Doesn't feel like it, but that's what they've been telling me," she replied, then hesitated. "Are you mad at me?"

Sky stared at Ruby for a moment, somewhat confused. "Mad? Why would I be mad?"

"For accusing your uncles of attacking me," Ruby replied softly, then became animated. "But it was them, I swear. I called you that night because I overheard two men talking about you out back. It wasn't until they ambushed me by my car that I realized it was Cyrus and Carlton."

"Yes, we found out the hard way," Sky remarked, then drew a deep breath. "They tried to kill me yesterday afternoon. Apparently, it was one of many attempts."

"I'm so sorry, Sky," Ruby gasped, shaking her head. "I wish I could have gotten that warning to you sooner. Detective Garland has my statement about that as well as the attack."

"You almost died trying to warn me, Ruby," Sky replied. "You did more than enough."

"Considering Detective Garland just left with my statement, I assume he didn't get to tell you everything I overheard that night," Ruby announced.

"No, he didn't tell me anything," Sky replied.

Ruby shifted uncomfortably, both physically and emotionally. "When I overheard the men talking outside behind the bar," she began, then hesitated. "When I heard Cyrus and Carlton talking, one of them mentioned your parents' car accident." She held her breath a moment before continuing. "Sky, I think they were responsible for that accident. I think they wanted your Uncle Nash to inherit the ranch."

Sky was momentarily stunned at the news. It all suddenly made sense. For a moment, she was filled with hate and rage, but quickly realized it was over. The three people who were responsible were already dead.

"When they ambushed me in the parking lot, I realized calling your Uncle Nash was probably what nearly got me killed."

"And you'd be right," Sky replied, then frowned. "But it wasn't my Uncle Nash who tipped off Cyrus and Carlton. My aunt texted them a warning while you were talking to him. It was easy for them to slip around the side of the building and ambush you on her orders. Selma was responsible for your attack."

Ruby stared at Sky with horror. "Aunt Selma?" she almost cried out. "She was in on it?"

"It was all her," Sky replied. "She'd been financially crippling Uncle Nash for years, but she couldn't touch my inheritance. She wanted the ranch, thinking it'd be sold, so she could steal my inheritance a little at a time without anyone noticing. When Uncle Nash took over operations instead of agreeing to sell and put it in escrow for me, it made her life less ideal, but at least she could still live the lifestyle she was accustomed to. Apparently, with only two years until I receive full custody of the ranch and my parents' money, she felt time was running out. Having me 'offed' was her last effort to inherit the ranch." Sky held her breath a moment. "With me gone, Uncle Nash would inherit everything."

"That bitch!" Ruby cried out then cringed, clutching her side in pain from the sudden action. She collected her emotions and again studied Sky. "Your family was like my family all those years. I remember the pain of losing your parents in that crash. I know I betrayed you, and you have every right to hate me. I accepted that. But when I heard that your parents' accident was premeditated murder, I had to let you know." Her eyes filled with tears. "I know you'll never be able to forgive me for Tony, but that won't change the fact that I still love you like a sister."

Sky hesitated, then placed her hand on Ruby's and gave it a gentle squeeze. "I still don't know how I feel about what you did with Tony," she replied gently. "But I know the sort of man Tony was turning into. I saw it happening before my eyes while we were still together. He was becoming increasingly frustrated with our celibate relationship and my wanting to wait until marriage. Tony put a lot of pressure on me, and I recently learned, from him, that he put even more pressure on you. He wanted to hurt me by using you and destroying our friendship."

Ruby managed a tiny smile and nodded. "But that still doesn't excuse what I did," she replied and wiped the tears from her eyes. "That's on me. I destroyed our friendship. I should have been stronger and resisted his advances. Instead, I just sort of let it happen. That whole 'attraction to bad boys' thing." Ruby tensed a moment and barely looked at Sky. "I haven't so much as kissed a guy since I realized how badly I screwed up our friendship and my life. I suppose it's my way of punishing myself for what I did."

Sky held her breath a moment, then exhaled and again squeezed Ruby's hand, causing Ruby to meet her gaze. "I've missed you, Ruby," she announced softly. "And I forgive you."

§

Sky's Jeep pulled up to the house later that afternoon and parked alongside Deputy Rhodes's police cruiser. When Sky got out of the Jeep, she saw Jerry, Tom, Marlon, and Dixie sitting on the porch and drinking iced tea with Deputy Rhodes, who leaned against the post closest to the steps. All five eyed her as she walked up the steps, sharing the same curious expression.

"How did it go?" Dixie asked.

Sky drew a deep breath, held it a moment, and then released it with a sigh.

"Ruby and I are starting over with a clean slate," she announced and was met with a few sighs of relief and only one groan.

"It's going to be strange seeing the two of you on speaking terms again," Jerry remarked. "But, considering everything that's happened, I think you made the right decision."

"Speak for yourself," Tom muttered while shaking his head. "I saw what you went through with that girl. A leopard don't change its spots."

Tom received glares from all five. He glared back with added cockiness. "What?" he scoffed.

Sky walked onto the porch and joined them, collapsing onto the railing near the second support beam opposite Deputy Rhodes.

"Well, you'd better put your feelings aside," Sky informed him. "Because I told her she could stay here for a week or so until she can be on her own in her apartment. No stairs. So she'll be staying in the small bedroom off the kitchen."

"I never knew her as your friend," Dixie announced. "Your friendship with her had already ended a few months before Marlon and I came to town. It'll be a little strange, to say the least, but if you were best friends at one time, I'm sure we'll all get along just fine."

Marlon nodded, then looked at Sky and grimaced slightly. "There's always something I wanted to ask, Sky, but I knew I shouldn't."

Sky was curious and stared back at her friend. "What's that?"

Marlon hesitated only a moment before finally responding. "Would you be mad if I asked Ruby out?" he asked.

Marlon received several surprised looks, a smack on the shoulder from Dixie, and a cheap snicker from Tom.

Sky managed a tiny smile and shrugged. "I think she might actually like that," she replied. "And for the record, I wouldn't have been mad even if you asked her out years ago."

"It wasn't worth risking our friendship over," Marlon informed her. "And Dixie wouldn't let me ask you."

Dixie gasped with surprise, then turned angry and again smacked Marlon on the shoulder. He shirked and cried out.

"Now that my brother 'jumped the shark' with that totally ill-timed question," Dixie announced, then indicated Deputy Rhodes. "The deputy was just giving us the good news."

Sky cocked her head and eyed Deputy Rhodes. "More good news?" she asked. "I could get used to this. What's your good news?"

"Well," Deputy Rhodes began. "The hidden camera footage from the illegal casino operation is still being reviewed, but there have already been several high-profile arrests made."

"Exactly who did they go after?" Sky asked, now curious.

"Don't worry," Rhodes announced. "None of the girls or employees were arrested. They just wanted the big fish."

"I'm glad to hear that," Sky replied, then cocked her head. "And who were the 'big fish'?"

"The mayor and Sheriff Burke, for starters," Rhodes replied while attempting to hide his grin. "Being the local law, he not only turned a blind eye to the entire situation, but he was also recorded gambling, taking bribes, and soliciting prostitution."

"So that leaves the sheriff's position vacant then?" Sky asked.

Deputy Rhodes maintained his grin. "Well, I'm currently filling that position," he replied. "As long as they don't find anything incriminating me on that recording, it'll be made official."

"Congratulations," Sky announced cheerfully. "Even if you do nothing, you'll still do a better job than Sheriff Burke had."

"The town was pretty much sanitized in one day," Rhodes reported. "I suppose we all have a clean slate now."

"And those gambling there?" Sky asked with some concern.

"None of the locals gambling there are in any trouble," Deputy Rhodes informed her. "Honestly, they were only interested in the mayor, Sheriff Burke, and Marcus, but that's an ongoing investigation, which I'm not being briefed on. Again, probation."

"I'm sure we'll find out soon enough," Jerry remarked. "Just give it some time."

Chapter 57

That evening, Sky sat on the window seat in her bedroom, holding her knees to her chest, and stared outside at the still-bright sky just before dusk. Vaughn placed his duffel bag on the bed, removed the bag of sex toys from the nightstand drawer, and stuffed them inside his bag. He finally cast a glance at Sky on the window seat.

"Are you sure you want to do this?" he asked somewhat timidly.

Sky looked back at him, came to life, and jumped up from the window seat. "Yeah, I'm sure," she insisted as she approached him.

Vaughn drew a deep breath and sighed as he picked up his bag and slung it over his shoulder. "Okay, then," he announced and headed for the bedroom door.

Sky followed a slower-moving Vaughn from her bedroom and walked down the hall. He was far more hesitant than she was. It was like walking in a funeral procession. Both then turned and entered her parents' bedroom at the end of the hall. Vaughn looked around the master bedroom as he set his bag on the foot end of the bed.

"Uncomfortable?" Sky asked and offered a tiny, sly smile.

"A little," Vaughn reported. "I mean, it is your parents' room. You left it 'as is' for eight years, essentially making it a shrine." He shuddered slightly. "Feels almost disrespectful when I think of violating you in their bed."

"It's a much bigger room with a larger bathroom," she insisted. "I think it's time I moved in here." She then smiled and moved into his arms. "It also puts an entire room between us and Uncle Nash."

Vaughn chuckled warmly while holding her against him. "Yeah, but you should have thought about that before you told Moose he could have the room next door. You know he's going to critique me through the wall."

"Come on, Vaughn," Moose announced while passing the open doorway with his duffel bag slung over his shoulder like a sailor on shore leave. "Everyone knows you're a dead fuck."

Vaughn groaned and let his head fall on Sky's shoulder. "See what I mean?"

"You're the one who said it was a package deal," she reminded him.

"I didn't mean they had to live under the same roof," Vaughn announced. "And certainly not in the bedroom next door."

"No take-backs," Ox called out as he passed the open doorway with his duffel bag.

Vaughn released Sky, approached the door, and slammed it shut. "Seriously," he informed her. "I can't live with them. We need to discuss an alternate living space for them."

"I said we'd build an apartment above the new barn addition this fall," she informed him. "You can live with them for a few months."

Vaughn groaned, then muttered something under his breath. He approached his duffel bag, opened it, and removed the bag of sex toys.

"Okay, which nightstand is mine?" he asked, shaking the bag of toys while grinning.

Sky eyed the bag and the cheap grin on his face, then chuckled. "You can have the one on the right," she informed him.

Vaughn approached the nightstand, opened the drawer, and dropped the bag inside. "Okay, I'm all moved in," he announced as he shut the drawer and turned to face her with a grin on his face.

"Then you can help me move my stuff," she informed him.

"In a minute," Vaughn announced as he returned to his bag.

Vaughn removed a large caliber revolver, approached the head of the bed, and stuffed it between the mattress and the box spring. Both were surprised when they heard a metallic clunk. Vaughn seemed puzzled, then reached between the mattress and box spring.

"What is it?" Sky asked while approaching him, even more curious than he was.

"I'm not sure," Vaughn remarked while feeling around. "Maybe your dad liked to keep a loaded gun there, too."

Vaughn pulled his hand out and stared at the red fuzzy handcuffs. He cast a look at Sky and raised his brows.

"Hmm," Vaughn announced while attempting to hide his grin. "Now that's interesting."

"Well, I guess now we know why Selma hated my father," Sky remarked.

Vaughn chuckled, humored by it. "And now we know where you get your naughty side from."

§

Later that evening, Sky and Vaughn came down the back stairs into the kitchen, where Moose and Ox were steaming clams for dinner while Jerry and Tom were on the back porch grilling some steaks. Sky was a bit surprised when she saw her Uncle Nash setting the table with Dixie and Marlon. He had a small strip of tape on his temple covering the stitches he'd received from his near-death experience.

"Uncle Nash," Sky announced, smiling. "I didn't know you'd be home tonight. Did everything go okay in the city?"

"Better than expected," Nash informed her and managed a tiny smile. "My sisters-in-law and I agreed we'd have Selma and her brothers cremated in the city without any sort of service or memorial. Their life insurance policies will be paid out, so all three of us can at least get a little bit of our lives back."

Sky placed her hand on her uncle's shoulder. "Are you okay, Uncle Nash?" she asked with compassion. "I know what she did was horrible, but you were married to her for almost twenty years."

Nash patted her hand on his shoulder and managed a smile. "I'm fine, Sky," he informed her. "Maybe, one day, I'll be able to look back on the good times, but that's not going to be for a long time. I never knew she resented the country life so much that she was willing to kill you to get her hands on your inheritance."

"If you want to move back to the city--"

"That's the thing," Nash announced while turning to face her. "She resented you for us being stuck here, but I'm the one who wanted to stay. I never wanted to leave you or the ranch. I like it here. And now that Marcus is gone, it'll be even better."

"You haven't even heard the best part," Vaughn announced while pouring water into the glasses at the table. "Roscoe and Foster turned evidence on Marcus.

They confessed everything they knew about his operations and all of his dark little secrets."

"All of it?" Sky asked while glancing at Vaughn.

"Everyone Tony and Marcus had killed or ordered killed, the illegal gambling, prostitution, and drugs," Vaughn informed them. "On Marcus's orders, Tony arranged for Gus's *accident* at the feed store to acquire his property and the hit on Candy at the hotel. Tony suspected she was turning over evidence on Marcus. Apparently, it wouldn't have made any difference if I had stayed with her. They were already questioning my loyalty and complicity with her actions."

"How did they manage to kill Candy in her hotel room?" Sky asked.

"Detective Garland found evidence that they'd tampered with the connecting door lock," Vaughn replied. "Tony rented the room connected to hers under a false name, doped her up after the maid went through Saturday morning, and then went back later Saturday night, avoiding all the security cameras, and killed her. The FBI is handling her death now, and they're also reviewing my brother's cell phone for additional evidence."

"What was on his phone?" Moose asked, now joining them at the table.

"Sebastian recorded a conversation on his cell phone with Marcus discussing his body dump with Tony," Vaughn replied. "He wanted evidence to take to the FBI so he could run away with Candy without looking over his shoulder for the rest of his life. Apparently, Marcus ordered the hit on Sebastian after he refused to dump a body for him. Having non-team players on his team was an act of war. Tony killed my brother, then made it look like Sebastian robbed the bar. When the FBI recovers the bodies from Marcus's dumping ground, I assume they'll find Sebastian's body."

"I'm so sorry, Vaughn," Sky announced sadly.

"No, it's okay," Vaughn replied and managed a tiny smile. "I knew Marcus was responsible for my brother's death from the beginning. I just came here to make sure he paid for it, which he will, and we'll be able to give my brother a proper burial--alongside Candy. They both would have wanted that. Mission accomplished."

Jerry and Tom entered with two platters of freshly grilled steaks and set them on the table while Moose and Ox brought over the steamed clams. Everyone approached the table and took their seats, making themselves comfortable. When Dixie reached for her iced tea, she realized she was seated between Ox and Jerry. While one offered her the basket of rolls, the other offered her the butter tray, each with overly attentive smiles. Dixie's expression dropped as she eyed each man's telltale grin and the position she'd put herself into. She smiled politely at both, then slowly sank into her chair, minding her roll.

"So are we staying and finally putting down some roots?" Ox asked, seeming almost a little too cheerful while casting a quick glance at Dixie, who was attempting to hide in her chair.

Vaughn eyed his friends, then looked at Sky and smiled. "I know I am," he announced proudly. "Until Sky says otherwise, I'm still officially engaged to the rancher's daughter."

"Oh, God," Tom muttered while shaking his head. "They're never leaving."

The End

Other books by Holly Copella!
Reviews left on Amazon are appreciated!

"The Battle for Andrea Maria"

A cruise ship attack turns six survivors into overnight celebrities after they take credit for the heroic act of a stowaway who died saving them.

The cruise is just what Jess needed--a bit of harmless fun far from her daily grind. But what begins as a relaxing vacation turns into a desperate fight for her life when terrorists take over the ship and start piling up bodies. Teaming up with a mysterious stowaway, Jess attempts to send out a distress call but knows they cannot wait for help to come. If she or the few remaining passengers have any hope for survival, Jess must act now. The papers dub it "The Battle for *Andrea Maria*," but to Jess it is the moment she fought side-by-side with her enigmatic Romeo, saving the ship--and losing him. She thinks the story ends there, but really, the nightmare is just beginning...

"Insanely Deadly"

When the dead return to life, it's up to an admiral's daughter and a mildly insane, former war hero to save their small town.

Jetta Cross, a Navy Admiral's daughter, is tasked with keeping her father's comrade, a former war hero turned town crazy, grounded in the real world. Capt. John Hunter is still fighting the war in his head, where imaginary dead people are part of his world. When a viral outbreak brings about a zombie uprising, Hunter is left to his own devices. He must resume his role as a one-man commando unit in order to destroy the ravenous undead. With Hunter still fighting his own inner demons as well as the undead, the townspeople fear their zombie neighbors may not be the only threat. Stranded at the island's luxurious resort with a handful of workers, Jetta is forced to live up to her father's reputation and take charge of the deteriorating situation at the hotel. She must wage her own war against the infected before the government declares her hometown a total loss.

"Deadly Institution"

A town recluse suspected of killing his wife teams up with a young woman in order to stop a killer.

After being accused of murdering his wife, Konrad Churchill turns his back on the town that once adored him. Ten years later, he still holds his grudge and the title of the most feared man in town. With the reopening of the burned mental institution, where his wife had died, former employees are now murdered one by one, throwing suspicion back on Churchill. A young local reporter, Jacey, is forced to reveal her long-time friendship with the infamous recluse in order to clear his name not only in the recent murders but to exonerate him in the death of his wife as well. Will Jacey's relationship with Churchill invite the killer closer to her? Or is the killer already in her life?

"Death Displacement"

A grief-stricken man travels back in time to seek revenge on the woman who murdered his girlfriend, but inadvertently falls in love with her.

Kane is about to marry the woman he loves. His life is perfect. A few weeks before the wedding, a vindictive woman from his girlfriend's past mysteriously arrives and kills her. He learns of a traumatic accident that happened five years earlier, which triggers Riley's hatred for his girlfriend. Distraught over his girlfriend's death, Kane uses an antique time machine to travel into the past in order to find and destroy the woman responsible. When he runs into Riley's younger self, he realizes she's not the monster she later becomes, and he can't bring himself to destroy her. With a little help from his oddball friend from the past, they formulate a plan to prevent the accident that sends Riley down her destructive path. Kane's plan backfires when he falls for the younger Riley. His new tortured existence is further complicated when future Riley, his girlfriend's killer, shows up with her own devious agenda that doesn't include him. Will he be able to stop the time ripple, which ultimately ends with his girlfriend's death? Or will future Riley take him out of the timeline forever--

"Dead Village"

After strange happenings isolate a small resort town from the rest of the world, nearly one hundred residents seek refuge at the closed hotel. Only eight survive the night. And that's just the beginning...

One day after the entire population of Fox Ridge Village disappears, a car wreck forces several unsuspecting crash victims to seek help at the closed summer hotel. Within the hotel, they discover the grisly aftermath of a brutal slaughter. Crash victims Vander and Devon, a reluctant clairvoyant, team up to solve the riddle of the "haunted hotel" and the mass hysteria plaguing the remaining survivors. By the time they discover the hotel's secret, they're already drawn into the hysteria. As the body count continues to climb, it's a race to isolate the source and bring everyone back to reality before they kill one another. Will Devon be able to communicate with the traumatized spirits before their fate becomes her own?

"Town Darling"

After surviving a brutal attack that claims the lives of those she loves, a young woman seeks revenge on a corrupt town.

Going back home is never easy, but for Casey, it means returning to her corrupt hometown, where she barely survived a brutal attack. Accompanied by two family friends, she seeks justice for the night that destroyed her life. Her physical scars are nothing compared to her emotional ones, forcing the local sheriff to believe that the town darling is back for revenge. As the conspiracy for her revenge appears to be leading up to the coveted town fair, the sheriff is determined to stop her from fulfilling her vengeful scheme...but guilt over his role on that fateful night continues to haunt him. Will his desperate need for Casey's forgiveness be his undoing? Or will Casey's desire for revenge destroy them both?

"Basement Dwellers"

A viral outbreak at a hospital leaves a mortician, sheriff, and coroner fighting for their lives against a horde of undead and the CDC.

After a massive car wreck leaves several survivors in critical condition at the local hospital, a surgeon uses experimental drugs on his critical patients and accidentally causes a zombie outbreak. When local mortician, Lexx, receives an infected corpse as her client, she becomes stranded in the hospital basement during CDC quarantine along with the local sheriff and the coroner. The infamous surgeon struggles to find a cure for his infectious blunder by using the other survivors as test subjects. Meanwhile, Lexx and the sheriff attempt to locate his missing sister, who's stranded somewhere in the battle zone that once was the emergency room. It's a race against time and the ravenous undead. Can they survive the undead before the CDC sanitizes the hospital of all infection?

"Misfits, Inc."

A seemingly ordinary young woman meets four misfits who claim she has given them supernatural powers.

While on a business trip to a remote island paradise, a bored secretary, Hailey, has her world turned upside down when her path collides with a psychic freak, Skyler. He attempts to convince her that they had met in his dreams, and she had chosen him as one of her four mystic warriors. After Skyler foresees a woman's death, they discover an unidentified creature has killed one of the guests. They are joined by a lounge pianist and a rich playboy, who also claim they had met her in their dreams. If Skyler's prophecies are genuine, the evil entity controlling the ravenous creatures needs to destroy Hailey to ensure its survival. Reluctantly accepting her fate, Hailey has to locate the last and most powerful of her chosen warriors, The Guardian. Their fate is in doubt when The Guardian turns out to be a self-absorbed, former cat burglar with a bad attitude. Can Hailey turn her company of misfits into an elite team of mystic warriors? Or will The Guardian's secret agenda destroy them all?

"Deadly Institution 2"

When blackmail turns into murder, a young woman finds herself caught in the killer's crosshairs.

The small town of Stony Ridge is no stranger to scandal and persecution of the innocent. When a brutal killing shakes the town's prestigious country club, Jacey McMurray seeks help from a self-proclaimed vigilante, Konrad Churchill. As her professional and personal worlds collide, Jacey fears the stress of the country club killings have finally taken their toll on Churchill. Can a stressed-out vigilante stop the killer before he strikes again?

"Witness Protection"
Also available in audiobook!

After witnessing an execution, a resourceful young woman attempts to disappear while being pursued by a hitman and a handsome federal agent.

A helicopter pilot, Jackie Remus, reluctantly agrees to go on a date with one of her clients, but her date is unexpectedly cut short when she witnesses a man being murdered. After narrowly escaping with her life, she is placed into protective custody. When the safe house is breached, Jackie makes a daring escape from both the hired killers and the handsome FBI agent, who wants to return her to protective custody. With a little help from her sly and crafty friend, Monroe, Jackie is convinced she can disappear until the trial. While on her journey to meet with her friend, she solicits help from a few shady but lovable characters along the way. Although she manages to stay one step ahead of the hired killers, the federal agent remains in hot pursuit. Will Jackie reach Monroe before she's captured by the FBI and returned to protective custody? Or will the hired killers silence her first?

"Unconditional"

A young woman puts her life on hold to care for an unstable, highly skilled combat soldier, who believes someone is trying to kill him.

A botched military coup leaves a team of elite fighters injured, with one clinging to life in a coma. When Harlan wakes from his coma, he's left with no memory of his past life. His commander's daughter, Indy, takes it upon herself to care for the fallen war hero. She's challenged with more than just his physical care as she combats with not only his memory loss but also his newly found desire for her. His infatuation with her becomes the least of her worries when he sinks back into his role of a combat soldier. Believing his life is in danger, his fighting skills emerge, transforming him into an unpredictable and dangerous man. Will his memory return to him before Indy is forced to commit him? Or will he finally find his nemesis, "the coyote", and possibly claim the life of an innocent person?

"The Pen Pal"

In order to save her friend, she must enter the mind of a serial killer.

When her best friend is abducted, no one believes Jolynn saw it in a psychic vision. With nowhere to turn, Jolynn reluctantly joins Agent Harris Slade and his team on their hunt for a sadistic serial killer known only as "The Pen Pal". Finally confronted with the killer, Jolynn realizes she must enter the mind of the psychopath in order to stop the brutal killings. But when her vision reveals a particularly disturbing death, can Jolynn sacrifice her lover for her friend?

"Witness Protection 2"
The Return of Whiskey Tango Foxtrot

Believing she holds the clue to millions in missing laundered money, a young woman is placed into the protective care of a former Navy SEAL team.

Feeling sorry for her recently separated co-worker, Leeann invites Wiley to join her and her friends on their night out. Little does she know that finding her co-worker murdered is just the beginning of her nightmare. Leeann unknowingly holds the key to fifty million dollars in potentially laundered mob money. With hired killers pursuing her, the FBI places her into a different kind of protective custody. Former Navy SEAL team Whiskey Tango Foxtrot reunites to keep Leeann alive at their secret hideaway. What should be an easy assignment takes an unscheduled turn when secrets, lies, and betrayal threaten to derail their mission. Is the team prepared for a war on their own doorstep? Will Leeann's misguided trust endanger the lives of those sent to protect her?

"Witness Protection 3"
Alpha Mike Foxtrot

A helicopter pilot risks her life to help a team of retired Navy SEALs rescue two girls from a killer.

When former Navy SEAL team Whiskey Tango Foxtrot asks for a simple favor, Jackie reluctantly offers her air-taxi services. What could go wrong? What begins as a search and rescue for two girls turns into a fight for survival against a heavily armed drug cartel. Wanted by the law with the cartel in hot pursuit and their home base breached, the team is forced to call in a favor from a questionable ally. Unfortunately, their new safe house isn't what it seems. Without knowing who the real enemy is, can Jackie and the team save their young witnesses from the hands of a killer?

"Already Dead"
Supernatural Collection

From the already dead to the undead. Three supernatural tales of "things that go bump in the night".

"Bloodletting" - A vampire-themed resort allows guests to *participate* in their Bloodletting Ritual to celebrate the island's legendary vampires.

"Reaper of Souls" - A young woman must outwit an evil sorcerer in order to save her brother or become one of his minions forever.

"Already Dead" - When Flight 220 crashes, ten passengers make it to an isolated island, but only one man lives to tell the lie.

"Witness Protection 4"
O-Dark-Hundred

A simple assignment turns deadly when a retired Navy SEAL team uncovers a plot to kill a notorious mob boss.

When Whiskey Tango Foxtrot embarks on a simple stalking case, they're not prepared for a trip to a private island paradise owned by an infamous mobster. With one of their own suffering from traumatic head injuries, the team is left scrambling to decide what is real or imagined. The situation escalates even further when they uncover an assassination plot where everyone is a suspect. Now targets themselves, can the team survive their trip to paradise?

"Witness Protection 5"
Outside the Wire

After suffering several casualties on their last assignment, a retired Navy SEAL team discovers their misery is just beginning.

When Whiskey Tango Foxtrot returns home after suffering a devastating loss, they're hit with even more bad news regarding the rest of their team. Their grief is cut short when they discover their names are all on the same hit list. Hunted by relentless assassins, the scattered team must decide whether to remain safely hidden or find the man who put the price on their heads. Against the wishes of her teammates, Jackie strikes out on her own in order to save a friend who wants her dead. In a kill-or-be-killed situation, will Jackie's emotions finally betray her?

"The Murder of Emily Fisher"

After finding their favorite teacher murdered, the lives of two teenage girls are forever changed.

Everyone loved Emily Fisher. While walking home one afternoon, two teenage girls, Sidney and Trisha, stumble upon a gruesome murder scene. The brutal murder of Emily Fisher, a young, attractive schoolteacher, shocks the small town of **Marilina**. After graduation, Sidney moves far away from the memories of the small town, while Trisha retreats deeper into denial. Eight years after the murder, Sidney receives a desperate call from her childhood friend, forcing her to return home. Trisha believes Emily's killer was falsely accused, and she manages to turn the entire town against her while attempting to prove it. When Trisha receives a death threat, Sidney realizes there may be some credibility to her friend's wild accusations. Is Trisha's mental breakdown a result of childhood trauma? Or is the real killer actually attempting to silence her? In order to save her friend, Sidney must answer the eight-year-old question. Who murdered Emily Fisher?

"Once Upon a Disaster"

A young homicide detective finds herself at the mercy of a hitman in the aftermath of an earthquake.

While investigating the murder of a hitman, Detective Jade Wesson pursues a lead connecting the dead man to a break-in at a computer programming company. She's drawn into the world of a nightclub owner and front man for the mob, Cody Riley. Her investigation continues to point to Cody's right-hand man and possible hitman, Vahn Lott. Despite her efforts to keep her investigation on track, Vahn has plans of his own for the attractive detective. When an unprecedented earthquake rocks their east coast town, Jade must put her life in Vahn's hands if she wants to survive. Can she trust a man who might be the killer she's hunting?

"Awaken the Dead"

A grieving innkeeper struggles to keep her haunted hotel out of foreclosure.

After losing her parents in a suspicious boating accident, Harley Brandon is determined to keep the family hotel out of foreclosure. Unfortunately, the hotel ghosts have other plans. Built with tainted money, the century-old Horizon Hotel thrives on a tradition of murder, scandal, and suicide. As the paranormal activity increases to alarming levels, Harley discovers the truth about the hotel and its residents. Can Harley save her friends from the hotel's frightening hidden secrets?

"Castle Bloodshed"
Murder Collection

From a deadly island paradise to haunted castles. Three novella-length tales of murder, mystery, and malicious intent.

"Castle Bloodshed" – A tour of Wesley Castle turns into a fight for survival as six stranded tourists discover the haunting secrets within the castle walls. A mystery writer teams up with an uptight butler in order to stop a killer who may already be dead. Novella-length paranormal murder mystery.

"Fleshies" – Is Uncle Rutger crazy? Five years ago, four business partners died within their newly purchased, fixer-upper castle. Their bodies were never found. The surviving partner, Rutger, claims a demon keeps him as its slave. Rutger's nephew schemes to save his uncle by sacrificing the lives of a group of stranded motorists and a high-profile novelist. Novella-length supernatural murder mystery.

"Demon Island" – A group of strangers are invited to a remote island for the reading of a will. The guests soon discover they were brought to the island to be executed one by one. It's up to a private detective and a tenacious young woman to solve the murders and find a way to escape paradise. Novella-length murder mystery.

"Brighton Island"

When a psychic visits a haunted island mansion, he inadvertently awakens the ghosts' tortured souls.

Something's not right with Simon. When Jacklyn brings her eccentric friend to her uncle's island mansion, she doesn't expect him to slip into psychic overload. As Simon attempts to solve a decade-old double homicide, Jacklyn is confronted with the possibility that she could be next to join the mansion ghosts. When they find themselves stranded on the secluded island, her Uncle Hyland wages his own war to save them from a flesh-and-blood killer. Will her uncle's "shock and awe" military tactics save them or get them killed? Can Simon bring peace to the tortured souls or unexpectedly join them?

"A.L.F. Resort"

A fantasy vacation turns into a nightmare when the resort's artificial life forms are compromised.

Welcome to A.L.F. Resort, where you can live out your fantasies with safe, state-of-the-art artificial life form robots! When a young journalist and a photographer are sent to A.L.F. Resort to do a story for their magazine, Shay and Becka believe they've hit the jackpot of all work-cations. The engineers pull out all the stops to make their fantasies a memorable experience. Unfortunately, the newly designed A.L.F., the Gen X, is smarter than his programming and creates havoc within Shay's fantasy. A computer malfunction removes their safety inhibitors, and the A.L.F.s play out their own hostile fantasies. Zombies, bikers, and mobsters run amok, turning fantasies into nightmares. Shay gets more of a story than she anticipates, but will she survive long enough to write it?

"Jungle Princess"

While stranded on a prison island, a young woman discovers a creature of "unknown" origin.

After their cruise ship sinks, Alex and two of her shipmates are stranded on a deserted, tropical island. Unfortunately, the castaways soon realize they're not alone. They discover an abandoned prison with over two dozen inmates living on the island's south side. While avoiding the prison on the far side of the island, Alex discovers a strange but loveable creature of unknown origin. When one of her fellow castaways is in trouble, Alex reluctantly seeks help from the prisoners. After the brutal murder of several inmates, their questions surrounding the abandoned prison are about to be answered. What really killed over one hundred prisoners? And is it still out there?

"Murder in Wax"

A series of brutal murders plagues a quiet farming community when beautiful women audition for the same acting job.

While all the young women in town are fighting over a once-in-a-lifetime acting opportunity, Devon Vincent is excited about her new job at the local wax museum. Although supportive of her friend's acting aspirations, Devon has a hard time understanding the rivalry among the women in town. When the aspiring actresses are brutally murdered one by one, Devon fears her friend may be the next victim. Devon finds herself in the middle of a murderous revenge plot that leads back to the wax museum's doorstep and possibly implicates her boss as the killer. Will Devon's newly found feelings for her boss bring a killer closer to her? Or is the killer already in her circle?

"Witness Protection 6"
Alpha Dogs

An easy rescue turns into a wild ride for retired Navy SEAL team Whiskey Tango Foxtrot when everyone wants to kill their client.

It was a simple task. Rescue a young woman from her mob boss father-in-law. Little did Jackie and company realize that rescuing the young woman was the easy part. Keeping her alive would be a massive undertaking, especially when everyone wants a piece of the mafia heiress. The team fights for survival against their toughest adversaries yet. How many innocent people must die in order to save one woman? Can the team survive the ultimate battle between mercenaries and assassins?

"Midnight Requisition"

A series of brutal murders leaves a traumatized young woman on a hunt to find a killer.

When they were just babies, Scorpio and her twin brother, Kane, tragically lost their parents under mysterious circumstances. Refusing to accept his father was dead, Kane set off on a mission to find a man he'd never met. A home invasion gone wrong leaves Scorpio grieving the loss of those she loves. Out of the tragedy of her loss, two fallen heroes are thrust upon her. Scorpio soon realizes someone wants her dead, and the killer may already be in her circle. As her entire life unravels in a web of betrayal and lies, can Scorpio trust her new, slightly questionable friends?

"Until Death"

Liars, cheaters, blackmail, and murder. It would be a wedding no one would forget.

Despite knowing he's making the biggest mistake of his life, Raina Steele reluctantly attends her father's third wedding. What should have been a boring reception turns into a web of lies, betrayal, and murder. With no one above suspicion, Raina must put aside her feud with the arrogant yet insanely handsome butler in order to catch the killer before he finds his next victim. With a murderer waiting to strike and lives hanging in the balance, the real question remains...the bride is wearing white? Seriously?

"Tainted"

What happens at the Dark Forest Hotel, stays at the Dark Forest Hotel...for all eternity.

What secrets surround Dark Forest Hotel? After her parents die under mysterious circumstances, sixteen-year-old Jeri escapes foster care and seeks refuge at a "closed for the season" hotel. Over the next six years, Jeri graduates from teenage runaway to the hotel's assistant general manager. When she learns a convention is secretly held every year in her absence, she demands answers from her boss, friends, and co-workers. After getting conflicting stories, Jeri sets out to discover the truth. She's suddenly thrown into a horrifying new world where vampires and vicious creatures are craving her virgin blood. After six years of being lied to, is there anyone she can trust?

"Witness Protection 7"
Bravo Foxtrot

An Army deserter on the run brings mayhem to a retired Navy SEAL team when his teenage daughter is caught in a mercenary's cross-hairs.

A weekend of fun turns into a race for survival as Monique and Colleen's surrogate big brother, Bogart, rescues the girls from mercenaries hunting Colleen's Army deserter father. With the girls safely stashed at their Colorado hideaway, trouble brews when the team discovers Colleen's father was framed by his former commander over a stolen, high-tech weapon. In order to clear Colleen's father and bring him home, the team must fight one of their toughest adversaries yet...a high-ranking military officer with countless mercenaries and the U.S. military behind him.

"Midnight Requisition 2"
Amateur Night

A brother and sister duo team up to catch a potential kidnapper.

After finally reuniting with her not-so-dead brother, Scorpio and her friends are taunted into helping him with his new case. A wealthy cattle rancher believes someone wants to abduct his daughter, but the team suspects her ex-boyfriend is pulling off an elaborate scheme to win her back. What appears to be a slice of paradise in the Colorado Mountains turns out to be a venomous snake pit filled with lies, lust, betrayal, and murder. Surviving the depraved family becomes the least of the team's worries when a botched kidnapping turns into murder.

"Cemetery Stalkers" Horror Collection

Four tales of horror from flesh-eating alien monsters to blood-sucking vampires.

"Night Creatures" − When a rescue party becomes stranded on an abandoned cruise ship, they discover the terrifying secret unleashed from the cargo hold. What starts out as a rescue mission rapidly deteriorates into survival as a frightening creature with a taste for human flesh hunts the small group. Novella-length horror book.

"Ravenous" − After escaping a carjacking in the back woods, a young woman seeks refuge in a mysterious mansion with a terrifying secret. Despite promises of a ride to town in the morning, she's convinced she's being held prisoner by a cult leader. Short paranormal story.

"The Feast" − Five years ago, a killer went on a murderous rampage at the church picnic. Despite eyewitness accounts of a non-human killer, the local law refused to believe the town's citizens. When a group of teenagers stumble upon the contained remains of the killer, they unwittingly set him free to continue his terror upon the small town. Novella-length paranormal book.

"Cemetery Stalkers" − When 'The Reaper' stalks a cemetery, death follows. Following a series of bizarre incidents within the cemetery, a young woman fears for the safety of her friend, who lives in the middle of spook central. Short horror story.

"Jumpers"

When a cruise ship is exposed to a deadly virus, the fate of the world rests in the hands of a lounge dancer and a conman.

An infectious outbreak threatens the passengers and crew of the "Queen Anita" and the entire world if the virus escapes back into civilization. Lounge dancer, Maxine, must find a way to prevent the destruction of the world, but in order to do that, she needs to trust a conman with unique insight into the virus.

"Witness Protection 8"
Midnight Requisition

A brother and sister duo find themselves on an explosive collision course with a team of retired Navy SEALs.

Obsessed with the belief that his father is still alive, Kane Wayland embarks on a foolhardy mission to confront the elusive former Navy SEAL, Zack Kinsley. Despite heavy protests, Kane's sister, Scorpio, joins him on his quest. The disastrous "reunion" comes with a steep price that none are prepared to pay. With the haunting reality of the botched mission, Midnight Requisition, still looming over each of them, can the two teams pull together in time to prevent another tragedy?

"Midnight Requisition 3"
Circular Run

A brother and sister reopen a hotel with a tainted history, only to discover its past refuses to stay dead and buried.

Scorpio and Kane Wayland finally realize their dream of reopening their grandfather's old, cliffside hotel in Maine. With the hotel's checkered past behind it, the relaunch is a dream come true. Unfortunately, history has a tendency to repeat itself. When guests mysteriously vanish, the hotel's somewhat seedy clientele are all now suspects. In order to save their hotel, Scorpio and Kane must stop a killer. When your guests are mercenaries, bounty hunters, and mobsters, who can you trust?

"Raven Force"

An innkeeper becomes involved in a game of espionage after picking up a mysterious hitchhiker.

After surviving a nightmare of a date, Maxine Croft didn't think her evening could get any worse...until she nearly hits a stranger on a dark back road. This unprecedented meeting would turn Max's world upside down as she's thrust into a world of murder, corruption, and deception within her own backyard. As she gets in deeper with an elite, special task force, Max inadvertently puts her sisters' lives in danger. Will Max and her sisters become just more "collateral damage" to facilitate the team's mission?

"Midnight Requisition 4"
Charlie Foxtrot

A mob convention at a remote cliffside hotel has murderous consequences.

Hotel owner, Scorpio Wayland, reluctantly books a "mob" convention at her quiet, cliffside resort. What could go wrong? When former mob boss Salvatore Romano invites friends for a "family" reunion, disaster swiftly follows.

"Witness Protection 9"
S.N.A.F.U.

A notorious mob boss turns to a retired Navy SEAL team to keep his son alive.

They were made an offer they couldn't refuse. When his son is accused of murdering known mobsters throughout Colorado, Giovanni turns to the retired Navy SEAL team of Whiskey Tango Foxtrot to keep his boy alive and prevent a war between the "families". With the mobster's son in the crosshairs of every hitman and bounty hunter on the West Coast, Jackie and the boys need to find Marco and go completely off-grid. But is the team risking their lives to protect a serial killer?

"Witness Protection 10"
Bravo Zulu

It's all hands on deck when the mob declares war on the team and those they love.

Whiskey Tango Foxtrot reunites with Midnight Requisition when war is declared by a notorious mobster and his army of highly trained soldiers. After several deadly attacks shake both teams, their skills, loyalties, and limitations are tested in an explosive and bloody rampage that will scar and change their lives forever.

"Pretty Little Dead Things"

Romance, scandal, and an unsolved murder. Welcome to snob central!

After a disastrous evening at the exclusive country club gala, Marley Temple doesn't think her life can get any worse. When someone close to her is murdered, Marley is left devastated. Although everyone else seems to move on after the unsolved homicide, Marley can't let it go. She's suddenly thrust into the inner circle of a wealthy playwright recluse, whose stage actress wife was brutally butchered just two years earlier. Although Marley fears falling for the infamous Devlin Ryker, forming a strange alliance with him brings her closer to solving the perplexing murder. But as she gets closer to learning the truth, the killer gets closer to her. Will Marley discover the killer's identity before she becomes his next victim?

"Dead Again"

After barely surviving a murderous attack, a young woman believes a cold-hearted cattle rancher holds clues to that night.

After the murder of her mother in an attack that nearly claimed her life as well, Sage Remington believes moving to the country with her sister will heal her emotional scars. Sage's near-death experience leaves her with memory loss surrounding that fateful night. A bizarre encounter with an infamous cattle rancher, Jackson Morgan, brings back fragments of Sage's lost memory. If she wants to piece together what happened to her mother, Sage needs to get closer to Jackson, who somehow holds the clues. Unfortunately, discovering Jackson's secrets opens the door to a whole other world where nothing is what it seems.

"Dead Woods"

Two magazine reporters get more of a story than they want while investigating strange happenings in a cursed forest.

While interviewing a small-town hero, two adventure-seeking magazine reporters, Kara and Lenox, hike into the infamous Dead Woods in search of a story. Their simple outing takes a chilling turn, and they soon find themselves involved in the town's haunted history filled with curses, witch burnings, and zombified minions. Narrowly escaping with her life, Kara runs into local legend Daemon Archer, a distant relative of a man accused of witchcraft and burned in Town Square in the 1800s. In order to survive a panic-stricken village prophesizing 'evil will take a mate', Kara has to trust the town's most feared citizen.

"Cinderella of Yardley Manor"

Never believing in love at first sight, a young woman finally thinks she's met the man of her dreams, only to discover he's the wrong man.

After graduating college, Ramsey O'Connell reluctantly agrees to travel with her uncle on his business trip to England. However, when she discovers her uncle's true intention--to fix her up with his wealthy colleague, William Yardley —she has some reservations. Falling in love was the last thing she expected, but falling in love with an emotionally unavailable man turns her fairytale into a nightmare.

"Protect and Serve"

Celebrating her birthday with friends on a luxury cruise ship, a young heiress is looking for a little romance on the high seas. Instead, she's confronted by kidnappers and assassins.

Kasey's birthday celebration cruise was supposed to be ten days of sun, sea, and fun with her friends. That is, until her uncle insists she take her bodyguard along. Although her bodyguard, Hunter, is undeniably handsome, he's a little rough around the edges. When her uncle's enemies exact their revenge on Kasey, the cruise turns into a nightmare. If they want to survive, they have to trust Hunter. But sometimes, the enemy is not who you think.

"Crime Scene"

The cast of a popular television crime show finds themselves stranded in a small town after a real-life murder mystery intrudes on their world of make-believe.

After weeks of filming on location, the cast of a highly acclaimed crime show becomes stranded when their luxury bus breaks down in the middle of nowhere. An inconvenient overnight in a small town turns into the beginning of a murder investigation with the cast of "Crime Scene" high on the suspect list. To save the cast's reputation, the show's writer assists the handsome but guarded sheriff and his K-9 deputy in the murder investigation. As alibis unravel, lies pile up, and the suspect list grows, can they catch the killer before he strikes again?

"Midnight Requisition 5"
Sierra Hotel

A Christmas wedding, mistletoe, and murder.

Only a few days before Christmas, a very pregnant Scorpio and her friends are planning Mac and Maverick's wedding. Little did they know that Santa would be delivering a few early presents. What was supposed to be a merry Christmas turns into an epic whodunit when a helicopter crashes on the hotel grounds, leaving eight stranded passengers and a dead man. Their once silent night is filled with accusations, alibis, and mayhem. With the assistance of former Special Agent Holden Falcone, can they solve the murders before the next body drops?

"The Rancher's Daughter"

When her town, ranch, and life are threatened, a young woman teams up with the enemy's top enforcer to reclaim what is hers.

Skyler Winchester's small hometown has become more corrupt in the five years since her parents' car accident. Little by little, wealthy business tycoon Marcus has been buying buildings, property, and people. As one of the largest ranch owners and the object of Marcus's lust, Sky has always been immune to the corruption and dirty dealings, but her friends aren't so lucky. After forming an unholy alliance with one of Marcus's top enforcers, it appears that Sky's immunity has been revoked. When her life is threatened, will the man she trusts most be the one sent to eliminate her?

ABOUT THE AUTHOR

Holly Copella has been writing since the age of twelve when her frustration at a book's poor plot drove her to author her own story. Over the last decade, she's written a number of screenplays, some of which she's now adapting into novels. Her fascination with zombies and other darker material lends an edge to her writing, which tends to lean toward horror. As a fan of Agatha Christie, she appreciates the craft of a good plot and the importance of creating significant characters.

Hailing from Pennsylvania, Copella lives in the Endless Mountains on a farm with her horse, Maverick, new puppy, Darth, and other animals. In addition to writing and reading fiction, she enjoys riding horses and traveling to Las Vegas

www.ingramcontent.com/pod-product-compliance
Lightning Source LLC
Chambersburg PA
CBHW070351260626
47161CB00001B/105